PENGUIN BOOKS

Who Gets Fluffy?

Who Gets Fluffy?

JUDITH SUMMERS

PENGUIN BOOKS

PENGUIN BOOKS

Published by the Penguin Group
Penguin Books Ltd, 80 Strand, London WC2R ORL, England
Penguin Group (USA) Inc., 375 Hudson Street, New York, New York 10014, USA
Penguin Group (Canada), 90 Eglinton Avenue East, Suite 700, Toronto, Ontario, Canada M4P 2Y3
(a division of Pearson Penguin Canada Inc.)
Penguin Ireland, 25 St Stephen's Green, Dublin 2, Ireland (a division of Penguin Books Ltd)
Penguin Group (Australia), 250 Camberwell Road, Camberwell, Victoria 3124, Australia
(a division of Pearson Australia Group Pty Ltd)
Penguin Books India Pvt Ltd, 11 Community Centre,
Panchsheel Park, New Delhi – 110 017, India
Penguin Group (NZ), 67 Apollo Drive, Rosedale, North Shore 0632, New Zealand
(a division of Pearson New Zealand Ltd)
Penguin Books (South Africa) (Pty) Ltd, 24 Sturdee Avenue, Rosebank, Johannesburg 2196,
South Africa

Penguin Books Ltd, Registered Offices: 80 Strand, London WC2R ORL, England

www.penguin.com

First published 2008
1

Copyright © Judith Summers, 2008

Typeset by Palimpsest Book Production Limited,
Grangemouth, Stirlingshire
Printed and bound by Clays Ltd, St Ives plc

ISBN: 978-0-141-03627-4

www.greenpenguin.co.uk

Penguin Books is committed to a sustainable future
for our business, our readers and our planet.
The book in your hands is made from paper
certified by the Forest Stewardship Council.

For Tabby, Hannah, Joshua and Nathaniel

One

'Let me run through this again, Mrs Curtis.'

The lawyer on the other side of the mahogany desk sat forward in his chair, ran his hands anxiously over his receding silver hair and, after adjusting the half-moon lenses of his reading glasses, peered down at the notes he'd been making.

'First, there's no question of a reconciliation between you and your husband?'

'None whatsoever, Mr Williams.'

'You're quite sure you wouldn't rather opt for a judicial separation at this point?'

'Absolutely.'

'Okay, so we'll go ahead and serve the petition against Mr Curtis on the ground of the irretrievable breakdown of your marriage, without naming the co-respondent with whom he committed adultery. Now, if your husband expresses no wish to contest the divorce –'

'I can assure you he won't.'

'Well, then, in that case he'll return the signed Acknowledgement of Service to the court. Then we can apply for the decree nisi, and the process will be well under way.'

'Good!'

Williams glanced up as if he was surprised by my

enthusiastic reaction. 'As it happens, Mrs Curtis, your husband has already consulted a solicitor.'

'Yes, I know,' I said. 'I told him to. I said I'd pay.'

'You did?' He frowned. 'May I ask why?'

I shrugged. 'Since I'm going to be represented by you, it seemed only fair.'

He raised the two dark, overhanging ledges of his eyebrows. They were in dire need not only of threading, I noted, but of clipping with hedge-trimmers. 'Fair is not a word one often hears from a petitioner's lips in such cases,' he muttered, then picked up a letter that was lying on his desk. 'Her name's Martha Greenwood, of Greenwood and Broadhurst,' he read out. 'I've already received this from her, outlining a proposed financial settlement.' He returned to his notes. 'Apparently you've talked about giving your husband fifty per cent of the marital assets. To include half the value of your flat, a one-bed loft in Islington that you bought, in your name, two years before you met him and which has gone up in value three-fold since then. Plus you've said he could have the Audi Avant that you bought, again in your name, last year. Can this be correct?'

'Yes.' The fabric of my black Armani trouser suit made a comforting rustle as I sat back in my chair and crossed my legs.

Williams frowned again, then jabbed with his fat Mont Blanc fountain pen at a line halfway down the page. 'You've also offered him first choice of all your personal chattels. To wit, the contents of your home, this choice to include your new Bang & Olufsen hi-fi system, a vintage fifties Charles Eames chair and footstool, which you bought Mr Curtis as an anniversary gift two years ago, and a signed original lithograph – entitled *Welcome to Hell* – by . . . Who's the artist? I'm afraid I can't quite read my writing.'

'Banksy.' I spelled it for him.

'Not one of the Impressionists, then?' He smiled fleetingly at his joke. I could almost hear the lines round his mouth crack. 'The signed *Banksy* print your husband gave *you* – *this* Christmas? The one that's just past? A print valued at around eight thousand pounds?'

'It's probably gone up by now. But, frankly, it's more his taste than mine.'

Williams cleared his throat. 'In addition, even though you've been the only breadwinner throughout the marriage . . .'

I held up my hand. 'To be precise, the main breadwinner. I provided the daily organic ciabatta, so to speak, while Mark brought home the occasional crust of Mother's Pride.'

'Right.' He altered his notes, then continued: 'Even though you have been the *main* breadwinner for the last few years, Mrs Curtis, am I to understand that you have expressed your willingness to divide all your other savings and assets with your husband? Assets accrued before and after the aforementioned period of your marriage, as I understand, and amounting to some . . .' he flicked through the pages until he came to a long list of figures '. . . one hundred and sixty thousand pounds in cash?' He raised an eyebrow. 'That's quite a substantial sum.'

I was almost embarrassed by the amount – though why

I should have been in front of a man to whom I was paying £350 an hour I hadn't a clue. 'Annual bonuses,' I said apologetically. 'And a profitable venture into the buy-to-let market. I struck lucky, that's all.'

His gaze didn't waver. 'You've suggested to Mr Curtis that you're willing to hand over half of all this to him? Without a fight?'

'That was the idea.'

Williams shook his head, and a shower of dandruff, light as the first flakes of a snowfall, tumbled into his eyebrows and over the slate-grey shoulders of his ill-fitting suit jacket. 'Mrs Curtis, as the solicitor who will be representing you in this unfortunate case, I'm duty-bound – no, obliged – to advise you that you're erring very much on the side of generosity here. "Erring" being the crucial word.' He raised his chin and, after a passing glance at the cleavage revealed by the open neck of my Vivienne Westwood shirt, peered at me disapprovingly from under lowered eyelids. 'As I understand, your husband brought no financial assets to the marriage, and has contributed almost nothing to your joint finances. The irretrievable breakdown of your marriage can be said to be, at least in part, his responsibility. Even had the concept of no-fault divorces already been on the statute book in this country . . .'

I couldn't help feeling a surge of anger when I heard those words. I mean, it was a joke. No fault that Mark was a lying, conniving bastard? No fault that he'd promised me heaven, then thrown me into hell? No fault that, while I was flogging my guts out to pay for him to sit around on his arse at home all day long, endlessly writing and rewriting the first bars of the chart-topping guitar solo he felt he had in him, he'd wiled away the empty hours by shagging other women?

'It was his bloody fault!' The words fell from my lips before I could stop them.

Williams seized on them like a starving dog grabbing a juicy bone. 'Aha! Precisely my point! Your husband's infidelities. One with his – what was she? – his psychotherapist?'

I cleared my throat, shifted in my seat and stuffed my anger back where it belonged, which was deep inside me. 'Actually, she was our Pilates instructor,' I said, as if I didn't care.

He barely suppressed a snigger. His lips parted, showing a line of vicious teeth, and as his heavy eyebrows collided over the top of his nose he looked exactly like a feisty Schnauzer spoiling for a fight. 'You could hammer him over his adultery, you know. Not to mention unreasonable behaviour. You'd probably get away with a much smaller settlement.'

I gave him a pitying look. 'Mr Williams, I don't expect you to understand this for one minute, but I'm a very fair person, and I'm not trying to get away with anything. I love my husband.' It wasn't until he frowned at me that I realized what I'd just said. 'I meant *loved*, of course. We both loved each other. Very much – before our marriage fell apart, that is. And since that's the case, I don't want what was once a wonderful relationship to end in bitterness or pettiness. Mark feels the same.'

'I'm sure he does. Particularly since he has everything to gain by it financially.'

I winced. 'It was I who suggested that we split everything fifty-fifty.'

Williams's mouth fell open. 'It was?'

'Yes. I don't think Mark wants anything from me but, as I said before, I want to be fair to him. He's got nothing of his own, you see. And, despite his weaknesses, he's a very unusual person. Money's the last thing on his mind. He scarcely knows the value of it. He's very gifted. One day he's going to be really well known. At the moment he's just . . .' I searched for all the expressions I'd used in the past to defend Mark to my friends and family: 'unworldly', 'temporarily resting', 'professionally retrenching', 'an unappreciated talent'. But the phrase that eclipsed them all was the one my father frequently used: 'an idle, sponging sod'. I shoved it back into my psyche, along with my anger. 'Not everyone can be good at earning a living,' I snapped.

'Don't get angry with *me*, Mrs Curtis. Save that for your husband. I'd be acting negligently if I didn't speak bluntly to you. What Martha Greenwood is proposing in this letter is unacceptable. What you say you've offered your husband – albeit of your own free will, as you suggest – is not so much a settlement as complete capitulation at the opening shot. I can only say "*Cur ante tubam tremor occupat artus?*"'

'Sorry?'

'It's Latin. Virgil. "Why should fear seize the limbs before the trumpet sounds?" Ms Greenwood will be expecting us to negotiate on the basis of this letter, you know.'

'Negotiate?' I gave a sad laugh. 'Mr Williams, this isn't

some business deal we're talking about. And I assure you that Mark and I aren't at war. Ours is going to be a civilized divorce.'

His upper lip curled into a sneer. 'Mrs Curtis, let me tell you that in my experience – and it is not negligible – there is no such thing as a civilized divorce.'

I sneered back. 'Well, Mark and I are about to disprove that. Believe me, neither of us has any wish to hurt the other. We just want to go our separate ways as soon and as painlessly as possible.'

Williams sighed. 'Well, if you're absolutely sure you want to give him half of everything?' I nodded. 'However, I want it on record that I tried to dissuade you.' He put his digital recorder close to his lips, repeated what he'd just said, then scribbled something at the bottom of the last page of his notes. Then, he placed his pen on top of the pad, turned it so that it was facing me and manoeuvred it across his cluttered desk. 'I'd like you to check through this very carefully, Mrs Curtis.'

While he paced up and down the overheated, book-lined room, hands clasped behind his back, pausing now and then to gaze out of the sash windows at the winter-bare branches of the ancient plane trees in Lincoln's Inn Fields, I stared at his notes. I must have been having trouble with my contact lenses because the loopy, semi-legible handwriting, written in blue ink on lined yellow paper, blurred before my eyes.

'Of course, you're lucky you don't have children,' Williams mused, half to himself. 'Divorce is always so much easier when there are no young ones involved. I can't tell you some of the mucky battles I've seen in the family courts. The gut-wrenching fights over residency and maintenance. The mud-slinging. The name-calling. The devious lengths some people will go to in order to sway the judge in their favour. Even so ... I must say, I'm glad all my clients aren't as reasonable – not to say generous – as you are. I'd be out of a job! I might be anyway, with the divorce rate falling so fast. As for quickie Internet divorces ... Pah! They'll be the death of the profession. Still, I suppose there's always the palimony cases to look forward to, with this complex new partnership legislation the government wants to introduce.'

On and on he rambled. I tried to concentrate on the words in front of me, but I suddenly felt utterly miserable. What a way to start the New Year. All the hopes I'd had on my wedding day had come to this: a list of my assets on a pad of paper. Other people's marriages might splinter on the rocks, but until Christmas Day, just a month before, I'd honestly believed mine would last.

How could I have been so naive? We hadn't even made it to five years.

Suddenly I wanted to get out of Williams's office. I wanted the entire divorce to be over so that I could put it behind me and forget I'd ever met Mark. I stood up and grabbed my oversized black-patent YSL Downtown tote bag, the shiny, obese bulk of which was occupying the chair next to mine. 'It's fine,' I told him, groaning as I heaved it on to my shoulder. 'Just go for it and get it over with. I honestly can't be bothered to quibble over details.'

'Then I'll draft a reply. I think we've covered everything.' He walked back to his desk, picked up the letter he'd received from Mark's lawyer, and skimmed through it again. 'Oh, my! I have been negligent. I was forgetting Ms Greenwood's postscript. There's just one last minor matter we need to settle.'

'Oh?'

'It shouldn't take more than a moment to clear up.'

He smiled at me, as if the matter was so trivial he was almost embarrassed to raise it. Then he said, 'Apparently your husband wants the dog.'

Presuming I'd misheard, I smiled back. 'Can you say that again, please?'

'Your husband wants the dog!' he repeated jovially.

I fell back into the chair, clutching my Downtown tightly to my chest.

'I told you it was an unimportant matter,' Williams continued blithely. 'Shall I add it to the list?'

He reached for the yellow notepad, but I clamped my hand on it. 'There must be some mistake,' my voice rasped.

'No, no.' He peered at the letter again, his pupils magnified by his spectacles. 'Here it is, in black and white.' He cleared his throat and began to read in the kind of slow, rather jaunty voice one might use to tell an amusing story to a child: 'PS: my client wishes to have sole custody of his dog, Fluffy.' He pronounced the last word slowly, lingering on the Fs.

I felt as if the air had been sucked out of my lungs. 'But Fluffy's not Mark's dog,' I managed to gasp. 'He's mine. Mark knows that.'

A pair of watery blue pupils regarded me over the top of the spectacles, then Williams said cautiously, 'It seems that he doesn't, Mrs Curtis. It clearly says here, "full custody of *his* dog".'

'What do you mean, "full custody"? Give me that!' My Downtown thudded to the floor as I snatched the letter from him. My hands were shaking so much that the words danced before my eyes. But there they were: 'full custody . . . *his dog*'. I let go of the sheet of paper, which fluttered on to the desk. 'This can't be right,' I said. 'Mark knows what Fluffy means to me. He'd never try to take him from me!'

But he would. He was intending to. Mark, who'd once been more devoted to me than he was to his vintage Gibson guitar, now wanted to get me where it really hurt. As if he hadn't hurt me enough. I stared blindly at the notepad and, picking up Mr Williams's Mont Blanc, absentmindedly began to draw small circles in the margin. I, who always kept my head at home and at work – even on days when I was rushed off my feet – couldn't think straight. There was a tightness in my chest, and I felt peculiarly ill. As so often since Mark and I had decided to divorce, I was overcome by panic. But now there was some other emotion, too, one that I'd done my best to suppress during the past few years but which now throbbed inside me like a fast-swelling abscess.

The solicitor resumed his seat opposite me. 'Are we talking about a valuable animal, Mrs Curtis? Is this . . .' his lips twitched '. . . this *Fluffy* a pedigree breeding champion, perhaps?'

'He's a cross,' I muttered. 'Part lurcher, part Tibetan terrier. And probably part Jack Russell. The vet thinks there's probably some sheepdog in him, too.'

'Ah. You mean a mongrel. What our brothers and sisters across the Pond call a *mutt*.'

'Would you like to see him?' I picked up my bag, pulled out my BlackBerry, and showed him the screensaver: my favourite photo of Fluffy, curled up asleep on the bed with his nose between his paws and his hair falling over his eyes. I could see Williams struggling to keep a straight face.

'In that case – in my *humble* opinion,' he went on in a tone that implied it was anything but, 'a mutt is a very small demand compared to all the others. Half the value of your flat. The pick of the contents. A valuable car. A half share of all your assets. If you want to get this over quickly and easily, as you say, it might be worth your while to use him as a bargaining tool.'

My jaw dropped. 'Are you seriously suggesting that I let Mark have Fluffy? Are you crazy? What about all that stuff you said before about not capitulating? Besides, Fluffy's mine!'

I felt the abscess burst, flooding me with something pernicious and exhilarating: poisonous, white-hot rage.

'Ye-es . . . but –'

I heard my voice getting louder: 'There's no but about it, Mr Williams. *He's – my – dog*. DO YOU UNDERSTAND?'

There was a long pause. Williams was no longer looking at me. He was staring down at the desk – more precisely, at his notepad. The notes he'd jotted on it were now obliterated by wild blue scratches, and the paper was covered with deep puncture holes where I'd stabbed through it with his pen.

'I gather,' he said, as he took his Mont Blanc cautiously

from my hand and examined its ruined nib, 'that this is one point we won't be conceding.'

With as much dignity as I could muster, I scooped my Downtown from the floor and stood up to leave. Though my knees threatened to give way, my mind was crystal clear. 'Mr Williams,' I said, 'you can tell my husband's solicitor that, when it comes to the dog, that bastard Mark can go fuck himself. If he wants a fight he can have one. Fluffy is mine. Full stop. He stays with me.'

Two

Out on the street, with the door of Crawley, Hurte & Williams closed behind me, I pulled up the collar of my winter coat against the late January wind and checked the time on the Dolce & Gabbana my father had given me for my last-but-one birthday. I'd already lost half an afternoon at Haines and Hampton, the department store where I worked, and I had a client booked in at five – a famous, throaty-voiced stage actress in urgent need of an evening dress to wear for the BAFTA awards. If I found a taxi now, I'd just about make it back to Chelsea in time.

I hailed a cab and jumped inside, but instead of directing the driver to the store I gave him my home address in Islington and threw myself on to the seat. I couldn't face all those 'dahlings' and 'fahbulouses' in the changing room, not after what Mark had just done to me. I felt like a lollipop lady who'd been flattened on a zebra crossing by a yummy mummy driving a Chelsea tractor – sick, bewildered and stunned by the unfairness of it. After rummaging for a couple of minutes in the depths of my Downtown, I finally found my BlackBerry and dialled work.

'Hello. Personal Shopping at Haines and Hampton. Charlotte speaking. Have a nice day. How may I help you?' purred the plummy voice of our receptionist.

'It's me,' I said abruptly.

'Hello, Annie. Charlotte speaking.' Unlike me, Charlotte came from an upper-class county family. Thick as two planks, she'd survived her British public-school education without learning anything, it seemed, other than how to enunciate her vowels like Princess Anne.

'Yes, I know it's you, Charlotte. You've already said your name.'

'Have I? Sorry, Annie. How may I help you?'

'You "may help me" by putting me through to Eva, please.'

'Hold the line please, Annie. Have a nice day.' I held on, impatient for Eva Wyrzykowski to answer her bleep. Three years earlier, when Eva had started at the store as a cleaner, she'd been unable to speak anything but her native Polish. Now she spoke fluent English, passable French, a smattering of Russian, and was persuasive enough in Arabic to sell bikinis to our full-veiled Saudi Arabian clients. She'd not only risen through the ranks to become my favourite assistant, she was also halfway through an Open University degree course in management skills. Meanwhile, no one else in the personal-shopping department – myself included – had learned to pronounce her surname.

'Hold on, Annie, I'm putting you through to Eva now. Thank you for your call. Have a nice day.'

I made a mental note to tell Charlotte to cut out the American-style telephone jargon she'd recently taken to using. It was too annoying. Our clients were, on the whole, busy people who, like me, didn't have the patience for all that nonsense. Besides, I wasn't having a nice day. Far from it. How refreshing it was when Eva answered her telephone with a simple, efficient 'Hello?'

'Eva, it's me.'

'Yes, Annie?'

'Something's come up. An emergency. I have to go home. Could you . . .'

'. . . telephone your next client, make an excuse and reschedule the appointment for tomorrow if poss?'

'Yes. It's . . .'

'. . . Fenella Marshall,' she finished for me. 'Of course. I have her numbers here. Shall I tell her you suspect you're getting laryngitis? No actress would want to catch that.'

'You're a genius, Eva. Thanks.'

Next I selected my father's number from the call list. Then I thought better of it because, though it was now four weeks since Mark and I had decided to get divorced, I hadn't yet plucked up enough courage to tell Dad. Instead I dialled my best friend Clarissa, but when her number was engaged, I gave up.

All of a sudden I couldn't breathe. I forced my ribcage to expand and contract so that my lungs would too. I wasn't going to cry, I told myself. That bastard – for that was how I now thought of the man who, until this morning, I had called Mark, and had even addressed within living memory as 'darling' – wasn't going to get to me. Ever again.

Then I burst into tears. Me, Annie Curtis, née Osborne, who hadn't cried in front of another human being since my mother had disappeared when I was eight.

The cabbie glanced at me curiously in his rear-view mirror. I guessed he was about to say something comforting, so I looked away. By the time he'd lurched over the trillions of huge speed bumps that had turned the Islington back-streets around where I lived into the Swiss Alps, I'd pulled myself together and restored my face to something resembling normality with the help of some compact foundation and a slick of Chanel Rouge Noir. Hiding behind my shades, I paid him off and, instead of ringing the intercom bell four times in quick succession to let Mark know I was coming, as I usually did, I let myself into the block and stomped furiously up the three flights to the top floor.

As I reached our landing I heard the clatter of paws across wood. A moment later the shadow of a nose appeared at the crack under our front door and, after the brief but loud snuffling, the usual frantic barking began.

Fluffy.

Feeling sick at the thought that I might lose him, I tried to fit the key in the lock, but my hands were shaking so badly I couldn't do it. Eventually the door opened from inside. Like a greyhound let out of the traps, Fluffy hurled himself at me. Manic with happiness – after all, he hadn't seen me since I'd left home for the store at seven o'clock that morning, and for all he'd known I was never coming back – he leaped into the air like a circus dog, then stood on his hind legs and scrabbled at my coat buttons with his front paws. One tufted ear pointing upwards, the other pointing down, he grinned at me with demented devotion from under the haystack of his black-and-white fringe.

I glared over his bobbing head at the dishevelled monster slouched in the doorway behind him. Its knobbly pink feet were planted firmly in a pair of canvas summer sandals, from which its legs sprouted like hairy, muscular stalks. It was dressed in its usual daytime, all-year-round gear: a pair of old khaki knee-skimming baggy shorts teamed with its favourite Fair Trade tree-hugger sweatshirt – a washed-out grey garment emblazoned with the remarkably appropriate word *UseLess*. Its face was creased, its long, curly dark hair unwashed and uncombed. It was half past five in the afternoon but, as usual, the monster looked as if it'd been up all night in some jazz club, and had only just rolled out of bed.

This creature, this unkempt *thing* was my husband.

The man over whom I had once swooned breathlessly. The man I'd promised to love, and who'd promised to love me, until death us did part. The man I had once trusted implicitly, and believed was the nicest, kindest, most humane human being on earth.

The man of whom my doting father had often said, in less-than-dulcet tones, 'Call me a moron, but I just don't known what you see in him, love.'

'Hi!' Mark smiled his usual mild, imperturbable smile, shoved his hands into his shorts pockets and swayed towards me to plant a chaste kiss on my cheek.

But rather than let him make contact, I turned away at the last minute and instead embraced the ten kilos of exuberance, which was, at that moment, doing its best to knock me down. 'Hello, Fluffy-wuffy!'

Mark wiped some sleep from the corner of his eye. 'How's tricks?' he said. I ignored him. And instead of realizing it was his fault that I wasn't speaking to him, as he should have done, he automatically presumed I'd had a bad day at work. 'Failed to sell any ten-thousand-quid handbags today, did you?'

It was an old joke of his, a tired one. At the best of times it would have merited a weak grin. This afternoon I scowled at him as I shrugged off my coat and threw it over the back of the sofa.

'Where's Mickey Mouse?' I said to Fluffy, scratching his ears. 'Fetch Mickey, Fluffy!' All spindly legs, wagging tail and swaggering derrière, Fluffy scooted off across the living room to retrieve his favourite toy from his basket. He picked it up in his pointy muzzle, brought it over and, hovering a few feet from me, growled as he tempted me to take it from him. When I lunged for it, he shied away. 'Drop it, Fluffy!'

'Annie?'

'Drop it!' I warned Fluffy, then lunged again. Quicker off the mark this time, I grabbed Mickey's leg and, after a short tussle, wrested the toy from between his teeth. As I flung it the length of the room, with more force than I knew I possessed, I imagined I was hurling it at Mark's head.

Puzzled by the lack of communication, Mark shifted thoughtfully from foot to sandal-clad foot, until at last the penny dropped. 'Why are you wearing your sunglasses in the house?' he asked. 'Aren't you talking to me or something?'

'Talking to you?' Fluffy came running back with Mickey. This time he stayed well out of my reach, growling. I turned to my husband, removed my shades and gave a bitter laugh. 'About what, Mark Curtis? There's really nothing to talk about any more, is there? And you know perfectly well why.'

He spread his hands. 'No, actually, I don't.'

I took a deep breath. 'I've just been to see my solicitor. He told me about Fluffy.' Mark opened his mouth to say something, but I wouldn't let him speak. I shook my head incredulously and went on, 'I can't believe you're trying to do this to me. I *hate* you. No, that's not strong enough for how I feel – I *loathe* and *despise* you, you – you rotten, lazy, scheming, unfaithful, two-faced *bastard*! And I never want to speak to you again as long as I live!'

And having made this pre-emptive strike, I grabbed Fluffy's collar, dragged him into what until that morning had still been Mark's and my bedroom, and slammed the door on the bitter dregs of our marriage.

Overcome with exhaustion, I lay down on the expensive memory-foam mattress – a mattress imprinted with the memory of how tenderly we had once made love – and kicked off my shoes. Fur flying, Fluffy jumped up to join me, and attempted to straddle my chest. After I'd pushed him off a few times he got the message and trampled circles on the duvet, then stretched out comfortingly across my feet.

How had this happened? I brooded, as I picked up the TV remote, switched on our thirty-two-inch LCD and, without the slightest interest in what he was saying, watched a high-definition George Alagiah read the BBC News at Six.

My marriage was over. History. In the bin-bag.

And only weeks earlier, on the morning of 25 December, I'd started the day thinking it had never been so good.

Three

It was Christmas Day in the Workhouse, and from outside Islington's Institution for the Destitute looked as grim and oppressive as it had when it had first opened its doors to the parish paupers way back in the 1840s.

From the inside, however, it was a different picture. Where once there had hung lists of rules – *No Disorderly Conduct, No Smoking but Abroad, No Obscene or Profane Language* – there now hung Damien Hirst prints and plasma screens. Where once rough wooden clogs had thudded against splintery pine floors, the soft soles of Tod's loafers padded across planks of polished American oak. And where, in the old days, there had been only one communal cold-water tap on each landing, shared by up to a hundred inmates, the old Institution now boasted a glut of en-suite bathrooms, shower rooms and wet rooms, all equipped with state-of-the-art Philippe Starck sanitary fittings.

Back in the nineteenth century, the working classes of the parish had dreaded the degradation of entering the building. Nowadays their descendants could only dream of it. Like the area's run-down terraced houses, which had long ago been gentrified by future prime ministers, the Workhouse (as the old institutional building had recently been renamed by the developers who'd turned it into 'lifestyle apartments') was now the preserve of the well-to-do.

The high walls surrounding it had once kept the local unemployed from breaking out. Now those same walls stopped their great-great-grandchildren breaking in. Watched over twenty-four hours a day by a bank of CCTV cameras and a team of African or Eastern European concierges, the gated development was reputed to be the most secure in the N1 postcode. Even the Ocado delivery drivers had a hard time gaining access to the car park to drop off the organic provisions and luxury quilted lavatory paper that the owner-occupiers had ordered on the Internet during quiet moments at work.

This high level of security, however, proved more of a provocation than a deterrent to the gangs from the surrounding sink estates. Hard-faced hoodies, who wore their ASBOs like military decorations, bare-legged school-girls, who dressed like hookers in micro-skirts and vertiginously heeled boots, they congregated round the Workhouse's main gates at all times of day and night, drinking, smoking, swearing and making threatening gestures at the residents when they roared down the street in their VWs and Porsches, frantically waving their remote controls at the car park's automatic barrier as if their lives depended upon it.

This being Christmas morning, however, the hoodies and hookers were at home opening their Christmas presents, and Winston Churchill, the Workhouse's daytime concierge, had – uniquely of the building's occupants – gone to church. Down in the basement communal gym, which was a steaming cauldron of testosterone, sweat and Calvin Klein eau-de-Cologne on working days, the Power Plates and treadmills had yet to be switched on.

At least half of the Workhouse's occupants had left London for Christmas in Klosters, Gloucestershire or Ibiza and, as a result, the huge Victorian building creaked like a deserted ship.

As Mark and I lounged about in our towelling bathrobes up on the third floor, we felt deliciously alone.

Mark was pottering about at the kitchen end of our open-plan living room, while I was lying on the big white rug beside the steel-clad free-standing fireplace – one of the many wow-factors that had made me decide to buy the place when I'd first viewed it seven years before. Fluffy lay on the rug beside me, snoring gently, his long hind-quarters stretched out behind him and his muzzle resting peacefully between his paws.

Though the sky outside the huge sash windows was a leaden grey, it felt wonderfully cosy indoors. The gas fire's roaring flames, turned up to the maximum, cast a warm glow over the exposed-brick walls, and a dozen star-shaped paper lanterns, strung between the cast-iron roof girders, sent flickering shadows dancing across the vaulted ceiling. Our eight-foot-high Christmas tree twinkled with coloured baubles, ropes of garish Woolworth's tinsel, and skeins of flashing LED lights, and a giant plastic snowflake, covered with sparkling glitter, was pinned to the bathroom door. The final touches were the dancing mini-Santa, which was gyrating on the glass-topped table, and the Christmas CD *Krazy Karaoke Karols* blasting out from our B&O.

When I'd rushed off to work two days earlier there hadn't been a sign of Christmas in the apartment. But as soon as I'd left, Mark had walked Fluffy up to Chapel

Street market and raided its Christmas stalls. By the time I'd got back that evening he'd already put up everything.

'Whaddayathink?' he'd asked, slouching in the doorway as Fluffy ran round and round the flashing tree, manically chasing his hairy question-mark of a tail.

I'd regarded it with a professional eye. 'I'd say it's part nineteen-sixties trailer trash, and part Hamley's Santa's Grotto. Totally tasteless, kitsch and over the top. And I adore it, darling! Next year you should design the windows at Haines and Hampton. All that's missing is a light-up sleigh on the roof.'

Mark had taken my hand and led me to the bedroom. Fluffy had followed at our heels. Suddenly his ears had flattened and he'd growled. A moment later he'd changed from a docile mutt into a mad werewolf and had thrown himself at the sliding windows. A life-size inflatable plastic reindeer with a glowing red nose was staring in at us from our decked balcony.

'Where on earth did you get *that*?' I'd gasped.

'It was part of a job lot with the dancing Santa. I think the bloke who was selling it wanted to go home.'

I'd thrown my arms round my husband's neck. 'How can I ever thank you enough for doing all this for me?'

Funnily enough, he'd immediately thought of the perfect way. And the bed had been just behind us.

Since then, everything had been great between us – much better, in fact, than it had been for ages. Mark hadn't sniped at me for not sorting out my rubbish for recycling, and I hadn't snapped at him for kicking off his muddy walking boots on the white living-room rug. He hadn't accused me of monopolizing the en-suite first thing in the morning, and I hadn't complained late at night that his music was keeping me awake. He'd cooked me my favourite food without having to be asked – spaghetti carbonara, pan-roasted cod with home-made chips and designer mushy peas, and Chocolate Nemesis from the *River Café Cook Book*. In return I'd scoffed the lot without once mentioning that I was still on the low-carb diet I'd been following, without success, for the last three years.

So, as I stared into the gas-flamed fire on Christmas morning, and Mark wandered towards me, carrying two freshly made cappuccinos, I counted my blessings. How nice was *this*, to be sitting in front of a fire, singing along out of tune to a karaoke version of 'O Little Town of Bethlehem' with the two beings I loved most in the world for company? Plus, there was the sweet, slightly medicinal scent of the huge Nordic fir in my nostrils, and the tantalizing smell of slow-roasting pheasants, wrapped in pancetta and stuffed with Calvados-soaked apples, wafting from the oven.

As usual Mark, who was a brilliant cook, had gone to town over our Christmas meals, but I was so content that morning that I didn't give a stuff what we ate for lunch – it could have been Turkey Twizzlers for all I cared. Ours might not have been the liveliest or most sociable Christmas Day – my father was in Barbados with his girlfriend, Norma, and her two teenage sons, and Mark's parents, Jackie and Dennis, were cooking lunch for their customers at the Dog and Fox, their pub outside Norwich – but it felt perfect for Mark and me to be at home together. After we'd eaten, we'd get dressed and drive over to Hampstead for what had become, during the five years we'd been together, our traditional Christmas Day walk on the Heath. What could be nicer than a private, domestic twenty-four hours after the fraught, sozzled build-up at work to the holiday season? There was only so much Bollinger, bonhomie and speculation about which designer dress, eye-shadow and clutch bag looked best on a client that a woman could stomach without feeling she'd had enough of the high-end fashion business for good.

There was another reason, too, why I felt so happy that Christmas morning. There were only six more days left until 31 December. This meant that Mark and I had made it through another year. There had been times during the past twelve months when I'd feared we wouldn't. Just like I'd feared the year before. Oh, yes, and the year before that. But here we were on the brink of New Year's Eve, still very much together, I thought smugly, as I skimmed the cocoa-sprinkled froth from my cappuccino and sucked it off my teaspoon. It was, in fact, a Christmas miracle. Not quite the Virgin Birth, but a miracle nevertheless.

'So, who wants presents?' said Mark, squatting beside me.

'Me, please!'

He put down his mug and crawled under the Christmas tree, revealing as he did so a glimpse of marble-white, naked buttock under his towelling robe. After some scuffling, he emerged with a pile of boxes and packages all beautifully wrapped in red-and-gold paper and tied with silver ribbon – presents he'd wrapped especially for

Fluffy and me. On impulse I leaned over and kissed him.

'Mmm. What have I done to deserve that?' he said, with a smile.

'Nothing. You just happen to be rather buff, that's all.'

'"Buff"? What kind of word is that? Something you've learned from your teenage assistants, I suppose. Don't you mean suave, sophisticated and irresistible?'

If there was anything Mark wasn't, it was suave and sophisticated. But irresistible? I looked at his full, smiling mouth, and the crinkly blue eyes set wide apart in his craggy, weatherbeaten face, softened by the halo of unruly dark curls that surrounded it. At forty, he was still seriously attractive, even more so than when he'd first walked into my life, aged thirty-five.

'Oh, I wouldn't go so far as to say you're irresistible,' I said, as I brushed away a sprinkling of pine needles that had got tangled up in his hair.

'Why not?' Puckering his lips into a huge mock kiss, he lunged at me and, as we larked around like kids, I accidentally hit Fluffy's nose with my elbow. He woke with a yelp, leaped to his feet and, in an attempt to join in the game, grabbed the hem of Mark's bathrobe and tried to rip it off him, knocking over Mark's cappuccino in the process.

First it was Fluffy's turn for presents. We'd spoiled him terribly, but I can't say he appreciated it. Not even an organic hand-baked carob-flavoured dog biscuit in the shape of a snowflake could tempt him to enter the new, fake-fur bed we'd bought him; he much preferred the paper it was wrapped in, which he promptly tore to shreds and scattered all over the floor. He looked great in the Burberry collar and leash set I'd got with my employee's discount from Haines's luxury-gift department, though rather more like a flash *nouveau-riche* rock star than the pedigree country gentleman I'd hoped for. But, then, with his thin, lurcher-like body, his extra-long back, his loping gait, his jutting hip-bones and the cartoon-like black and white fur that sprouted from the top of his head like an old-fashioned floor mop, Fluffy wasn't exactly the pedigree type.

Still, the sterling-silver bone-shaped dog-tag we'd had engraved with his name did lend him a rather upper-class air. Not that Fluffy was impressed by designer accessories. In fact, the only present he expressed any real interest in was the cheap Christmas stocking stuffed with packets of rawhide chews and liver-flavoured treats that Mark had picked up at our local pet shop, and which Fluffy polished off in minutes (along with half of its nylon net wrapper), despite our warnings that it would ruin his appetite for lunch.

Next we took it in turns to open our presents. I'd given Mark the new Eric Clapton autobiography. He'd given me a voucher for a day at London's swankiest spa. I'd given him a Paul Smith sweatshirt. He'd given me the fabulous red patent Vivienne Westwood bag I'd been eyeing all season. I'd given him Bose earphones for his iPod. He'd bought me the eight-thousand-pound Banksy screen print – to which he'd taken a fancy when we'd seen it in an exhibition in Soho several months before.

Anyone looking at those gifts might have thought

that, compared to my over-generous husband, I was miserly. However, they should know that everything Mark and I had bought for each other on our credit cards would eventually be paid for out of our joint bank account. I say our joint bank account because both our names were on it. We both had cheque books, cash cards and equal access to the Internet banking service. Everything that came out of the account was, thus, joint expenditure.

The only thing that wasn't joint about the account was the money that went into it.

It was all mine.

As I often told my father when he moaned about Mark, apart from the reversal in our sexes there was nothing unusual about our financial situation which was replicated in millions of marriages all over the world. I, as the main breadwinner, brought home the bulk of our income, and my spouse, who earned pin-money, helped me spend it. And spending money happened to be one of the three things my spouse was good at. The other two being cooking and sex.

'Wow!' I said, as I unwrapped the Banksy. 'You actually bought this!'

'Yeah.' He looked at it proudly and smiled. 'I sneaked back to the gallery later that week with my Visa.'

'Amazing!'

'Are you pleased with it?'

'Of course! It's lovely!' As lovely as it could be, considering it was an image of a rat holding a placard on which were scrawled the words, 'Welcome to Hell'. 'I'm just . . . well, I'm surprised you splashed out on it, that's all.'

'I know it's incredibly extravagant,' Mark went on, looking at me doubtfully, 'but I thought you'd like it.'

'Oh, I do! Very much! I mean, it's *great*, Mark. A *brilliant* present! Thanks *so* much! Where do you think we should hang it?'

'Well, I'm not sure. I was thinking up there, maybe.'

He pointed at the small mezzanine level that overhung part of the kitchen. This was our study area, where Mark kept the digital piano I'd bought him for his last birthday in the vain hope that it would inspire him to compose a number-one hit.

'Mmm.'

His face fell. 'Why do you say it like that, Annie?'

'Like what?'

'Suspiciously. *Mmm?* Like you think I bought the Banksy for myself.'

I cursed him for being such a mind-reader. 'Mark! What a horrible thing to say!'

'I just think it'd look good up there, don't you?'

'Yes. Terrific.'

'Really? Look, I know it cost a lot, but I figured it'd be an investment. I mean, as well as being a present. I'm sure I read in the *Guardian* that the price of Banksy prints keeps shooting up. Doesn't it?'

'Oh, yes!'

'And I thought you deserved something special for Christmas.' He suddenly looked ashamed. 'I wanted to spoil you. You've worked so hard this year, and done so well, while I . . . Well, I've been sodding useless, haven't I? As usual.'

'You haven't!'

'Cut the crap, Annie.'

Mark's bursts of self-deprecating candour always made me melt. I couldn't bear to see him upset. He was so committed to composing guitar music and writing lyrics, which he'd been doing ever since he'd left university a hundred years before – having gained, according to my father, an honours degree in slothfulness. He worked so hard at composing, but to little effect. From the snatches I'd heard of his songs – when he deigned to play them to me – I was convinced they'd be successful – when he eventually found someone to record them, that was.

But when would that be? No wonder he felt demoralized. While my career had gone from strength to strength since we'd got married just under five years ago, his had gone precisely nowhere. He had ambition – well, sort of – but did he have enough talent? I thought his music was great, but unfortunately the people in the business didn't seem to agree. Year after year, Mark persevered, endlessly honing, rewriting and repolishing his compositions until he'd quite worn through them. His desk was piled high with rejection letters from music publishers, record producers and singers' agents. Some were gentle let-downs of the my-client-list-is-already-so-full-that-I-would-not-be-able-to-do-justice-to-your-obvious-talent variety. Others were downright insulting, and some agents didn't even bother to reply to him. They probably didn't listen to the CDs he sent them – just hurled them straight into the dustbin, as I did the DVDs of vintage TV sit-coms that seemed to come free with every Sunday newspaper.

'Oh, darling, don't be crazy!' I said to Mark now. 'You're a brilliant composer!'

'I'm rubbish.'

'You're not! I believe in you.'

'Thanks. But what do you know about music?'

This was Mark's mildly insulting answer whenever I praised his work. 'Well, I listen to the radio. And I watch MTV sometimes. Besides, you know I couldn't do what I do without you. Work such long hours at the store, I mean. Who'd take care of Fluffy if you had a full-time job? And who'd look after me?'

Eventually I managed to cajole him out of his mood and we went back to bed. While Fluffy dozed on the rug, snoring rhythmically, we made love with more tenderness than we'd done in a long while. I even surprised myself by not having to fake my orgasm – something I'd been doing rather too frequently lately. It wasn't that I'd gone off making love with Mark, I was just so tired by the time I got home from work that I'd rather have had a cup of Ovaltine than the night of passion that was on offer. Perhaps I was getting old.

Afterwards we cuddled up in bed watching a DVD of *It's a Wonderful Life*.

'What's that's smell?' Mark said suddenly. 'Something's burning. Oh, shit, it must be the pheasant!' He leaped out of bed and ran stark naked into the kitchen, Fluffy bounding at his heels.

Grinning to myself, I propped myself up on our large pile of pillows, and listened to the domestic symphony issuing from the kitchen: the clank of a roasting tin as it was taken out of the oven, the rustle of aluminium foil, the rattle of the knife drawer followed by a string of expletives.

'Don't panic, Nurse,' he called. 'She may have third-degree burns but I think I can save her. However, we may have to amputate.' A couple of minutes later, he reappeared clutching a charred drumstick and asked, 'Would you say this is cooked through yet?'

While I fell about laughing, Fluffy snatched the burned offering and, balancing it between his big front paws, settled down to demolish it on the bedside rug. To his fury Mark snatched it back, in case the bones splintered in his mouth. Then, shutting our disgruntled mutt in the bedroom with me, he returned to the kitchen to rescue the remains of Christmas lunch.

Married life! There was nothing to beat it, I reflected as, furious at being excluded from the kitchen, Fluffy first whined at the door, then crawled under our bed on one of his frequent seek-and-destroy missions. How right I'd been to stick with Mark! After I'd found out about his affair with Fern, our Antipodean Pilates teacher, eighteen months before, my best friend Clarissa had warned me that he was congenitally immature and would never settle down. However, over a bottle of Chilean Sauvignon Blanc and a big bowl of salted almonds in the Roach and Parrot in Upper Street, I'd assured her she was wrong.

'Mark says he only had an affair because he was unhappy and frustrated,' I'd said defensively. 'It was partly my fault.'

'*Yours?*' Scandalized, Clarissa had sat forward in her chair. Even in an old pair of black trousers and a navy-blue jumper of her husband's that was not only three sizes too big for her but had seen better days, my tall, slender friend had managed to look as elegant as Erin

O'Connor. She'd even looked good in our navy blue school uniform – a feat never achieved by any other girl. 'Poise is in her blood,' her mother had once told me, in the living room of the family's house in Cadogan Square – a gloomy place full of heavily varnished portraits of her ancestors and dark Victorian furniture that, like the Garland family's finances, had seen better days. 'You see, Clarissa's grandmother was a duchess, dear. And breeding will out, as we all know.' Perhaps the Hon. Mrs Garland had been trying to warn me off being friends with her daughter: with my background, good breeding was something I'd never possess, at least in her eyes. But the nice thing about Clarissa was that she'd never given a toss about any of that, even at the age of eleven. She and I were inseparable from our very first day at school, even though I called my grandmother 'Nan' rather than 'your ladyship', dropped my aitches and scooped peas from my dinner plate with the inside of a fork (though my new teachers had soon put a stop to that).

Anyway, it had turned out that Clarissa was desperate to let down the crumbling aristocratic side of her family, rather than prop it up. As soon as she'd left school, she'd joined the Socialist Workers' Party and shacked up with James, a penniless Welsh miner's son who was a left-wing law student. Seventeen years on, James was a QC and a stalwart of the local Liberal Democrats, while Clarissa was a social worker and the harassed, somewhat worn-out mother of their four ravishing young daughters, Rachel, Rebecca, Emily and Miranda. More importantly, at least to me, she was still my best friend.

'I haven't been paying Mark enough attention lately,

you see,' I'd gone on to explain. 'I can't have been loving enough to him. I've been too preoccupied with my job.'

Clarissa had shaken her long, lank, mousy hair. 'That's because you're brilliant at what you do! You've made an incredible success of running Haines's personal-shopping department. *Vogue* didn't call you 'the make-over queen' in their last issue for nothing, darling. Mark should understand that. He ought to be proud of you.'

'Oh, he is. I'm sure he is.'

'Does he often say so?'

'Yes,' I'd said. But when Clarissa had narrowed her eyes at me, I'd admitted, 'Well, not for some time.'

'You mustn't feel guilty about doing well, Annie. You have a real talent for helping people to change their appearance for the better. I mean, just think what you did for Whatsername.'

'Who's Whatsername?'

'You know – the shadow secretary of state for Whatever-it-is. One minute the tabloids are calling her a political liability. The next, every glossy mag in the country was slapping her on the front page.'

'Well, it wasn't hard to make her look better because she couldn't have looked worse.'

'Mark should be grateful to you. One of you has to earn a proper living, for God's sake.'

'I know that. But I don't think he understands how much everything costs.' I'd crunched up some almonds, then washed them down with a big gulp of Sauvignon. 'And then there's the baby question.'

'Ah. The bloody baby question,' Clarissa had enunciated,

with her cut-glass consonants, 'which keeps raising its ugly, bald little head.'

'It isn't funny. It's a real issue. You can't blame Mark for wanting to start a family.'

'I guess not. Men have such pathetically frail egos that they need to prove they're virile by spawning. Just think of James. Well, call me old-fashioned, but I don't think sleeping with another woman is the best way to go about getting one's wife knocked up.'

'I guess not. But you know me, I'm not ready for motherhood.'

Clarissa had raised her arched, aristocratic eyebrows. 'You *are* in your late thirties, darling. Tick-tock and all that bullshit.'

'Thanks for reminding me. You sound like Mark. *And* my father. You see? Even you secretly agree that I've driven Mark away because I don't want to have children yet!'

'Well, you must have expected him to want them some time. After all, he does come from a big, jolly family. How many sisters does he have? Six? Seven?'

'Three. I've lost count of all the nieces and nephews.' I'd pushed the half-empty nut-bowl to her side of the table. 'Don't let me have any more, please. On pain of death. Except these,' I'd added, as I'd scooped up a last handful. This was definitely not the right time to stick to my permanent diet. When was? 'I suppose I'll have to make more effort to please him in future, if I want to stop him having another affair.'

'Good idea,' Clarissa had commented drily. 'Have lots and lots of babies just to make Mark happy. A brood of screaming brats overrunning the flat – that should stop him straying.' Clarissa had shaken her head in despair. 'You should listen to yourself, Annie. You sound like a battered wife, blaming herself for her husband's abysmal behaviour, then going back for another beating.'

As I lay in bed on Christmas Day I tried to put this conversation out of my mind and concentrate instead on the black-and-white images of 1946 small-town America flickering across the TV screen in *It's a Wonderful Life*. But even as I watched a desperate George Bailey, a.k.a. James Stewart, tell Clarence, his guardian angel, that his life had been a total failure, I was thinking about Mark's affair.

Despite what Clarissa had said after I'd found Fern's disgusting red thong nestling among the manky socks in his sports bag, I knew I'd been right to stick with him. After all, the affair had only been a *Brief Encounter*, if you'll forgive the pun. Except that, unlike Celia Johnson and Trevor Howard, the lovestruck stars of one of my favourite black-and-white films, Mark and Fern had actually had sex, rather than just thought about it. And, they'd had it quite a few times, if my suspicions had been right. Still, Mark had insisted he'd only done it because he'd been so depressed and disillusioned with our relationship, and he'd promised it would never happen again. And when you weighed up the rights and wrongs of the situation in the scales of justice, lacy thongs and all, what were a few meaningless shags when weighed up against our marriage?

In *It's a Wonderful Life* the good folk of Bedford Falls gathered together to save George Bailey from financial ruin, while his wife Mary stood by with tears of pride in her eyes. As I snuggled under the bedclothes, I congratu-lated myself that things between Mark and me really had changed for the better during the last year. It hadn't been easy, but we'd managed to avoid talking about difficult issues such as money, and Fern, and having babies, and money, and Fern, and the long hours I worked, and the long hours he didn't, and Fern, and money, and as a consequence we hadn't quarrelled nearly as much as we used to. During the build-up to Christmas he had seemed happier and more relaxed than he had earlier in the year. He was even making good progress with a new song. Once his talent was recognized, his self-esteem would be restored and, I persuaded myself, we'd live happily ever after, just like George and Mary Bailey.

There was a rustle under the bed, and the end of Fluffy's long bristly tail, which was sticking out from under the valance, swished excitedly from side to side. He'd obviously found something of interest among the junk we'd shoved there and, from the ripping sounds I could hear, he was tearing it to shreds.

'Fluffy?' I leaned over the side of the bed, raised the valance and peered into the darkness. Though he knew I was there, Fluffy took absolutely no notice of me, even when I tapped his hindquarters. 'What are you doing?' Still he ignored me. Whatever he'd found – an old pair of knickers, a half-eaten biscuit, some balled-up tights – I knew it wouldn't be good for him. He'd probably eat it, retch for a while, then throw it up. I'd lost count of the times Mark and I had had to clear up the regurgitated aftermath of Fluffy's destruction-fests.

What had he found now? 'Drop it!' I said, in my most

commanding voice. I might as well have saved my breath. It was hopeless telling Fluffy anything. Mark, who had a way with dogs, said he was the most disobedient animal he'd ever come across.

'Did you hear me, Fluffy? I said *drop it*!' Fluffy threw me a defiant glance, his eyes flashing yellow in the gloom under the bed, then carried on with what he'd been doing. I heard another rip, followed by a crunch. I jumped out of bed, threw on my bathrobe, grabbed him by the haunches and hauled him out. Though he gave a menacing growl, I knew he wouldn't bite me. Fluffy might pretend to be aggressive, but as a rule he abhorred violence – the exception being the occasional tussle with other dogs.

'Okay, that's enough!' I said. 'Give it to me!' Thinking he was being clever, Fluffy let go of whatever he'd been chewing just before his muzzle emerged from under the bed. Though he gave me an innocent look, there were flecks of red and gold paper on his lips.

I let go of him and, before he could scramble back under the bed, I reached in and rescued his soggy prey. As I threw it on to the mattress, he leaped up after it, barking excitedly. I followed suit, and snatched the thing out of his reach. 'Get off!' I said, standing on the mattress while Fluffy pirouetted into the air with snapping jaws. 'Get down! Bad dog! Down!' At last he slunk back on to the floor, where he sat to attention and eyed the parcel with longing.

He'd found another Christmas present, wrapped in the same expensive red-and-gold paper as the Banksy. I read the message on the card: 'Darling,' Mark had scrawled in his spidery script, 'A little something for our walks on the

Heath.' The words were followed by his trademark signature to me, a long line of Xs, followed by a star. He must have forgotten to give it to me earlier, I thought. Or maybe he'd been keeping it as a special surprise for later in the day.

I felt all warm inside.

I smiled to myself. Yes, I actually smiled.

I thought, Aren't I a lucky woman?

'Everything all right in there?' Mark yelled from the kitchen. 'It's almost ready.'

'Great!' I yelled back. 'Couldn't be better. I'll be out in a sec.'

I knew I should put the present straight back under the bed and wait until Mark remembered to give it to me, but curiosity got the better of me. What *had* he bought me for our walks on the Heath? A cashmere scarf from N. Peal's in Burlington Arcade? A Nicole Farhi hat? Or perhaps that pair of yellow fur-lined Marc Jacob gloves I'd eyed the other week when I'd gone spying in Harvey Nicks?

Taking care not to tear the paper any further, I prised it apart and peeped inside.

My heart stopped. Curled up like a snake in a nest of cellophane and gold tissue paper was a dog collar and a leash. The leash was hand-stitched and made of the finest, shiniest ostrich skin. Hanging from the matching collar was a multitude of tiny charms: enamelled stars, a silver kennel, a mobile phone with tiny diamanté buttons, and a dog bowl, all interspersed with little silver hearts.

It occurred to me that they must have cost Mark a

fortune – they really were the most beautiful collar and leash I'd ever seen.

There was only one thing wrong.

The colour.

It was pink.

After going through a moment or two of fuzzy confusion, my brain achieved a horrible clarity. This pink collar-and-leash set wasn't meant for our very male dog. *Ergo*, that line of kisses on the gift tag wasn't intended for me.

'Lunch is on the table!' Mark called cheerfully, from the living room. 'Hurry up, angel!'

Unable to speak, I sank down on the bed with the soggy, half-unwrapped parcel dangling loosely from my hand. Fluffy nosed in to reclaim it. This time I let him fish out the end of the leash and chew it. What did I care if it was punctured with toothmarks? I tried to work out which was the greater betrayal: that Mark was having another affair, or that he'd hidden the present he'd bought for his new mistress under our bed. Knowing it was there, just beneath us, how could he have held me in his arms as he'd just done, and made love to me as if he'd meant it, and not have felt torn apart with guilt? If he *had* felt guilty, he'd hidden it better than he'd hidden the bloody present. I must be completely insensitive to his feelings. Because I simply hadn't been able to tell.

What a fool I was!

I had to think quickly. What was I going to do about this? Garrotte Mark with the leash when he sat down to eat Christmas lunch? Or shove the parcel back where it had come from, say nothing, and try to forget I'd ever found the damned thing? I'd attempted to do that with Fern's thong, but – unlike Mark, obviously – I'm hopeless at hiding my feelings, and it had only taken a matter of six broken mugs in as many seconds for him to work out that something was seriously wrong between us.

A second later the decision was taken out of my hands as Mark burst through the bedroom door.

'The burned offering's getting cold on the plates, babe,' he said. ' Come and . . .' His voice petered out when he saw the thin line of pink ostrich skin which was now stretched between my hand and Fluffy's clenched teeth. He froze. Our eyes met, and the colour drained from his face.

'Oh, shit!' he said. He came to me and, pushing Fluffy aside, knelt penitently at my feet. 'I know what this looks like, darling,' he said, putting his hand over mine and squeezing it. 'But, believe me, it was a stupid fling. It doesn't mean anything.'

I digested this for a moment, then said, 'Not to you, perhaps.'

'I'm so, so sorry, Annie. It just sort of happened. You see, I –'

I cut him short, and pulled my hand away. 'I don't want to hear your excuses.'

'Please, darling, let me at least try to explain.'

'You can't,' I said. 'Not this time.' I sighed. 'Not ever again.'

'Annie?' he said. 'What are you saying?'

I looked into my husband's gorgeous blue eyes, and I knew that, whatever he did or promised, I'd never be able to trust him again. 'Look, Mark,' I said, 'we both know this marriage isn't working. Not for either of us.'

And then I said the four little words that started off this whole, ghastly chain of events: 'I want a divorce.'

Four

My mother's most treasured object was her dressing-table.

It was kidney-shaped, made of cream-painted wood and embellished with gold-burnished rococo swirls – bog-standard cheap bedroom furniture, in the nineteen sixties, but nowadays back in fashion as retro 'French shabby chic'. Though my parents' bedroom in the 1950s council-owned maisonette in Hackney where we then lived was not exactly spacious – there was barely room to see the patterned Cyril Lord carpet between the bed and the walls – Mum's dressing-table was squeezed into a corner by the metal-framed window, with a small, matching stool, upholstered in striped Regency-style fabric, tucked underneath it.

The top of the kidney was covered with a sheet of thick glass, beneath which was sandwiched a group of family photographs. These included a black-and-white snap of my maternal grandparents standing outside their greengrocer's shop in Stepney, a cute nude studio portrait of myself as a baby, and a picture of my mother, Julie, sitting with a female friend on Brighton Beach, both in bikinis. Mum must have been around twenty when it was taken, and looked terribly young and carefree.

The dressing-table's five drawers – two deep ones on either side of the kneehole, and a long, thin one above it – were treasure troves of things that she had either bought or inherited from her own mother, who'd died the year I was born. In the top drawer on the left-hand side there were some nylon chiffon squares in bright colours, a pair of cream kid evening gloves with tiny pearl buttons at the wrists, a stash of plastic hair-combs and some Kirby-grips. The drawer below it contained embroidered handkerchiefs, unused and in their original boxes, an old-fashioned bone-handled chamois nail buffer, and hairnets as fine as cobwebs, made from knotted real hair. The drawers on the other side of the kneehole housed my mother's jewellery: old fifties brooches set with rainbow-hued paste stones, a pair of large silver hoop earrings, and colourful Perspex necklaces and bangles, one in a black-and-white op-art design. There was also my grandmother's old sewing-kit, a felt bag that contained a metal thimble, a packet of needles and a skein of interwoven multi-coloured threads, which Mum used now and then to sew on buttons. If I remember correctly, this was about as domestic as she'd ever got.

The drawer above the kneehole was my favourite because it contained Mum's makeup. Within its shallow wooden divisions were stowed pots of rouge with fan-shaped brushes, half-used cakes of Rimmel eye-liner, sticks of Max Factor Pan-Stik, a bottle of white Mary Quant nail varnish, and old plastic face-powder boxes that leaked their soft, pale contents into the dusty corners. There was also a big collection of oily pink lipsticks, all in greasy gold cases, and all worn down to the same, uneven U-shaped stump, formed by my mother's particular way of applying the colour to her lips.

It was at this dressing-table, on the matching stool, that my mother sat to adorn herself before she went out to the local pub once or twice a week. As I lay on her bed in my ruffled pink baby-doll pyjamas, watching her put on what she called her war-paint with her right hand while clutching an ash-dripping menthol cigarette in the left, I would see each side of her profile reflected in the matching triple mirror balanced on top: her green eyes large, almond-shaped and framed with thick false lashes, her long blonde hair straight and glossy, her nose small and upturned, her gorgeous high cheekbones accentuated by the application of silvery Miners highlighter, underscored with stripes of brown Mary Quant face-shaper.

After she'd sashayed out of the flat, swathed in a long, fake-fur Biba coat and reeking of Estee Lauder's Youth Dew, I would take her place on the stool, put her cold, lipstick-stained cigarette butt in my mouth and deck myself out in her finery. This was, I suppose, the first of the thousands of fashion makeovers for which I later became famous. I certainly had my work cut out. Instead of my mother's fine features and streaming blonde locks, I'd inherited my father's strong chin, high forehead, flat, boxer's nose and straight, mousy hair. I think I knew even then that, no matter how much makeup I plastered on, my looks would never be a patch on Mum's. Still, I enjoyed playing at being a glamorous adult. From my eight-year-old perspective I imagined growing up as a kind of small, rocky hill with a plateau on top of it. By the time I was twenty, I'd have reached the summit, married the man of my dreams and found everlasting happiness. The future would stretch ahead of me like a smooth, grassy plain.

Were my parents' lives like that? On the surface Julie was gregarious and always game for a laugh, and nothing ever seemed to faze Bob Osborne, my genial, hardworking dad, except his losses at the local betting shop, where he threw away most of the cash he earned selling cut-price, out-of-date cosmetics on his market stall. But looking back now, I remember silent family meals when you could have cut the atmosphere with a bread knife, my mother's snide comments about Dad's gambling, and shouting matches behind closed doors in which 'bastard' and 'bitch' were bandied back and forth as fast as the balls at a Chinese table-tennis tournament. It didn't really worry me at the time. This was what family life was like in our house: a series of laughs, interspersed with rows. Sometimes my parents were at loggerheads, at others they were like the lovebirds I'd seen in the local pet shop, billing and cooing side by side on a wooden perch. But when Mum and Dad sat close together on the sofa watching *Coronation Street*, and my father put his arm round her shoulders and pulled her close, I sometimes had an uneasy feeling – as if I knew that, deep down, she tolerated his caresses and kisses rather than enjoying them.

One night their shouting woke me up, and in my half-conscious state I was aware of a commotion in the hall. When I stole into my parents' bedroom the following morning, as I often did to climb into the warm, safe place between them, Mum was missing, Dad was slumped against the pink Dralon headboard, red-eyed and desolate, and the dressing-table's drawers were hanging open; they looked as if they'd been ransacked.

'What's happened? Where's Mum?' I asked Dad.

46

'She's not here, love,' he sobbed, into a half-empty glass of gin. 'And she's not coming back!'

'What do you mean?'

He wiped his eyes with the back of his hand and sniffed loudly. 'Your mum's gone and done a bunk on us, hasn't she?'

Never having heard that expression before, I presumed he meant she'd 'done a bank', like his brother James, who was then halfway through a fifteen-year sentence for armed robbery. So, when Mum didn't come home that night, or the next, or any time that week, I thought that, like Uncle Jimmy, she was away at Her Majesty's pleasure, and would be home when the Queen deigned to let her out.

Six months later, on a visit to my paternal grandmother in Stepney, I plucked up courage to ask Nan when my mother would come out of prison. Her prune of a face turned puce beneath her red-rinsed hair, and she said, 'Coming out? She ain't never coming out, love, because she never went in, did she?'

I felt confused. 'What do you mean, Nan?'

'Your mum's not inside, darlin'.'

'Then where is she? Dad told me she'd done a bank!'

Nan shook her head. 'She done a *bunk*, love. She only ran off to Panama, didn't she, with Gordon, the man what used to run the Feathers down Stepney High Street?' And having thus spoken, she turned away, pursed her wrinkled lips, and spat into the clown-shaped Murano glass ashtray that held pride of place on her side table.

I had the feeling that, had my mother indeed been caught holding up the local branch of Barclays Bank with a sawn-off shotgun, she would have earned my grand-mother's deepest respect; after all, Uncle Jimmy had achieved almost legendary status by pulling off exactly that stunt. As it was, Nan held Mum in the deepest contempt. I wasn't sure which was worse in her eyes: that Julie had abandoned her eight-year-old daughter, or that she'd done the dirty on Nan's precious eldest son. Either way, her daughter-in-law's name was never to be mentioned in the house again. Even going to see *Mary Poppins* was banned because of Julie Andrews.

The news that my mother had left me of her own free will brought my unclouded childhood to an abrupt end and plunged me into an acute case of early adolescent self-doubt. Why had she walked out on us? What did the mysterious Gordon from the Feathers have that my dad and I didn't? Why did Mum never phone or write? Was it something I had said or done? Perhaps it was because I wasn't beautiful, like she was. It must be that, because otherwise wouldn't she have taken me with her to Panama? It was a place I knew nothing about, other than it shared its name with a summer hat. I racked my brain to recall any cross words that had passed between us, but the only thing I could come up with was my last, dismal, school report.

'It's just you and me now, Annie,' my father said, when he came home from work that night to find me sitting at my mother's abandoned dressing-table, scrawling 'Mum' on the triple mirror with the one pink lipstick stub that remained. 'And let me tell you something, doll,' he added.

'What?' I wailed.

'You may not have your mother no more, but I promise you ain't never going to want for nothing else, not never again.'

I tried to decipher what he meant by all those double negatives, but soon gave up. Luckily I understood the spirit of what he was trying to say: he'd look after me from now on. He'd make sure I was okay.

Dad proved true to his word. From then on, he flogged his guts out to make up to me for my mother having left us. He no longer gambled away his profits, and soon became a small-time entrepreneur. As well as the out-of-date cosmetics he traded on his market stall, he took to selling fake designer perfumes, which he manufactured by mixing cheap eau-de-Colognes on the kitchen table, decanting them via a plastic funnel into second-hand expensive scent bottles, and repackaging them as if they were new.

A brush with the Old Bill, and a short spell in Wormwood Scrubs alongside Uncle Jimmy, soon put an end to that. But by the time my father was released, and reclaimed me from Nan, with whom I'd been living, he'd had a brilliant idea. By starting a bona-fide company of his own, Osborne Perfumes, changing the names of the scents he made and slightly altering the packaging, he could sell them and stay legit.

From then on, instead of designer rip-offs under the counter, Dad sold Osborne Channel No. 5 over it, along with Osborne Saint Lawrence Rive Coach, Osborne Nino Richy's Lair Dew Temps, and the unforgettable Osborne Diarrhissima. Maybe the people who bought his scents were dyslexic, or had no sense of smell, for over the next couple of years demand for Osborne Perfumes grew so strong that production moved from our kitchen table to a small factory in Whitechapel, and my father acquired what soon became a chain of small shops in run-down neighbourhoods across the south-east of England, from which he could sell his wares directly to the public, thus cutting out the middle man and doubling his profits.

Then, as property prices began their inexorable rise, and those working-class neighbourhoods were gentrified, Dad found himself sitting on a valuable commercial-property empire. By the time I hit my early teens the perfumery business had been sold, and Bob the tradesman had become, by default, Bob the Builder, or rather Mr Robert Andrew Osborne, a suave, wealthy property-developer. 'This is the business, Annie,' he said to me one day, rubbing his hands together after having concluded the sale of a few dilapidated retail units on the Isle of Dogs for redevelopment as a housing estate. 'You just sit on your arse and the cash piles up round you. We're in the money, girl!'

No sooner were we in it than Dad started to spend it: on a detached, mock-Georgian house in Hampstead Garden Suburb; on meals in flash restaurants; on a first-class education for me at a girls' public day school in Central London; on cashmere overcoats, Italian sports cars and holidays in swish hotels on the French Riviera, which I have to admit were a distinct improvement on the boarding-house in Margate to which he and Nan had taken me soon after my mother had left. Most extravagantly, Dad spent money on a succession of stunning younger women, whom he traded in for newer and fancier models almost as regularly as he did his Alfa Romeos.

How did my father manage to inspire such devotion in these young women? My posh new schoolfriend Clarissa Garland and I speculated endlessly about this as, from the window-seat in my bedroom, we watched one of the old models exit down the semi-circular gravel carriage drive in floods of tears, only to be replaced by a smiling new arrival five minutes later. For it wasn't just his high living that attracted these women to Bob Osborne. Could it be his expansive, larger-than-life personality they liked, we wondered, or the challenge of trying to hook him, or his big-built, meaty body, which he now honed three times a week in a gym, or his skill between the sheets? His girlfriends seemed genuinely to adore Dad, and carried on doing so even when he dumped them, after which they continued to come round to the house to see him, often laden with presents for me in an attempt to get him back. 'Your dad's dusky darlings,' Nan called them, for they were all young and beautiful, black or so fake-tanned that they were dark orange, and all far too nice and intelligent to waste themselves on a middle-aged, under-educated ex-con and market trader, who clearly had no intention of being tied down. 'Once burned, twice shy,' was how Nan explained his compulsive womanizing. 'If my son's got any sense he ain't never going to let no woman hurt him never again.'

Neither would I. As the years passed, and I heard nothing from my mother, even on my birthdays, and the one chiffon scarf she'd left behind in her dressing-table lost its once familiar smell of Youth Dew, Mum stopped being a living presence to me and became a shadowy figure, then a memory, and later . . . Well, nothing. I simply couldn't remember her – not her laugh, not her voice, and certainly not her personality. I didn't miss her, for how can anyone miss what they can't recall? Looking at old photographs of her was like looking at a stranger. Who was that pretty, leggy woman, at my father's side in a striped mini-dress and hoop earrings, her mouth frozen in a perfidious pink smile?

Five

'A pink collar and lead? For *Fluffy*?'

It was early February, and my father and I were having Sunday lunch together. I'd pondered long and hard about when and where to tell him what had happened: how, on the morning of 25 December, I'd started off happily exchanging presents with my husband and how, by the time the Queen's Speech was broadcast that afternoon, my marriage resembled the debris of the Christmas wrapping paper Fluffy had had so much fun destroying. If I told Dad when he was at home, I knew he'd jump straight into his Jag, drive over to the Workhouse and throttle Mark with his bare hands, which he'd been dying to do since before we'd got married. However, seated at a restaurant table with rare steak, chips, salad, and a glass of mellow Merlot in front of him, as he was now, my father was far more likely to behave.

And the smarter the place was, the better he'd behave because he wouldn't want to let himself, or me, down in public. Particularly not here, at the fashionable Le Caprice in St James's, his favourite celebrity haunt, where every other table in the room was occupied by Joan Collins or Michael Winner.

'That's the point, Dad,' I explained. 'Mark hadn't bought them for Fluffy. The Christmas present wasn't intended for me.'

'Then who the bloody hell was it for?'

'As it turns out, a Weimaraner.'

My father's expression changed from confused to outraged. 'A foreigner? And a German! I might have known!'

'Dad!'

'So who is this Weimar cow he's having an affair with?'

I put my hand over his. 'The Weimaraner's a bitch.'

'That goes without saying!'

'I mean, she's a dog.'

'What? Ugly as well?' The cutlery rattled as he smacked the palm of his hand on the white linen tablecloth. 'Unbelievable!'

I sighed impatiently. 'A dog as in spaniel. Or Labrador. Or Dalmatian.'

The angry flush in my father's round cheeks deepened into an embarrassed purple. 'I knew that,' he said defensively. 'Of course I did. I was just having a laugh, wasn't I? Okay, okay, there's no need to snigger, young lady. Not everyone's had the benefit of your expensive education.'

'Yes, I know, Dad.'

'Some of us had to leave school at fourteen and work our fingers to the bone out in a cold street market to keep body and soul together.' He spread his large hands; his sausage-like fingers were now professionally manicured every week and permanently decorated with diamond-studded gold rings.

'Yes, Dad, I know you did.'

'I never had no opportunity to take no university degree.'

'And you know I'm eternally grateful to you for all the wonderful advantages you've given me.'

'Hmm!' he grunted sceptically, picked up his glass and swallowed the last of his wine in one gulp. Then, with a practised, sophisticated gesture, he signalled to a waiter to bring him another.

I took a deep breath and ploughed on with my sorry tale. 'Mark's . . . mistress . . . is the Weimaraner's owner.'

Dad's grip tightened round his steak knife. 'I'll kill him,' he hissed.

'She's married. With two kids. Apparently they met when they were both dog-walking on Hampstead Heath. Mark says it was only a fling, and a big mistake, and he only did it because he was unhappy.'

'He'll be a hell of a lot more unhappy by the time I've finished with him!'

I was torn between wanting to urge Dad on, and knowing I should try to calm him down. Luckily, good sense prevailed. 'Please, Dad,' I begged. 'This isn't very helpful.'

'How dare that idle bastard cheat on you?'

'Look, he swears he's very sorry and it's all over, et cetera. But . . . the trouble is, I don't really believe him.'

'Too right you don't!' he agreed.

'Because . . .'

'I always said he was a born liar,' he interrupted.

'No. It's not that. And please just listen. You see, the thing is . . .' I hesitated.

'What?' Dad looked concerned. 'Go on, love. You can tell me anything. I'm your father, after all.'

That was the trouble. 'First, promise me you won't go ballistic.'

'Have I ever?'

'Promise?'

He shook his balding head and sighed with resignation. 'Yes, yes. I promise.'

'Okay. The thing is . . . Well,' I took a deep breath, 'it's not the first time Mark's been unfaithful to me.'

Le Caprice or no Le Caprice, Dad dropped his cutlery on to his plate with a clang, pushed back his chair and sprang to his feet, 'WHAT?' he roared.

'For God's sake, sit down!' I hissed, tugging him back into his seat as everyone turned to stare and the front-of-house manager hurried over to ask if anything was wrong. 'Look, it was just the one time before.'

'*Just* one other time? I'll tear that bastard limb from limb!'

'Is everything all right, Mr Osborne?'

'Yes, Carlo. Thank you.'

'The meal is to your satisfaction?'

'Absolutely. As usual. Sorry about the commotion. I just, well . . . I had a bit of very bad news, that's all.'

'I'm sorry to hear it, sir. Anything I can help with?'

'No, thank you. Unless you know any hit-men for hire,' he muttered, as he waved Carlo away.

'Look, Dad, the affair didn't mean anything. I mean, not much to *Mark*, or so he says now. He says he only did it because he felt neglected. And because I . . . Well, never mind.' Now was not the time to tell Dad that Mark and I had come to an impasse six months earlier about having children. As always, he wanted us to try for a baby and, as always, I wanted to wait. 'The thing is, we haven't been getting on very well lately. For over a year, really.

And *so*,' I added quickly, as the angry flush deepened in my father's cheeks, 'I've decided to divorce him.'

'Oh!' Dad's eyebrows shot up, transforming his expression in an instant from apoplectic to almost joyful. 'Have you now?' he murmured. 'Well, well, Annie, that's a turn-up for the books.'

'I've already been to see a lawyer.'

'Have you?' He patted my arm. 'That's my girl! That's the spirit, Annie. Chew the little worm up and spit him back into the gutter where he belongs.'

Why did I feel so upset to hear him badmouthing Mark in this way when I'd already thought much worse myself? 'Please, Dad, don't. He's still my husband.'

'Not for much longer, luckily. If you ask me, it's high time you got rid of him.' He picked up his knife and fork and cut into his steak with relish, smiling grimly as the bloody juices oozed out and spread across the plate. 'I knew from the start he was no good. Didn't I say so when you first brought him home?'

'Yes, you did.'

'And now, clever clogs, you see that your uneducated old dad was right all the time. A fine husband Mark's been to you! Lazing around, twanging that bloody guitar while you worked your socks off for him.' He paused to chew his forkful of meat, and I toyed with the salmon fishcake on my plate. 'How can you respect a man like that? How can he respect himself? That's what I'd like to know.'

'Mark has worked. In his fashion.'

'Pah! The man wouldn't know what proper work was if it flew at him off the nearest lamppost, landed on his head and shat in his eye.'

I didn't reply, just laid down my knife and fork and gazed miserably at my plate. My father snorted like an angry bull. Ever since Mum had walked out on us, he hadn't been able to bear seeing me hurt. 'God help me, if he's broken your heart I'll break every bone in his body!' he muttered, through his mouthful.

My heart sank. 'You've never liked him, have you?' I asked.

Dad shrugged. 'Frankly, what's to like, love? He doesn't do much, he can't keep you, he's got no get-up-and-go. Granted, he always seemed to be a genial chap, and his parents are very nice people, hard-working, salt-of-the-earth and all that. But the work gene seems to have passed that slacker by. He's got no oomph, Annie, and you've got plenty. I'm very proud of you, you know.'

I did know, but it always boosted my confidence to hear it. And at the moment my confidence needed a rocket to get it off the ground. So I said, 'Are you, Dad?'

'A university degree – the first in the family to have one? A big job like you've got? A great salary? Buying your own home? Standing on your own feet like you've always done? Course I am.'

'Thank you.'

'Whereas *he* – he's all take, take, take. Here, love!' He delved into the pocket of his Aquascutum jacket, and brought out a linen handkerchief, beautifully ironed by his thrice-weekly cleaner. And as I dabbed away the tears that had sprung into my eyes, he went on, 'My little girl's very special, see? She's been through a lot and she's achieved a lot.' He chucked me under the chin. 'She deserves better than some forty-year-old wannabe rock star who, as it turns out, can't even keep his pecker in his pants.'

The tears spilled over. 'I hate him, Dad,' I blurted out. 'You can't imagine what he's doing – he's trying to take Fluffy from me!'

'What?'

'Can you believe it? He wants custody of him!'

'Oh, he does, does he?' Instead of blowing another fuse in my defence, as I'd expected him to, my father seemed strangely amused by this piece of news. 'Now that might be the only decent idea the bastard's ever had.' He chuckled, violently spearing a forkful of chips.

Six

It was on a Sunday afternoon in early July, five years previously, that I'd fallen in love with him. The TV weather reports had been predicting record temperatures throughout a week of grey skies and warm drizzle. Now, at long last, the heatwave had arrived. I hadn't been able to get to sleep for ages, and after I'd finally dropped off, at about three o'clock in the morning, I'd woken up so late that I was late leaving for lunch at Clarissa's house, between Camden Town and Primrose Hill.

I hopped on the Northern Line at the Angel, decked out in what I'd decided was the perfect funky Camden-on-a-Sunday outfit: a simple black cap-sleeved Gap T-shirt teamed with white Armani jeans and a pair of Manolo Blahnik wedge sandals, the latter two items bought from Haines and Hampton, with my generous employee's discount, as were all the designer clothes and accessories in my not-insubstantial wardrobe. A pair of olive green plastic retro-sixties chandelier earrings, picked up for three pounds fifty in an Oxfam shop, added just the right note of vintage glamour to what was, in effect, a classic look. There were works on the Northern Line, which meant there were cancellations, so the carriage was as packed as it was during the weekday rush-hour, and the air smelled of old burgers and sweat.

At Camden Town, I was swept out of the train on a

human *tsunami*, which washed me up on the wide, litter-strewn, gum-splattered pavement outside. There, I joined the denim-clad battalions on the march towards Camden Market. As always on a Sunday, the place was packed with tourists, teenagers, shifty-looking hoodies, save-the-universe chuggers, community-support officers in rolled-up polyester shirtsleeves, and pasty-skinned punks – the face of one was pierced with more metal studs than a silver Versace belt. Eager to get out of the crowd, I turned off the main street and into Jamestown Road.

And there he was in front of me, sitting on the pavement on a soiled blue sleeping-bag.

The temperature must have been above thirty degrees Celsius, but he was in the full glare of the sun. It was no wonder that his damp, sweaty hair was plastered to his head, or that his mouth was hanging open and his parched lips were were bleeding. He looked dehydrated, dirty, and so in need of a bath that, as I approached him, I automatically stepped into the road to give him a wide berth.

Was I afraid I might catch bubonic plague just by walking past him? Or did my instinct tell me that, like most members of his sex, he would turn out to be more trouble than he was worth? Trouble was the last thing I needed. As I often told Clarissa, who was nevertheless trying to fix me up with one of her husband's colleagues that very lunchtime, I was doing perfectly well by myself, thank you very much.

Had Fate not decreed otherwise, I might have walked past him unnoticed, and this whole sorry saga would never have started. But as I approached, he turned his head in my direction, and his eyes – those sad, beseeching eyes – looked straight up into mine. The hair on the back of my neck prickled. Because this was no ordinary look. I could have sworn he could see right through the dark lenses of my Prada shades deep into my soul.

He held my gaze so completely that, as I drew level with him, my feet stopped moving of their own accord. To my surprise I found myself unable to walk on. I stared down at him from atop my wedges, transfixed by his gaze, certain he wanted something from me. Was it simply a few kind words to comfort him? The offer of a drink, perhaps? Or a handful of coins dropped into the collecting tin that lay at his feet – a tin with 'Pleese Give Genrusly' scrawled in black ink on the side, and a loop of string forming a handle round the top?

All of a sudden, as if tortured by a terrible itch, he twisted round and scratched his backside with a big, hairy white paw.

'Spare any change?'

I tore my eyes away from the puppy's and switched them to the tramp slumped in the doorway behind him. I took in the dreadful stench, the long, russet beard, the soiled trousers with their half-undone flies, the frayed jumper riding up over the naked, dirt-streaked belly, and the greasy grey parka that seemed almost like an extension of his skin. Covering his feet were a pair of battered shoes, of which the uppers were coming apart from the soles, revealing toenails so long and dirt-engrained they made Dr Hoffman's *Struwwelpeter* look like an advertisement for luxury pedicures.

I knew I should walk on, but instead I unzipped my Marc Jacobs and reached for my wallet.

The tramp pushed back a lock of his hair, revealing a pair of bright blue but rheumy eyes and a zigzag scar on his forehead, which made me think of Harry Potter. He was probably the same age as I was – thirty-five – but he looked halfway to drinking himself into an early grave. 'God bless you,' he said, in a slurred Irish accent, wiping the back of his hand on the long coils of matted hair that cascaded over his shoulders like poisonous snakes. His words wafted up at me on a cloud of alcohol so strong that I automatically took a step back into the road.

'Um, how old is the puppy?' I asked. He didn't answer, but continued to watch me closely as I opened my wallet. 'He's far too young to have left his mother,' I went on. 'And won't he be dehydrated, sitting out in this heat? Shouldn't you give him some water?'

I took out a pound coin and bent down to put it into the collecting tin. Tongue lolling out, the puppy gazed at me with the same steady, meaningful look. He was sitting in a puddle of his own urine, I realized, and his ribs and hip-bones were jutting through his scaly skin.

'He looks hungry, too,' I went on.

The tramp narrowed his eyes at me. 'Sure I can't afford to feed meself.'

I took out a fiver. 'If I give you this will you promise to buy it something to eat?' He raised an eyebrow. 'As well as something for yourself, of course.'

'God bless you,' he said again. Even as he reached out his hand to grab the note, I knew he wouldn't spend any of it on the poor little thing. He seemed to know what I was thinking because no sooner had he got his filthy fingers on the filthy lucre than he immediately tucked it into the waistband of his even filthier trousers. 'He's all right,' he muttered, shoving the little creature roughly with his foot. It whimpered.

'Don't kick him!' I shouted, before I could stop myself.

Those bleary eyes blazed with anger. 'What the fuck is it to you?' he yelled back. Looking at me defiantly, he leaned forward and looped the collecting tin's string handle around the puppy's tiny muzzle. He didn't try to protest, just sat there, a trembling, fearful bundle of skin and bones, with the heavy tin dangling from his mouth. He rolled his dark eyes up at me and gave me a last piercing, suffering look, then cast them down to the ground.

'I'm going to call the RSPCA!' I said in outrage, aware that I sounded like one of those mad Englishwomen who devote their lives to saving stray dogs in exotic holiday locations. 'It's cruel to treat an animal like that! It really shouldn't be sitting out in the sun on a boiling hot day like this!'

'I'll take him home, then. To Buckingham Palace.' The tramp laughed, releasing a stink-bomb of bad breath from between his yellow teeth.

Just then, my Nokia rang. As I fished it out of my bag the name 'Clarissa' flashed up on the screen. 'I'm coming, I'm coming!' I said.

Her voice belted out through the earpiece, consonants as crisp as starched linen. 'Where *are* you, for God's sake?'

'Just round the corner. Sorry. I'll be with you in two minutes.'

'Everyone else has been here for hours,' she said reproachfully. 'Including Jake.'

'Who?'

'The *man*. James's partner. I've been plying him with Pimm's in the garden, and making excuses as to why you're late.' Just then the tramp let loose a barrage of expletives. 'What's going on?' my friend demanded.

'I'll explain when I see you.'

'Well, do hurry up. We're all completely plastered already, and we haven't even started on the wine yet.'

I gave the dejected puppy a last, lingering glance, then hurried off to Clarissa and James's, which was several streets away.

I tried to put my encounter with the tramp out of my mind during lunch in the patio garden of their run-down Victorian terraced house. But as I sat there in the shade of the lovely magnolia tree, drinking Pimm's and listening to Jake, a divorced father of three, drone on interminably about property prices, catchment areas and private-school fees, I kept thinking of the puppy, dying of hunger, heat exhaustion and thirst.

'Whatever's the matter with you?' Clarissa hissed, dragging me into the kitchen between the Jamie Oliver Pork Chops with Thyme, Lemon and Pesto and the Nigella Eton Mess.

'Mummy, can I have a chocolate biscuit?' whined five-year-old Miranda, the youngest of her daughters, who'd trailed into the kitchen after us.

Clarissa wiped her hands absentmindedly on her old,

out-of-shape, printed crêpe-de-Chine summer dress. 'No, you may not, Miranda! We're about to have pudding.'

There was no such thing as having a private conversation with Clarissa. However, twelve years after she'd given birth to Rachel, her oldest, I'd got used to sharing her attention with the girls. 'What do you mean?'

'I mean she can't have one.'

'No, I meant what you said about something being the matter with me.'

'Well, you're not joining in with the conversation, Annie, are you?'

'Please, Mummy!'

'No! And let go of me!' Clarissa prised away Miranda's grubby little arms which were now wrapped round her slim, bare knees. 'Honestly, Annie, you haven't *contributed*, or asked Jake a single thing about himself. Don't take one!'

'But I don't know what to say to him! He's a bit dull, isn't he? He never says anything remotely amusing.'

'Who were you expecting? Paul Merton? *Put that packet down!* Look, Jake specializes in company law. He earns a fortune. Plus he's single. Well, divorced. He's not *dull*, he's interesting.'

'I mean, he's very nice and everything, and I'm terribly grateful that you thought of me.'

'Sure.'

'It's just that –'

'What?'

'Mum! Mum!'

I shrugged. 'I can't say there's much chemistry.'

'God, you're so fussy, Annie. You should give him a

chance. You've really got to think sensibly about choosing a partner. After all, you're thirty-five now. Let go of my dress!'

'But I'm hungry, Mummy!'

'Then eat some more sausages. There are plenty left. I may sound hard, Annie, but you know I'm right. You'll have to make more effort if you want to find a husband.'

'Who said? It's you who wants me to find one.'

Clarissa ignored this. 'Jake is okay. More than okay. Nice. Well, nice enough. Not that he'll be interested in you, given the way you're behaving. All you've talked about so far is that filthy old dosser.'

Miranda burst into hysterical tears. 'Please! Please! Annie, make her let me have a biscuit!'

I picked her up, balanced her on my hip and gave her a kiss. 'Can't she have just one?'

'Yes, just one biscuit, Mum!'

Clarissa had reached breaking point, as all three of us had known she would. 'Oh, for God's sake! What do I care if you grow up without any teeth? Here, take the whole bloody packet! Frankly, I don't want to hear another word about that tramp's disgusting trousers,' she continued, thrusting a packet of chocolate digestives at her now-ecstatic daughter. 'It's putting me off my lunch.' She scraped some leftovers from a plate into the bin. 'I never knew you were so into animal rights, Annie.'

'I'm not. It's just that particular puppy. I swear he looked right at me in a really funny way. Almost as if he could see through me.'

'Can I go and see it?' Miranda said, her mouth full,

67

showering me with crumbs. 'I want to look at the puppy. And the man with his dirty trousers falling down!'

'*No!*' Clarissa and I said in unison. 'He was probably eyeing up your delicious handbag,' my friend went on. 'It was Heston Blumenthal in disguise. He thought a Marc Jacobs might be tasty if it was boiled for four days, roasted for sixty hours, set on fire for thirty seconds and served with triple-cooked chips.'

'Why are you talking rubbish, Mummy?'

'I'm talking about Heston Blumenthal, darling. He's an innovative chef who makes things like bacon-and-egg ice-cream. Look, Annie, there's nothing you can do about it. It's just a puppy and it's not your problem. Besides, it probably doesn't even belong to that tramp.'

'What do you mean?'

She stowed some glasses in the dishwasher. 'Lots of beggars use dogs or puppies to get money out of people. They pass them round from person to person. Surely you've seen them in Islington, sitting on the pavement by the Tube every morning, cadging money from the commuters, with some poor old dog lying next to them? The next day the dog's with another person. They're playing the sympathy card. Mostly the dogs are very well cared-for, often better fed than the homeless people themselves. I don't think anyone actually owns them. Here, put that monster down and make yourself useful while you're standing around.' Miranda slipped to the floor, and made off with her booty while her mother pushed a pile of used crockery in my direction.

'It was starving.' I picked up a dirty plate and threw away the paper napkin. There was a half-eaten sausage on the plate, and a meaty piece of pork. 'You're not going to throw this away, are you?'

'What else am supposed to do with it? I don't suppose anyone wants a doggy-bag to take home with them,' she said jokingly.

But I did.

Seven

Armed with a bottle of Evian, a foil packet containing the barbecue leftovers, and a warning from Clarissa not to do anything stupid without phoning her first, I made an excuse to leave and hurried back down Jamestown Road, my heart thumping in my chest. Ahead, I could see the puppy sitting out in the sun where I'd left him three hours earlier, still stoically holding the collecting tin by its string. His little head was bowed under is weight, and his front legs looked as if they were sinking into the ground. Some kind soul had put a plastic container of water beside him, but as it was full to the brim it seemed unlikely that he'd drunk much – unlike his owner, who was still slumped in the doorway, now fast asleep, mouth hanging open and a half-empty bottle of cheap whisky clasped in his hand. The money I'd given him – I must have been crazy to think he'd spend any of it on food, especially for the puppy.

This time, when I approached him, he didn't even have the strength to raise his eyes to me. Regardless of my pristine white Armanis, I knelt on the pavement beside him. Although the sun had now moved off him and he was in the shade, he was panting loudly, and the black teddy-bear button at the end of his short muzzle was hot and dry. I could see his ribs heave every time he took a breath.

'Here, you poor little thing,' I whispered as, gently, I unlooped the string handle from his jaws. Then I opened my bottle of Evian, poured some into my cupped left hand and put it under his chin. When he didn't take it, I dabbled the fingers of my right hand in the water, and then moistened his lips with them.

Slowly but surely, he began to lick my damp fingertips. When they were dry, I poured some more water into my cupped palm and offered it to him. This time he lapped thirstily, and when he'd had enough he lifted his downcast eyes to mine and gazed at me with the most meltingly grateful expression.

As I unwrapped the doggy-bag of leftovers, his nose twitched, and before I'd even broken a small piece off one of the charred sausages he'd grabbed it from my fingers with tiny white teeth. After chewing it for a long while, he swallowed it with difficulty – as if he wasn't used to eating. However, the next morsel I broke off for him disappeared in half the time. And the next. And the next.

Soon, I could scarcely keep up with him. He was ravenous. But gradually the rate at which he wolfed the leftovers slowed, then stopped. He'd had enough, he signified, licking clean his now greasy lips. His eyes rolled towards my face, this time adoringly. He crawled towards me and clumsily attempted to clamber on to my lap, but as he didn't have the strength I picked him up, cuddled him close, and stroked the top of his head. He snuggled up, and his eyes closed. Within a minute he was asleep.

I don't know how long I sat on the pavement, holding him to me and feeling the steady beat of his heart, before

71

I became aware that a pair of bloodshot blue eyes was staring at me from under the greasy snakes. 'Put him down!' the tramp growled, through lips crusted with cold sores.

Now that I was eyeball to bleary eyeball with him, he seemed far more menacing that he had when I was towering over him earlier. 'I – I brought him some food,' I stuttered. I showed him the remains of the foil parcel. Snatching it from me, he began to stuff the leftovers of the leftovers into his own mouth. He jerked his chin at the puppy. 'Put him down,' he ordered, with his mouth full.

'He was starving,' I went on. 'And thirsty. I – I gave you money earlier on to buy him something to eat. And something for yourself. But you spent it all on whisky, didn't you?' He ignored me but I persisted: 'You shouldn't have a dog if you can't look after it.'

'Fuck off out of here.' The half-chewed remnants of a piece of pork shot out of the tramp's mouth and landed on my face. Grimacing, I wiped it away, got to my feet and took a step back. At this point, the puppy woke up and squirmed against me. I looked into his trusting eyes. I remembered what Clarissa had said about dogs being well treated as they were passed round by people who were sleeping rough. In this case she was wrong. 'Look, I know it's none of my business, but this puppy really ought to be taken to a vet.'

The tramp attempted to pull himself to his feet. As he staggered upright, his unbelted trousers with their open flies slipped lower, and came perilously close to falling off. Unnerved by a glimpse of pubic hair, I lowered the puppy gently on to the sleeping-bag and backed off, but my new friend waddled towards me, twitching his thin, limp tail as if he didn't have the muscle power to wag it. 'Please look after him!' I said to the drunk, as he fell back into the doorway, collapsing on to a heap of rags. He picked up the bottle of whisky and put it to his lips. When he'd emptied it, he swore loudly and hurled it at me. It landed in the road, where it exploded into a thousand shards, narrowly missing a passing car.

It was time to get out of there. Shaking with anger, I turned away, brushed some of the dirt from my jeans, and forced myself, to leave. I'd done all I could for the puppy, I told myself as I scurried back towards Camden High Street. What happened to him now was neither my business nor my responsibility.

But if not mine, then whose was it? Could I just walk away from the poor creature and leave him to die?

Just before I turned the corner I made the mistake of glancing over my shoulder. Those soulful eyes were still fixed on me. He yapped once, as if to call me back. Then, as if he knew how useless it was, he lay down on the sleeping-bag with his nose between his paws.

I stopped. I retraced my steps. As I reached him he raised his head and blinked at me with those all-seeing eyes – eyes that were now full of desperate hope.

'Hello? Hello? Excuse me,' I said to the dozing tramp.

'Wha'?'

'How much do you want for this puppy?'

'Wha'?'

'I want to buy this puppy from you.'

'Wha'? That?' He shoved it with his foot again.

'Yes, that. And please don't kick him again.'

''Snot for sale,' he said, resting his head against the door behind him.

'Everything's for sale at the right price,' I retorted. 'So name yours.'

He seemed confused, as if he was too drunk to take in what I was saying. Then his mouth twisted into a sneer. 'A hundred pound!'

'But that's ridiculous!'

He laughed. 'You want him? He's a hundred pound.'

'No way.' I swear that the puppy understood what was going on, because his head drooped again. 'I'll give you twenty for him,' I said. The tramp chuckled, but said nothing. 'Fifty?' He wiped his nose on his jacket sleeve, then spat on the ground. I took a deep breath, and heard myself say, 'Okay, you can have a hundred.'

Was I crazy, I asked myself, as I took out my wallet and counted some crisp clean notes into the tramp's open palm. I must be. On the other hand, what was a puppy's life worth? Drunk as he was, I could see what the tramp was thinking – that he should have asked for double. 'Ten, fifteen, twenty-five . . .' Suddenly my wallet was empty. I scrabbled around in the bottom of my bag for coins, but could only find a few pound coins and a handful of pennies. 'Thirty's all I've got. Will you settle for it?' I said. 'After all, I gave you some money before.'

His fist closed round the cash. 'You agreed a hundred.'

'But I haven't got it.'

'There's one of them hole-in-the-wall machines round the corner.'

Obviously he wasn't as out of it as I'd thought. But neither was I that much of a fool. 'Okay,' I said. 'I'll go and get it. But first give me what I've just given you. Then, when I get back, I'll pay you in one lump sum.' I held out my hand for the money, but instead of giving it back to me, the tramp tucked it into his trouser pocket.

'I'll keep it,' he said.

'What?'

''S a deposit.'

We glared at each other for a moment, neither willing to give in. Then he shoved the puppy with his foot a third time, and I ran off down the street, its whimpers ringing in my ears. I turned the corner into Camden High Street and fought my way through the crowds to the bank on the corner of Parkway. It occurred to me while I was standing in the long queue to use the cash machine that, by the time I got back, the tramp would have vanished. I'd never see that thirty pounds or the puppy again.

But I was wrong.

Eight

He was mine. I'd rescued him! As I hurried to Camden Town station with him tucked under my arm, I felt elated, as if my Manolo wedges were floating on air.

It was only on the way home that I began to think about what I was going to do with him.

He peed on my white jeans as I held him on my lap on the Northern Line. He peed on my T-shirt as I got out at the Angel. He had diarrhoea when I put him down outside the Workhouse so that I could search for my keys, and when I placed him on the living-room rug, he threw up all the food I'd given him, coated with the kind of mushroom-coloured foam that Michelin-starred chefs spent hours whipping up to serve as an hors d'oeuvre.

I shut him into the bathroom while I got down on my hands and knees to clean, wash and disinfect the rug but, as with my jeans, the stains didn't come out. When I opened the bathroom door to see how he was doing, the stench was terrible and the place looked like a dirty protest cell. He'd had diarrhoea again, this time all over the granite flooring, and he was crawling in circles in it.

I kept him captive in the bath while I cleared up the new mess with one hand while holding a tissue soaked in perfume over my nose with the other. Afterwards I turned on the shower attachment and washed him with my best Aveda shampoo. Weak as he was, he struggled like a champion wrestler – being bathed seemed to revive him. The moment I took him out he slipped from my grasp, shook the water off himself, drenching my remaining clean towels, and disappeared through the door. A trail of water led me to my squashy cream sofa, upon which he was now frantically rubbing himself dry. I carried him back into the bathroom where he defecated again, this time on the bathmat. How could one tiny body contain so much shit? I wondered, as I threw the bathmat into the washing machine with the towels and my jeans. He'd only been mine for a couple of hours but he'd already ruined some of my favourite clothes, dirtied every towel I possessed and turned my spotless home into a lavatory.

Reality hit me in the face like a cold wet flannel. I had to be at work by eight thirty the following morning to see an early client. What was I going to do with a doubly incontinent puppy? There was only one thing for it. I'd have to get up at six and take him to Battersea Dogs' Home in the hope that they'd find him an owner who didn't mind spending all her time cleaning up after him.

Feeling lighter at heart, I knelt on the bedroom floor and, holding the wriggling puppy still with difficulty, dried him off with my Revlon Tourmaline Ionic. When I'd finished he shook himself violently, rolled over on the floor in an ecstasy of scratching, then sat down facing me. He was such a comical-looking creature. His ears pointed in opposite directions, his tail was much too long for his tiny body, and his hairy paws were almost as big as his head. Though he was terribly scrawny, the Aveda Pure Abundance had turned him from a drowned rat into a black-and-white pom-pom.

Buried in that fluff was a pair of big black eyes, which now met mine with a steady grateful gaze, just as they had in the street.

Then he opened his tiny muzzle and smiled at me. I swear he smiled.

My heart melted. I had never seen anything so adorable. I was in love. At that moment, I knew I could never give him away.

'Oh, what am I going to do with you, you little monster?' I said, picking him up and holding him at arm's length. When he squirmed, I put him down again. Without waiting to be invited, he clambered on to my lap, put his paws on my chest and tried to lick my chin. As an answer to the question I'd asked him, this was eloquent stuff.

Fluffy – for that was what I called him – shared my late-night supper of scrambled eggs. The day's momentous events had exhausted both of us, and we were soon curled up together on my bed, watching a late-night soap. As I stroked his little head, I suddenly felt incredibly peaceful. I think Fluffy did, too, because he dozed off before the first ad break off with his muzzle resting trustingly on my chest. And well before the second break, I was asleep too.

I woke in the early hours of the morning. My nightdress was damp and beads of sweat were crawling slowly down my back and along my legs. As I came to, I had an uneasy feeling that I wasn't alone.

I remembered Fluffy.

I switched on the bedside light. He was no longer on top of the bedcovers. I threw back the duvet to find him stretched out beside me on the bottom sheet. He raised his head and gazed at me adoringly, then tucked his black button nose between his outsize front paws and went back to sleep.

I was about to do the same when I noticed the yellow patch under him. The little monster had peed in the bed. And I was lying right in the middle of it.

I kicked the duvet right off, and caught sight of a brown speck scurrying across my left thigh. In an instant it had disappeared behind my knee. I leaped out of bed, shrieking, and tore off my nightdress. Those weren't beads of sweat I'd felt running down my body. They were insects.

I flapped my hands manically to brush them off. How many were there? Four? Five? Six? As one dropped to the floor I attempted to crush it with one of my sandals, which I'd kicked off when I'd gone to bed. Fat with my blood, it died with a squelch. Scratching like a maniac, I ran into the bathroom and jumped into the shower, but no amount of scrubbing could make me feel clean. When I emerged from the soapy Niagara I reached for a dry towel. Then I remembered there were none left.

I threw on my bathrobe, but not before I'd caught sight of myself in the full-length bathroom mirror. My torso, arms and face were dotted with big red welts. I looked as if I had a bad case of chickenpox. How could I go to work like this? Back in the bedroom, I stood at a distance from the bed, glaring at the culprit, who was lying on the sodden sheet, chewing through the straps of my sandal.

'Stop that! Get down! Get *off*! *Get off*!' I yelled hysterically.

It was no use. For Fluffy, jumping off the bed would have been like throwing himself off a cliff. Besides, he hadn't a clue what I was saying. However, the tone of my voice had obviously scared him rigid because he hung his head and shook with terror. 'I'm sorry, I'm sorry!' I cried. After all, it wasn't his fault he was lousy. I knew I should cuddle him, but I couldn't bear to touch him, so I ran into the kitchen, put on my Marigolds, picked him up at arm's length and put him back into the bath. Tentatively, as if they might attack me, I lifted the pillows off the bed, squashed another bug, then stripped off the pillowslips and the bottom sheet. Fluffy's pee had seeped through the mattress cover and penetrated the mattress topper. It was ruined.

It was now just past five a.m. Imprisoned in the bath, Fluffy yelped for attention. I shut the door on him, carried the soiled linen into the kitchen, shoved some into the washing machine and put on the first of four boil-wash loads. By six o'clock, my downstairs neighbour had been up to complain about her vibrating bedroom ceiling. By six thirty, a disgruntled man who lived along the corridor had rung my bell in his shorts to complain about Fluffy's barking. When he saw my spotty face he backed away and apologized, saying that he hadn't realized I was so ill.

Since it was the only way to shut him up, I took Fluffy out of the bath and gave him the run of the living room. He peed on the floorboards, vomited on the sofa cushions, then fell asleep on the rug. By seven a.m. he was yelping again. By eight, when Clarissa called me from her SUV during the school run, I was hysterical.

'Why aren't you on your way to work?' she shouted into her mobile phone, her voice rising above the noise of the engine and the chatter of her girls. 'You sound terrible.'

'I can't cope!' I wept.

'What? Do be quiet, Emily, or I'll drop you off here and you can walk the rest of the way. No, I don't care if you do miss assembly. What's up? Are you ill?'

'Oh, Clarissa, I've done something stupid.'

'What? Rebecca, don't pull Miranda's ponytail – and please hold the phone closer to my ear. I can't hear what Annie's saying. What do you mean, stupid? Oh, my God, what's that noise? *Shut up, girls!* Did I hear yelping in the background? Annie, you didn't!'

'Didn't what? What didn't she do?' piped up the chorus in the background, as Rebecca clicked on the phone's loudspeaker.

'I did.'

'What?'

'Oh, my God!'

'What? What?' yelled the girls. 'What did she do?'

'Oh, you idiot!' shouted Clarissa.

'I know,' I agreed.

'I bet she had sex!'

'I can't believe you were so foolish!'

'Maybe she had unsafe sex!'

'Annie had unsafe sex!'

'What is unsafe sex, Mummy?'

'Shut up, all of you!'

'I couldn't leave him there with that awful drunk. He'd have died. So I brought him home with me.'

'What? What did you bring home? A rent-boy?'

'What are you talking about, Rachel? How do you know about rent-boys?'

'It's on the syllabus. Mrs Nelson taught us in PSHE.'

It was time to cut out the middleman and speak directly to my young interrogators. 'Sorry to disappoint you lot, but it's nothing to do with rent-boys or sex,' I announced.

'Oh!' Their disappointment was audible.

'I bought the puppy I was talking about at lunch yesterday.'

They shrieked with delight. '*Oh!* A puppy! Wicked! Can we come and see it?'

'Bought? You mean, you actually paid money for him?' Clarissa gasped. 'How much?'

'The man wanted a hundred pounds.'

'Are you crazy?'

'The thing is, I don't think Fluffy's very well, Clarissa.'

'*Fluffy?* Oh, per-lease!'

'He keeps being sick. And he's got diarrhoea. And bugs.'

'*Ergh!*' went the chorus, with Clarissa leading it this time.

'I've been bitten all over.'

'*Ugh!*'

'And he wet the bed.'

'That's disgusting! What were you thinking of, Annie? Give him back to the tramp!' Clarissa shouted, over the other voices. 'Or take him to Battersea and get them to find him a home.'

'*She can't do that!*'

'I was planning to. But . . . well, although he's a bloody nuisance, he's really very cute, Clarissa. Adorable, actually. He smiles – honestly he does. I love him. I'd like to keep him if I can,' I heard myself say.

'Annie, be sensible! How can you possibly look after a mangy puppy when you're at work six days a week?'

How indeed? For the first time ever, I phoned in and took a sickie. It was some sort of contagious viral infection, I told my boss, Eileen Grey, and for good measure I listed symptoms that I knew neither she nor anyone else in the personal-shopping department would want to catch. They included nausea, diarrhoea, stomach cramps and, worst of all, a dreadful rash that had disfigured my entire body. The rash part was true, except that the red marks all over me were bites rather than an infectious disease. The nausea and diarrhoea were real, too, only it wasn't me who had them.

An hour later, instead of advising my morning client, a top female QC, on which clothes to take to the Maldives, I was sitting in the waiting room at the local vet's, trading pet stories with a woman in a green shell suit and her fifteen-year-old blind cat. Fluffy was on my lap, wrapped in a towel, his nether regions swathed in an old Tesco bag – I was determined that the distressed Diesel jeans I was now wearing wouldn't go the same way as my white Armanis had.

'Ingenious,' said Mr McClaw, the middle-aged vet, suppressing a smile as he ushered me and my bag into his consulting room. I placed it on the bench, and unwrapped Fluffy, who shook and trembled while I recounted the story of how I'd found him. Meanwhile the vet gave him a thorough examination, which included everything from peering into his ears with a light, to sticking a thermometer up his bottom.

'He has a slight fever,' he said, as he wiped it clean on a tissue. 'But I have to say that's the least of your problems. First off, he's extremely weak and dehydrated. You just have to feel his skin. It's stiff, dry, almost like thin paper. That's partly to do with the diarrhoea, of course. He's also severely undernourished, as you can see by his prominent ribs.'

'I did give him some pork fillet and sausages, and a bit of scrambled egg last night, but he threw it all up.'

'Far too rich for him. He may have gastroenteritis. And he has these odd sores around his mouth.'

'I think that's from the string handle of the tramp's collecting tin.'

He shook his head. 'Poor little mite. He's certainly been maltreated. From the size of him, I'd say he's ten or eleven weeks old. I guess he was probably abandoned by his mother – or dumped by her owners – soon after birth. It's likely he's been pretty much starving ever since. That would fit in with the way his front legs are slightly bowed. Here – you see? He might be developing rickets, which is caused by vitamin D and phosphorus deficiency. Luckily, his bones are still growing, so there should be plenty of time to rectify the problem, given plenty of TLC and a balanced diet from now on.'

'Is that it, then?'

Mr McClaw smiled at me again, this time with indulgence. 'Yes, apart from possible mange, as you can see from these little bald patches on his belly and back. Oh, yes, and then there are the other parasites.'

'Para*sites*, in the plural?'

'I'm afraid so. You've already found out about the lice, I see,' he said, glancing at my spotty face. He parted Fluffy's thin fur with his fingers, then brushed it gently to the roots with a fine-toothed steel comb. 'And see these tiny dark specks? They're evidence of fleas. I advise you to spray your entire flat against infestation when you get home. He also has ear mites – look – and almost certainly worms.'

'Worms?' My heart was sinking rapidly.

'Well, if you look underneath him – here – you can see that he's rather pot-bellied, despite being so malnourished. Now, that's likely to be a symptom of *toxocara canis*. Roundworms to you. You may have spotted some in his vomit?'

'I can't say I examined it that closely.'

'They're pretty long. Look like lengths of wriggling spaghetti? No? I've seen a female grow up to eight inches. In extreme cases they can block the intestines. They're amazingly fecund. An adult female can lay tens of thousands of eggs a day. They pass out of the host animal along with the faeces.' By now *I* was about to pass out. 'I should warn you that if they're accidentally transmitted to humans – under dirty fingernails, say – they can cause a serious infection called visceral larva migrans. In a worst-case scenario this can cause blindness, even brain damage.' As discreetly as I could I looked under my fingernails. Luckily I'd developed obsessive compulsive disorder since I'd woken up in my sodden bed, and I'd already scrubbed my hands about a dozen times that day. 'He might also have tapeworms and hookworms, of course.'

I tried not to panic. 'Mr McClaw, I'm also very concerned that Fluffy seems to be doubly incontinent.'

'No, not *incontinent*, dear. Just not housetrained. I think we can say that he's been brought up very much as an *enfant sauvage*, as the French would have it. Besides, he's still too young to have much control over his bladder and bowels. That should come soon, and with training. First, we've got to make the poor little mite well again. I can't promise miracles, but I'll do my best. I'll give him a general-purpose wormer now, which should help to shake all the little nasties out of him. And as soon as he's gained a bit more weight he'll need microchipping and vaccinating against the common diseases, such as distemper and kennel cough. In the meantime, you'd better keep him inside and away from other dogs. I'll give you some antibiotics for his stomach, some cleaner to squirt down his ear canals twice a day, and some invalid-puppy food, which he'll need to be fed at four- to five-hour intervals for the next week or so – I find demand feeding at night works best. You'll need a box of special substitute puppy milk and, of course, a litter tray and some litter. Here's a feeding schedule and a booklet that explains a little about housetraining. And you might need this – it's the address of your nearest puppy-training classes. Ask the receptionist to give you some insecticide to spray on him. And some for your bed and the rest of the house. Best to nip the problem in the bud. And some toothpaste and a brush – those sharp little teeth of his will be crawling with bacteria. I shouldn't let him lick you. Buy him a collar and lead, and you can start training him to wear them. I suggest a special anti-fungicide shampoo, for good measure. Wash him three times a week in it for the first fortnight, and leave it on for ten minutes before you rinse it off. You're taking on quite a commitment, you know. Are you sure you're up to it?'

'I think so. Fluffy's had such a horrible start in life. I don't want to give up on him.'

'Very admirable.' He patted me on the shoulder. 'Well, let me know if it's too much. We can always get one of the rescue organizations to rehome the little fellow, if necessary. Have you thought what you're going to do with him while you're at work?'

'I might be able to take him in with me for now. That is, if my boss lets me. He can sit under my desk in my handbag.'

He looked at me as if I was mad. 'In your handbag?'

'Well, he's very small.'

He suppressed a smile. 'Very soon he'll grow. Judging by the size of those paws – and, if I may say so, his substantial testicles – by quite some amount. And puppies and dogs don't sit still. They run around. They play. They chew things. They need plenty of exercise. I'm not sure that taking him to work is going to be a viable option – unless you have a very understanding employer, that is. Of course, once his vaccinations kick in you can get a professional dog-walker to take him out for you.'

'Really?'

'Oh, yes. Many of my clients use them. The receptionist

can give you a list of locally based people. A couple come highly recommended – one in particular, whom my female clients seem to find indispensable. Ask at the desk and they'll give you his details.'

Nine

And so Mark Curtis ambled into my life at three o'clock the following Saturday afternoon, more than an hour later than he was supposed to.

With hindsight, I realize that this was a sign I should have picked up on: that, from a desire to please people, Mark was in the habit of promising more than he could deliver. But what's the point in hindsight, other than to make you feel foolish for not having known better?

When I opened my front door to him, Mark was dressed in the canvas sandals and khaki shorts that he seems not to have taken off since. They were teamed that day with a washed-out white T-shirt that bore the slogan 'Wag the Dog Walks', the name of his dog-walking business.

Actually, to call it a business was something of a misnomer. The word implies offices, bank accounts, employees and profit-and-loss charts. Whereas Wag the Dog Walks consisted of Mark, his rusty VW camper van, and the old pay-as-you-go Nokia through which I'd contacted him earlier that week.

'Annie?' Mark ran a hand through the unruly sun-streaked dark hair that fell fetchingly over his forehead, framed his craggy, weatherbeaten face and skimmed his powerfully built shoulders. 'Sorry I'm late,' he said. 'I thought I'd be able to make it over here in time but the traffic was unbelievable.'

As he smiled at me, I felt something crawl down my spine. And since I'd sprayed Fluffy thoroughly with insect-icide three times that week, I knew it wasn't another louse. 'Never mind,' I heard myself say, although I'd spent the last thirty minutes silently rehearsing a tirade: I mean, what kind of reliability was I to expect from a dog-walker who turned up so late for our preliminary meeting? 'Do come in.'

'Thanks. Shall I take these off first?' He lifted one of his monumental feet, and peered at the sole of his some-what dusty sandal. 'I've probably brought half of Hampstead Heath with me.'

'Oh, I wouldn't bother. I don't think the floor could get much dirtier than it already is, with Fluffy around.'

I stood aside, and he ambled past me along the short entrance hall into the double-height living room. I waited for the estate agent's wow factor to strike him, as I knew it would. On cue, he stopped in the doorway, put his hands into his shorts pockets and let out a long, apprecia-tive whistle. 'Wow,' he said. 'What an amazing space!'

'Thanks.'

He wandered into the middle of the room and looked up at the high ceiling. 'The acoustics must be brilliant.'

'I suppose so,' I said, staring at his hairy, muscular calves. Christ, what was I up to? Lusting after a dog-walker, for God's sake! 'Do you know a lot about acoustics, then?' I simpered.

He nodded. 'I'm a musician. Bass guitar.'

'Oh! Are you in a band?'

'Not exactly.' He turned and grinned at me. God, he was good-looking when he smiled! Quite devastating, actually. 'Not at the moment,' he went on. 'The dog-walking stuff's sort of taken over recently.'

'Really?' I realized I was grinning back at him so, with a great effort, I pulled down the corners of my mouth.

'How long have you lived here?' he asked.

'About four years.'

'Do you, like, rent it?' he asked.

'Actually, I bought it a few years ago.'

I watched, almost embarrassed, while he did a 360-degree turn, taking in the free-standing fireplace with its steel chimney, the six-seater sofa and the industrial-sized stainless-steel kitchen fitments at the far end. 'Great kitchen,' he said, walking over to inspect it. 'I like this double range. That must be a joy to cook on.'

'Yes. It's brilliant!' Now wasn't the time to admit that the most I'd ever done in my state-of-the-art kitchen was to throw the ready meals I lived on into the microwave. 'Do you like cooking?'

'Very much.' Mark ran a hand over the unblemished granite work surface. Though his general appearance was untidy, he had elegant slim fingers, I noticed, and beautiful shiny fingernails. 'I kind of grew up with it. My mum and dad run a pub just outside Norwich. A real old-fashioned place – you know, wooden beams, horse brasses, log fires, comfy chairs.'

'How lovely.'

'It is, rather. Anyway, when I was about eleven they turned part of it into a proper restaurant. We lived upstairs, so my older sisters and I had to help out in the kitchen whenever Mum and Dad were short-staffed. They don't serve the sort of overpriced grub you get in all these London gastro-pubs nowadays.'

'You mean there's no fusion prawn and asparagus mousse with chilli and peanut dipping sauce? Or lamb shanks and ginger in maple syrup, surrounded by a lake of watermelon *jus* and mash?'

Mark laughed. 'I see we've been eating in the same joints. No, it's strictly traditional stuff, but really good quality. You know, roast chicken with all the trimmings. Proper butcher's sausages, cabbage and home-made mash. Ploughman's lunches with proper Cheddar cheese, decent ham, tomatoes from my dad's garden, and home-made pickles. Everything was home-made, even the bread. So I grew up knowing how to make a mean steak and kidney pie – suet crust and all. And my apple and blackberry crumble isn't bad, either. But pot-roast pheasant's my speciality. With apple and Calvados sauce, cabbage, chestnut stuffing and roast spuds with garlic.'

By now I was salivating, though whether over the thought of that food or Mark himself I couldn't tell. I managed a faint 'Mmm. I'm impressed!' Which was certainly true.

Mark was gorgeous. His voice – a rich, gravelly baritone with a slight Norfolk accent – tumbled from a sensuous mouth set in the lived-in face of a 1960s French film star, the kind who was never without a Gauloise clamped between his lips. He also had the sleepy-eyed look of a man who'd been making love all night and had only just fallen out of bed. He probably *had* just fallen out of bed, I thought – no doubt with some sexy girlfriend. That probably accounted for him arriving here so late. No sooner had this occurred to me than I found myself blushing. 'Heavens, this heatwave!' I said, running to one of the windows and flinging it open.

'So, how old is your baby?' he said.

I swung round. 'My *baby*?'

'Yeah.' He indicated the play-pen full of stuffed toys that was situated near the fireplace. 'I love kids. My youngest sister's got one, and my oldest sister's got three. Babies smell wonderful, don't they?'

'Well, actually, that's my puppy's play-pen,' I admitted. Sniggering, he went over to the circular mesh enclosure I'd acquired three days before from Argos, leaned over the top and fished out one of the many stuffed animals I'd bought to keep Fluffy company. 'You must think I'm completely crazy,' I said, as he started moving Mickey Mouse's arms about, 'but I bought it for Fluffy to sleep in. And for when I want to keep him out of trouble. I mean, what do you do with an out-of-control puppy when, say, you want to have a bath?'

The moment the words had left my lips, I wished I hadn't said them. Because when Mark turned and smiled at me I felt as exposed as if I was stark naked, about to step into the shower.

Mark nodded. 'You don't have children, then?' he asked.

'God, no!' I said. He gave me a funny look. 'Do you?' I batted back, after a short pause.

'Haven't reached that point yet.'

I asked Mark if he wanted to sit down, so he perched at one end of the low, six-seater sofa, while I curled up at the other.

'So, where's the little man?' he said, after a short pause.

'Fluffy? Oh, I shut him in the bathroom a few minutes ago. I'm trying to train him to use his litter tray. He's probably amusing himself by chewing through my other Manolo. He's already ruined one.'

Mark frowned fetchingly. 'What's a manolo?'

'You know, as in Blahnik?' He was still bemused. 'It's a brand of shoe, an iconic brand, actually. Manolo Blahnik's the name of the designer. His mother was Spanish and his father was Czech – that's how he got his wonderful name. He's a real artist. He started off designing shoes for Ossie Clark way back in the nineteen seventies, and since then he's made them for everyone from John Galliano to Isaac Mizrahi and Carolina Herrera.'

Mark shook his head. 'You're speaking a foreign language, I'm afraid.'

'They're all top fashion designers.'

'Ah. Fashion's not my strong point. As you can probably tell,' he added, pulling at his old T-shirt. 'You seem to know a lot about it.'

'Well, it's what I do,' I explained. 'I'm a makeover specialist, in the personal-shopping department at Haines and Hampton.' He still looked blank. 'It's a clothing store in Chelsea. *The* clothing store, actually. Haines is to the King's Road what Harvey Nicks is to Knightsbridge or Browns to South Molton Street.' None of this seemed to mean anything to him either. 'We sell everything from designer handbags to designer knickers.'

He raised his eyebrows. 'Designer knickers – interesting.'

94

I giggled. 'When you say *designer*, I suppose you mean expensive?'

'Yes, very expensive, on the whole.'

'And what's *personal shopping*?'

'Well, we run a sort of service. We help people to shop. Hey, do you want a drink? Tea? Coffee? Something herbal?'

'Thanks. Coffee would be great. So, tell me more about personal shopping,' he said, following me to the kitchen. I caught a glimpse of my reflection in the chrome kettle. God, I looked terrible! It had never occurred to me to dress up to interview my dog-walker, but now I wished I had. I ran my fingers through my flat hair to rake it into a windswept style, then turned. 'Well, all sorts of people come to see us, wanting to look better than they do or just different, or more *on trend*, as we say, but not knowing how to achieve the look they want. It's my job – and that of my colleagues – to go round the store with them, or on their behalf, and pick out something that's just right for them and within their budget.'

'Ah. So you're a shop assistant?' Mark said.

'Well, yes, I suppose I am.' I perched myself on the counter so that I could have a better view of him. Tall, slim, tanned and, I guessed, in his mid-thirties, Mark really was wonderfully handsome in a dishevelled, Heathcliffish way. 'But my job involves more than just selling,' I rambled on. 'The people we see – and they're almost all women – come in for a variety of reasons. Sometimes they're super-rich – you know, young heiresses or trophy wives with bottomless Chanel purses. George – the owner of the store, George Haines – he adores them because they spend an absolute fortune every time they come in. You wouldn't believe how much – tens of thousands of pounds at a time.'

Mark was clearly amazed. 'On clothes?'

I nodded 'Clothes, makeup, beauty stuff and, most of all, accessories. It's not hard in a store like ours. I mean, spending six or seven hundred pounds on a handbag is par for the course for the true fashionista. In fact, that's considered pretty reasonable! And, however much they cost, there are long waiting lists for them.'

'*Waiting lists* for *handbags*? And at those prices? You're having me on!'

I shook my head. 'Even for the Hermès Birkin, which is over a thousand. So you can imagine, if a woman wants a whole new outfit – bag, shoes, suit, accessories – and some of them do every week, the bill soon mounts up. One customer the other day spent over twenty-five thousand on something to wear for a charity ball. She could have just donated the money instead!'

'That's crazy!'

I laughed. 'I know. But to me those women are our least interesting clients.'

'Why?'

I shrugged. 'They can be very demanding, and most of the time they already own more clothes than they know what to do with. They come in wanting more of the same or, at least, the latest must-have designer whatever, whether or not it suits them or it's right for their age.' The kettle came to the boil, so I jumped down, opened a cupboard, and took out my jar of instant. 'Black or white?' I asked. 'I think I've got some milk left.'

'Er ...' Mark seemed somewhat doubtful, '... um, sorry to ask, but don't you have any real coffee?'

'You mean proper coffee? God, no. I can never be bothered to make it. Can you?'

He nodded. 'It's really easy. You should get yourself a cafetière. Or one of those electric espresso-makers.' Then he smiled apologetically. 'Sorry. None of my business. Instant's good. Tell me more about your customers.'

Feeling rather embarrassed about my slobbish ways, I spooned some brown granules into a mug and sploshed on the boiling water. 'Oh, the ones I really like are career women on tight salaries. They're teachers, lawyers or actresses, or they work in a bank, maybe even a shop. Or perhaps they're running their own business. One of the customers I deal with is a government minister – though I'm not allowed to say which. Our service is absolutely confidential, and we pride ourselves on being very discreet. Anyway, maybe whoever-it-is has got a special occasion coming up and she hasn't a clue what to wear. Or perhaps she's just turned sixty and has lost confidence in herself. Or her marriage has just ended, or she's scared it's on the rocks, or she's got the sack from her job. Or she's about to start a big new job, and she's worried about making the right impression on her new colleagues. What we do is try to understand what she wants, then help her to achieve her aim, whatever it is, at a price she can afford. To bring out the best in her, make her feel confident and good about herself.'

Those crinkly blue eyes blinked at me incredulously. 'And you do this by selling her outrageously expensive clothes?'

'Well, I know it sounds funny, but yes. You must have heard of retail therapy. Sometimes it's just a matter of helping someone choose an amazing bag or belt that will update her whole wardrobe. At other times I don't sell a customer anything – I just send her to our hair salon for a restyle and blow-dry, or get one of the assistants on the cosmetics counters to revamp her makeup. If you do that for someone, they may not spend much money – they may not spend anything at all, in fact – but they're ever so grateful. And you can bet anything you like that they'll come back to the store when they do have money to spend.'

'So, you're a kind of retail therapist?'

I laughed. 'That's a great way of putting it!'

Oh, Mark was nice that day. He was very, very nice, and not at all what I'd expected someone running a dog-walking business to be like. By now it seemed that I'd been talking for ever, and I was enjoying myself so much that when he suddenly said, 'Are you going to introduce me to him, then?' I'd forgotten what he'd come for, and it took me a moment to remember what he was talking about.

Leaving him on the sofa, I went through to my bedroom and, with trepidation, opened the door to the en-suite. Just a week earlier, it had been my personal mini-spa, a haven of peace, calm and order, stocked with piles of pristine white towels and colour-coordinated pots of expensive body scrubs, shower gels and lotions that I'd bought from Haines's. It had smelled wonderful – of the Chanel Allure I was addicted to, mixed with the grapefruit scent of the Jo Malone candle that Norma, my father's new girlfriend, had given me for my last birthday ('A flame from a flame,' as she'd sweetly put it). Now the counter above the swanky Philippe Starck circular wash-basin was lined with a chaotic display of large blue bleach containers, lurid packets of stain remover and bottles of crème-de-menthe-coloured disinfectant. Despite a tornado's worth of industrial-strength air-freshener – the kind that's meant to nuke smells, not just mask them – the room stank like a car-park stairwell crossed with a Glastonbury Festival latrine.

Fluffy had relieved himself on the granite floor again, I noted with resignation, and was now curled up asleep on the virgin sawdust in his litter tray, half covered by my bath towel, which he'd somehow managed to pull down from the stainless-steel ladder towel rail. He opened his eyes and blinked at me sleepily as I picked him up, then yawned and stretched in my arms as I brushed the sawdust from his coat and carried him out. As I came through the door, I saw Mark at the sink, surreptitiously pouring away his coffee.

I cleared my throat loudly. 'Here he is.' I sat on the sofa with Fluffy on my lap.

Mark came over and sat down next to me. 'Hello, little fella.' He chucked Fluffy under the chin. Fluffy rolled on to his back, looked at him with a twinkle in his eyes, opened his mouth and began to chew one of Mark's fingers. 'Oh, you're a right little cutie, aren't you?'

'Do you think so?' I squinted at Fluffy critically. For the first few days I'd had him he'd been terribly ill, and had run a high temperature. But the invalid-puppy food, supplemented by substitute puppy milk given at four-hourly intervals throughout the night, plus the occasional scraps of M&S delicacies from my plate, had, I realized, worked wonders. His patchy skin was softer and more supple, his eyes were brighter, and he seemed to have more energy to play. After six broken nights, I, on the other hand, looked like one of my many washed-out J-cloths.

'Ouch!' said Mark, as Fluffy gnawed his thumb.

'Stop it, Fluffy!'

'It's okay. I'm tough. I can take the pain. How old is he?'

'I don't really know.'

I gave Mark a précis of how I'd rescued Fluffy from Camden Town the previous Sunday. 'It's brilliant of you to take him on,' he said, when I'd finished, 'but how're you going to manage? How will you juggle a dog with all that personal shopping?'

It was the question Clarissa had asked me on Monday morning. And Mr McClaw, the vet. And Dad and Norma when I'd invited them over on Tuesday evening to meet the new arrival – although my father had been rather more blunt in the way he'd put it: 'You must be bloody mad paying good money for that mangy rat!' he'd barked, as he'd sat on the sofa disapprovingly. 'What the bloody hell are you going to do with him?'

'Oh, don't be such an old misery, Bob! He's beautiful!' Norma had purred as, with Fluffy, she'd crawled round the rug in knee-high black-leather boots, skin-tight, low-cut jeans and a spray-on fuchsia T-shirt that covered every curve of her voluptuous breasts like a second skin. Instead of getting older and more mature as the years passed, my father's girlfriends became younger and more glamorous. At thirty-eight, Norma was only three years older than I was. Although she was the single mother of two teenage boys, Jason and Shane, and ran a successful business supplying decorative platters of chocolates to the catering trade, she dressed and looked like a twenty-year-old. Off-duty and away from her sons, she acted like one, too. 'You're well cute,' she went on, picking Fluffy up and hugging him. 'You know, Bob, I think we should get one of these!'

'We?' Dad had been horrified. 'What's this *we* all of a sudden? Leave it out, Norma. And if I were you I'd put that animal down before he *wees* all over you!'

'Your father – he just cracks me up!' Norma had fallen about laughing at Dad's pun. Then she'd shrieked, 'Oh, my God! He has!'

'Disgusting animal!'

I'd rushed him into the bathroom in the vain hope that he'd learn to associate his litter tray with urinating, and when I'd come back in, Dad had asked again, 'So what're you going to do with that thing when you're working? Well, Annie? Have you thought about it? And while we're on the subject, young lady, why weren't you at work today? I called you at the store at lunchtime.'

'I'm off sick this week.'

'Yeah,' my father had grunted. 'Sick in the head, that's what you are. With Mad Dog Disease!'

Worrying about how I was going to look after Fluffy when I went back to work had kept me awake ever since I'd got him. I worked six days a week, from nine in the morning – sometimes earlier, if a client required it – until six or seven at night. Thursday was the store's late shopping evening, so we were open until nine. Even though I was second in command of the department – my boss, Eileen Grey, was coming up for retirement – I knew there was no way I could take Fluffy in with me. Like most department stores in London, Haines and Hampton operated a strict no-dogs policy, except in the case of guide dogs for the blind or hearing dogs for the deaf. Besides, I didn't even want to imagine what his indiscriminate bowel and bladder habits would do to the velvety white carpet that had only recently been laid in the lounge and changing rooms that made up the personal-shopping suite where I was based.

Now it looked as if I'd found the answer to my prayers, in the shape of Wag the Dog Walks. But, as with designer clothes, perfection didn't come cheap.

'I do two sixty-minute walks a day,' Mark explained. 'At nine o'clock in the morning, and again at midday, so you can choose which you'd prefer. He can go on both walks, if you want. If you'll be out at work all day, it'd probably be best if I took Fluffy out at lunchtime, because it'll break up the long day for him. I'd collect him from here and bring him back afterwards.'

'It sounds wonderful. Can I ask what you charge?'

He looked embarrassed. 'Ten pounds per walk. I know it's steep but it's the going rate, I'm afraid. And unlike some of the other dog-walkers I know, who go round with packs of up to a dozen, I never have more than four with me at any one time because I feel that's all I can control. Anyway, I don't think it's fair to the dogs to take more than a few, because if there were too many I couldn't give them enough attention. But you're not old enough to go for walkies yet, are you, Fluffball?' he said, turning his blue eyes on Fluffy, who had crawled on to his lap, the better to chew the surprisingly long and pointed fingernails of his right hand.

'That's true. He hasn't had all his injections yet. And he's still on medication. He's not going to be allowed to mix with other dogs for the next month. Frankly, I haven't a clue how I'm going to manage until then.'

'Well, I could do pet-sit visits till he's old enough to come out with me,' Mark suggested.

'Pet-sit visits?'

'I'd drop in once or twice a day to feed him, or give him pills if he needs them, play with him, and sort of generally see that he's all right.'

Mark was an angel sent from Heaven. '*Really?*' I gasped. 'That would be incredible. But . . . wouldn't it work out very expensive?'

The angel shrugged his hefty shoulders. 'Well, actually, I'm not that busy at the moment so I'm sure we could come to some arrangement. I mean, it would only be for a month max, wouldn't it? Then Fluffy'd be able to come out for walks with me. Anyway, I'm pretty flexible about money – you could always give me shares in a designer handbag as part payment.' He smiled. 'Besides, it wouldn't be much trouble because I don't live very far away. Just over in Finsbury Park, in fact. And this place is almost on the way to Hampstead, where I go twice a day on my walks. Does fifteen pounds a day for a couple of home visits sound too much? Because if it is, I'm sure there's room for negotiation. And while I was here I could also help with training Fluffy, if you wanted me to.'

'Housetraining?' I said eagerly.

'That, plus a few basic commands – sit, stay, roll over, you know the sort of thing. I have a way with dogs. Probably comes from growing up in the country, surrounded by Labradors and retrievers.'

I sighed. 'It sounds like you had an idyllic childhood.'

'I guess it was,' Mark said, rather wistfully. 'Didn't you?'

I was beginning to think I'd talked more than enough about myself for one day, so I just said, 'Not exactly,' and left it at that.

'The trouble with having such a nice childhood is that no one ever warns you that being grown-up is harder,' Mark went on, sounding almost regretful. Then he glanced at his watch. 'Shit! It's five o'clock. I'd better be off. So, Annie, would you like me to pet-sit Fluffy?'

I looked at my puppy, and did the mental arithmetic. Hiring Mark to visit him at home would cost me a small fortune over the next few weeks but I could just about afford it – and if I wanted to keep Fluffy, I couldn't afford not to. 'Yes, please, Mark. It'd be a huge relief to me.'

'Great.' He put Fluffy gently on the floor, and stood up to go. 'I'll start on Monday, if that's okay with you. Sunday's sacrosanct – I sleep till three. All I need is a set of keys from you, and we'll be in business.'

'Keys?'

'So I can get in to look after Fluffy when you're at work. Look, if you're worried about security, you can always call some of my other clients and ask for references.'

'That won't be necessary,' I answered. 'I'm sure I can trust you.'

Ten

This was how I, who'd always shied away from commitment, handed over my front door keys to Mark Curtis, a virtual stranger, and permitted him unfettered access to my life. Since I was out at work all day, I had no idea how often his battered VW, with the paw-marks and 'Wag the Dog Walks' painted on it, pulled up alongside the gleaming Audis and Porsches in the car park (I'd instructed the day-time concierge to let Mark in through the security barrier whenever he showed up).

Nor did I know how long Mark spent in the flat with Fluffy, or what he did while he was there. Sometimes he'd text me to reassure me that everything was fine. On days when I didn't hear from him I'd fret all afternoon that he'd forgotten to show up, and I'd rush back to the Workhouse in the evenings feeling frantic. But when I opened the front door, feeling guilty for having left Fluffy alone so long, the money I'd put out for Mark that morning was always missing, and Fluffy was curled up as usual, in his play-pen, fed, calm, contented and ready to play with me.

Mark proved to be a treasure. He seemed to know just what Fluffy needed, and to get it for him without my having to ask. For instance, when I got home from work one night towards the end of the second week, I found a green rubber ball in the play-pen that I'd never seen before. When I threw it across the living room, Fluffy scooted after it as if he'd been trained to, his little legs splaying outwards as he slid comically on the wooden floor. Another day I came home to find him gnawing a bone-shaped dog-chew covered with little plastic nodules. 'Bought this designer teether from the pet shop in Queen's Crescent market,' read an almost illegible Biro note on the coffee-table. 'Thought it'd save my fingers – and those Manolo Blah-blahs! Hope you don't mind vast expense – £2.50.' The note was signed 'From Fluffy's Personal Shopper'.

The following morning I left the extra money out for Mark, along with a note thanking him for taking the initiative. Two days later, as I was standing in the changing rooms helping an American producer to decide between the green Vera Wang evening dress she'd set her heart on to wear for the London première of her new film, and the printed Issa sheath that suited her better, I received a text on my Nokia: 'New initiative: have moved litter tray from en-suite into hallway in hope Fluffy might reach it in time to use it. Okay?' Though it felt odd to think of Mark wandering into my bathroom I soon got over it: that night, when Fluffy and I were watching television together, he suddenly jumped down from the sofa, toddled out into the hall, climbed into his litter tray and, to my amazement, peed in it.

As I told Clarissa smugly when she called from Cornwall, where she and James were renting a holiday cottage, Fluffy was thriving and everything was running like clockwork, all thanks to Mark. In fact, my dog-sitter was proving more and more of a treasure. One day that week he'd sent me a text, offering to take Fluffy to the vet for his check-up so that I wouldn't have to take time off work to do it. On another, he'd phoned from Sainsbury's; he was doing his shopping, did I need anything picked up? When I said I didn't think so, he told me that the milk in my fridge was sour and that I was running low on washing powder – or so he'd noticed when he'd looked under the sink for something to mop up after Fluffy's latest accident. When I got home a packet of detergent was on the counter, a carton of fresh milk in the fridge and a bag of doggy dental sticks on the counter next to a note that read, 'A present for the boy'.

'Hmm. Sounds like a bit of a stalker,' Clarissa remarked down the telephone, in her usual acerbic way. 'A bunny-boiler. Or, in this case, a puppy-boiler. Poking around in your fridge, smelling the milk. Weird.'

'He was probably just making himself a cup of tea,' I said, in Mark's defence, as I threw myself on to the living-room rug beside Fluffy, who was curled up in a ball, fast asleep.

I heard a Cornish bird tweet in the background and Clarissa take a gulp of the wine she'd told me she was drinking. 'I'm not so sure,' she said suspiciously. 'I think that Mr Wag-the-dog may have a bit of a thing for you.'

Since I already had a bit of a thing for Mr Wag-the-dog, my heart leaped at the thought of it. But I knew it was too good to be true. 'Nonsense!' I said, as I picked up my glass of Pinot Grigio, which was balanced on the edge of the raised fireplace. 'Mark never even sees me.'

'Maybe that's why he likes you. Or perhaps he's attracted to you because you're a bitch!' She laughed.

I could always rely on my friend to bolster my confidence. 'Ha-bloody-ha, Clarissa. Thanks a bunch. Anyway, my relationship with Mark is strictly professional. We only ever communicate by text or phone.'

She sighed wistfully into the receiver. 'Sounds perfect. Maybe I could suggest it to James. Thank God he's taken the girls out tonight to find the nearest fast-food outlet – they've been gagging for some e-numbers ever since we got here. For one night at least I don't have to pretend to be a Domestic Goddess and whip up Nigella's fairy cakes and a shepherd's pie, or make conversation with James.'

'How hard can that be? You've been married for centuries.'

'Precisely. Honestly, Annie, we're just not used to spending so much time together any more. I swear we only communicate through the children when we're at home. We ran out of things to say to each other on the hellish journey down here. Five hours of sweets, pit-stops and rows about what cassette we were going to listen to. *Harry Potter* and *Horrid Henry* versus Kylie, or Danny Kaye singing "Tubby the Tuba".'

'I'd be for "Tubby the Tuba". And stop complaining about James – you know you adore him.'

'I suppose so,' Clarissa admitted, somewhat reluctantly, 'much as one would adore a younger brother – the kind you want to throttle every other day. Yes, of course I love him. I just wish he wasn't so . . . well, so bloody hearty. He has so much energy – for everything except sex. A little of that wouldn't go amiss, I can tell you. It's all "Let's play rounders!" Or "Who fancies a game of Monopoly?" Or "Let's go and visit the local gnome museum!" Or "I know, everyone, let's build a sandcastle in the shape of the Old Bailey!"' Her mimicry of James was spot on, and I started to laugh. 'Honestly, it's like living with a hyperactive Boy Scout leader. I'm supposed to be on holiday, relaxing and being pampered, but I swear I have less time to myself down here than when I'm at work. When James and the kids are out of the house, like now, the peace is utterly blissful. I tell you, this is the first moment I've had to myself all week. I'm sitting in a hammock in the garden as we speak, enjoying a healthy supper of Chardonnay and sour-cream-and-chive Kettle Chips. Perfect.' There was a loud crunch in my ear as she bit into one. 'What's he like, anyway?'

'Who?'

'The dog-walker.'

'Oh . . .' I gulped my wine. For some reason I felt reluctant to expose Mark to Clarissa's scrutiny. 'I don't know. I've only seen him once.'

'And?' she persisted in her usual nosy manner.

'What can I say? He's very nice. Tall, dark –'

'And devastatingly handsome?' she interrupted, with a giggle. There followed another crunch.

'Yes, I guess so.'

The Kettle Chip came spluttering out of her mouth, and I waited to hear her fall out of the hammock. 'Really?' she asked, when she'd finished choking. 'Is he single?'

'How on earth should I know?'

'Haven't you asked him?'

'No, I haven't. What do you expect me to say? "Hello, Mark, what time are you collecting Fluffy today, and are you shacked up with anyone?" He's probably married. Or, at least, in a permanent relationship. Anyway, what does it matter? He's just my dog-walker. I haven't really thought about it.'

Actually, I had thought about it – more often than I cared to acknowledge, even to myself. Did Mark have a bit-of-a-thing for me, as Clarissa put it? And did I reciprocate? Although after our initial meeting our conversation had never gone further than Fluffy, our brief, slightly flirtatious phone calls and Mark's texts lit up my days at work. And, once I'd got over the shock of his moving the litter tray into the hall, I'd found the thought of him prowling around my flat when I wasn't there oddly comforting. So when, one day towards the end of August, Mark called me at work and asked if I'd mind if he brought his guitar round occasionally and practised in the living room while he was pet-sitting, because he'd been asked not to at his place, I told him that would be fine as long as he didn't disturb my neighbours.

When I got back from Chelsea that night, there was a thank-you note for me on the kitchen table, along with a small bunch of wild flowers he said he'd picked on Hampstead Heath. The vase in which they were casually arranged was an old favourite of mine – a pink china jug I'd taken from Nan's flat when she'd died three years before. As I rarely used it, it had been stowed at the back of one of the highest kitchen cupboards. He must have gone to great lengths to find it – in fact, there was no way he could have known it was there without standing on the stepladder I kept in the hall closet and undertaking a thorough search.

The following day Mark brought his electric guitar over. A week later he said there seemed little point in taking it away every night only to bring it back the following morning, so I agreed to him leaving it overnight. From then on, it took up permanent residence on a black metal stand in the corner of the living room, along with various electrical cables, a large subwoofer, and an old Wills tobacco tin containing an assortment of plectrums. Sometimes, at night, Fluffy would wander over and give the paraphernalia a good sniffing. Apparently he responded to music – or, as Mark put it in a text to me later that week, 'Ruff likes riff.'

By now it was early September, and Fluffy was unrecognizable as the pathetic, sickly creature I'd brought home from Camden Town on that fateful Sunday in July. The bald patches on his skin were covered with downy fur, the diarrhoea had cleared up, and his lips, previously disfigured by sores where the string handle of the tramp's collecting tin had rubbed them raw, were as soft and pink and moist as his tongue. Sleeping in the sunshine on the balcony, combined with liberal amounts of cod-liver oil mixed into his meals, had made his coat glossy and seen off the rickets; unfortunately it had also made his breath smell like stale mackerel on a hot day. Although his paws turned inwards, as they always would, his legs were growing straighter, stronger and longer. Instead of coming up to my ankles, his head was now at mid-calf height. Like a Russian vine, he seemed to grow every day. When he scrabbled at my legs to be picked up, as he often did, his little claws left scratch marks all the way up to my knees. From weighing just a kilo, he now tipped the vet's puppy scales at four.

Most satisfying of all, his tail never stopped wagging, and his mouth hung permanently open in what looked like a cheesy grin.

'It's as if he knows he's landed in clover,' Mr McClaw remarked, when I took Fluffy in for his final inoculation. 'When I think of what he was like a few weeks ago – he's unrecognizable. Congratulations.'

I flushed with pride. As a makeover job, Fluffy was perhaps my greatest success story so far. Despite his crazy multi-directional salt-and-pepper coat, which was becoming less fluffy and more wiry by the day, and his large hairy ears, one of which stuck up to the ceiling, the other of which bent over and pointed to the ground, he carried himself with an elegant, almost raffish air. His muzzle was elongating into a foxy point, and his tail growing longer and hairier. Full of bounce, he leaped around the flat like a gazelle, brimming with playfulness. When I came home from work he threw himself at me with such unalloyed pleasure that it was as if we'd been separated for a lifetime. On Sundays – when I was at home all day – he lolled around the flat with me, following me from room to room, and chewed up the newspapers as I finished reading them; like me, he seemed to have a penchant for the fashion pages.

Fluffy wasn't completely housetrained yet, but he was getting there. He had realized what his litter tray was for, and most of the time he used it, though his aim wasn't brilliant, particularly now that he had almost outgrown it. Though I put it out on the balcony when I was at home, and cleaned it whenever it was dirty, a stale odour still pervaded the apartment, and there were frequent accidents. Very frequent, actually: perhaps because he was still being fed so often, Fluffy seemed to defecate three or four times a day. 'Helen of Troy,' my father called him, 'the face that launched a thousand shits.'

Now that he'd been fully inoculated, Fluffy was allowed out for proper walks, which would hopefully mean an end to the litter tray, and certainly the end of Mark's pet-sitting rate, which, while reasonable for the amount of time he was putting in, worked out at a substantial ninety pounds a week. Had I had a spare room, I could have had a live-in au pair for less, dedicated to looking after Fluffy. So, on the Sunday following our visit to the vet, I rang Mark to discuss our future plans. Though it was three o'clock in the afternoon, he sounded half asleep.

'Have I woken you up?' I asked him nervously.

'No, no.' He yawned. 'I came to a good hour ago. Though I haven't managed to get out of bed yet.'

I wondered who was keeping him there. 'Sorry if I'm disturbing you.'

'You're not. I'm not doing anything. Or, rather, I'm fully occupied with relaxing my hamstrings, Sunday being my day of rest. Actually, I was going to call you about the arrangements for this week.'

'Right. That's what I'm calling you about.'

'Well, I was thinking, even though Fluffy'll be allowed out now, rather than take him to the Heath with the other big dogs straight away, we ought not to rush things. It would be better to get him used to being outside gradually.

So, I think I should still pop into your place, like I usually do, and take him out for a walk in the street by himself.'

'Really?'

'You know, get him used to being out on a leash for a week or so. A long walk on the Heath every day might be too much for him.'

'I suppose so. After all, he's still only little, isn't he?'

'And he might be intimidated by some of the other dogs. You see, I take out a Rottweiler three days a week. And a huge mastiff on Thursdays and Fridays.'

'I see what you mean.'

'Actually, Maisie – the Rottweiler – is as gentle as can be. In fact, she's a dreadful coward. She got spooked by a miniature dachshund on Parliament Hill the other day.' I laughed. 'Still, Fluffy might find the size of her intimidating.'

'Mmm. He might. And, anyway, you're right, an hour-long walk might tire him out, I suppose,' I said. 'Well, if you don't mind carrying on doing home visits for a bit longer . . .'

'Not at all. Anything to oblige.'

'The only thing is . . .'

'Yeah?'

'After a couple of weeks I'll have to make do with just one walk a day.'

'Oh!'

'It's just that . . .' I took a deep breath. 'I'm not saying you're expensive, Mark – in fact, I think your rates are awfully reasonable for what you've been doing and I certainly couldn't have managed without you. But I can't afford to keep paying out so much every week, not *ad infinitum*, just so that Fluffy won't be alone. I don't like the idea of leaving him for long stretches but . . . I was thinking that if I took him out early in the morning, and he went for a long walk with you at lunchtime, do you think that would be enough – I mean, to work towards – now that he's getting older?'

There was a long silence at the other end of the phone. 'The thing is,' Mark said eventually, 'I rather like hanging out with the little monster.'

'He is adorable, isn't he?'

'Yes. And then . . .'

'Yes?'

'There's my music.'

'What about it?'

'The acoustics in your big room are something else. I kind of find it really stimulating playing there – it sort of gets my creative juices flowing in a way nothing else has in a long time. Actually, I'm bang in the middle of composing a new song.'

'Are you?'

'Mmm. A sort of bluesy, jazzy number with pop over-tones – think the Oscar Peterson trio, *circa* 1959, crossed with Kylie Minogue's *Can't Get You Out Of My Head*.'

'That sounds amazing!'

'Yeah. Well, without being big-headed, I think it could be, I really do. It might even end up quite commercial, if I can get it right. But it still needs a lot more work on it.'

'I see.' I was about to point out that I could scarcely keep paying him to dog-sit just so he could carry on composing in my flat when he came up with his own suggestion:

'So ... Let's think about this ... How about if you were to pay me to take Fluffy out in the morning, and I kept coming over to the Workhouse in the afternoons anyway? Without charging you, I mean.'

'What – nothing?'

'Fluffy wouldn't be alone all the time, and in return for keeping him company, and taking him out now and then, I'd be able to work there.'

I digested this for a moment. 'So you'd use my flat as a kind of studio?'

'Yeah. No different from what I've been doing for the past few weeks. It would be sort of a fair exchange, wouldn't it?'

'A form of barter, you mean?'

'Yeah. A use-of-premises-in-exchange-for-services-rendered swap, right? I can't afford to rent somewhere just to work in, and you can't afford to keep paying me so much, so it makes sense, doesn't it? And you're out all day so I wouldn't bother you when I was there, would I? And if for any reason you *were* at home, and wanted the place to yourself, well, you could tell me to piss off for a while. And I would. Whaddaya think?'

Alarm bells were ringing in my head, but I blocked my mind to them. 'It's an interesting idea.'

'Yeah. It is. Plus ...'

'Yes?'

'I could always make myself useful in other ways.'

I found myself smiling. 'Such as?'

'Well, I could do your shopping for you. Or sweep the

117

floor. Dust that big yucca in the living room. Put up shelves.'

I stopped myself laughing. 'Thanks, but I already have more than enough shelves.'

'That's true. Okay, then, I'd change your lightbulbs when they went.'

'Funnily enough, that's the one bit of DIY I can do by myself.'

Now we were both laughing. 'Look, if it doesn't work out,' he went on, 'we'll call it off. Simple as that.'

I took a deep breath. 'Okay.'

'*Okay?*' Mark sounded startled. 'Do you mean okay about calling it off or okay about starting it up?'

'Both, I guess.'

'That's brilliant! Fucking brilliant, Annie!' Mark sounded ecstatic. And then he added prophetically, 'I promise you'll never regret this.'

I should have got that in writing.

Eleven

Around six weeks later, on a Wednesday afternoon in mid-October, I was lying on the sofa in the personal-shopping suite's private lounge with my shoes kicked off and my feet up, halfway through a glass of Champagne. A complimentary bottle of Bollinger was always on ice for our best customers, who viewed it, and the triangles of freshly made mini-sandwiches that accompanied it, as an integral part of our service. But ever since I'd joined Haines's personal-shopping department ten years earlier, as one of the store's graduate management trainees, I'd made it a habit never to drink while I was working.

This day, however, had proved the exception. I'd just finished with a potentially important new customer, who'd been with me since eleven o'clock that morning, and I really needed a shot of something strong. Tiffany George was the twenty-two-year-old wife of Ralph, a hot provincial footballer who'd recently been signed up to play for Arsenal. *Hello!* was doing a feature on the couple's new double-fronted home in Mill Hill, and Tiffany had come to see me in search of some outfits to wear for the photo-shoot.

Poured into a pair of Lycra jeans, teamed with a cropped pink Stella McCartney T-shirt so tight it seemed to have been sprayed on to her cosmetically enhanced boobs, Tiffany had arrived two hours late for her appointment, trailing a badly behaved toddler, an overtired baby and a clumsy, pasty-faced nanny; she obviously wasn't going to risk losing her husband to some voluptuous au pair.

When Eileen Grey brought her into the spacious suite where I was waiting for her, I noticed that my boss had a rather fixed smile on her face. A slim, elegant woman, who wore her long grey hair pulled back in a chignon and always dressed in minimalist dark clothes, like her role model Jean Muir, Eileen had been at Haines and Hampton for more than thirty years, first as a buyer, then as head of the personal-shopping department, which she had started. During that time Haines had become the most famous stop on London's high-fashion circuit. When I'd joined the store, she'd taken me under her wing and taught me everything I now knew about style and clothes.

'Tiffany, this is my assistant, Annie,' she said. 'I'm handing you over to her because I'm sure she'll be able to find the perfect outfits for you.'

Tiffany gave a silicone-enhanced pout and dumped her Louis Vuitton Murakami bag on a chair. 'Whatever,' she said, in a bored voice.

Eileen smiled crisply. 'Annie, I know you'll do your best for Mrs George. She's all yours.' As she hurried out of the door, she mouthed, 'And good riddance!' at me behind Tiffany's back.

Though she was a natural beauty – tiny nose, big blue eyes, to-die-for body and long silky blonde hair – Tiffany's orange skin, gold acrylic talons and blinding bling made her look hard and tarty. Her sour expression and high-handed manners spoiled her appearance even more. While

Acapulco, her three-year-old son (conceived during a stay in a five-star Mexican spa), threw chocolate and tantrums all over the white carpet, and the depressed nanny did her best to cope with the crying baby, Croydon (conceived on a visit to Tiffany's parents), she worked her way sulkily through the two racks of fabulous clothes I'd selected for her earlier that day without once unplugging the head-phones of her iPod – that season's must-have accessory. She demanded that we lend her the clothes, and when I told her politely that it was the store's policy never to do that, she asked for a 50 per cent discount. When I told her even more politely that we didn't do that either, she found fault with everything.

'This is fucking crap!' was her most eloquent phrase as, gyrating to the music we could hear throbbing through her earpieces, she wriggled out of Vivienne Westwood dresses, Burberry Prorsum blouses, Dries Van Noten trousers and Pringle jackets and dropped them unceremoniously on the floor. Unchecked by his mother, who appeared totally indifferent to him, Acapulco fell on them, pawing them with grubby fingers before we could pick them up. After emptying half a litre of Bollinger down her throat, and picking the filling out of the sandwiches without offering one to either her toddler or the nanny, Tiffany flounced out without buying anything, saying she was off to find some real style at Harvey Nichols.

As the demoralized nanny pushed the pram out after her, dragging the screaming Mexican city by the wrist, I thrust a large bag of makeup samples at her. 'Here, these are for you,' I whispered. She looked so grateful that for a horrible moment, I thought she was going to burst into tears.

'Hey, what's in that bag?' I heard Tiffany demand, as they waited for the lift.

'Oh, just a dirty nappy,' the poor girl stuttered. Good on yer! I thought, smiling for the first time that day.

'How did you get on with Cartier Whatsername?' George Haines, the store's managing director, asked eagerly when he phoned down from his office on the top floor.

'She's called Tiffany, Mr Haines. Although Ratner would suit her much better – Rat for short. Let's just say that I'll never be able to wear my silver Tiffany earrings again. If that cow ever comes back, you can deal with her.'

'Now, now, Annie, that's no way to talk about one of our customers.' George, a mild-mannered gentleman of the old school, sounded shocked.

'You're absolutely right. However, the word "customer" implies someone who buys something, so in Tiffany's case it doesn't apply.'

'What? She bought nothing?'

'No. She didn't even spend a penny.'

My dire joke was lost on him. 'Dear, dear, Annie,' he said anxiously. 'I was really hoping we could entrap her. Where one overpaid Arsenal footballer's wife puts her dainty little foot, surely the others would follow?'

'Many of them already use our personal-shopping service and they're all absolutely charming. Believe me, you wouldn't want someone like her wearing our clothes.'

When he hung up, I set about polishing off the dregs

of the Champagne before my next client came in. Just as I was finishing the bottle, my Nokia rang. 'I've got a problem,' Mark said straight away.

I put my glass on the coffee-table. 'Has something happened to Fluffy?'

'No, but only you can help me.'

By now I was envisaging all sorts of domestic crises. 'What *is* it, Mark?'

'Is Fluorescent Green the New Black?'

'*What?*'

'Is Fluorescent Green going to be the New Black this winter? I need to know because I'm in Chapel Street market and I'm buying some trainers and they only have fluorescent green ones in my size.' I started to laugh, as he continued, perfectly seriously, 'The bloke in charge of the stall says fluorescents are coming back into fashion.'

'I'm not sure they were ever in. At least, not since 1970s disco chic.'

'Ah. So you advise against it?'

'Well, wouldn't it rather clash with the grass on Hampstead Heath?'

'You've got a point there. Also,' he went on, 'Fluffy's with me, and we wondered if you needed any food for tonight.'

'Tell him that's very nice of him.' Since we'd started our new arrangement towards the end of August, Mark and I had developed an easy, bantering telephonic and texting relationship that revolved around my dog, our only point of contact. Mark had also made himself more and more indispensable, not only as a dog-walker and pet-sitter, but around the flat which, since he'd imported his electronic keyboard, computer and second guitar into it, was beginning to resemble a music studio. However, the burgeoning technological clutter in the corner of the living room was worth putting up with: having Mark around was like having a live-out housekeeper. Not only was Fluffy looked after in my absence, when I returned from work every night the place was tidier than when I'd left it in the morning. The floor was swept, my dirty cereal bowl had been washed up and, instead of being draped over the taps, the tea-towels were neatly folded away. Now Mark was buying my groceries, too.

'Actually, I could do with a new bag of Hill's Science Diet,' I said. 'The rabbit-and-rice flavour.'

'I thought that was Fluffy's. I didn't know you ate it as well.'

His deadpan humour always made me smile. 'Yes, well, I want my coat to be glossier, and I'm trying to grow a tail,' I quipped back.

He sniggered. 'Seriously, Annie, what are you going to eat? There's nothing there except a mouldy lump of Cheddar, two stale eggs, some out-of-date hummus and a withered lemon.'

'Have you spent *all* day with your head stuck in my fridge? I thought you were meant to be writing your song.'

'I am. I was. But I was taking a little break and I couldn't help noticing that your fridge is the barest I've ever seen it.'

'Don't worry. I'll pick up something at M&S on my way home.'

'Why do that?' he countered. 'I'm standing in front of

a proper butcher's shop. In fact, Fluffy's pulling at the leash to get inside. *Control yourself, freak!* Look, shall I go inside and pick something up for you? You really ought to support your local small shops, you know, or England will be wall-to-wall supermarkets. How about some nice bangers? Or chops? There's some great fillet steak in the window, too – properly marbled and all.'

'Marbled? What does that mean?'

'You know, with fat running through it.'

'That sounds disgusting.'

'It's not. Fat keeps the meat moist by melting and sort of basting it internally while it's cooking. Really, Annie, didn't your mum teach you anything in the kitchen?'

'I didn't have a mum,' I said, before I could stop myself.

There was a short pause, during which I could hear the sound effects of Chapel Street Market in the background. 'What?' Mark said eventually.

I, too, hesitated. 'I mean, I had a mother, of course. But she wasn't much of a *mum*, if you know what I mean. She walked out on me and my father when I was eight. I haven't seen or heard from her since.'

I could tell that Mark was embarrassed, because he went silent again. Then he continued, as if I hadn't just confessed my darkest secret, 'There are some nice pheasants in the window.'

'Thanks, but I wouldn't know what to do with one, other than stick its feathers on a hat.'

'It's easy. All you do is shove it in the oven with some butter up its bum and –'

'Really, forget it, Mark. Please. Look, I've got to go

now. Don't worry about me. As I said, I'll get something myself.'

At seven o'clock that evening I arrived back in Islington. The food aisles of M&S opposite the Angel Tube station boasted their usual contingent of Workhouse residents who, like me, were buying their supper on the way home from work. I recognized a woman who lived on the ground floor, as well as the guy from along the corridor who'd complained about Fluffy on the morning after his first night with me. We acknowledged each other with an unsmiling nod, as we did whenever we encountered each other in the Workhouse's lobby, then walked on, our eyes skimming the refrigerated counters for something that could be reheated in a microwave in three and a half minutes flat. Wholesome cauliflower cheese made with real West Country farmhouse Cheddar, succulent chicken tikka with saffron-yellow pilau rice, Italian beef lasagne, flavourful salmon steaks with watercress sauce – this wasn't just any chill-cooked food we were buying, it was sophisticated, sexy chill-cooked food especially designed with singleton workaholics like ourselves in mind. It occurred to me suddenly that there was something rather sad about all of us young professionals sitting in solitary splendour on our stylish sofas in our fancy flats, watching our expensive flat-screen televisions or scanning the lonely-hearts ads while balancing our reheated, single-portion gastro-meals on our laps. What the building needed was a communal kitchen, or even a restaurant, where the singleton residents could get together, eat and talk to each other about their lonely lives – a sort of cross between Central Perk and the Samaritans.

Relationships, as opposed to friendships, had never been my strong point. In fact, since getting dumped at the age of sixteen after two weeks of dating my long-time heart-throb Melvyn, who'd lived round the corner from us in Hampstead Garden Suburb, I'd made a point of steering clear of them. I'd had the occasional lover, naturally – there had been four to date, an extremely modest number for a woman of my age by modern standards – but whenever things had looked like turning serious, I'd got out as fast as I could.

By now I was used to being single; I rarely gave it a second thought. According to Clarissa – who, since she'd been a social worker, was full of psychobabble – this was because I was unconsciously afraid of commitment so avoided it. Since my mother had left me, she said, I subconsciously refused to put myself into a position where I might get hurt again.

Rubbish, I'd told her. On the whole I was perfectly happy on my own.

Nevertheless, there were times when I felt lonely and, in the past, coming home late from work had been one of them. Now all that had changed. I was no longer one of the many Workhouse residents buying just enough food for myself on the way back to an empty flat, because my flat was no longer empty. And it wasn't just a flat any more, it felt like a real home. Fluffy was there, and I couldn't wait to see him. Lately he'd seemed to anticipate my arrival. As I'd climb the stairs, or leave the lift, I'd hear him snuffling at the crack under the front door; and as I stood in the corridor, fishing in my bag for my keys, he'd start barking, and scrabbling to get out. Eyes gleaming with joy, long pink tongue lolling out, he'd throw himself at me the moment I opened the door, and welcome me home as if we'd been separated for years.

Tonight, however, there was no snuffling as I walked out of the lift. Instead, the corridor was filled with rock music, and it was coming from my flat. Hesitating, I put my ear to the front door and listened. I could also hear the sound of a male voice, singing along off-key. As I pushed the door open slowly, a delicious smell met me. A pair of muddy, canvas-strapped sandals was lying on the hall floor, with a gaoler's size bunch of keys and a thin, stripy plastic bag which contained a pair of lurid green trainers.

I walked quietly towards the living room and stopped on the threshold. Mark was standing behind the stainless-steel island unit at the far end, singing to himself as he expertly chopped some celery. There was an open bottle of red wine and a half-empty glass beside him, and behind him a saucepan and a frying-pan were sizzling on the hob. As for Fluffy, he was sitting upright in front of the island, ears pricked, following Mark's every move with slight turns of his head. At last Mark took a scrap of meat from the chopping board and tossed it to him. Without jumping up, Fluffy caught it.

'That's the last of the scraps for you, Greedy-guts,' Mark said to him, 'You'll have to wait till after supper now.' Then, gathering up the chopped celery in both hands, he threw it into the frying-pan.

Fluffy was the first to notice me as I walked in. But

instead of running over to greet me, he turned his head in my direction then, tail swishing, looked back eagerly at Mark, who had now picked up the frying-pan and, singing at the top of his voice, was shaking the vegetables about in the totally professional manner of a chef.

'Mark?'

With a terrible clatter, he dropped the pan on to the hob and swung towards me. 'Shit! I didn't hear you come in.'

While he went over to the sound system and lowered the volume, I walked over to the island unit, stopping to greet Fluffy on my way. I put my M&S bag down, and peered at some dismembered limbs that were marinating in a bowl. 'What's this?'

Mark strolled back across the floor in his bare feet, picked up a fork and turned a piece over. 'It's the pheasant. From the butcher's. They were such a bargain I just had to buy one. And seeing as you said you hadn't a clue how to cook it, I kind of thought I'd do it for you.'

'That's very nice of you.'

He frowned. 'I hope you haven't got other plans for this evening? Have you? Fuck it, I didn't think about that!'

'Well, as a matter of fact I did have plans.' His face fell. 'Putting my feet up and eating this.' I took my single-portion packet of pasta out of the carrier-bag and put it on the work surface.

'What's this?' Mark picked it up. 'Spaghetti carbonara?' He looked at the ingredients list, then shuddered. 'Buying that's a crime, Annie. Do you have any idea how quick and easy it is – not to mention inexpensive – to cook this from scratch?' I shook my head. 'I can see I'll have to teach you.'

'But cooking's so complicated. I mean, I can grill chops and stuff. And heat beans and do a fry-up. I had to cook for my father and me when I was growing up – you know, after my mother left. But we never had anything fancy like this. Except later, in restaurants, of course.' I looked at everything he'd spread out on the counter – apples, vegetables, chopped-up rashers of bacon, olive oil, and a plastic packet containing brown knobbly things. 'What on earth are those?'

'Vacuum-packed chestnuts. To go with the cabbage. Buying them like that's cheating, really, but it isn't the right season for fresh ones.'

'There's rather a lot of food here for just one person.'

'Well, I thought you might not mind sharing it with the chef.' Mark pushed his long curls off his forehead with the back of his wrist. Since the one and only time we'd met face to face three months previously, I'd forgotten how good-looking he was. Standing behind the island unit in his white Wag the Dog Walks T-shirt and knee-length khaki shorts, with a tea-towel tied round his waist, the hair on his bare, muscular arms glistening under the halogen spotlights, and his crumpled-paper-bag face creased into a grin, he was devastating.

'That sounds great,' I said. 'Thank you.'

'All part of the service.'

I watched him go straight to the cupboard where the wine glasses were kept and get another out. He filled it and handed it to me. He seemed thoroughly at home in my kitchen – I'd almost say more at home than I was. 'So, do you run this service for all your clients?' I asked. 'A sort of dog's dinner service?'

'Well, it will be a dog's dinner unless I get on with it. So, if you'll excuse me . . .' He turned back to the sizzling pan. 'I hope you're hungry.'

'Actually, I'm ravenous. And shattered. I've had the most appalling day.'

'Well, go and have a shower or whatever it is women do, and I'll have it on the table in thirty minutes. And please take Fluffy with you. I made the mistake of giving him some scraps, and now he won't leave me alone.'

An hour and a half later – as I was to learn, Mark's timing was always on the optimistic side – we sat down to eat the most delicious home-cooked meal I'd ever tasted: pot-roasted pheasant, with celery and onion, flambéed in the leftovers of a bottle of brandy that had been hanging around at the back of one of the kitchen cupboards ever since I'd moved in. It was served with cabbage sautéed with the bacon and chestnuts, and accompanied by roasted-apple sauce. Before we'd started eating, we'd fed Fluffy an extra bowl of his rabbit-and-rice pellets in the hope that he wouldn't beg at the table. But the fabulous smells coming from our plates proved irresistible to him, and as Mark and I sat opposite one another tucking into the scrumptious feast, Fluffy positioned himself midway between our legs, in turn whining and scrabbling at our knees.

Maybe it was all the wine we'd drunk while we were waiting for the food to be ready, but conversation flowed as easily between us as our bantering texts usually did.

Talking to Mark was, I discovered, almost as easy as talking to Clarissa. It was as if we'd known each other for years.

'I see you went for the fluorescent green in the end,' I remarked, as I tucked into my second helping of pheasant.

'You mean my new Jimmys out in the hall?'

'Jimmys?'

'It's the new Cockney rhyming slang. You know – Jimmy Choos, shoes?'

I smiled at him across the table. 'Very clever. My father, who really is a Cockney, used to call them his ones. As in one-and-twos. That was before he made money and started buying them at Gucci.'

'What did he call them then?'

'His Guccis, of course. He's a believer in the if-you've-got-it-flaunt-it school of philosophy.'

Mark laughed. 'Well, I don't have it, and I doubt I ever will. But I'll certainly be able to flaunt it in those green trainers. Do you think they'll pass muster with the fashionista Fascists?'

'I'd say they were fresh, vibrant and ironically witty. Which is fashion-speak for outrageously bad taste. Naughty dog! Stop that!'

'What's he doing down there?'

'Scratching my knees. You'd certainly make an impression if you wore them at London Fashion Week. You might even start a new trend. By the way, I thought you knew nothing about fashion.'

'I don't.'

'So how do you know about Jimmy Choos? And, come

132

to think of it, expressions like "fashionista" and "the New Black"?'

Mark shrugged in an embarrassed way. 'Well, you know . . .'

'No, I don't know. *Go away, Fluffy! Sit!*' Fluffy flounced out from under the table, threw himself on to the floor, put his nose between his paws, and gave me a sulky, reproachful stare.

'Well,' Mark continued, 'sometimes when I'm here in the afternoons, playing my music, I make myself a cup of tea.' He stopped.

'And?' I prompted.

'And . . . while I'm waiting for the kettle to boil, I, er, sometimes sit down on the sofa for a while.'

'And?' I urged him.

'And . . . well . . . sometimes I just sort of vegetate. And sometimes . . .'

'Yes?'

'Well, sometimes I kind of have a look through those.' He jerked his chin towards the enormous pile of glossy fashion and style magazines stacked on one of the side tables – magazines I had to read as part of my job.

I was amazed. 'Really?'

'What's wrong with that?' he said, rather defensively.

'Nothing. I'm just surprised you'd be interested in them.'

He shrugged. 'Some of them aren't bad, actually. *Tatler, Marie Claire, Cosmopolitan, Style.* I like *Wallpaper* best. That's pretty cool. And, of course, there's all those Vogues – American *Vogue*, Italian *Vogue*, *Vogue for Men*, British *Vogue*, British *Vogue for the Stylistically Challenged*.

I bet they do *Vogue for Dogs*, don't they? You should get it for Fluffy. He'd enjoy chewing it up. It's not the pictures of the models that I like – they're a bit skeletal for me, and the weird photos make it difficult to see what they're wearing. What I like best is . . .' He stopped again.

'Yes?'

'It's nothing.'

'Oh, go on. You can't stop now.'

'Well . . .' He took a deep breath. 'I kind of like the free sachets stuck on to some of the adverts. You know – shampoo and face cream and stuff. You never seem to use them. Tearing them off the pages and picking the lumps of glue off the back is kind of satisfying. And some of the creams are quite nice too. There was one I found the other day that was full of adenoids.'

I attempted to control the urge to burst out laughing. 'Do you mean retinoids?'

'Yeah, that was it. It made my hands really smooth and soft. My favourites, though, are those lift-the-flap ads – the ones that have a nice smell inside which comes off on you if you rub them with your fingers.' The thought of macho Mark trying out the free samples of cream and perfume was so incongruous that, by now, I had practically collapsed over my plate. 'I knew you'd laugh at me if I told you,' he said, turning scarlet.

'I'm sorry! You're just so terribly funny.'

'That's not what my ex-girlfriend called me. I think pain-in-the-arse was the expression she used.'

'Perhaps she didn't appreciate your wit.'

'She thought I didn't have any wits at all. But, then,

she wasn't a bundle of laughs. Come to think of it, I don't remember us ever having fun together.'

'Sounds like a great relationship. How long did it last?'

'On and off, about five years.' Our eyes met across the table, and Mark said, 'How about you?'

'Me?'

'Yeah. Why isn't there a Mr Annie Osborne in your life?'

I felt a hot flush begin to rise. 'How do you know there isn't?' I said.

Mark pushed a stray lock of hair out of his eyes. 'Let's just say I haven't noticed any evidence of one.' I felt my cheeks turn red. 'I mean,' he went on, 'there are no rolled-up black socks festering under your bed. No shaving cream in the bathroom. Only one mug of coffee on the counter in the mornings. Only one toothbrush. And the cap on the toothpaste tube's always screwed on tight.'

'I guess that's conclusive evidence, then.' By now my embarrassment was turning into anger. I remembered what Clarissa had said about Mark being a puppy-boiler and stalking me. 'Tell me something, do you spend all your time here going through my things and spying on me?'

He looked horrified. 'Spying?'

'Yes. The fridge. My bathroom cabinet. Poking around under my bed.'

'I wasn't poking. I was trying to get Fluffy out,' he said lamely. 'He was stuck under it, eating something.'

Closely followed by the puppy in question, who jumped up the moment I did, I gathered up some dirty crockery, walked behind the island unit and dumped it in the sink. There was a long pause. Then Mark asked, 'Are you angry with me?'

'It doesn't matter,' I snapped, as I flung open the dishwasher and, while Fluffy scampered eagerly about my feet in the hope of more scraps, started to load in the cutlery.

Mark watched me in silence. At length he took a deep breath. 'I haven't been spying on you. It's just that I couldn't help noticing.' He sighed. 'You don't believe me, do you?' I didn't answer. 'Oh, shit. I've blown it, haven't I?'

'Blown what, exactly?'

'*It*. My chance.'

'What chance?'

'I kind of thought I might have one. The thing is, Annie, I really like talking to you. You know, on the phone. And I was kind of hoping there might be a sort of opening for me here.'

I turned on the taps and started manically rinsing the plates. 'I don't understand you.'

'An opening. You know, a Situation Vacant.'

'I wish you wouldn't speak in riddles. What are you talking about?'

'Like they advertise in the papers. "Boyfriend Wanted for TLR. NS. GSOH. Must be DWGWFS".'

The floorboards seemed to tilt beneath my feet and I felt my scowling mouth twitch into a smile. I turned my back on him and put the plates into the dishwasher. 'I know about Tender Loving Relationship and Good Sense of Humour. But what does DW whatever stand for?'

'DWGWFS? Dog-walking Guitarist With Fluorescent Shoes, of course.'

My shoulders were shaking with laughter now. When I'd managed to control myself, I said, in a choked voice, 'So it's not just *Vogue* you've been reading, it's the lonely-hearts ads, too! Do you ever do any composing while you're here?'

'Sure. But I get bored easily. There are always more interesting things to do.'

'Like counting the toothbrushes, or lack thereof?'

'Yeah, that took me a couple of days. And wondering whether I'm ever going to get to see you in the flesh again, rather than just texting you.' Mark got up from the table, walked over to me and slipped his arms round me from behind. They felt strong and comforting and I didn't resist when he pulled me against him.

'And what if I was looking for a dog-walking guitarist with fluorescent shoes?' I said quietly.

He blew the hair off the nape of my neck. 'Well,' he said, planting a kiss on it, 'I was sort of thinking I might apply for the job.'

I turned to face him. And the next thing I knew we were kissing passionately.

Then Fluffy was barking like a maniac and jumping up in his first jealous attempt to push us apart. Mark and I broke off, and said in unison, 'Oh, Fluffy, do *shut up*!'

Twelve

'You're going out with a geezer who does *what* for a living?' my father said when, six weeks later, over Sunday lunch of roast beef and Yorkshire pudding at Simpson's-in-the-Strand, I told him I was seeing Mark.

'He's a dog-walker. I mean, he runs a dog-walking business.'

'Employs a lot of people, does he?'

'Well, I don't know how many.' My father narrowed his eyes at me. 'Okay, it's just him,' I admitted. 'But he's awfully nice, Dad. He's a wonderful person.'

He put a forkful of Yorkshire pudding into his mouth and chewed it thoughtfully, then washed it down with a sip of Beaujolais. 'He certainly must be ambitious to have a job like that.'

I put my hand over his. 'There's no need to be sarcastic. Mark only walks dogs as a sideline. He's a talented musician.'

I'd thought my father couldn't look more upset than he already did. However, I'd been wrong. 'What sort of a musician?' he grilled me suspiciously

'A ... well, a rock musician,' I said, as casually as I could.

Dad froze. 'He's in a rock group?'

Now it was my turn to reach for the wine. 'Well, he

was. But for the last few years he's been trying to strike out on his own.'

'Trying, you say? So he's out of work?'

'No!' I gulped down some more Beaujolais. 'He's self-employed.'

'By which you mean unemployed.' He shook his head in despair. 'Well, I must say, you seem to have picked yourself a real winner, love. Just the kind of man I've always wanted for my one and only daughter – an unemployed rock musician who takes dogs for walks! Couldn't you have found someone more on your level, Annie? And you with all that expensive education, and a university degree in business studies!'

'Look, Dad, I don't know why you're being so horrible about Mark,' I said defensively. 'He's from a really nice family, and you haven't even met him.'

'I don't need to,' my father said stubbornly. 'I've heard enough. A bloody rock star.'

'He's not a star.'

'And that's supposed to make me feel better? I suppose he takes drugs?'

'No, he does not!'

'Rubbish, Annie. All rock musicians take drugs. Just think of the Beatles. And look at that geezer who was married to Whatsername.'

I put down my cutlery, reluctantly abandoning my roast beef to get cold. It was a pity, because it was delicious. However, my father's negative attitude was putting me off. I wished I'd waited until after I'd had pudding to tell him about Mark; I'd spotted apple crumble with custard on the menu, but now my appetite was ruined. 'Who's Whatsername?'

He speared a roast potato with his fork and waved it at me. 'You know, the one on telly with short dark hair and the pretty mug.'

'That could be anyone, Dad.'

'You know! They've got their own show! And he wears dark glasses!'

'Are you talking about The Osbournes?'

But my father's momentary interest in the drug habits of rock stars had lapsed, and he turned his attention back to cross-examining me. 'Tell me something, why does a beautiful young girl like you want to throw herself away on a useless piece of work like this geezer?'

There was no point is reminding my father that, although I knew how to make the most of my neat figure and square-jawed features, I wasn't exactly beautiful, and at the age of thirty-five, neither was I a young girl. So I just said, rather angrily, 'Mark's certainly not useless. He's a wonderful composer. He happens to be writing a big hit at the moment.'

'Huh! Says who, young lady?'

'And I'm not throwing myself away on him. I'm not marrying him, for heaven's sake! We're just going out, that's all! Like you and Norma.'

As it happened, Mark and I weren't just going out. We were doing an awful lot of staying in. In fact, less than a month after our first kiss he'd moved into the Workhouse. There'd been no great decision about this, it'd just happened. There seemed to be little point in his going home at night when he was due back at half past eight the following morning to collect Fluffy for his morning walk. Besides, it was cold and wet outside. It didn't get light until almost eight o'clock, and the darkness closed in by five. The nights seemed endless, and since we spent most of them in bed – making love, eating the delicious delicacies Mark cooked and cuddling up to watch DVDs of old black-and-white films – that suited us perfectly.

I'd told Clarissa about my marvellous new living arrangements when we'd met one evening for a quick drink in a tapas bar in Upper Street on the way home from work. She, too, had been oddly sceptical. In fact, she'd seemed distinctly worried when I told her the news. She had taken a big gulp of her Sauvignon Blanc. 'Darling, that's great, but . . .'

My hand had frozen halfway to my mouth with an anchovy-stuffed olive. 'But what?'

'Isn't it a little too soon to let Mark to move in with you?' she'd said.

'*Soon?*'

'Well, darling, you've only been seeing him for a few weeks.'

I'd put the olive back in its little saucer. 'It's been ages, Clarissa!'

'Mmm . . . Not really. No.' She'd speared a ring of fried squid with a cocktail stick. 'In fact, it's been no time at all – certainly not long enough to know that want to live with someone.'

'But I do know. And so does Mark. We love each other.'

While Clarissa had finished chewing, she'd given me a measured look. 'Annie, you and Mark hardly know each other.'

'That's just not true!' I'd protested. 'We met back in July, remember? Besides, he's been practically living at my place since the first time we slept together. I mean, he was already pet-sitting Fluffy *and* working at my place, and his guitars were already there, and his keyboard and computer. And since the evenings were the only time we could see each other – apart from Sundays – he was staying with me every night anyway. So now he's officially at my place all the time. *And* he's bought me an electric cappuccino machine! Isn't that incredible? I'm so blissfully happy, Clarissa!' I finished, finally throwing that olive into my mouth.

'That's wonderful, darling.' Her smile was unconvincing. A minute later she came out with another 'But . . .'

I sighed. 'But what?'

'Look, I'm really glad you're having such a nice time with Mark. Honestly I am. But what's the hurry? Surely it's not a good idea for him to give up his own flat and move in just yet.'

'Well, we've done it now, so that's that. And, besides, we want to be together as much as possible. And it seemed a waste of money for him to keep paying the rent on his place when he was never in it. Never mind the cost of petrol driving to and fro.' Annoyed, I'd drained my glass and signalled to the waiter for the bill. 'Look, I've got to go now. Mark'll have supper on the table and be wondering where I am.'

What was it with Clarissa and my father? For years they'd been nagging me to stop being fussy and find a nice partner. During that time, I'd scarcely met anyone I'd liked. Now that I'd actually fallen in love with an extraordinarily nice man – now that Mark had walked into my dull, deserted grotto of a life and, with a wave of his hand, transformed it into a sequin-studded, fun-filled, gourmet-food-fuelled winter wonderland, they seemed to spend all their time telling me to be cautious.

But caution was the last thing on my mind in those first heady months. I simply couldn't believe my luck. One minute I was a single woman. The next, Mark and Fluffy were in the frame. By Christmas Day I felt as if we'd been a family for ever, and I didn't think life could get any better. But Mark had a surprise for me.

That year Dad had taken Norma and her two teenage sons to Paris for the holiday. Naturally he'd invited me to go with them, but I hadn't wanted to leave Mark. Delighted to be by ourselves for forty-eight hours, we got up late on Christmas morning, opened our presents, shared some venison stew with Fluffy, then drove to Hampstead Heath in the Wag the Dog van for the first of what, from that day onwards, became our traditional Christmas Day walks.

A leaden sky hung heavily above us, threatening rain, and a bitter east wind was blowing. When we let Fluffy off the leash he disappeared into a small copse behind Parliament Hill and wouldn't come back when we called. By the time we eventually found him, knee deep in mud with his head stuck down a foxhole, it was nearly dark, my teeth were chattering and my hands had turned to ice inside the leather Miu Miu gloves that Mark had generously spent a whole month's wages on.

'You're cold because you're not dressed properly,' he told me, as he took them off and blew on my frozen fingers.

I laughed. 'You sound like my old headmistress. She used to say, "There's no such thing as cold weather, only bad dressing."'

'Well, the old bird was right. You need thermal undies – mmm, sexy! – and a proper outdoor jacket, not this little itsy-bitsy thing you're wearing.'

'It's not a bitsy thing, it's a MaxMara!'

'It's far too short,' Mark said. 'It's showing your midriff. No wonder you're shivering. Come on, I'll race you to the top of Parliament Hill. That'll warm you up!'

I tried my hardest to beat him up the steep, grassy slope in my kitten-heeled black suede ankle boots, but I sank into the mud, and both he and Fluffy were far too quick for me. I puffed up the final metres after them, breathless and panting. Standing on the otherwise deserted summit, silhouetted against the fast-darkening view of the city, with his wild hair blowing in the wind, Mark held out his arms to me, and when I reached him he pulled me to him and wrapped the sides of his open anorak round my back. Meanwhile Fluffy ran in mad circles round us, barking into the wind.

'This is a very nice way to spend Christmas,' Mark said, kissing the tip of my frozen nose.

'Perfect,' I agreed, snuggling into his warmth.

'I'm so happy when we're together, Annie,' he murmured.

'Are you?'

'No. I'm lying. You know,' he said dreamily, 'I really want us to stay together.'

'Do you?'

'Yeah.' After a short pause he added, 'Always.'

'That's a very long time.'

'Not if you're having fun. And we do have fun together, don't we?' I nodded. Then Mark said, 'I kind of want us to grow old together, Annie. We could have puppies together. Maybe even babies.'

'Puppies, yes. But babies? I'd have to think about that!' I said lightly, and kissed his lips.

He looked down at me. 'Look, I know I'm not much of a catch for someone like you, but . . .' He hesitated. 'Would you . . . I mean, I really kind of want this to work out, you know. So . . . Well, will you marry me, Annie Osborne?'

And to that question there was only one answer I could give.

Thirteen

The following morning my fiancé of less than twenty-four hours' standing shook me awake at dawn. 'Time to get going, darling.'

I forced my eyes open, then closed them quickly and pulled the bedclothes over my head, but not before Mark had landed a soft kiss on my naked shoulder. 'Darling?' He lifted the sheet and planted another on my ear.

'Wha'?'

'I've made you a cappuccino.'

With a burst of joy I remembered that this was the first morning of our engagement. Then I remembered it was Boxing Day, and a rare chance for me to sleep in. I rolled over on to my back and looked up at him. 'What time is it?'

'Around seven thirty. Ish,' he said evasively.

This certainly wasn't the first time Mark had woken me at some ungodly hour, but usually he was still in bed, lying beside me – or even half on top of me – and wanted us to bonk. This morning he was already dressed, his hair glistening from the shower, and Fluffy was sitting at his heels, licking his lips as if he'd already been fed. Was this a taster of what married life would be like, I wondered, all domesticity and no sex?

I pulled myself into a sitting position, leaned back against the pillows, and let Mark hand me a giant cup of coffee. 'Look, I've made it exactly how you like it,' he purred. 'Ninety-five per cent foam.'

I spooned some of the chocolate-sprinkled froth into my mouth and began to feel better. 'Mark, darling, why are you up so early? More to the point, why am I?'

'Well, I thought it would be really nice to spend Boxing Day in the country,' he said brightly.

I glanced out of the window. 'But it's still dark!'

'Yes, but it won't be, will it, not by the time we get there?' my new fiancé explained patiently. 'And if we wait until later to set out, well, the days are so short at this time of year that it'll be dark again before we arrive.' He leaned over and kissed me. 'Come on, Annie! Please! Fluffy wants to go. Don't you, you rascal? He'll love it, Annie. He can do country things like shoot pheasants, and hunt foxes, and shag sheep.'

'But . . .' I cast around for an excuse not to leave our lovely warm bed and venture out into the cold, damp world. 'Mark, I don't have the right outfit for a walk in the country!'

He burst out laughing. 'Annie you have more clothes than anyone I've ever met! Wardrobes of them! Anyway, we're going to the *country*. It doesn't matter what you wear as long as it's warm. Besides,' he added, pulling the duvet off me, 'you know I like you best when you're wearing nothing at all.'

Mark knew how to get round me. A little over an hour later, kitted out in two rather out-of-shape sweaters, one of his fleeces, my oldest, shabbiest Levi's and a pair of cream Uggs, which Mark said were exactly like his grandmother's slippers, I was sitting in the passenger seat of his Wag the Dog Walks rust-bucket, breathing in the distinctly doggy air, and we were heading out of London on the fog-bound M11. Fluffy was on my lap, nose lifted, ears pricked, dark eyes peering curiously out of the window, and Mark was behind the wheel, happily humming a new tune he'd had in his head for the last few weeks. Life was perfect.

'Do you know exactly where we're going?' I shouted, above the clatter of the inefficient heater.

'Of course,' he muttered.

'Will there be somewhere nearby for lunch?'

He smirked to himself. 'There most certainly will.'

'How long will it take to get there?'

'Mmm ...' he mused '... if the fog clears ... in this old thing, well, it's about four hours' drive.'

'What?' I squeaked. 'Mark, where on earth are we going?'

He flashed me a boyish grin. 'Norfolk. I thought we'd go and tell my parents the good news.'

I stared in disbelief at his smugly smiling profile. Then I exploded, 'Why on earth didn't you tell me?'

He frowned. 'I dunno. I suppose I wanted to surprise you, darling. Besides,' he confessed, 'if I had told you, you'd still be standing in front of your wardrobe, deciding what to wear.'

'Well, I certainly wouldn't be wearing these!' I pulled at my torn jeans. 'And I would have washed my hair, and put on some makeup! Honestly, you'll have to turn back!'

'You must be joking!'

'No, I'm not!' I protested. 'I can't possibly meet your parents looking like this!'

He glanced at me again, smiled, then shook his head. 'Chill out, Annie! Mum and Dad will love you. They don't give a toss about appearances.'

The Curtises' pub, the Dog and Fox, was situated on the edge of Minhampton, a picture-postcard village just outside Norwich. Built of the local flint, and covered with a thick toupee of thatch pierced by smoking chimneys, it was a long, rambling building, two storeys high, with a car park at one side and a small slate board nailed to the wooden porch, upon which was written in chalk, 'Home-cooked Roast Turkey, Roast Pheasant, Spiced Apple Crumble'. Another, propped up against a large stone by the roadside, advertised 'Real Ale & Open Fires'. Nervous as I was about meeting Jackie and Dennis Curtis, I couldn't wait to get inside. Not only was I was desperate to use the loo after the four-hour journey but the van's heater had given up its struggle for survival just south of Cambridge, and even though I'd been clutching Fluffy to me as if he was a hot-water bottle, I could no longer feel my fingers, and my feet had turned to stone.

The van turned into the car park, which was filled with four-wheel drives, gleaming Mercedes and old bangers. Mark pulled up in the middle, leaned over and opened my door. 'You get out. I'll drive round the corner, and park in the lane at the back.'

'No,' I protested. 'I'm coming with you. I'm not going in without you!'

'It's a pub, not a lion's den, Annie!' he said indulgently. 'My parents don't bite, darling! Besides, the lane's always incredibly muddy at this time of year. Those boots will get ruined.'

That clinched it for me. 'Okay. But I'll wait out here for you,' I insisted.

I jumped down from the VW, leaving Fluffy with Mark, who said that, after four hours in the van, he could probably do with a short walk. Spouting clouds of exhaust, the VW reversed out of the car park into the road, then sputtered out of sight. I walked up and down in the cold damp air, banging my hands against my thighs and stamping my feet to get the circulation going while I waited for Mark and Fluffy to reappear.

Minutes passed, but they didn't turn up. I jumped up and down and, with childish pleasure, watched my breath freeze into little clouds. Through the pub's small windows I could see people smiling and drinking. I could hear them laughing, and the clink of their glasses. I checked my watch: Mark had now been gone for seven minutes. Surely he'd parked the van. Had something happened to him? Or had he forgotten about me?

I waited five more minutes. Then, desperate to get out of the cold, I reluctantly went inside. The interior of the Dog and Fox was as Mark had described it to me: an old-fashioned cosy jumble of gleaming horse-brasses, dark oak floorboards, small round wooden tables, and shabby but comfortable-looking armchairs. Ancient beams criss-crossed the low, whitewashed ceiling and, at either end of the long room there were brick inglenook fireplaces, with log fires burning in their grates. The room smelled of woodsmoke and Christmas trees – garlands of branches, baubles and pine cones hung beside each fireplace, and were pinned to the overhead beams, with a small red-and-gold Merry Christmas banner. There was also the unmistakable aroma of roasting meat; the pub's small restaurant, Mark had told me, was in a separate section to one side.

Standing behind the bar – a highly polished wooden counter complete with old-fashioned beer taps, glasses hanging in a rack above it, rows of spirits and liquors lined up at the back – a small, bird-like woman, pale-skinned and with short grey hair, wore a rather dour expression. I presumed she was Mark's mother, and didn't know whether or not to introduce myself. But as she pulled a pint for a customer, she saw me. Feeling distinctly nervous – I'd never had to introduce myself to a future mother-in-law before, and didn't quite know how to do it – I went over to her. 'Excuse me, are you Mrs Curtis?'

'Ah,' she said, in the lilting, local accent that Mark had once told me was called Broad Norfolk. 'I know who you are! So, you've turned up at last!'

'Oh, I . . .' I stammered. 'I didn't realize you were expecting us.'

'Actually, we was expecting you a good hour ago.'

'Well, it took ages to get here.'

She nodded. 'Thanks for coming to help us out.' Before I could say anything else, she turned her attention to the elderly man in a Barbour who was waiting at the bar, and handed him the pint. 'Here you are, Michael.'

'Thanks, Jackie,' he said. 'Chalk it up on the slate, will you?'

'Well, it is Christmas, so you can have it on the house,' she said, with a smile that lit up her face.

'Cheers! And have one on me later!'

Now Jackie turned her attention back to me, rather unsmilingly, I thought. 'Dennis has already started serving the lunches, love, so can you go straight through and give him a hand, please?'

It was probably a future daughter-in-law's role to be helpful around the house, or, in this case, the pub, so I said, 'Sure. Of course. Which way is it?'

'Just come round the bar, and go through this door. You'll find him in the kitchen. And you'd better leave that jacket under the bar here. My,' she said, as I took off Mark's fleece. 'You've come very casually dressed for Boxing Day. I thought he'd have told you to dress up a bit. But never mind, love. Willing hands is what we need. It's just through here.'

By now I felt terrible. This meeting with my future in-laws was turning into a minor disaster. So much for Mark telling me his parents didn't give a stuff about appearances: Jackie had seemed quite miffed when she'd seen my baggy old jeans. And where the bloody hell was Mark, anyway? I thought furiously. What on earth had happened to him? Talk about throwing me in at the deep end! The least he could have done was be here to introduce me to his parents.

Jackie opened a door behind the bar that led directly into a small, old-fashioned but spotlessly clean restaurant kitchen, where a young man was carving slices from a huge turkey and arranging them on plates, while a tall man in a white chef's coat stood in front of a stainless-steel stove covered with saucepans, stirring a pot with one hand and shaking a large frying-pan with the other. 'She's here at last, Dennis!' Jackie called. 'Okay, love, I'll leave you to it,' she said to me, then disappeared back into the bar.

Dennis – Mark's father – still had his back to me, but even from behind, I could see a resemblance to Mark – they shared the same broad shoulders, the same shaped head and the same curly hair, though Dennis's was shorter, greyer and balding at the back. 'The aprons are hanging up in there, love.' He jerked his head towards a cupboard. Not so much as a hello, I thought. The Curtises certainly didn't stand on ceremony.

I opened the cupboard, got out one of the big white aprons folded up inside it, and slipped it over my head. Then, making up my mind to be more upfront and assertive, I went across to Dennis, stood right next to him and held out my hand. 'Hi, I'm Annie,' I said.

He glanced at me for a split second, flashed me Mark's grin, then returned to his cooking. 'Annie, is it?' he muttered, as he tossed what turned out to be a steak in the pan. 'That's odd. I thought he said your name was Juliette.'

Who the hell was Juliette? I wondered. I made a mental note to ask Mark the moment he showed up. The next minute a tall, rather buxom woman in her thirties came pushing through some swing doors, holding a huge pile of dirty plates against her ample breasts. 'Two turkeys and trimmings, one pheasant and one smoked-eel salad, table four, please, Dad,' she said. 'And where's the steak and pheasant for table ten?'

'Just coming up, Lizzie.' Within seconds, Dennis had produced two beautifully garnished plates from his pans.

Lizzie – Mark's sister – dumped the dirty plates on the side and turned to me. 'Take them in for me, will you, love? Table ten's on the right at the back. My corns are killing me! I've got to sit down for a minute or I'll scream.'

Before I knew what was happening, two hot plates had been thrust into my hands, I was through the swing doors and standing in a small pretty restaurant with about a dozen tables, all occupied. With my fingers burning, I stumbled along until I came to a table with just two people sitting at it.

'Steak?' I asked the women. 'Pheasant?'

'No thanks, dear,' said one of them. 'We've had our mains. We're waiting for dessert.'

'I think those must be ours,' said a man at the next table. I plonked the plates in front of him and his wife and rushed back to the kitchen, stopping on the way to pick up some empty plates from another table. Just as I was about to go into the kitchen, yet another customer signalled to me. 'Excuse me, Miss, could we have some more water? And another bottle of this?'

I looked at the wine bottle's label, then dashed back to the kitchen. 'Another bottle of Côtes du Rhône something or other 2006 for the table by the window,' I shouted, before more plates were thrust into my hand and I careered back into the restaurant.

When I returned, Mark burst into the kitchen through the bar door. 'Has anyone seen a – There you are, Annie!' he exclaimed. 'I've been looking for you everywhere!' He took in my apron, and the pile of dirty plates I was holding in amazement. 'What on earth are you doing?' he said. 'Dad? Lizzie? What's going on?'

'What do you mean?' Dennis said. 'Do you know Annie? Your mother and I thought she was the girl from Norwich who'd come to give us a hand!' Mark burst out laughing. 'Do you mean she isn't?'

'No, Dad. This is Annie, my girlfriend from London. Actually,' he added, putting a possessive arm round me, 'she's not my girlfriend any more, she's my future wife. Dad, we're getting married!'

After that, the Boxing Day lunch service at the Dog and Fox went awry. Still, none of the customers seemed to mind. Mark was getting married, everyone was told by a beaming Dennis, it was drinks on the house and Champagne flowed even in the kitchen. Stripped of my waitress's apron, I was seated with Fluffy in a place of honour beside one of the inglenooks and fussed over by everyone, including Mark's two other sisters, Katie and Emma who, with their husbands and children, had driven over from the neighbouring villages where they lived to meet me. My anxiety about meeting Mark's family evaporated as we fell about laughing over the case of mistaken identity; luckily the real waitress had turned up soon after Mark.

And where had Mark been while I was doing my waitressing stint? It turned out that, on the way to park, he'd realized that the van was running out of petrol. The nearest garage was in the next village, so he'd driven straight there to fill up before it closed.

Once she'd found out who I was, Jackie was terribly apologetic, particularly over her comment about my clothes. I warmed to her. Plainly dressed, her face devoid of a trace of makeup, she emanated warmth and calm. There was something wonderfully honest and open about her. It was almost as if her pale skin was transparent, and you could see her inner goodness, her lack of guile, shining through.

Thrilled that their footloose son was intending to settle down at last, she and Dennis gathered me into the bosom of their family as if I was another of their daughters. By the end of the day, I felt so at ease pulling pints and dishing up helpings of Christmas Crumble with everyone else that, when Mark and I left for London, it seemed strange to be going – I felt so at home. When Jackie kissed me goodbye in the car park, and told me, 'I already feel like you're part of the family, Annie,' I knew exactly what she meant.

If only my father had felt the same way about Mark.

Fourteen

We got married at the end of April. The bride wore a full-length, sleeveless, bias-cut Vivienne Westwood sheath in cream silk jersey, teamed with a pair of khaki satin Giuseppe Zanotti stilettos. The groom wore his old Levi's, which he'd washed and pressed for the occasion, teamed with a brand new powder-blue Gap shirt, the fluorescent green trainers and a baggy cream tuxedo he'd picked up in our local Oxfam shop. 'Nice of him to make an effort,' my father commented drily, when we met up outside the register office. But I knew that, of the two of us, Mark looked the more stylish.

After protracted negotiations with Islington Council, which, like Haines and Hampton, usually only allowed guide dogs or hearing dogs to enter their hallowed premises, Fluffy was permitted to join what passed for a ceremony, sporting a red satin bow instead of his usual leather collar. I'll draw a veil – the only one of the day – over his attempt to hump the female registrar's leg while Mark and I read our marriage vows. It was his last chance for pre-marital sex, Mark told her, when he gave her the money to have her suit dry-cleaned.

Dad threw a small party for us in the private room at the Ivy. This wasn't the big wedding he'd dreamed of giving me, which had included a grand church service somewhere unpretentious such as St Paul's Cathedral, followed by a bank-balance-busting dinner-dance at a swanky hotel. However, Mark and I were adamant that we didn't want a big function. Which was just as well, really, because although Dad never said it in so many words he intimated that a lunch party for thirty (albeit at one of London's most fashionable restaurants) was a more-than-good-enough send-off for me, seeing that I'd insisted on getting hitched to a man with, as he saw it, no ambition and little hope of ever earning a proper living.

With tears in his eyes, and a glass too many of Champagne clutched in his hand, he stood up in front of the guests, who included Norma, George Haines, Eileen Grey, Clarissa, James and the girls, and, of course, Mark's family, and made a toast to the bride and groom. He attempted to sound as enthusiastic about his new son-in-law as Dennis and Jackie obviously were about me but, to my ears and Norma's, he couldn't pull it off. Mark was a one-off, a real character, Dad said, and although he wasn't quite the son-in-law he'd imagined for his wonderful daughter, he seemed to be a nice enough bloke who appeared to make her happy – though Dad couldn't quite understand what she saw in him (a remark that was received as a great joke by Mark's family). Still, Dad continued, he'd always wanted a son-in-law who'd win the knobbly-knees contest at Butlins, and since Mark nearly always wore shorts, he stood a good chance. Dad went on to say that it was a canny move on my part to have married my dog-walker for at least I'd no longer have to pay him to walk my stupid mutt (pause for laughs again).

He followed this with a heartfelt eulogy on my sterling qualities – my sweet nature, strength of character and beauty, et cetera, not to mention the kind heart that made me a sucker for picking up stray animals, regardless, he added, with a sideways look at Mark, of the trouble it got me into. Most of all, Dad went on, he admired the strong work ethic that had led me to do so well in my chosen career, personal shopping, a skill I had perfected at his expense during my teens (shouts of 'True!' from Clarissa). I ought to use my talent for doing fashion make-overs on my new husband, my father added. He could do with a bit of smartening up! (Pause for 'Hear, hear'.) In short, Dad concluded, his new son-in-law was bloody lucky to have bagged such a treasure, and if he ever let me down or treated me badly in any way, he would person-ally seek him out and throttle him.

There was wild applause at this, which was taken as a joke. Only Norma and I knew that Dad was being truthful. To everyone but my father, the prospect of our relation-ship breaking down seemed unlikely. Even Clarissa, who'd been doubtful when Mark had moved in with me, had realized that he and I were made for one another. 'You lucky cow, you don't deserve him,' she said, when we came back from our week's honeymoon in Sussex at the only deluxe hotel we could find where dogs were allowed and I was boring her with the photographs: Mark, Fluffy and me lying in a medieval four-poster; Fluffy and me, on the beach; Mark and Fluffy standing on a breakwater; me and Mark kissing in the gardens, which we'd snapped by holding the camera at arm's length.

'Honestly,' I said, 'if I'd only known how wonderful

married life was, I'd have got hitched years ago.' We were sitting at Clarissa's kitchen table; she'd invited us for lunch, and after we'd eaten James and Mark had taken the children for a walk on Primrose Hill.

'Make the most of it,' Clarissa said, in an unusually sour tone. 'Believe me, it's not always like that.' She drained her glass, picked up the wine bottle, found it was empty and grabbed James's glass. She finished that off too.

Then she burst into tears.

I stared at her in astonishment. In all the years I'd known her, I'd only seen my best friend cry once, and that was when she was twelve and had broken her ankle in the 100-yard sprint at our school sports day. And she'd only cried then because she'd wanted to win, not because she was in pain. 'Clarissa, what is it?'

She covered her face with her hands. Her fingers, I noticed, were covered with some sort of allergic rash. 'I'm sorry,' she said, 'I don't mean to be a killjoy. It's just that you're so happy, and I . . . Well, frankly, I'm so jealous!' And she laughed through her tears. 'Can you please stop telling me how wonderful everything is?'

It turned out that while Mark and I were having fun and wild sex – in the shower, on the stairs up to the mezzanine level, on the beach in Sussex, and once even in the back of the van – James and Clarissa weren't having any of either. The combination of two careers, four daughters under the age of twelve, his mother, who had Alzheimer's, shopping, cooking and cleaning had sapped their libido. Domestic life, she told me, was not conducive to romance.

'By the time we get to bed at night, we're both

completely shagged out.' Clarissa sniffed into a crumpled tissue she extracted from the sleeve of her cardigan. 'And, believe me, that phrase has a different meaning when you've been married for a hundred years. If one of us is in the mood for sex, the other isn't, and on the rare occasions when we *both* feel like it, it's only a matter of moments before one of the children wakes up and comes in to disturb us. Usually it's Miranda. Sometimes I think she has a built-in anti-sex radar system. James and I only have to snap each other's knicker elastic and she wakes up screaming with a nightmare, bursts into our room and climbs into bed with us. Not just *with* us, either, but between us. Talk about barrier contraception. She probably wants to make sure she remains the youngest child.' She sighed. 'Please don't mention this to Mark, darling – James'd kill me if he knew I'd talked to you about it, but I honestly can't remember the last time he and I had a really passionate bonk. The last time we did it *at all* was on New Year's Eve – that's five months ago, Annie! And I'm sure we only did it then because we both felt it was expected of us. How miserable is that?'

'Pretty dire,' I agreed.

'The worst thing is,' she said, glancing at me through red-rimmed eyes, 'I've completely lost confidence in myself. As a woman, I mean.'

'Instead of losing confidence in yourself as an alien? Or a dishwasher?' I just about succeeded in making her laugh.

'Dishwashing is about all I'm good for nowadays,' she said. 'I mean, look at me!'

Usually it was Clarissa who switched into professional

161

mode to help me through my problems. Today it was my turn. I tried to look at her dispassionately, as if she was one of my clients. She was wearing a typical Clarissa outfit: a faded floral print dress in pinks and blues, teamed with an out-of-shape black cardigan worn thin at the elbows that looked like a cast-off of her mother's, which it probably was. Instead of seeming slender and elegant in her Cinderella rags, as she usually did, Clarissa looked scraggy, as if she'd been too busy feeding and caring for everyone else to bother with herself. Her long hair, mousy and streaked with grey, needed washing, cutting and colouring. Most depressing of all, her usually flawless skin, which I'd always envied, had lost its translucent glow. Instead she was pasty and sallow, with dark circles under her eyes and a small spot erupting on her chin.

'Mmm. I'm not sure that dress brings out the best in you,' I said, as diplomatically as I could.

'*Per-lease*, Annie! Don't insult me by trying to be *nice*.'

'Sorry.' I took a deep breath. 'Okay, if you want to know the truth, your hair needs attention, and you could do with a bit of makeup – some mascara and lip-gloss at least. As for that dress, it's appalling.'

She winced. 'That bad?'

'It's completely shapeless and washed out. And, look, there's a stain on the skirt, and the hem's coming down at the front. Why on earth are you hiding your lovely slim body under *this*?' I picked a couple of woolly bobbles off her cardie. 'It looks like a leftover from an Oxfam shop.'

She gave a grim smile. 'You must be a witch. It was from a Cancer Relief jumble sale. Five years ago.'

'Well, it's high time you binned it!' I said firmly.

'I know.' She sighed. 'And, believe it or not, this is one of my better outfits. I suppose it's not surprising that James doesn't have the hots for me any more.' She held up the eczema-covered hands with chewed nails. 'These used to be really nice. Now they they belong in some old-fashioned Fairy Liquid ad – as the "before" picture. I'm the woman who scrubs the dishes with caustic soda.'

'You need to look after them,' I said. 'Stop biting your nails, and wear rubber gloves.'

'I'll never remember.'

'Have a paraffin wax treatment now and then.'

'A beauty treatment? When do I have time for that? Or the money?'

'Well, slather lots of really good cream on them. Eve Lom or Crème de la Mer.'

Her big blue eyes widened. 'Annie, what parallel universe are you living in? Oh, yes, I forgot – the childless one. I can't afford brands like those!'

'Then I'll cadge some samples for you from work. Talking of which, why don't you come into Haines one day and I'll give you a proper makeover? That'd make you feel better.'

'What? Trying on outfits I can't afford to buy? Thanks, but no thanks, darling. I'll have to resign myself to a sexless existence, and to James running off with one of his trendy young clerks one day or having an affair with my best friend.'

'Hey, I'm your best friend!' I reminded her crossly. 'And, much as I love James, I have no intention of having an affair with him — I've just got married, for God's sake!'

'Oh, you know what I mean!' Clarissa said, in despair.

I thought for a minute, then said, 'What you and James need is some time to yourselves.'

'How? When?'

'Can't you go away together? You know, for a dirty weekend.'

'Every weekend's a dirty weekend in this house,' she muttered darkly. 'Dirty clothes, dirty floors, dirty children, dirty dishes . . .'

'Stop being so negative! Couldn't you ask your mother to look after the girls for a few days?' This was such a stupid suggestion that we fell about laughing. Clarissa's mum, the Hon. Mrs Toffee-nosed Garland, hadn't improved with time. Looking after children — even her own grandchildren — was not something she did. Nor was spending the weekend in Camden Town. She seldom left Belgravia nowadays, unless it was to go to Knightsbridge or what she called the 'cunt-treh' and, as she'd made clear to Clarissa and James when they'd first moved to Primrose Hill, she considered NW1 a district where only servants and railwaymen lived.

'God! Can you imagine her ferrying the kids to their classes on Saturday?' Clarissa said, when she'd recovered. 'Or grilling fish-fingers? Never mind mucking out the hamster's cage! No, darling, it's impossible. I've got to face facts. James and I aren't going to get any privacy — or sex — until Miranda leaves home.'

'But that's not going to be for at least thirteen years!' I looked at my exhausted, distraught friend, and said, on the spur of the moment, 'Mark and I could always look after the girls one weekend. I'm sure he wouldn't mind.'

The moment I'd said it, I regretted it. Luckily I knew that Clarissa would turn me down.

'Oh, Annie! Thanks, darling, but I couldn't possibly say yes,' she said, as I'd expected. I breathed a sigh of relief. 'That's way beyond the call of duty,' she went on. 'After all, you've only been married a month. You want to be alone together, don't you? It's far too much to ask.'

She was silent for a moment. Then, biting her lip, she ran to the dresser, grabbed her Filofax and leafed through it. 'How about the weekend after next, darling?' she said brightly. 'Starting on Friday night?'

Fifteen

'The hamster food's at the bottom of the larder, in case Rachel forgets to feed Hamlet, but I've told her she mustn't on pain of death. And I've written the telephone number of the vet, and the emergency vet, on the wall just beside it. This is the number of the doctor's surgery, and these are the instructions for the boiler. But you probably won't need them, because the pilot light doesn't go out that often. Only every time someone's taking a shower. Don't look so horrified, Annie, I'm joking. It's not *every* time, honestly. Oh, hold on, I was forgetting, no one's at the doctor's surgery at weekends but they do have emergency locums if one of the girls goes down with something in the middle of the night. And if there's a real crisis, like a broken bone or something, there's always A and E at the Royal Free.'

'For God's sake, Clarissa, Mark and Annie aren't idiots!'

It was twelve days later, and Mark and I were back in Clarissa's basement kitchen. James stood by in an old North Face parka, alternately tapping his feet and jiggling his car keys in his impatience to get away to the sumptuous Gloucestershire hotel-cum-spa I'd suggested they stay at. Clarissa was running frantically through the myriad instructions she'd already sent me by email *and* explained on the phone. Though I was nodding manically at everything she told me, like one of those toy dogs that used to sit in the back windows of cars, I was feeling more and more apprehensive at the idea of being responsible for four children for two days. By contrast, Mark was strumming his guitar at the kitchen table, and looking perfectly cool. Equally laid back, Fluffy was happily hoovering up fish-finger crumbs and dropped peas under the chairs.

Wearing makeup for a change, as well as her best navy trouser suit, teamed with the cream Nicole Farhi cashmere sweater and red Hermès belt I'd lent her, Clarissa was more like her old, beautiful self than I'd seen her for years. She seemed a different person from the tearful drudge of ten days earlier.

'Here's the phone number of the hotel where we're staying,' she went on, pointing to one of the dozens of overlapping handwritten Post-its with which she'd temporarily turned the fridge-freezer into a pink and yellow armadillo. 'This is James's mobile number and this is mine –'

'Don't you think Annie knows that off by heart?' James interrupted. 'You two are never off the phone to one another.'

'Yes, of course she does, James,' Clarissa said crisply. 'But she's going to be at work all day tomorrow, aren't you, Annie? And what if something happens when you're not around, and Mark needs to get in touch with me urgently?'

'Well, he can always –' I began.

'Nothing urgent *is* going to happen, poppet,' James said, in a long-suffering voice, 'except that the girls are going to have a ball playing Mark and Annie up, and Mark and Annie are going to curse themselves for having been stupid enough to volunteer to look after them.'

Mark raised a hand. 'For the record, I didn't volunteer, I was press-ganged into it.'

'Pussy-whipped already,' James said sadly. 'How long have you been married?'

Mark and I smiled at each other in the gooey-eyed way that was our habit. 'Five weeks and three days,' we said in unison.

'Christ!' said James. 'I wish I hadn't asked. I think I'm going to be sick. Now just relax, poppet.'

'I am relaxed, for God's sake!' Clarissa snapped back. 'And please don't call me poppet. It reminds me of those cheap bead necklaces Annie and I used to wear when we were kids. Or were those poppers?' She ran her hands through her hair, which, I was glad to see, she'd washed and even blow-dried. 'Look, Mark, darling, here, just under this Post-it, which has Rachel's mobile number on it, is their timetable for tomorrow.'

'Timetable?' my husband said. 'But tomorrow's Saturday, not a school day.'

'These are their *hobbies*, darling. Rachel's got violin at nine thirty but it's only round the corner, and she can walk there. Then there's ballet at ten fifteen in Hampstead for Miranda and Emily. Their shoes and leotards are in bags in the hallway. And don't forget Rebecca's Kumon maths. That's at eleven in Finchley Road.'

My husband put down his guitar. 'What's Kumon maths when it's at home?'

James sighed. 'Well might you ask, Mark. It's a form

of Japanese mental torture, employed by pushy North London mothers who are convinced that their perfectly run-of-the-mill sprogs are – what do they call them nowadays? – gifted children, and want them to graduate from nursery school to Oxbridge. It involves driving them insane by forcing them to do twenty hours of repetitive sums every day.'

'That's so unfair, James!' Clarissa interrupted. 'It's only twenty minutes a day – and I'm not pushy! Rebecca happens to love it.'

He raised his eyebrows. 'Really? That's not what she told me when I dropped her off there last week.'

'Well, she hasn't said anything to me about it. And I'm sure she would if –'

'Clarissa, if we have to discuss this fascinating issue, could we please do so in the car? If we don't leave now, we'll never get there.'

'What? Yes. Of course, darling. I'll just be one more sec.' Clarissa stared wildly at the Post-its again. 'I'm sure there's something else I meant to tell you both,' she muttered. 'Oh, yes. Please make sure they do their homework, particularly Rachel, who'll do anything to get out of it. And, in case you get locked out, the spare keys are Sellotaped behind a loose brick to the left of the dustbins in the cellar area.'

'For this, we have to have an expensive burglar-alarm system,' James said drily. 'Why don't you just tape them to the front door, with a sign saying, "Who Dares Enters"? Now, come on, love, please!'

'Don't rush me!' Clarissa looked even more panic-stricken than I felt. 'I'm sure I've forgotten something.'

'Well, if you have, you can just ring Annie!' her husband said, losing patience. 'And if she and Mark need to know something, they can ring you. We're not setting off on a three-month trek through Outer Mongolia, for fuck's sake, we're driving to Gloucestershire! For two nights! And unless we set off soon it'll just be one night!'

'Yes, all right!'

'Don't worry! Mark and I will take care of everything,' I promised. 'How hard can it be?'

She smiled grimly. 'You have no idea.'

'Okay, poppet, let's get going.'

'James, please! I just asked you not to call me that. Do you ever listen to a word I say?'

The atmosphere between them didn't bode well for a weekend of passion, I thought, as Mark and I followed them up the creaking stairs to the hall. Nevertheless, five minutes later, after giving us one final instruction – 'Don't let them have too many sugary things' – and dozens of hugs, kisses and goodbyes in the street, not to mention tears from Miranda, who clung to her mother's legs, screaming, 'Don't go!', Clarissa and James's ancient Volvo estate drove into the distance.

'Oh, Mark, what have I let us in for?' I whispered, as Miranda beat her hands on the back of the front door, sobbing, 'Come back! Come back!'

Mark kissed the tip of my nose. 'We're going to have fun, that's what.' He smiled his most disarming smile. Then he scooped up Miranda, threw her high into the air and caught her. She stopped crying and squealed with delight.

'Guess what, Miranda?' he said, as he hoisted her on

to his shoulders, and gave her a piggyback ride downstairs to the kitchen.

'What?'

'I think this calls for a chocolate-biscuit fest, don't you?'

After supper, which consisted of Mark's mild Thai green chicken curry in coconut sauce, followed by home-made pancakes with sugar and lemon (Mark again), Mark suggested that we take Fluffy for a torchlit walk on Primrose Hill. When we reached the summit, and Emily said she was bored, Mark had the brilliant idea of lying down on the grass and rolling to the bottom, so everyone else did the same. Back at the house, we stripped off our muddy clothes, put on dressing-gowns and sat in front of the open fire. Instead of turning on the TV, Mark got everyone to play a heated game of Junior Monopoly, which didn't finish until after eleven, by which time both five-year-old Miranda and eight-year-old Emily were asleep. Instead of waking them, Mark picked them up from the sofa, hoisted them over his shoulders and carried them upstairs.

On Saturday morning Emily woke us at six by jumping up and down on Clarissa and James's bed in her pyjamas. Instead of telling her to bugger off back to her own room, which was my inclination, Mark allowed her to crawl under the duvet between us, then read aloud *The Wind in the Willows* to her. By seven, when I threw myself into the dodgy shower, Fluffy, Miranda and ten-year-old Rebecca were also tucked up with them, howling with laughter at the funny voices Mark adopted for each character.

While I was putting on my makeup, Mark took Fluffy for a quick run. By eight thirty, he was back, showered, in his shorts and T-shirt, in the basement kitchen, dancing to Radio 1 while baking blueberry muffins for breakfast. With their long curly hair tied back in ponytails, so that it didn't get covered with flour, the three youngest girls were helping him, while twelve-year-old Rachel quietly got on with her geography homework. Meanwhile, Hamlet was rolling around the kitchen floor in a see-through plastic exercise ball, with Fluffy in hot pursuit.

'Are you sure you can manage by yourself?' I called guiltily from the doorway before I left for work – the easy option, since Mark would be coping with the entire household until I returned.

'Absolutely.' He smiled at me reassuringly across one of the three mixing bowls they were using.

'Don't let Fluffy break open that plastic thing and eat Hamlet.'

'I won't.'

'Thanks. You will be good for Mark, girls?'

'*Yes!*' they chorused.

'Don't give him a hard time, or anything.'

'*We won't.*'

'Do what he tells you.'

'*We will.*'

'Okay. Goodbye, then.'

''*Bye!*' they called, without looking up from what they were doing.

I hesitated by the door.

'Why are you still here?' Mark asked, when he looked up and saw me standing there.

'I feel mean leaving you all,' I confessed. 'Look, if you'd like me to, I could call in sick, and spend the day here?'

Four horrified childish faces turned towards me. '*No!*' went the chorus. '*Don't!*'

Mark raised his eyebrows. ' Don't worry, we'll be all right, won't we, you lot?'

'*Yes!*' they cheered.

So I left.

I didn't realize how upset I was until Clarissa called me on my mobile when I was halfway to the Tube station. 'Well?' she said.

'Everything's fine, thank you,' I said tightly.

'Why do you say it like that?' she said in alarm. 'Like something's wrong. What's happened?'

'Nothing. It's all one hundred per cent hunky-dory. I've just left Mark and the girls making blueberry muffins for breakfast . . .'

'Ooh!'

'. . . and Rachel's doing her geography homework.'

'Without being nagged?'

'Of course.' For some reason I felt disgruntled now. 'I don't know why you make such a fuss about coping with a few children, Clarissa. Motherhood's obviously a piece of cake. Everything's totally under control. Mark's control,' I added grudgingly.

'Ah! So that's what you're so annoyed about!'

'Annoyed? Why should I be *annoyed*?'

'Yes, darling, why?'

I thought about it for a moment, then said, 'Oh, you old witch, you're right. Maybe I'm being silly, but I feel a bit redundant. I mean, the girls all used to adore me, didn't they? They couldn't wait for me to come over and see them. Now that Mark's larking around with them like a *Blue Peter* presenter, they can't wait to see the back of me.'

'Oh, Annie, I'm sure that's not the case!'

'It is. Mark's so bloody good with children, Clarissa. And so wonderful in the kitchen. Wonderful at everything. Like a cross between Supernanny and Jamie Oliver.'

'Perhaps he'd like a job as my live-in housekeeper.'

I rounded the corner towards the Tube. 'Anyway, I'm being horribly selfish, talking about me. How are you?'

'Little me?' she said. 'I thought you'd never ask. Oh, I'm just sitting up in a sumptuous designer bed, a tray in front of me loaded with organic croissants, freshly squeezed organic orange juice and organic cappuccino – apparently everything's organic here, probably even the loo paper. Oh, yes, and I'm watching a DVD of *My Big Fat Greek Wedding* on a very non-organic wall-mounted plasma screen, which is about the same size as the one at the Leicester Square Odeon. That's probably no novelty to spoiled brats such as yourself, but it's bliss to us mere mortals. Oh, yes, and guess who was checking in when we arrived last night?'

'Who?'

'Gwynnie! This place is celebrity paradise. How on earth did you hear about it?'

'Oh, we in Personal Shopping have to know about these things.'

'I'm booked into the spa later on to have something called a Cloud Nine Massage, followed by a Cascade Facial. What do you think that means? That they shove your face under a tap? I love it so much here that I don't think I'm ever going to leave. I'm sure you and Mark won't mind staying on for ten years to bring up the girls.'

'So?' I asked pointedly.

'So what?'

'You know! Can you talk?'

'If you're asking is James lying beside me, breathing down the cleavage of your mauve La Perla nightie – thanks for letting me borrow it, by the way – the answer's no. He's gone to explore the local footpaths.'

I was shocked. 'Why didn't you go with him? You're meant to be doing things *together* this weekend!'

'Because it's raining in Gloucestershire, darling, and I've no intention of being in anything but a horizontal position all weekend.'

'Talking of which, I'm about to go down into the Tube station, so put me out of my misery,' I begged.

'Well,' she confided, 'you'll be pleased to hear that I'm no longer a born-again virgin.'

'That's wonderful! Congratulations!'

'Thanks. I wouldn't say that the earth moved, but the bed did. Sort of.'

Sixteen

It was the middle of the afternoon and, after a morning of phone calls to Mark, asking how he and the girls were managing without me (answer every time: 'Perfectly well, thank you very much') I was in the changing room with a wonderful new customer, and had quite forgotten what awaited me back in Camden Town.

If Tiffany George had been the personal-shopping client from Hell, thirty-two-year-old Jessica Harrison seemed to have been sent to us from Client Heaven. A highly successful businesswoman whose company had recently been floated on the Stock Exchange, Jessica, who was a perfect size ten, had worked so hard while she was building up her Internet dating agency that she'd never had time to put her nose inside a department store, and had bought all her clothes online or from postal catalogues. Now she had £20 million in her pocket, the time and inclination to spend some of it and wanted me to help her. Recommended to me by the wife of one of her employees, she'd arrived two hours earlier, and we'd spent the afternoon touring the store together, picking out an entire new-look wardrobe of clothes and accessories. Jessica had loved everything, and everything had suited her.

By four o'clock there were three trouser suits, four coats, five dresses, three jackets, countless tops and skirts and an array of jeans hanging on the rail in our biggest changing room, not to mention handbags, shoes, belts and costume jewellery that I'd picked out to go with them. From these, I was helping Jessica to make a final 'capsule wardrobe' selection when Charlotte put her head round the door. 'Excuse me, Annie, I'm very sorry to disturb you . . .'

'Yes, Charlotte?'

'Sorry to interrupt and everything, but I've been sitting at the reception desk for ages, and, the thing is, your mobile phone is in your office.'

'Yes, I know that, Charlotte. I left it there. And?'

'Well, it rang,' she said.

Oh, for God's sake! I thought. Charlotte could be so stupid at times, and this was one of them. 'Well, whoever it is, I'll call them back later,' I said, smiling at her as sweetly as I could manage. 'As you can see,' I added, widening my eyes at her in what I hoped was a meaningful way, 'I'm very busy at the moment.'

'Of course,' she said slowly, but she stayed where she was, biting her lip and frowning.

I returned to Jessica Harrison and tried to ignore Charlotte, but when I looked round again, she was still there. 'Yes, Charlotte? What's the matter now?'

'The thing is, Annie, your mobile . . .'

I sighed. 'Yes?'

'It rang more than once. Six times, actually. So, um, I took the liberty of going into your office, and I got it out of your Mulberry, and I answered it for you. I thought that might be the right thing to do.'

'That showed great initiative, Charlotte, thank you.'

'So you don't mind?'

'No.'

'Look, Annie,' Jessica Harrison said, touching my arm, 'do you want to go and deal with this? I really don't mind.'

'No, don't worry,' I reassured her. 'I'm sorry. Whoever it was can wait. Well, who was it, Charlotte?' I asked pointedly.

'I thought it was Mark – I mean, Mr Curtis – because it was his name that was flashing up on the screen.'

By now I wanted to strangle her. 'Right, and did you say I'd call him back and tell him to have a nice day?'

Looking even more unhappy, she shook her head. 'Well, no. I didn't. You see, it wasn't him who answered. It was a girl. I think she said her name was Rachel.'

Rachel? Suddenly I remembered Clarissa's children and grabbed Charlotte's arm. 'What did she say? Is she okay?'

'Oh, yes, she's fine! Absolutely!' she said, with a bright smile. 'Apparently, it's only Mark who isn't. Rachel said he'd fallen off a ladder and he can't get up off the floor.'

Leaving Jessica Harrison in Charlotte's incapable hands – Eva was off that afternoon, and no one else was free to look after her – I grabbed my Mulberry, ran out into the King's Road and, rudely pushing past the customer who was about to climb into it, threw myself into the taxi that Manny, Haines and Hampton's uniformed doorman, had just flagged down for her.

Manny was outraged. 'Hey, Annie, what do you think you're doing?'

'Sorry, it's an emergency!' I shouted, as the driver pulled away.

All the way back to Camden I was on my Nokia, alternately advising Charlotte about what she should be telling Jessica Harrison and telephoning Clarissa's house. A terrible disaster scenario was playing in my head: there'd been a fire, armed gangsters had broken in and, as they'd shot at the children in cold blood, the building had collapsed due to a massive earthquake. I was pretty certain that the Victorian terraces around Primrose Hill hadn't been built on a major fault line, but that didn't stop me worrying about it. I worried that something dreadful would happen to the girls if there was no one to supervise them, in which case I'd never be able to face Clarissa or James again.

During the journey I barked myriad instructions for Rachel to relay to her sisters: don't touch the kitchen knives; don't turn on the gas in case there's an explosion; don't leave the house, in case you get kidnapped; don't let them eat anything in case they choke and there's no one to perform the Heimlich Manoeuvre.

'For fuck's sake, Annie,' Mark snapped, when Rachel put the phone to his ear, 'They're fine, and doing their own thing. They're not babies, and it's not like they're alone, anyway. I'm still here. I just can't get up off the living-room floor.'

It turned out that he'd done nothing more serious than pull a muscle in his back by falling off the top rung of James's stepladder. What had he been doing up it in the first place? I demanded, when I came in, by which time he'd dragged himself on to Clarissa's tatty black velvet

179

sofa, and was spreadeagled on his back, rather like Sophie Dahl in those old Opium ads, only clothed in shorts and a T-shirt, and as if he was in the throes of agony rather than orgasm. Fluffy was keeping guard over him, intermittently pushing his nose into Mark's face.

'I was pinning that to the ceiling,' Mark said, pointing to a big yellow sheet that was now lying in a heap on an armchair.

'Why?'

'Because we were going to put on a surprise show for you when you came back from work,' Rebecca said, 'with singing and dancing.'

'And Mark was turning this room into a theatre,' Rachel added. 'This end was to be the stage, and that was supposed to be the curtain.'

'And now Mark says we can't do the show!' Miranda cried, throwing herself at my knees. 'And I was going to dress up as a fairy and sing "How Much Is That Doggie In The Window" with Fluffy!'

'Never mind, darling.' I bent down, unclasped her hot hands and hoisted her on to my hip. 'We'll do something else instead.'

'I miss Mummy! And I'm hungry!' she wept. 'And Mark promised to make scones for tea. You do it, Annie!'

'I would, sweetie, but I'm not a very good cook.'

Her big eyes filled with tears. 'Mark promised!'

My heart sank. 'Okay, I'll try.'

Mark lifted his head from the cushions and gave me a helpless look. 'Sorry to land you in it, darling. I suppose I could have sort of managed to keep going till you came home, but I thought we ought to call and tell you. I thought you'd want to know. I hope we didn't interrupt anything at work?'

Only the biggest single sale I'd have made all year, I thought. But I was a newly-wed, so I merely said, 'It doesn't matter, darling. I'm just glad you're okay.'

Slipping into Domestic Goddess mode, I went down to the kitchen, got out some ingredients and, tossing my fringe out of my eyes in what I hoped was an irresistible manner, plunged my hands into a bowl of flour while Mark called out instructions from upstairs. By the time I put the misshapen blobs into the oven, burning my arm as I did so, it was almost time for supper, everyone was starving, and everything within sight, me and the girls included, was covered with the remnants of the sticky white dough.

How something so soft and malleable could turn into something as hard and unyielding as the shrivelled lumps that eventually came out of the oven was little short of a miracle, Mark said, as we examined the finished product. He went on to suggest that it hadn't been a cake that King Alfred had left too long in the oven but a giant scone, and that was where the name of the Coronation stone, the Stone of Scone, had come from; my efforts, by contrast, were scones of stone. Rebecca suggested we take them down to Camden Market, set up a stall and sell them as paperweights, which I pretended to find as exceedingly funny as Mark genuinely did.

Inside I felt useless. Why hadn't I locked everyone out of the kitchen, climbed out of the window, run to Marks and Sparks, bought scones and pretended they were my own? No one ate one except Emily, who loyally said it was delicious, and Fluffy, who took the half Emily slipped him into a corner of the living room and spent a good part of the evening gnawing it. Even his sharp little teeth failed to make much of an impression.

'What are we going to eat?' Miranda wailed. 'I'm hungry!'

'And who's going to help make up the sofa-bed in my room?' said Rachel.

'Why do we need to do that, darling?'

'For Helena, Jasmine and Posy, of course!'

'Sorry?'

'They're my best friends! Didn't Mummy tell you I was having a sleepover tonight?'

This was something Mummy had forgotten to mention, deliberately no doubt. But there it was, scrawled on a pink Post-it at the bottom of the armadillo fridge: 'Sleepover! Oops! Sorry! Love you, darling!' followed by another half-dozen exclamation marks and a row of kisses. And there was the doorbell. Suddenly the hall was filled with precocious twelve-year-olds wearing mini-skirts and crop tops, hugging and kissing like starlets greeting each other on the red carpet at Cannes. And before I could tell their parents to take them away again, they were driving off in their Porsche four-wheel drive, shouting, 'We'll be back from Glyndebourne to pick her up at five tomorrow,' and 'I presume Clarissa warned you about her nut allergy?'

Then Fluffy ran out of the front door, in pursuit of a cat he'd seen across the street, and there was no one to run after him but me.

I returned to find the walls throbbing to the starlets dancing and singing along with Destiny's Child. Ten-year-old

Rebecca was sitting on the stairs, texting someone she said was her long-term boyfriend, and Miranda and Emily were in the kitchen, nagging to be fed. Mark was still lying on the sofa. I looked down at him, overcome with an emotion I mistook at first for profound pity. Then I realized it was the urge to strangle him.

'Darling, how am I going to manage for the next twenty-four hours?' I said, in as calm a voice as I could muster. 'And what am I going to give them to eat?'

This was not a matter of choice. Both Mark and I were aware that, like the old joke, there was only one thing I knew how to make for dinner. A reservation.

Leaving him with Fluffy and a packet of Clarissa's Nurofen Plus – luckily for Mark, she'd always suffered from painful periods – I marched my charges across the painted railway bridge to Chalk Farm Road, feeling rather like Snow White with the Seven Dwarfs. In the welcoming tiled depths of a restaurant called Marine Ices, where my father had taken me as a child to buy ice-cream cornets, we tucked into pizza, Coke and sundaes. By the time we returned to the house, I'd firmly re-established myself as number-one adult. Looking after children was easy, I told Mark, as I handed him a takeaway Quattro Formaggi with added pepperoni: you just gave them everything they wanted, and they were yours for life.

'Do you think maybe you shouldn't have let them have quite so many fizzy drinks?' he suggested at half past one in the morning. We were lying side by side in Clarissa and James's sagging bed, listening to the whoops of laughter that were coming intermittently from Rachel's room above us, along with karaoke Robbie Williams.

I sighed. 'What can I do about it?'

He gave me a nudge. 'You could always make love to me.'

'What about your back?'

'It seems a little better now,' he murmured, slipping a hand under my nightdress.

'Well, if you really think it won't hurt you . . .'

'I'm sure I'll survive. But it's definitely a case of "Girls On Top" tonight. Mmm.'

We kissed. I sat up. Mark winced as I clambered over him.

'Does it hurt terribly? Do you want me to get off?'

'No, no. I'll grin and bear it – just for your sake, you understand.'

We began to make love very slowly, but for the first time I didn't feel carried away. Mark sensed it almost immediately. 'What's wrong?' he asked.

'Nothing!' I said, as I listened to Rachel and the starlets thunder downstairs on their way to the kitchen to prepare a midnight feast. I heard them stop and giggle outside our door, which made Fluffy crawl out from under our bed and growl. I flung myself on to Mark in an attempt to be my usual passionate self, but I couldn't stop thinking of the seven girls, aged between twelve years old and five, who were in the house with us. Rachel and her friends, all as high as kites on Coke, Emily and Rebecca ditto, and Miranda who, when I'd last checked on her, had been fast asleep in the room next door, separated from us only by the paper-thin walls.

But Miranda wasn't asleep. Neither was she in her room. She was in ours or, at least, standing in the open doorway, with a doll under her arm. The first I knew of this was when a little voice said, 'Annie, why are you sitting on top of Mark?'

I vaulted off him a hundred times faster than I'd ever got down off the horse in our school gym. 'Just massaging his bad back!' I ran my hand through my tangled hair and smiled at her, trying to look like her favourite auntie, not a guilty sexual wanton caught mid-coitus. 'How come you're awake, darling?'

'I wet the bed,' she said, without a trace of embarrassment. 'Can I get in with Mark while you change the sheets for me?'

Seventeen

Mark's back had been okay enough to have sex at one thirty in the morning, but five hours later, when Fluffy woke us because he wanted to go out, my husband was in so much pain he couldn't get up. I pulled on my jeans, threw his sweatshirt over my nightdress, clipped on Fluffy's lead and, careful not to wake the sleeping children, crept out of the house to take him for an early-morning walk. By the time I returned fifteen minutes later, ready to crawl back under Clarissa's thin, washed-out bed linen, Emily and Miranda were tucked under the duvet beside Mark, who, flat on his back and holding the book directly above his head, was reading them another instalment of *The Wind in the Willows*.

'Sorry to be a pain, but is there any chance of you bringing me up a coffee, darling?' he asked apologetically.

'Can I have hot chocolate?' asked Emily.

'Me, too, please, Annie,' begged Miranda. 'Let's all have breakfast in bed! Can we – please?'

Down in the kitchen, the work surfaces I'd cleared before I'd gone up the previous night were now buried under piles of dirty bowls and glasses, open cereal boxes, empty Haribo packets, and the last remaining litre of milk in the house, which had been left out beside the Aga and gone sour overnight. While the kettle boiled and Fluffy dogged my footsteps, yapping to be fed, I made a pathetic stab at clearing up, but there was nowhere to put the bowls because I'd forgotten to put on the dishwasher the night before, and nothing in Clarissa's battery of eco-friendly cleaners could remove the wax Mini-Babybel skins that had been ground into the floor. I ended up on my knees, scraping them off with my fingers, getting a splinter under my thumbnail and chipping my carefully applied Chanel varnish. Then the telephone rang.

'How's it going?' Clarissa asked.

I threw myself on to a kitchen chair, and surveyed the chaos. 'Absolutely fine. Everything's still under control,' I said. 'Thanks for warning me about the sleepover, by the way.'

She drew in a sharp breath. 'Darling, do you hate me?'

'Not totally. It was fine.'

'They didn't keep you and Mark up all night?'

'Not *all* night.'

I heard Clarissa wince. 'Annie, what can I say except I'm sorry and I owe you one?'

'Only one?'

'The thing is, I thought you might change your mind about staying if I told you. And I was so desperate to get away.'

'I can understand that.' I certainly could. 'Do you want to speak to the girls?'

She hesitated. 'Not particularly. Frankly, if they're not missing us, I'd rather leave well alone.'

'How's the spa – and everything else?' I asked meaningfully.

'Fabulous. All of it. We're still lying in bed, eating breakfast and reading the papers, aren't we, James? And we've spent the last hour and a quarter listening to *The Archers* omnibus, without being disturbed once! The cultural event of our year! We have to give up this gorgeous room soon, worse luck, so we're going down to the spa for a swim, and James is booked in for a Reiki massage, aren't you, darling?'

I spent the rest of the day in a blur of clearing up and making snacks under Mark's supervision. The dishwasher got stuck mid-cycle, and needed baling out. Miranda fell over and cut her knee. Then Hamlet's plastic exercise ball bounced down the stairs and broke, so I had to rescue him from Fluffy's jaws. Rachel dropped her mobile phone down a lavatory and I had to don rubber gloves to fish it out. Shortly after that the starlets turned nasty, quarrelled among themselves and sent her to Coventry. She came to me in tears, complaining that everyone was bored and her friends hated her.

'Why don't you get them out of the house? That'll change the atmosphere,' Supernanny suggested, from his sickbed.

'But where can I take all seven of them?'

'I don't know, darling! Why not go for a walk on Primrose Hill.'

'No!' Rachel said. 'That's, like, *so* boring! They'll *so* hate it.'

'She's right,' I said to Mark. 'The only walk I can see those girls enjoying is a catwalk.'

Mark's face lit up. 'And there you have it! Annie, you're a genius! How much makeup do you have with you?'

'Just what I usually carry around with me. Which is more than enough.'

With the help of all the towels in the linen closet, some Alice bands, James's dressing-gown, two boxes of tissues and a drum of cotton buds from the corner shop, Rachel's bedroom was soon transformed into the starlets' very own makeover studio. I spent the rest of the afternoon pinning hair into crazy styles, giving the starlets advice about what colours suited them best, and showing them how to apply eye-liner, blusher and lip-gloss. Politically correct it was not, but they loved it, even Miranda, who insisted on using my purple Lancôme eye shadow as foundation, and my mascara wand to brush her eyebrows. By the time the starlets' parents came to pick them up, no one wanted to leave. They told Rachel they'd had the best time ever and wanted to be stylists, not brain surgeons, when they grew up.

After the last one had gone home, Rachel threw her arms round me. 'Thank you, Annie! I love you *so* much!' she said, which almost made me cry. But I didn't have time. I had to get the house cleared up again before Clarissa and James arrived.

The moment we left Camden Town, Mark staged a remarkable recovery. The nearer we got to Islington, the less he complained about his pain; even jolting over the speed-bumps – uncomfortable in the van at the best of times – caused him no concern. When we pulled up in the Workhouse car park, he almost jumped out of the van, picked up our overnight bags without a murmur and threw them nonchalantly over his shoulder. In the building, he didn't bother to wait for the lift, as I did, but raced Fluffy upstairs, taking the treads two at a time.

Since I was too exhausted to do anything, he fed Fluffy, then made us apple pancakes flamed in Calvados for supper. Afterwards he ran me a hot bubble bath, placed lighted candles all over the en-suite and climbed in with me, holding two glasses of red wine. Later – after much erotic splashing about – we put on our bathrobes and lay in each other's arms on our comfortable bed, with Fluffy warming our toes. Then Mark made popcorn and put on a DVD he'd bought from a stall in Chapel Street market.

Called *The Awful Truth,* it was my favourite kind of film – a 1937 screwball comedy. It starred Cary Grant as a high-society millionaire called Gerry Warrener, and Irene Dunne as his wife, Lucy. The Warreners lived in an elegant Manhattan mansion, where their uniformed maid served them cocktails from a trolley while they swanned around in evening dress, having witty conversations about the nature of trust within a marriage. They also had a cute fox terrier, Mr Smith, which, I think, was why Mark had chosen the DVD.

It started happily enough, but under the glittering surface all was not well within the Warreners' marriage, and before long I was stuffing popcorn nervously into my mouth, overcome by presentiments of doom. Gerry lied to Lucy about where he'd spent the weekend, Lucy stayed out all night with her suave French music teacher, Armand Duval, and before you knew it, the Warreners were in the divorce court, both demanding custody of

Mr Smith who, it turned out, had brought them together in the first place.

'Just like Fluffy brought us together!' Mark planted a kiss on my forehead. 'Otherwise we might never have met.'

'Mmm. No wonder this film's called *The Awful Truth*,' I said, snuggling closer to him as the courtroom scene began. 'It truly *is* awful. What's going to happen?'

Mark grabbed a handful of popcorn. 'I don't know, darling.'

'I can hardly bear to watch.'

The judge decided that Mr Smith would make up his own mind who he'd live with. He ordered Gerry and Lucy to call their pet: whoever he ran to would get custody of him. But poor Mr Smith couldn't decide – until Lucy produced his favourite toy from inside her white fur muff; forget designer handbags, a muff was the must-have fashion accessory for women in the 1930s, indoors and out. Mr Smith ran to her.

'But that's terrible! So unfair!' I cried. Gerry was as upset over the loss of his dog as he was over the breakdown of his marriage.

'Unimaginable,' Mark agreed. 'Nothing like that will ever happen to Fluffy and us!'

As if he knew he was being talked about, Fluffy lifted his sleepy head from his paws and looked up at Mark. I did the same. 'Won't it, darling?' I asked, wanting to be reassured, although I knew such a thing was out of the question.

Mark kissed me. 'No, darling,' he said firmly. 'You and I will never get divorced.'

'Good.' I snuggled closer to him, and plunged my hand into the almost empty popcorn bowl again.

'Unless you eat that,' Mark added. 'It's mine. You've already guzzled most of it!'

I opened my fist and let the polystyrene grains fall back into the bowl. 'It's a high price to pay, but I'm prepared to make sacrifices. Can we turn this film off? I don't think I can take any more. It's too upsetting. Besides, I'm zonked.'

'Sure.'

Mark grabbed the remote and put Jerry, Lucy and Mr Smith out of their misery. We wriggled out of our dressing-gowns and crawled under the covers, trying not to disturb Fluffy.

'It was a wonderful weekend, wasn't it?' Mark breathed into my neck as we spooned up for the night.

'Mmm,' I said noncommittally.

'It's so great to have kids around, isn't it?'

'Mmm!' So great? More like so exhausting. The two days we'd spent at Clarissa's had given me a new insight into why she looked so worn out nowadays. It was because she *was* worn out. And I knew now exactly why she and James never had sex when they were at home.

'The girls are lovely,' Mark went on.

'Yes, I adore them. Not so sure about the starlets, though.'

'Oh, they were just being little girls, Annie. All children play up. They can't be perfect all the time.'

'You're really good with kids,' I muttered.

I felt Mark's shoulders shrug against my back. 'Not particularly. I've just had lots of experience with my nieces and nephews. And I like mucking around with them.' A moment later he mumbled, 'You're really good, too, darling.'

'No, I'm not. I'm hopeless at everything to do with domesticity, and you know it.'

'That's just not true!' Mark propped himself up on an elbow and turned me round to face him. 'You heard what Rachel's friends said – they had the best time ever.'

'Only because I did makeup and stuff with them. It's a good thing they weren't boys. I'd really have been stuck.'

'Face it, you were brilliant, Annie. I'm so sorry about landing you in it, by the way.'

'There's no need to apologize. It was an accident, wasn't it?'

'Yeah,' Mark breathed, after the shortest of pauses. We snuggled up again, but just as I was about to go to sleep he stroked my side very gently. 'Annie?'

'Mmm?'

'Let's try for a baby,' he whispered.

My eyes snapped open, and I stared ahead into the darkness. 'What?' I said quietly.

'Let's have a baby.'

A strange feeling, halfway between fear and revulsion, came over me. 'What – now?' I breathed.

'Well, not this minute.' He kissed the back of my neck. 'I'm not sure I'm up to it after that bath. But soon. I do so want us to have children together, darling, don't you?'

'Of course.' I took a deep breath to try to calm my heart, which was pounding. 'But we've only just got married.'

'Yeah. I know that.'

'Things are lovely as they are,' I went on, 'aren't they? You, me and Fluffy?'

'Of course.' Then he added, 'But wouldn't a baby make everything that much more perfect?'

'Mmm.' After my experiences of the past couple of days, it certainly wouldn't. 'But I'm on the Pill at the moment.'

'You could always come off it,' he wheedled.

'I'm not sure that now's the right time – I mean, work-wise.'

'Okay,' Mark said. And I closed my eyes with a sigh of relief. 'But will you promise me something, Annie?' he went on, rather urgently.

'What, darling?'

'Promise you'll think about coming off the Pill?'

My eyes opened again. 'Okay,' I said quietly. 'I promise I'll think about it.'

He tightened his arms round me. 'Thank you, darling.'

And, over the next few years, I kept my promise.

I thought about it.

Eighteen

It was too ironic.

It was 30 April, our fifth wedding anniversary, and Mark and I were going back to a register office – only this time it was the Principal Registry of the Family Division in High Holborn, and we were in the middle of our divorce.

In the past we'd marked our wedding anniversary by cracking open a bottle of bubbly. This year we were more likely to crack one over each other's head.

As I fiddled with the chain handle of the vintage quilted Chanel handbag I'd chosen to carry that morning, I wondered how Mark and I had ended up here, and so quickly, when we'd loved each other so much.

At least, I'd loved Mark.

I'd thought he was the nicest human being I'd ever met. He was so sweet-natured and so generous, so loving and accepting. He'd made me feel safe and precious, and my heart had skipped a beat every time I'd walked through a door and seen him. We'd enjoyed the same films and the same art exhibitions. We'd liked listening to the same music – Clapton, REM, Van Morrison, Amy Winehouse, the soundtracks of *The Sound of Music* and *West Side Story*, both of which we knew by heart. We'd liked mooching around the flat together, going to the supermarket together, watching sentimental black-and-white movies like *Top Hat*, *Dark Victory* and, of course, *The Awful Truth*. *Now Voyager* had been our very favourite. When Bette Davis walked down the gangplank of the ocean liner, in her platform shoes and white straw hat, transformed during the cruise she'd just been on from a repressed frump into a confident vamp, it reduced both of us to tears.

How happy I'd been during the first couple of years of our marriage, I reflected, as I walked down High Holborn with my solicitor, Mr Williams. Sometimes, when I'd sit reading on the sofa at night with Fluffy curled next to me, I'd look up to the mezzanine level, where Mark was playing his guitar, and feel overcome by my amazing good luck in having found such a talented treasure of a man.

So what had happened to spoil our happiness? What had come between us?

When, for instance, had I discovered that Mark might not be entirely perfect? When had I stopped finding his shorts and T-shirts sexy? At first I'd been so proud that he'd cared nothing for his appearance: he knew what was important in life – the inner not the outer man, substance not spin. Yet, gradually, the sight of his fat toes wriggling worthily in his old canvas sandals, his hairy knees on show all the time, and his collection of clapped-out tops with their ethical slogans – Save the Whales, Save the Rainforest, Save Energy – had palled, and later embarrassed me, like the occasion when he'd worn one to the Haines and Hampton staff Christmas party.

When had I lost faith that Mark had enough commitment to make it as a musician? The rot had set in relatively early when the sure-fire hit he'd been composing in my flat since we'd met was abandoned half finished, as were the rest of the songs he subsequently began with enthusiasm but never completed. Then the group he'd occasionally played gigs with had disbanded, and he hadn't bothered to find others to play with. A few months later, he had given up looking for session work in recording studios, too, because, he said, what with looking after Fluffy, spending time with me and running Wag the Dog Walks, he didn't have time for it any more.

Not that the dog-walking business was booming. With his laid-back attitude to time, efficiency and money, Mark would never make it as a candidate for *The Apprentice*. During the second year of our marriage the number of his clients had dwindled from twenty to fifteen, then from fifteen to twelve, and finally to six, and somehow he'd never got round to finding any new ones. And with taking out so few dogs, having to drive round and pick them up, then ferry them to and from Hampstead Heath twice a day, the amount he'd been earning had scarcely covered the soaring cost of his petrol, never mind the tax bill he'd have to pay if he'd ever got round to declaring what he earned. So, when his beloved camper van collapsed in a heap of rusty bodywork in the middle of Kentish Town Road one Tuesday afternoon, leaving him stranded on the pavement in the rain with Fluffy and three yapping pooches, Mark was all for giving up dog-walking. And he would have done, had I not insisted that we buy a brand-new Audi on credit so that he could use it for the business – or, rather, since he didn't have any money to pay the hire-purchase instalments, that I should buy it for us.

Luckily I could afford to that year because I'd been promoted. My boss, Eileen, had retired and I'd been her natural successor. To be head of Personal Shopping was the culmination of the dream I'd been nurturing ever since I'd joined Haines and Hampton as a twenty-five-year-old graduate trainee, and that wasn't because my salary had doubled overnight. Suddenly I was a minor celebrity on the London fashion scene, interviewed by *Vogue*, and profiled in the UK edition of *Vanity Fair*. Running the department, doing the accounts, having meetings with George Haines and the buyers as well as seeing clients meant I had to work twice as hard, even with the help of my newly acquired assistant, the invaluable Eva.

After my promotion, instead of getting back to the Workhouse by seven, I sometimes hadn't returned until eight or nine. Often I'd been so brain dead by then that I'd fallen straight into bed, and Mark would bring me my supper on a tray. Even though I was exhausted, I'd never let on that I was tired when he'd wanted to have sex and, from what I'd gathered, he'd seemed to enjoy it as much as ever. If anything it was I who'd lost interest. I could neither let go nor concentrate. Sometimes, mid-coitus, I'd catch myself planning what outfits to show my clients the following morning or, horror of horrors, wishing Mark would hurry up.

My professional star was rising while Mark's was waning – or going nowhere. Did he resent my success? He claimed to be thrilled for me. However, soon after my promotion he was dropping hints again about us starting a family. Out in the country, his sisters and brothers-in-law were procreating like rabbits. It seemed that every time his parents telephoned, it was to announce a new pregnancy or birth. Lizzie had had another girl, or Emma a boy, or Katie was expecting again. 'Ah, brilliant!' Mark would sigh wistfully down the telephone. Soon his hints about parenthood grew not so subtle, and trying for a baby became an issue between us. It wasn't the right time, I kept telling him. I wasn't quite ready.

Secretly I wondered if I'd ever be. The thought of pregnancy sent a chill through me.

So, had that been the real reason why, two and a half years after our wedding, Mark had resorted to meaningless shags with a Pilates instructor who had crap taste in underwear? And had I now driven him into the arms of the Weimaraner's owner, whatever her name was, because I was doing well and he had no career?

Whatever. The result was that we were getting divorced. And the man who'd once loved me to bits now hated me so much that he wanted to take away from me the one thing I loved as much as I'd once loved him. Fluffy.

We had already received our decree nisi – the first legal step in our divorce – but, unable to come to any agreement through our solicitors over who should have custody of our precious pet, we hadn't yet been able to apply for a decree absolute, which would end our marriage. So, to try to resolve our differences, we were about to have a First Directions Appointment combined with a Financial Dispute Resolution, chaired by a district judge.

As Williams explained to me, when we stopped for a cappuccino in the local Costa's, sometimes a First Directions Appointment took place first, as the name implied, with the Financial Dispute Resolution following a few weeks later. But in relatively simple cases, such as ours, the two meetings were often combined, and we could get them over with together, saving ourselves time and money. This morning would be a good opportunity for Mark, me and our legal representatives – Williams, and Mark's solicitor Martha Greenwood – to thrash out our differences in a non-confrontational manner. If we managed to come to an agreement about who should have Fluffy, it would avoid the expense of taking our divorce to a full court hearing.

It sounded very civilized, until Williams and I made our way into the register office and bumped into Mark with Martha Greenwood. As we brushed past each other, with only a cold nod of acknowledgement, I felt as if we were duellists accompanied by our seconds, prepared to fight to the death.

Williams had advised me not to move out of the flat, and I had a feeling that Martha Greenwood had told Mark the same thing. Consequently he and I were still living together, and seemed destined to do so until such time as our divorce was finalized, the flat was sold and we split the proceeds of the sale. We'd scarcely exchanged a word for weeks other than the occasional frosty civility – *yes, no, have you finished in the bathroom? That's my milk you're using, so put it down, please!* It had taken its toll on both of us.

As for poor Fluffy, he hadn't a clue why his pack had suddenly changed its habits. Why was I, his mistress, spending so much time alone in the bedroom rather than curling up in front of the fire with him? Why was Mark sleeping on the sofa, instead of cuddling up with me in the comfortable bed where Fluffy, by degrees, had always inched his way between us during the night? He was used to hurtling through the flat at top speed, hurdling the furniture. Now the door between the bedroom and the living room was permanently shut, with Mark on one side of it and me on the other. Fluffy scrabbled at it, howling for his racetrack to be opened up again.

After a short wait in a corridor, the case of Curtis v. Curtis was called, and Mark and I were summoned before the district judge. She introduced herself as District Justice Robarts, and invited Williams to outline the case from my side; since I was bringing the petition against Mark, my solicitor apparently had the right to talk first.

Williams outlined the reason for the irretrievable break-down of our marriage – Mark's adultery – then read out my 'without prejudice' financial offer to him: half the flat, the car, his choice of the furniture and half my other financial assets to effect a clean break. Expressionless, except for the occasional raised eyebrow and nod, District Judge Robarts listened attentively while Martha Greenwood, Mark's solicitor, then outlined the divorce from his side. Although her client accepted that he had not contributed greatly to the couple's joint finances, she said, he'd taken on the role of home-maker on his marriage, thus allowing the petitioner to pursue her career unfettered by domestic burdens. The respondent was happy with the financial settlement on offer from the petitioner – in fact, he conceded that it was generous. He would also like to point out that he'd only committed adultery after his marriage had irretrievably broken down.

'That's not true!' I interrupted. 'Everything was okay between us! And, anyway, what about Fern?'

'Please, Mrs Curtis.' The judge gave me a brief smile. 'Let your husband's lawyer finish. You'll have your say afterwards.'

'That about wraps it up, your honour,' Martha Greenwood said. 'As I said, my client is quite happy with the proposed financial settlement.'

The judge frowned. 'Well, if everyone's so happy, and there's no dispute, I'm not sure why you're wasting my time,' she said, addressing Greenwood and Williams. 'Why haven't you simply gone through the usual channels to a decree absolute without recourse to a family court?'

'Because,' Williams said, 'there's one unresolved issue.'

She was clearly bemused. 'Well, have you suggested mediation to Mr and Mrs Curtis?'

'My client refuses to compromise on the issue, your honour,' Greenwood said.

'And so does mine,' said Williams. 'It's about residency.'

'Residency?' District Judge Robarts leafed through the open file on the table in front of her. 'I wasn't aware there were any children in this marriage.'

'There aren't,' Williams said. He gulped. 'It's about my client's dog.'

'*My* client's dog,' corrected Greenwood.

'Fluffy's not Mark's,' I snapped at her across the table.

'Come off it!' Mark said. 'You know he's more attached to me than he is to you.'

'Rubbish! Anyway, he's mine, Mark. I bought him.'

'And, in case you've forgotten, I brought him up!'

'Am I to understand that the petitioner and the respondent are at loggerheads over which of them should have custody of their *pet dog*?'

'Yes, your honour,' Williams said, somewhat nervously. 'He – Fluffy – is my client's dog, and she naturally wishes that he should remain so.'

'And my client insists that Fluffy is *his* dog, and that it is in Fluffy's best interest that he should live with him after the divorce.'

District Judge Robarts shook her head in wonder. 'Mr and Mrs Curtis, I trust that your solicitors have explained the legal situation to you both?' she asked, in the kind of tone you'd use to talk to very small children. 'Now, you may be deeply attached to your pet – Fluffy, is it? But you must understand that, in the eyes of the law, he, she or it is no more and no less than any other chattel acquired before or during your marriage.' She looked down at the list of our – my – assets. 'No more and no less than your loft flat in Islington, say, or your Audi Avant. He's an object, a piece of marital property. Imagine him, if you like, as your stainless-steel Magimix.'

'In which case I should definitely have him,' Mark said drily, 'because Annie hasn't got a clue how to switch ours on.'

'Fluffy's not a Magimix!' I protested. 'He doesn't have a switch. He's an animal with feelings and needs!'

'Yes, Annie. Needs that I can meet much better than you!' Mark batted back.

'Mr and Mrs Curtis, as I've explained, as far as the

law is concerned your dog is simply another of your possessions –'

'One that I paid for!' I interrupted.

'– an inanimate thing that has no needs.'

'But he does have needs!' Mark insisted. 'And if they're not going to be taken into account, that's terrible!'

District Judge Robarts smiled coldly at him. 'It might seem so to you, sir, but that is the law. Now, I'm not here to make a ruling. At this stage I can only give directions for this case. And I'm going to suggest that you reach agreement over Fido – or Fluffy, or whatever he's called – right now in this courtroom. Otherwise you could end up with a full hearing, which would cost you tens of thousands of pounds. Do you really want to go down that road? Can you even afford to?' Mark and I glanced at each other, then shook our heads. 'Good. I'm glad we've got that clear. Now, have you thought of sharing custody of Fluffy? One week on, one week off, for example? For instance, one year he goes on summer holiday with one of you and spends Christmas with the other. The next year it's the other way round.'

'If I might put in a without-prejudice offer here?' Martha Greenwood said. 'My client would be prepared – very generously – to let the petitioner have Fluffy for every Christmas holiday, and every bank holiday, with visitation rights every Sunday, providing he has full residency at all other times. In return, he is willing to forgo possession of the car during the division of the assets.'

'So, you think that's what Fluffy's worth to me, do you? The Audi?' I said scornfully.

'You can have the lot, as far as I'm concerned!' Mark

retorted. 'The flat. Everything. He's the only thing I really want!'

Williams sat forward eagerly. 'Oh, I think my client might be prepared to accept that offer from the respondent!'

I turned on him. 'No, I would not.'

'Look,' said the judge, 'divorced couples manage to care for their children by sharing residency, so I'm sure you two could manage it with your dog.'

'It wouldn't work, your honour,' Mark said. 'I'm not trying to stop Annie seeing Fluffy. Far from it. But he's got to live with me because she can't look after him.'

'*What?*' I turned to the judge. 'I don't know what he's talking about!'

'Yes, you do,' Mark said. 'You're out at work all day, six days a week.'

'Yes, but –'

'So how can you take care of Fluffy better than I can?'

'Well, now that I'm head of the department I can take him in with me – sometimes,' I said, off the top of my head.

'Don't be stupid!'

'And if I have to leave him at home, I'll hire a dog-walker to take him out.'

'That seems rather unnecessary when I *am* a dog-walker,' Mark said, the embodiment of reason.

'I'll hire you, then,' I said. Then I added, 'Oh, I forgot – I already did.' Mark looked daggers at me.

Williams cleared his throat. 'That's how my client and her husband met, your honour,' he explained.

'Since I'm an extremely responsible dog-owner, I needed someone to take Fluffy out for walks in the middle of the day when I was working,' I explained.

'When weren't you working?' Mark muttered bitterly. 'You were never at home!'

'Order, please.'

'Do I have to remind you that one of us needed to earn a living, Mark? I wouldn't have had to work such long hours if you'd had a proper job!'

'That's crap, Annie. You work long hours because you love what you do!'

'Yes, but I've also worked hard because *you* were too busy shagging strangers to contribute anything to our finances!'

'Order!' said District Judge Robarts.

Mark clenched his fists. 'It was only one woman on the Heath. And she wasn't a stranger.'

'Not after you'd shagged her she wasn't!'

'Mr and Mrs Curtis! Do I have to remind you that this is a court of law, not a mud-wrestling match?'

But all the anger Mark and I had been suppressing for months, maybe even years, was spilling out of us, and not even a judge could stop us. 'And what about Fern?' I said. 'You didn't meet *her* on the Heath, did you? You met her in the gym – the gym I paid for! Like I've paid for everything else during our marriage.'

Mark glared at me. 'That's it with you, Annie. Everything always boils down to money!'

My mouth fell open at this unwarranted attack. 'That is *so* not true, Mark Curtis! I've always shared everything I had with you!'

'And don't I know it! Why do you think I turned to Fern? Because you made me feel useless. Because you emasculated me!'

'I can't believe you said that!' I turned to the district judge. 'I always appreciated everything he did for me. And I did everything I could to encourage his music career! I was always telling him he was talented! I bought him an electric piano when he said he wanted one. And I tried to get him to expand Wag the Dog bloody Walks!'

'Wag the what?' Robarts said.

'Wag the Dog Walks, your honour,' Greenwood explained. 'My client's dog-walking business.'

'I even bought the Audi for you when your VW broke down,' I carried on, 'just so you could carry on ferrying those muddy creatures to the Heath.'

'So you could stay in control, you mean.'

I shook my head in disbelief. 'You must be crazy.'

Mark stared at me with what looked like hatred in his eyes. Then he said, more quietly, 'Just think about it, Annie. You're even in control of our divorce.'

There was a long pause. Then I said, more quietly, 'What are you talking about?'

'If you don't like what's happening to us, just remember that it was *you* who instigated it.'

'Yes, but only because *you* were unfaithful to me – for the second time!'

'Yes, but it was *you* who said you wanted a divorce. You who said you'd pay for my lawyer. *You* who made out I wanted half of everything you own.'

Williams perked up. 'My client would be willing to back down on this issue, your honour.'

'But mine wouldn't,' said Greenwood.

'Order, please! Order!'

'I was just trying to be fair!' I turned to the judge. 'Look, this just isn't right. All I'm asking for is my dog. I've offered Mark half of everything else I have.'

'A without-prejudice offer,' Williams muttered.

'Half my savings, half the flat . . .'

'A property my client bought well before the marriage,' Williams put in again, 'and on which she has always paid the mortgage. The respondent's name isn't on the deeds.'

'Yes, it is,' said Martha Greenwood, quietly.

'*What?*' Williams and I said in unison.

'Mr Curtis's name *is* on the deeds,' she said, in her prim voice. 'As of last month. I directed him to add it. For his own security.'

I stared incredulously at Mark, who'd turned away, probably out of embarrassment. 'Can he do that? I mean, legally?' I asked Williams.

'I'm afraid so. He's your spouse.'

I felt like I'd just been hit. I looked at Mark again. This time he had the decency to look shame-faced. 'I'm sorry, Annie,' he said. 'I had no choice. I needed to protect my position.'

'From me?'

There was a short, acid silence.

'Well, Mrs Curtis,' Robarts said, 'since you seem happy to split everything else fifty-fifty with your husband, why don't you split the dog as well? Go and get him now – or should I say, "*Fetch*"? I'll get a machete and chop him in half down the middle. One of you can take the front –

whichever of you doesn't mind his barking – and the one who doesn't mind dealing with what comes out of his rear end can have *that*.' Mark and I both looked at her as if she was mad. 'Has neither of you heard of the Judgement of Solomon?' She raised her eyebrows. 'Get real, Mr and Mrs Curtis! You're wasting the court's time, not to mention mine, and a great deal of your own money.' She turned to our lawyers. 'Have you given your clients an estimate of how much a full court hearing could cost them if they can't settle this between them?'

'I have the figures, your honour.'

'Well, I suggest you make sure Mr and Mrs Curtis study them. In detail.' She regarded us both sternly. 'Now, I want you to listen to me very carefully. This is my advice to you. Forget about going for a full hearing. Instead, sit down together over a bottle of wine, and thrash out this issue between you.'

Mark shook his head. 'I'm not going to change my mind,' he said. 'You see, it's not about the money. I honestly don't care about that. I don't want Annie's money. What's at issue for me is Fluffy's well-being. He'd have a terrible life if I wasn't there to look after him.'

'That's nonsense, your honour!' I said. 'Fluffy would be much happier living with me. And I'm willing to do anything to prove it.'

'So am I!'

'Right. I've heard enough.' The judge turned to our solicitors. 'Please, take your clients out of here. If they're determined to go for a full hearing, they can get on with it. I'm not going to waste any more of my time trying to dissuade them. We'll set a date for late August. Until then,

Mr and Mrs Curtis, I order that you take turns looking after your dog. One of you should have him for one week, the other for the next. And so on. Seven days on, seven days off. Will you both accept that?'

Mark and I glanced at each other sheepishly and nodded.

'Good,' District Judge Robarts said. 'I'm glad you can agree about something. And before you leave today,' she added grimly, 'let me give you one final piece of advice. If you take this divorce all the way to a full hearing, I can guarantee you'll live to regret it. Not least because I don't know a single judge in Britain who'd look favourably on this ridiculous battle between you.'

And, having made this chilling prediction, she dismissed us from her presence with a wave of her hand.

Nineteen

Wladyslaw Wyrzykowski, a six-foot-tall, shaven-headed hulk, scaled the creaking wooden staircase in front of me two steps at a time, carrying two huge, overstuffed suitcases, one in each hand, with a third tucked under his Schwarzenegger-sized arm.

Half an hour before, it had taken me three separate trips to lug those same cases into the Workhouse's lift.

'I'll take that for you,' Mark had snapped, when he'd seen me heaving one out of the front door.

'No, thanks,' I'd replied curtly. 'I don't want your help.'

'Don't be stupid, Annie. You'll hurt yourself.'

'Not as much as you've already hurt me.'

He'd sighed with frustration. 'You can't even pick it up!'

'Yes, I can.'

'Give it to me.' Mark had grabbed it from me. 'Jesus! What the hell have you got in here?'

'The rest of my life. Put it down, please, Mark. I don't need you any more. Not for anything.' So saying, I'd summoned Fluffy and clipped on his lead. Then, holding it with one hand, I'd dragged and kicked the three suitcases down the corridor one by one.

Arms akimbo, Mark had stood in the doorway, watching me. 'It's ridiculous, you taking Fluffy with you on the day you're moving out,' he called, as I waited for the lift. 'Why don't you wait till you've settled in, like I suggested?'

'Because it's my turn to look after him this week. He was yours last week.'

'God, you're so pig-headed!'

'I am not! I just don't want you scribbling it down in some little book that I couldn't cope with Fluffy without you, then using it as evidence against me.'

'Like I'd do such a thing, Annie!'

'Yeah, right! Like I should trust you not to, I suppose.'

Downstairs, Fluffy had jumped happily into the back seat of the minicab I'd ordered, while the poor Afghani driver had almost given himself a hernia trying to squeeze the three suitcases into the boot. However, when we'd reached the Fulham house I was moving into, Wladyslaw had run down the front steps to greet us in his white paint-stained overalls, scooped up the cases and carried them into the tall, forbidding, grey-brick terraced building as if each was as light as a cashmere sweater. After three flights, he wasn't even breathless. When he got to the fourth-floor landing, he swerved to avoid hitting his head on a bare lightbulb that dangled from a wire in the ceiling, then flashed me a boyish grin.

'Only one more flight of fucking stairs left to go now, Annie!' he said, in his thick Polish accent.

'How long has the lift been out of order?' I said, as I puffed up after him.

'Today.'

'Just my luck – or, rather, yours – that it should break down on the day I move in.'

'No, no – *two* day. One, two. Since Friday. When it break down, I say to myself, "You must fix it before Annie come!" I work all night Friday, no shit, but big problem with electric motor. It's like Russian worker, eh? Bastard don't want to get going. So, I already order new one from Germany on iPhone. It will arrive day before tomorrow, for sure.'

On the landing, I dumped my heavy Downtown on the bare, dusty planks. My shoulder usually hurt from carrying the giant patent-leather tote bag, but today, as well as its usual contents – tissues, makeup, BlackBerry, wallet, crumpled receipts for long-forgotten purchases, two-litre bottle of Evian, hairbrush, Smints, Moleskine notebooks, leaking biros and a selection of grubby unused tampons, which had long ago lost their hygienic cellophane wrappers and now festered like so many dead grey mice – it also contained my jewellery, passport, laptop and charger, my BlackBerry charger and my divorce papers, plus the entire contents of my bathroom cabinet, including my sonic toothbrush, Eve Lom cleanser, Clarins Flash Balm, my precious supply of Boots Protect and Perfect, and the dozens of virtually unused lipsticks, foundations and blushers I'd impulse-bought over the last twenty years in the mistaken belief that they'd suit me, and had hoarded ever since in the hope that one day they would.

'Ah, is hard work, climbing stairs, no?' Wladyslaw said cheerfully. 'But good for body as two-hour workout in gym, yes?' He jerked his chin towards my giant bag. 'You want I take that?'

'No, no. I can manage it, thanks,' I said valiantly. 'You've got enough to carry.'

'No fucking problem, love!' He slung the Downtown over his shoulder as easily as if it had been a pillowslip full of feathers and, like a pack animal loaded for a trip over the Andes, continued up the final flight. 'Lift motor come Wednesday, for sure. Thursday, maybe. Latest by last week. But when it come, I mend lift in five minutes, no problem. I do everything good, you know, even speak English like proper Englishman, innit.'

'You certainly do.'

'Under no circumstances should you move out of the marital home,' Williams had warned me, the last time I'd spoken to him. But it was all right for him to talk – he didn't have to live with Mark. The two of us had attempted to behave in a vaguely civilized fashion in the weeks since our First Directions Appointment with District Judge Robarts. We'd even done what she'd suggested and, with a bottle of wine to help lubricate our conversation, made a stab at sorting out the Fluffy question. However, before we'd finished our second glasses, our civilized discussion had disintegrated into an even worse row than the one we'd had in the courtroom. Mark's resentment of the time I spent working, his lack of ambition, my controlling nature, his overspending, my close relationship with my father (from which, it turned out, Mark had always felt excluded), that I never put my toothbrush back on the charger and that he occasionally forgot to flush the lavatory after he'd had a pee – the floodgates were open, and all the anger and vitriol we'd held back for so long just kept pouring through them, as unstoppable as molten lava. It had culmin-ated with me locking myself into the bathroom, and Mark crashing out of the flat, shouting that he hated me.

From then on, living together had grown ever more unbearable. It was as if both of us were trying to pretend that the other didn't exist. If we'd passed in the hall, we'd swerved round each other without speaking. If he was in the living room, I'd sit in the bedroom with the television on at full volume. If I was reading in the living room, he'd go upstairs to the mezzanine above the kitchen and play music so loudly that, on one occasion, a neighbour had come up from the ground floor and complained. When it came to mealtimes, we'd bristle past each other behind the kitchen counter in hostile silence, each preparing our own food, Mark by cooking himself something delicious from fresh ingredients, me by shoving something ready-made into the microwave. Then we'd take our plates to opposite ends of the room and eat by ourselves. The only one to profit from this had been Fluffy, whom we'd both bribed to sit with us by offering him liberal titbits. For the first time in his life, our skinny dog was putting on weight. Even his jutting hipbones were now padded with a layer of fat.

It was extraordinary what had happened to our relationship. Once upon a time I couldn't bear to be parted from Mark for five minutes. By the end of May, I could no longer bear to sleep under the same roof as him. In fact, I could scarcely remember what I'd ever seen in him, apart from his looks.

'He took you in with that supercilious smile of his,' my father said when, over dinner at the Wolseley in Piccadilly, I'd confessed how bad things had got between us. 'But, as your nan used to say, love, handsome is as handsome does.'

'I know that now, Dad. Listen, despite what my solicitor said, I've decided to move out.'

Dad almost choked on his Eggs Benedict. 'Why the bloody hell should *you* move out of the Workhouse, Annie? Why should *he* carry on living there, when you're the one still paying the mortgage?'

'Because Mark can't afford to move out *or* pay the mortgage, Dad.'

'Pathetic! You should turf him out on the street.' He took a sip of his Chablis. 'I'm only sorry it should be costing you so much money and trouble and pain to have found out what he's really like.'

'Oh, I'm all right. At least, I will be.'

'That's my girl!' he said. 'You will. When you're finally shot of the bastard, that is.'

Sensibly, Dad had suggested that instead of renting a flat, which I could ill afford to do, I should move home until the divorce was over, the Workhouse flat was sold and I had enough capital in the bank to put down a deposit on a new place. After all, since he stayed at Norma's house in Willesden two or three nights a week, our house in Hampstead Garden Suburb was often empty nowadays, and it was so spacious that it seemed a crime not to use it. However, the thought of moving home at my age – back to my lilac-hued teenage bedroom with its flowery Laura Ashley Austrian blinds, its faded Duran Duran posters, and the single wooden bedstead, which still had Brenda and Tiger, my battered teddy bear and stuffed cat, sitting on the pillows – was too depressing. Besides, Hampstead Garden Suburb was even further away from Chelsea than Islington was. And if I was going to be able to look after Fluffy properly, during the alternate weeks when he'd be with me – until the full court hearing, after which I hoped he'd be mine for good – I needed a place near enough to Haines and Hampton for me to get back there relatively quickly.

It was Eva who'd suggested that I contact Wladyslaw, or Vlad, as he was called for short. As she'd explained, her brother was that walking cliché, a Polish plumber who'd come to England to earn some money. He'd arrived six years before, and had spent his first twelve months on a building site in Peckham, where he'd learned to speak what he'd presumed was the Queen's English from has foul-mouthed South London navvy. By sleeping on Eva's floor, and living off vacuum-packed *bigos*, *flaki wolowe*, sauerkraut and *klopsiki*, which their mother sent from home, he'd saved enough money to set up his own plumbing business, Drainy Days – Eva had thought up the catchy name.

Inspired by watching *Property Ladder*, and in thrall to its presenter, Sarah Beeny, Vlad had saved enough after a year to put a down-payment on a tiny run-down studio flat in Clapham, which he did up while he was living there and sold on six months later, easily doubling his initial investment. Three years on, Drainy Days had become a small but profitable business, and Vlad was a full-time property-developer. With his team of fellow Poles – all family members and childhood friends whom he ferried to and from Krakow in his rattling Transit van – he bought near-derelict houses in West London and, in a matter of weeks, divided them into small, stylish flats aimed at the first-time buyer, with neutral Ikea kitchens, cheap and cheerful bathroom fittings, and ubiquitous laminate wood floors.

Vlad's latest project was a bit of a departure for him – an ex-bed-and-breakfast hostel overlooking some gasworks. He was in the process of turning it into a hive of furnished flats destined for the rental market; in other words, his very own buy-to-let empire. Even though the development was not yet finished – electric cables were coiled up like spaghetti on every landing, the walls were only half painted and copper pipes protruded like toadstools from the bare floorboards – he'd already found tenants for six out of the eleven flats in the building. I was to be his seventh.

Eva had brought me to see the development a week earlier. With no furniture in it, the attic flat had seemed the perfect bolt-hole. The bedroom had a largish fitted wardrobe and a romantic sash window, which looked out on to the neighbouring rooftops. It even had a tiny en-suite, which, while not exactly state-of-the-art, had brand new fittings and a decent power-shower over the small bath. The open-plan living-room-cum-kitchen was what an estate agent might describe as compact yet characterful. It had sloping eaves, and French windows on to a small decked balcony that was just big enough for me to sit on. The best thing about the flat was that, because he was still working on the development, and I was a friend of Eva's, Vlad said he'd charge me only half of the market rent for the first three months of my lease.

Now, as I finished climbing the stairs to the attic, I felt elated at the thought of having a place of my own again, far away from my ghastly husband. But when Vlad unlocked the flat door, swaggered into the now-furnished living room and put my cases beside the kitchen fitments, I was dumbstruck.

Something weird had happened since the last time I'd been here.

The flat had shrunk.

I took in the main room with dismay. The pale cream two-seater sofa that Vlad had installed took up a third of the minimal floor-space, the flat-screen TV another quarter, Vlad, Fluffy and I the rest. The sloping eaves I'd thought so atmospheric on my previous visit consti- tuted so much of the ceiling that there was scarcely anywhere in the room where anyone could stand upright. I bent my head, inched past my giant landlord's massive biceps and poked my nose into the bedroom, to find that I could only just squeeze the rest of me in. With Fluffy following, I sidled past the newly installed double bed and, by standing to one side of it, managed to open the wardrobe doors. The number of rails and shelves inside it had halved. Where would I put all my clothes? I'd have to leave them in the suit- cases – except there wasn't room to lay any of them flat on the floor.

'Everything okay, love?'

'Yes,' I said, in a strangulated voice. 'Fine, thank you.'

The bedroom door swung open – or, rather, as open as it could without banging into the divan – and Vlad's large, beaming face appeared round it, like a cheerful moon. 'Got everything you need?'

'Oh, yes.' Everything except room to breathe.

'Then I leave you to settle in, innit. You want something,

you call me. I am downstairs on second floor, buggering up the wiring.'

I listened to his boots stomp down the bare treads to join his compatriots, whose hammering and banging in one of the lower flats were echoing through the house. Then I squeezed back into the living room, which seemed only slightly more roomy without Vlad in it. Fluffy sniffed round the skirting boards, as if he was trying to find a doorway to the rest of our new home. 'I'm afraid this is it,' I told him, with a lump in my throat. Feeling claustrophobic, I flung open the French windows. Cool air poured in, and the drone of heavy traffic. With Fluffy, I went out on to the three square feet of decking and peered over the low parapet. A steady line of buses and cars trundled past far below, farting purple clouds of exhaust.

My spirits plummeted, like a well-loaded Mulberry Roxanne dropped from a catwalk. I thought of my beautiful, quiet flat at the Workhouse, with its acres of space – now occupied by Mark bloody Curtis. Why, this entire flat would fit into my old bedroom, with room to spare! I hadn't so much downsized as miniaturized.

Tears of self-pity filled my eyes, but I refused to let them fall. This was a temporary measure, I reminded myself. I wasn't here on a life sentence, just until the divorce was over and the Workhouse flat was sold. Besides, there was nothing wrong with the place, other than that it was small. Tiny. Okay, minuscule. However, there must be a bright side to miniaturizing from a spacious loft into a rooftop eyrie. I ought to look on it, and not be so spoiled. I could sweep the floor simply by blowing, for instance, or clean the entire kitchen *and* the living room without moving my feet. I could do the washing-up while sitting on the sofa, and answer the front door without getting out of bed. At a pinch, I could entertain guests – and even cook for them – while I was on the lavatory. I might need to, actually, since apart from the sofa and a kitchen stool beneath the mini breakfast bar, there was nowhere else to sit down. If I found the space cramped, I'd have to take the stool out on to the balcony and hope I didn't topple over the parapet.

As for Fluffy, well, he'd be fine during the weeks he was with me. The flat was larger than the pens in boarding kennels – just. I'd take him for lots of walks. There was a small park several streets away, where he could stretch his legs. After all, he was a dog, and dogs were adaptable. As long as they were with the one they loved, they didn't care where they were or what they did. When left to their own devices, they slept most of the time.

I began to feel more positive about my new life and surroundings. As soon as I'd unpacked, fed Fluffy and made myself a cup of tea, I knew that both of us would start to feel at home. 'Come on, Fluffball, let's get going!' I said. Thinking I wanted to play, he took up an alert position at a one-metre distance, which was as far from me as the cramped space allowed. Since I'd left his toys at the Workhouse, I screwed up an old letter from Williams I found in my Downtown and threw it across the room for Fluffy to chase. Before he had a chance to move, it rebounded against the sloping eaves and landed at his feet. Head to one side, he looked at it, puzzled. I picked it up and flung it through the bedroom door. Wagging his tail and barking, Fluffy disappeared after it, and was back in front of me, holding it, in all of two seconds.

I clicked on the nineteen-inch LCD TV and tuned into one of the shopping channels, which always cheered me up when I was feeling low. While a bald male demonstrator sprayed hair volumizer on to a lank-locked, anorexic model, I opened one of the suitcases and, followed each time by Fluffy, made the first of a dozen-odd micro-treks into the bedroom laden with tops, trousers and underwear. By the time I'd put them away the wardrobe was full, the bedroom floor was covered with shoes, and I still had two more suitcases to unpack. By doubling up on coat-hangers, and cramming everything tightly on to the shelves, I managed to empty the second case. But what would I do with the contents of the third, never mind the cases?

I shoved all three into a corner of the living room, under the lowest eaves, then stood up, bumping my head. I collapsed on to the sofa, hauled Fluffy up beside me, and stared blankly at the LCD. By now the hair model resembled a stick of candy-floss, and the balding man had been joined by Yvonne, one of the channel's regular sales presenters. 'Amazing, Carlos!' she said. 'Just look how big and thick her hair is!'

'Yes, Yvonne, and with no trace of stickiness!' he intoned, running his fingers through it.

'Usually one atomizer of Ultra Lift Hair-U-Grow retails at nineteen pounds seventy-five,' said Yvonne, smiling at me, 'but today Carlos and I have an unrepeatable special offer for you, viewers. An amazing *two* atomizers of Ultra Lift Hair-U-Grow, *plus* the special

Hair-U-Grow Ultra-Volumizing Gloss Daily Shampoo *and* a full-size bottle of Hair-U-Grow Big Hair Double-Gloss Conditioner, *plus* the special Hair-U-Grow Ultra Locks Big Hair Hairbrush. This collection has a recommended retail price of one hundred and twenty-five pounds. But call in now, and the package is all yours for twenty-one pounds ninety-nine!'

I had to admit that it was a real bargain, and that Hair-U-Grow Volumizer certainly worked. But this was one product I wouldn't be buying while I was living in this attic. Big hair – big anything – was the last thing I needed.

Fluffy seemed unusually restless. He slipped off the sofa, sniffed round the kitchen units, then sat down in front of me, put a paw on my lap and whined. I extracted the small bag of his Science Diet from my third suitcase, opened up the Ikea Kitchen Startbox Vlad had left on the tiny kitchen counter, and poured some dry rubble into one of the cereal bowls. Fluffy wolfed it in fifteen seconds. Then he sat down in front of me again, and stared at me, as if to say, 'What do we do now?'

I met his puzzled expression with despair. Then a wave of raw anger washed over me – not just at Mark but at the entire male species. I was through with love! Through with romance! And, yes, I was even through with sex!

To prove it, I ran into the bedroom, emptied the contents of my Downtown on to the unmade bed, and rummaged among them for my contraceptive pills. One by one, I popped them out of their foil pack, then plopped the lot down the loo.

Back in the living room, I flung myself on to the sofa,

buried my face in the cushions and screamed, 'I hate you, Mark Curtis!' into the fire-retardant foam. 'I hate you! I hate you, you bastard! I hope you rot in hell!'

Fluffy whined in sympathy. I heaved him back on to my lap, but although I scratched his ears and stroked his head, he wouldn't settle. Jumping down on to the floor, he attempted to scratch his balls with a back leg, then trotted over to the front door and scrabbled at it.

That night I lay in bed, eyes wide open, listening to the unfamiliar noises: a drunk shouting in the street; the throb of traffic; a gush of water in the pipes as one of the downstairs tenants flushed their loo. Thoughts about the divorce circled in my head, causing waves of panic to well inside me and leaving me sweaty and breathless. Just after I'd dozed off, Fluffy woke me by jumping down from the bed and nosing open the door. I could hear him prowling the other room like a caged wild animal, his claws tapping against the laminate as he paced back and forth. From time to time he stopped and sniffed deeply at the crack under the front door, evidently searching for the scent of freedom. After a while, he came back into the bedroom, jumped up beside me and, after circling two or three times, curled into a tight, miserable ball, pressing his body into mine.

My alarm went off at six o'clock – just minutes, it seemed, since I'd fallen asleep again. My plan was to walk Fluffy for a good hour before I left for work so that he'd sleep until lunchtime when I'd rush back and take him out again, before returning to the store for the afternoon. With any luck, that would last him until I came home in the evening and could take him out a third time.

I crawled out of bed and fell into the en-suite's mini-bath. I turned on the power-shower and hot water washed over me in a healing gush. But just when I'd lathered in my Aveda, the temperature changed from hot to scalding, and then to an icy trickle. No amount of fiddling with the controls warmed it again. Gasping, I rinsed my hair as best I could, tried to restore my circulation by roughly towelling myself dry, then threw on the first garments I could winch out of the overstuffed wardrobe: a two-year-old cotton mini-dress, and a tight black leather Topshop jacket. With no time to dry my hair, I shoved my feet into espadrilles, grabbed my keys and opened the flat door. The moment I did, Fluffy was off like a greyhound from the traps, pulling me behind him. Yelping with desperation, he clattered down the stairs, stopping only to vacuum up a couple of filter-tipped fag-ends on the second-floor landing. I hissed at him to drop them, and to be quiet, but he took no notice. Alternately choking and barking, he threw himself out of the house.

It wasn't until he was christening the nearest lamppost that I realized I was wearing odd espadrilles with different height wedges. Rather than go all the way back upstairs, I limped on. By the time I'd reached the local park I could limp no further, so, like a drunken hooker after a heavy night, I threw myself down on the nearest graffiti-covered bench and, too tired to stop him, watched Fluffy root among the dog shit, used condoms and syringes that littered the patchy grass. After ten minutes or so he plonked himself in front of me, and nagged me to throw him a ball. When I failed to produce one he lay down on the path with his head between his paws, the very embodiment of disappointment.

An hour later, cold, bored, fed up and hungry, we returned to our new abode. As we approached the front steps, Fluffy pulled in the opposite direction, like he did when I took him to see the vet.

'Come on, Fluffy!' I said enthusiastically. 'It's time for breakfast!'

He dug in his heels. I pulled on the leash. He planted his bottom on the pavement and glared at me. 'What's the matter?' I asked him. He lowered his head and growled. 'Well, it's tough,' I told him firmly. 'There's no point in making a fuss. This is your new home. Our new home. And we'll get used to it.' He turned away his head, indicating that he, for one, had no intention of doing so.

'Come on, get up!' I gave the leash another tug, but Fluffy wouldn't move. 'Please don't be difficult!' I begged. 'I can't take it this morning.' Instead of responding, he rolled his eyes reproachfully, showing the bloodshot whites.

I opened the front door, then went back down the stoop, picked Fluffy up, and hauled him over the threshold. By a mixture of cajoling and sheer force, I dragged him upstairs. By now I was desperate for a coffee, but I didn't even have a jar of instant, let alone milk, in the place.

I banished from my mind the memory of the frothy cappuccino with which Mark used to wake me every morning.

He was never going to make me cry again.

Twenty

Later that morning, puffy-eyed and anxious, I slumped in one of our changing rooms while a handsome woman stood in front of the floor-to-ceiling wall-size mirror in her Janet Reger slip. She examined her reflection with a critical eye, then ran a hand through her straight, dark, bobbed hair; the grey roots were in need of touching up.

'Oh, Annie,' she sighed, 'I look awful today.'

'No, you don't, Mrs Barclay.'

'Yes, I do.' She corrected the strap of her bra, which had fallen over her left shoulder, and adjusted her slip. 'My body's falling to pieces.'

'Well, we'll just have to stick it together again, won't we?' I said as cheerfully as I could, and handed her one of our in-house white cotton kimonos to slip on.

Though she didn't spend a fortune when she came in, fifty-four-year-old Marion Barclay was perhaps my favourite client. A civil servant at the Home Office, married to a university professor, she'd first visited us four years before after she'd had a mastectomy. During a course of chemotherapy, she'd lost most of her hair, and with it her self-confidence. She'd just been invited to her god-daughter's smart wedding, and she'd been dreading it. To her, it wasn't going to be a celebration but an ordeal to be got through – just like the chemo, she'd said. 'I can't stomach the thought of everyone thinking I'm destined for the knackers' yard,' she'd confided in me and Eileen Grey. 'I want to look presentable. And like I'm here to stay.' In her mind's eye she'd pictured herself in a plain, well-cut dress in which she'd blend into the background.

However, after searching the designer floor on her behalf, I'd come back with a long-sleeved, brightly printed Emilio Pucci dress from his Fall 2003 ready-to-wear collection. Made of soft silk jersey, it was covered with a bold, eye-catching, red, white and grey geometric design. 'I'm not wearing that!' Mrs Barclay had exclaimed. 'You must be out of your mind! It's far too bright and flashy!' But once I'd persuaded her to try it on – after all, what was the harm in that? – and shown her how to wrap the matching scarf round her head in a kind of turban, she'd been sold on it. 'I'm amazed! It really suits me!' she'd said. Although she'd never spent more than a hundred pounds on a dress before, she'd bought the Pucci, saying, with dark humour, that if her husband complained about her extravagance she'd remind him that it might be the last time she'd go clothes shopping.

As it turned out, it hadn't been. Four years on, Mrs Barclay's cancer was in remission, her hair had regrown and she was now a loyal customer who came to see me once or twice a year – whenever she needed something for a special occasion. Today, although it was June and the sales were about to start, she was looking for a suit: she had to go to a job interview at the end of August. 'None of those big prints, or garish colours you usually put me in, Annie,' she said firmly. 'This time I want to look efficient. I'd almost say severe. Businesslike and understated.'

'We don't have much as it's the end of the season, but I'm sure we can find something to make you look just that, perhaps in Armani. What job is it?'

She gave me a measured look. 'I'm not sure I'm going to tell you. I don't know what you'd think of it.'

'That sounds intriguing.'

'Well, let's say it's something in my usual area, which is law and order – but outside Whitehall this time. And quite a departure for me, in that I'd be dealing directly with people, rather than paper-shuffling. After twenty-two years as a bureaucrat, I've had just about enough of sitting at a desk all day.'

'Would you like a trouser or skirt suit? You have such lovely slender ankles, it seems a pity not to show them. Because, of course, if you're buying a good suit you want to be able to wear it on other occasions. In fact, it should last you for years. And with a bit of dressing up or down – with the right top and accessories – it will take you anywhere from the interview to the smartest dinner party.'

'I'm not sure my ankles will be a help in this case,' she said, 'but see what you can find.'

'I'm just going downstairs,' I told Eva, who was at the reception desk. 'Keep an eye on things for a few minutes, will you?'

'Sure, Annie.' Eva pushed her long blonde hair behind her tiny ears and looked at me curiously. 'Was everything all right at the flat last night?'

'Fine, thanks. Why?'

She frowned. 'I hope you don't mind me saying so, but you look a little frazzled. Could you do with some help this morning? Would you like me to go downstairs and find an outfit for Mrs Barclay? I know this must be a difficult time for you.'

I felt quite choked by her concern. 'Thanks for asking, Eva, but I'd rather keep busy.'

Taking one of our portable dress rails with me, I rode the goods lift down to the first floor where I headed towards the MaxMara and Armani concessions in search of some size 42 suits, picking out the odd blouse and jacket from other designers' sale rails on the way. Walking round the store and knowing what was in stock was as much a part of my day-to-day job as dealing with customers. Consequently everyone who worked at Haines and Hampton, from the buyers to the restaurant staff, knew who I was, and I was on first-name terms with most of them. As usual, a chorus of good mornings greeted me, but I barely heard them. It was now almost midday and, after a virtually sleepless night, I hadn't had time for so much as a sandwich.

On autopilot, I entered the Armani outlet, where I told Antonella, the Italian assistant, what I was looking for. But as we sorted through the racks of clothes, my mind was in the flat with Fluffy. Was he distressed all alone, I wondered, as I selected a shirt and hung it on my rail.

'This suit here, the cut is *bellissimo*,' Antonella said, 'but we only have it in cream, in a thirty-eight.'

'Great.' Perhaps Fluffy thought that I was never coming back. Perhaps he was desperate for a pee. If I left the store as soon as I'd finished with Mrs Barclay and grabbed a taxi, I should be at the flat by twelve forty-five to take him out for another walkies.

'And I have this model, with the slightly narrower lapels, and wide-legged trousers . . .'

'Terrific.' Fluffy might be fine in the flat without me. He was probably fast asleep and perfectly happy. But what if something had happened to him? I picked out a couple of blouses and hung them on my rail, then pulled it across to MaxMara. Suddenly I remembered all the shoes I hadn't been able to fit into the wardrobe. They were lying in piles beside my bed. Fluffy would have found them by now, and destroyed most of them. Ruined shoes I could live with – even ruined Jimmy Choos – but what if Fluffy had swallowed a buckle and choked on it? This was likely, given his penchant for destroying things. I'd probably return home to find him stretched out on the floor, dead, in a pile of leather straps and vomit.

I stared at my dress rail, and my mind went blank. Suddenly I couldn't remember for whom I was shopping, what size she was, or for what occasion she wanted something.

'Annie, are you all right?' Justine, the department's manageress, asked.

'I think so. I want a dress, Justine. Or maybe it was a suit. You'd better give me both. Suitable for a dinner party. Or work. Look, give me anything.'

'Anything?'

'Yes, in a size 40. No, I think it was a 38. And as fast as you can, please.'

With apocalyptic visions of Fluffy playing in my head, I ran towards the lift and waited impatiently for it to arrive. It was only when I'd ridden it up to the second floor, that I realized I'd left the rail behind.

While Eva went to retrieve it, I shut myself into my office. Lined from floor to ceiling with white-painted MDF shelving that overflowed with designer brochures, old fashion magazines, odd accessories, dusty shoeboxes and swatches of cloth, this was little more than a converted, windowless store-cupboard, as messy and full of junk as the public areas of the personal shopping department were minimalist and clutter-free. I sat down at my desk, rummaged in my bag for my BlackBerry and phoned Vlad.

'Ah, Annie! I am just thinking of you!' he said cheerfully.

'Why? Is there a problem?'

'No, no problem! I am in house, making it beautiful for you! As I promise you, the lift engine it come today. I set to work installing it pronto. But . . . big, big but, I am afraid – big butt like fat American tourist ass, geddit? – there is missing part. I am sick as a dead parrot. Sod's fucking law, innit. So, I have telephoned manufacturers and I, like, read Riot Act. I say, "Send me parts express post, Nazi bastards, or I come over there and sort you out good and proper." To what I owe the pleasure, love?'

'I was just wondering if Fluffy was all right. You know, my dog.'

'Ah! Well, when I come in this morning, he was barking good and proper. Tenant downstairs, he even complain to me.'

'Oh, God, did he?'

'I tell him, "Fucking hell, he's guard dog, mate, he keep burglars away. You should be grateful. Like having free Chubb Alarm and Securicor." Anyway, for last hour or so, Fluffy is not barking no more.'

'What? Not at all?'

'He is – how you say? – silent as the grave, innit.'

I was about to call a minicab and rush home when Eva stuck her head round the office door.

'Sorry to disturb you, Annie, but I took the clothes in to Mrs Barclay, and she's trying them on now. There seems to be a problem. I'm afraid I might have brought up the wrong rail.'

I hurried back into the changing room to find Mrs Barclay in a lime-green shirt in a retro floral print that not only did nothing for her but was blatantly unsuitable for her to wear at an interview. She was also in the process of trying to squeeze her ample hips into a pair of tiny low-cut trousers.

'I'm devastated, Annie.' She sighed, as she attempted to yank the waistband over her bottom. 'I hadn't realized I'd put on so much weight.'

Twenty-one

What with having to reassure Mrs Barclay that she was the same size as ever, and that it was my fault for bringing her outfits which were much too small for her; and what with having to go down to the Armani concession again, to choose more appropriate suits in Mrs Barclay's right size; and what with persuading Mrs Barclay that the navy blue suit with slightly puffed shoulders and pencil skirt I had subsequently picked out for her, teamed with a cream silk Burberry shirt, was so versatile it was worth six hundred and seventy pounds; and what with waiting while Inez, our alterations lady, pinned up the skirt and shaved a third of an inch off the sleeves of the jacket; and what with promising Mrs Barclay that, when the outfit came back from being altered, I'd keep it for her to pick up when she came back from the long summer holiday she was taking; well, what with all that, I didn't leave the store until past one.

So by the time I got back to Fulham, I was almost hysterical. As was Fluffy, who'd spent the morning trying to scratch his way through the flat's front door and chewing up the kitten-heeled ankle boots I'd worn on the day Mark had proposed to me.

I returned to Haines and Hampton at around two thirty, bowed down under the weight of a massive red canvas super-sized handbag. Manny, the doorman on duty at the main entrance, winked as I got out of my cab.

'What 'ave you got in there, Annie?' he asked, jerking his chin at it. 'A double bed? Mind if I join you in it?'

I grimaced at his terrible joke – it wasn't the first time I'd heard it since big bags had become a hot fashion trend, and I knew it wouldn't be the last. Leaning heavily to one side, I dragged it past the sign that said 'No Dogs', and through the revolving doors. Instead of stopping to chat with the sales assistants in the cosmetics department, I made my way straight to the customer lifts, and waited for one to come up from the basement. When the steel doors slid open, who should be standing inside it but the store's owner, George Haines. Just my luck.

'Ah, Annie!' He beamed at me. 'What a nice surprise!'

Instead of getting in beside him, I took a step back. 'Mr Haines!'

'Come in, come in.'

'Oh, I . . .' I racked my brain for an excuse to run away, but I couldn't think of one so I prayed for the steel doors to slide shut and whip him out of sight. After what seemed like a hundred years, but was probably more like three milliseconds, they began to close, but George put his finger on the button. They stopped midway, then slid apart again.

'Hurry up, dear,' he said, with a small frown. 'Mustn't keep the customers waiting, must we?' There was no way to get out of it, so I gritted my teeth and went in. 'Second floor, I suppose?'

'Please,' I squeaked. He pressed a button, and the doors slid shut, trapping us together. A flush rose up my torso, and gathered in a swimming-pool of sweat between my breasts. I felt as guilty as a drug smuggler cornered with a stash of heroin by a Customs officer at Heathrow. As gently as I could, I rested my bag between my legs on the floor, coughing to cover the scuffle that issued from inside it. I fanned myself with my hands. 'Gosh, it's hot, isn't it?'

'Actually, I find the air-conditioning a little chilly.' He stared curiously at the bag sandwiched between my trembling knees. Against all known laws of gravity, my stomach lurched into my throat. 'Now, I know I'm an old stick-in-the-mud,' George muttered, 'but, really, that handbag's almost as big as the trunk I used to take to boarding-school!' I pulled my lips into a watery smile. 'I'm afraid this trend for oversized handbags is one fashion too far for me,' he went on. 'How on earth do you women carry them around all day?'

'Oh, we manage! You know what they say – one has to suffer to be beautiful.'

'But why on earth would you want such a bag? What are they *for*? What do you put in them?'

'Oh, all sorts of things!'

'May I?' Without waiting for me to say yes, George grabbed the bag's handles. 'Good Lord! I can scarcely pick it up! Is this one of ours?'

'Mmm.' I cleared my throat loudly, then babbled on, 'It's a last season Orla Kiely. The accessories department sold lots of them. Here, let me take it from you before you hurt yourself.'

'Do you know,' George mused, 'I'm beginning to think we should stick up some sort of disclaimer or health warning downstairs. "Big Bags May Harm Your Health".

That sort of thing. After all, we don't want to be sued. Perhaps I'll have a word with the buyers.'

'Brilliant idea!' As the doors opened at the second floor, I practically fell over in my rush to get out. ''Bye, Mr Haines,' I called over my shoulder, as the doors closed on him. Phew! Though I was a dyed-in-the wool atheist, I thanked God for saving me. And to show Him how grateful I was, I swore that from now on I'd always pay over the odds for my weekly copy of the *Big Issue*, I'd sign up with every chugger who stopped me in the street and I'd never tell lies again.

But I wasn't home and dry yet. I had the rest of the day to get through. Hoisting my bag over my shoulder and humming to cover the grunts now coming from inside it, I made my way through Casualwear and into the lobby of the personal-shopping suite, where Charlotte was rearranging the long-stemmed white roses that always graced her desk.

'Good afternoon, Annie. How are you?'

'Same as I was an hour ago, thanks, Charlotte. Is Eva around?'

'She's currently with a client. You know, Su Lee Somethingorother? The businesswoman from Shanghai who comes in every now and then?' Her eyes lit on my bag. 'Hey, isn't that last season's Orla Kiely?'

'Very observant of you.'

'What *have* you got in there? It looks like it's moving!'

'It's a handbag gremlin,' I quipped. 'Haven't you heard? They're the latest thing in Milan.' She laughed uneasily, unsure whether or not I was joking. 'Look, when Eva's finished with her client, ask her to come and see me in my office, will you? But please don't let anyone else disturb me – and that includes you, I'm afraid. I'm going to be up to my eyeballs.' There went my promise to God never to lie again. It was a good thing I didn't believe in Him or I'd be done for.

'Sure. Have a nice –'

'Please don't say it, Charlotte!' I interrupted her. 'Because I'm not.'

Once in my office, I put down my bag and unzipped it. The handbag gremlin stuck his head out of the top. As he struggled to get his legs out, I unwrapped the silky scarf I'd tied round his muzzle to stop him barking as I brought him into the store. 'Ssh! Don't you dare make a sound,' I whispered. He shook himself violently, put his paws on my lap and licked my hands to show how grateful he was not to have been left behind in Fulham. I told him to be a good boy and, praying he'd stay silent, made him sit under my desk. Wonder of wonders, he did exactly as I asked. I turned to my computer, clicked on to my email, and stared blankly at the endless list of new ones that flashed up on the screen: one from the Prada press office, another from George's PA, two or three from clients, and 167 offering me cut-price Viagra, penile extensions, breast reductions, or '45 tips for Orgasm'.

As I set about deleting the spam, which was about all I was fit to do, Fluffy reached his boredom threshold, got to his feet and set about exploring my office. I watched nervously as he sniffed the stack of old *Vogue*s and *Tatler*s piled in one corner, crawled through the concertina files of press cuttings on the floor, then stuck his pointed nose into my overflowing wastepaper basket, from which he retrieved a screwed-up Cadbury's Fruit and Nut wrapper, which still had vestiges of chocolate in it.

Holding it between his front paws, he settled down to cleanse it, while I watched him closely, ready to throw myself on top of him if he so much as whimpered. Suddenly he tried to swallow the wrapper and choked. I got down on my hands and knees, and, while he growled at me, I prised apart his jaws and attempted to fish the slimy thing out of his throat. When his concentration lapsed, I managed to get it. I deposited it in my desk drawer. Thinking that this was a game, Fluffy sat to attention by my chair, fixed me with his beady eyes and gave a single bark. 'Shut up!' I hissed. 'No dogs are allowed in this building! You'll get me into terrible trouble if you make a noise!'

But it was too late. A moment later there was a knock at my door. 'Yes?' I called out.

'It's just me,' said Charlotte's voice. 'Are you all right, Annie?'

'Yes, thank you.'

'It's just that – well, I could swear I just heard a funny noise coming from your office.'

Just then, Fluffy gave another short sharp bark. I put my hand round his muzzle. 'You mean *that*?' I said. 'It's my smoker's cough.'

'I didn't know you had one. In fact, I didn't even know you smoked, Annie.'

'I don't.' Oh, God, what was I saying? 'I mean, I didn't. I started the other week. Okay?'

'Sure.' There was a long silence. I thought Charlotte might have gone away. But when I put my ear to the door, I heard her breathing. 'I know it's none of my business,

Annie,' her voice boomed, 'but it's awfully silly of you to begin smoking now. I was reading an article about it in *Cosmo* last month. Do you know it gives you deep lines round your lips?'

'Yes, thank you, Charlotte. I am aware of that.'

I could see that Fluffy was about to bark again, so I gave an ostentatious cough myself and handed him back the chocolate wrapper. He pounced on it, and lay down with it between his paws, ready to devour it. I coughed again. I prayed that Charlotte had finished lecturing me and gone back to Reception. But no such luck.

'Annie?'

'Yes?'

'Look, I know you said you didn't want to be disturbed . . .'

'That's right.'

'But . . . May I make you some herbal tea? Or ordinary tea? Or a coffee? Would you like me to pop out and get you some cough medicine or something?'

'That's very sweet of you, Charlotte. You're very thoughtful. But no, thanks, I'm fine, really I am.'

Once he'd eaten the Fruit and Nut wrapper, Fluffy got to his feet again and set about another seek-and-destroy mission. This time his prey was a pair of opaque black Lycra tights that had once been used in the changing rooms and had festered on one of the lower shelves in the office ever since. Sod it, I thought, and let him get on with it. He'd chewed up enough pairs before for me to know they wouldn't kill him.

I jumped at a brisk double knock on the door. 'Yes?' I called suspiciously.

'Annie?'

It was Eva. I knew there was no point in hiding the truth from her because, unlike Charlotte, she was far too bright not to guess it and, besides, ever since I'd given her a job she'd been 100 per cent loyal to me. 'Hold on a sec,' I called. I grabbed Fluffy's collar and opened the door a crack. When she squeezed through and saw him, her blue eyes opened wide, and she shut the door quickly behind her. 'Oh, Annie, what have you done?' she whispered, squatting to let Fluffy throw himself at her – he liked nothing better than an appreciative audience, and seemed to know that he'd found a new admirer.

'I had to bring him with me, Eva. He was going crazy shut up alone in the attic.'

'But how did you get him past Security?'

I pointed at my Orla Kiely, and we giggled, me rather nervously. 'And guess what? I came up in the customer lift with George – he didn't notice. We'll have to keep Fluffy secret. In fact, you're the only person who knows he's here.'

'Of course.' She stood up, and brushed dog hairs off her skirt. 'Look, can I borrow you for a few minutes?'

I glanced at Fluffy, who was scrabbling at her skirt. 'Can't it wait?'

She shook her head. 'I've got a client who's torn between two dresses, which both look great on her. I thought you might be able to advise her which she'd find most useful.'

I knew I had to go, but how could I keep Fluffy quiet in my absence? A quick root around in my desk drawer unearthed an old Digestive biscuit, which I sealed in one

241

envelope, then another, which I dropped on to the floor for him – getting at it would hopefully keep him amused for a few minutes. Then, shutting the door firmly behind me and feeling sick with worry, I followed Eva into one of the changing rooms. Several minutes later, my distracted conversation with her client was interrupted by a loud shriek, and Charlotte rushed in, her face pale.

'Annie!' she gasped. 'Excuse me . . . I'm sorry to bother you but . . . It's your handbag gremlin – it's escaped!'

'I don't know what to do about this, Annie.'

Half an hour later I was in George Haines's private office, as shame-faced as I had been on the day when Miss Robinson, my old headmistress, had chastised me and Clarissa for letting a colony of ants escape from the glass observatory in our school biology lab. It had been our responsibility that week to feed the creepy-crawlies their diet of water and honey, and since we were equally squeamish we'd done it in so much of a hurry that we'd forgotten to replug their waterhole with cotton wool. By the following day, there hadn't been a single ant left in the formicarium, as the disgusting earth-filled glass box was officially called, and a thin trail of sandy soil stretched all the way to the opposite end of the dissection counter, down the side of which the ants had made their getaway. Six months later the entire building had had to be treated for serious ant infestation. Dad and Clarissa's parents had been made to foot the bill.

Unlike the ants, which had taken half a year to resur-face, Fluffy had reappeared after only ten minutes. Leaving a trail of surprised customers and staff behind him, he'd raced from Personal Shopping to Lingerie, where he'd charged through the changing rooms, bringing down the curtains and emerging garlanded with a size 32D La Perla Black Label Pizzo balcony bra. Towing this expensive trophy, he'd bounded back towards my office, stopping only to christen the reception desk with his own holy water.

'I'm truly sorry, Mr Haines,' I grovelled. 'I don't know what got into Fluffy. He's never been dirty inside a building before.'

'He shouldn't have been here in the first place!' George glowered at me from under the grey arches of his well-groomed eyebrows. 'You've worked here long enough to know our policy on dogs, Annie. They are not allowed in the store at all, unless they're guide dogs or – what are they called? – hearing dogs. Haines and Hampton is not the place for pets, as that animal . . .' he jabbed a finger at Fluffy who, firmly attached to his leash, was now sitting penitently beside me '. . . has just proved. Why, even the Queen leaves her Corgis at the palace when she comes in to buy her Christmas presents! I'd have thought that you, of all people, would have realized that a department store of our stature has a certain reputation to maintain.'

'Of course I do!'

George banged his fist on his desk. 'A wild animal running amok in the lingerie changing rooms! It's just not on! As for the way you brought him into the store – smuggled him in under my nose! Well, do I have to tell you that I don't like sneaky behaviour?'

'You're right. I'm not going to try to excuse myself. I was caught on the hop.'

'Well, it's most unprofessional. I'm surprised at you! Surprised and, I have to say, very disappointed, Annie,' he went on. 'Whatever induced you to act in such a foolish way?'

'It was . . . an emergency.' Though I'd always kept my love-life, or lack of it, well out of the office and had never discussed anything personal with George, I'd always looked on him as a somewhat fatherly figure and was overcome with the desire to tell him everything. Surely he'd understand if he knew what I was going through. And if he did, maybe he'd even let me bring Fluffy in to work with me sometimes. 'The thing is, Mr Haines, Mark and I are splitting up.'

'Mark?' George had been at my wedding lunch at the Ivy, but I could see he was struggling to put a face to the name. At last he nodded. 'Oh, yes, I remember. He wore shorts to the Christmas party last year, didn't he?'

'Yes. We're getting divorced at the moment.'

'Well, I'm sorry to hear that. But what's that got to do with the dog?'

I started to explain the dreadful Fluffy custody battle and gave up at the look of mystification on George's face. 'Look, what can I say?' I said lamely. 'I know I shouldn't have smuggled Fluffy in, but I did and I'm sorry. Naturally I'll pay for the carpet cleaning and the La Perla bra. Unfortunately he seems to like nice lingerie.'

George's lips twitched. 'Okay, Annie,' he said. 'I'll let it go this time. But I expect more from my staff – especially you, one of my – up to this point – most trusted employees.'

By now I was close to tears. 'I give you my solemn word it won't happen again.'

But I think both of us suspected it would.

Twenty-two

That night, unable to work out how to use the microwave, I sat up in bed eating cold soup out of a carton and had a good moan to Clarissa on my BlackBerry. Fluffy was flat out on the floor beside me. His outing to Haines and Hampton, combined with the walk back to Fulham after we'd been sent home in disgrace, had exhausted both of us. He'd fallen asleep immediately after I'd fed him, and hadn't moved an inch since. But although I felt equally tired, I couldn't stop churning over the events of the last twenty-four hours.

'You can't imagine how awful it was,' I confided between icy spoonfuls of leek and potato soup. 'At one point I thought George was going to sack me.'

'I'm sure he couldn't do that, darling,' her soothing social-worker voice purred. 'Not for one little misdemeanour. There is such a thing as employment legislation, you know. You've worked at Haines and Hampton for ever, and he'd have to give you a proper warning first.'

'Well, he just did.'

'Oh dear. I'm surprised he didn't see the funny side. It's hysterical about that La Perla. Fluffy's certainly developed expensive tastes since his humble beginnings in Camden Town.'

'I don't think you're taking this seriously enough, Clarissa. I need my job. I'd be lost without it. Besides, if

I'm not earning anything, how on earth am I going to pay for this mini-flat I'm stuck in, let alone keep up the mortgage payments on the Workhouse *and* pay Williams? Not to mention that bloody solicitor I told Mark to hire at my expense!'

'Honestly, Annie, you must have been out of your mind to do that.'

'You're not kidding. But at the time Mark and I were still on good terms – well, relatively good – and it seemed only fair. How was I to know he'd use her to take Fluffy from me?'

'Can't you get out of paying?'

'I suppose I could. But it might antagonize Mark even more.'

'Have you lost something up that nostril, Rebecca?' Clarissa suddenly said off-telephone. 'If not, take your finger out. Sorry, Annie. Look, do you think it might have been a mistake to move out of the Workhouse? Couldn't you go back?'

'No, I could not!' I dumped the now empty soup carton on the bedside table. A millisecond later Fluffy woke up, jumped up and grabbed it. 'Put that down, Fluffy!' I said, as he balanced it between his paws and set about destroying it.

'What's he doing?'

'Finishing off my soup – carton and all. Honestly, Clarissa, he's become so disobedient in the last forty-eight hours. I don't know what's got into him!'

'He might be upset at having his life turned upside down.'

'Great. Something else for me to feel bad about.'

Clarissa's sigh whistled through the earpiece. 'Look, darling, it might be awful, still sharing with Mark, but at least Fluffy'd have some continuity, and Mark could take care of him while you're at work. Stop that, Rebecca!'

'That's all Mark's ever been good for, isn't it? Dog-sitting!' I said, with disgust.

'I wouldn't say that,' Clarissa said, after a short pause.

'Oh? What *would* you say, then?'

'Well,' she went on cautiously, 'you were happy with him once upon a time, you know. Very happy, actually.'

'Thanks for reminding me. Before the bastard started shagging other women, you mean.'

'Yes, well, there was that.'

It was my turn to sigh. 'I couldn't carry on sharing the flat with him. You don't know what it's like living with someone you loathe and who loathes you. Not that this is turning out to be much better. I don't see how I'm going to juggle work with looking after Fluffy on the weeks I have him. There simply aren't enough hours in the day.'

'Tell me about it. I've got four children. Actually, there'll be three in a minute. Rebecca!'

'But, Mum!' cried a high-pitched voice, 'Daddy says that everyone picks their nose!'

'Yes. But in private. And definitely *not* at the kitchen table. It's bloody hard for you, Annie,' Clarissa went on, back with me again. 'Have you ...' she hesitated a moment. '... have you considered that Mark might be right?'

'Right?' I laughed. 'About what?'

'Well. You may not like me saying this, darling, but perhaps, under the circumstances, he *is* the best person to have custody of Fluffy.' Clarissa must have heard my gasp of disbelief, because she added, 'In the short term, I mean. Things being as they are at the moment.'

'Things only *are* as they *are* because that lazy bastard doesn't have a job!' I spat into my phone. 'He doesn't have to work, does he, because I'm still subsidizing him, aren't I? And at this rate I will be for the rest of my life!'

'I know that but –'

'But *what*, Clarissa?' I couldn't believe what I was hearing – and from my best friend. 'Don't tell me you're taking Mark's side? Because if you are, I'll never forgive you!'

'Don't be an idiot, Annie. I'm not taking anyone's side!'

'Well, you should be!' I wailed. 'Mine!'

'Darling, of course I'm with you, you know I am. I just think that . . . well, that there might be a teeny bit of sense in what Mark's proposing.'

I felt irrational anger well up in me. I picked up a Biro, which was lying on the duvet, and chewed hard on the end of its barrel.

'I mean,' Clarissa went on, 'be honest. If Fluffy did live with Mark during the week, and you had him every Sunday, wouldn't that be easier for you?'

'Clarissa!'

'Darling,' she added hurriedly, 'I'm only thinking of you, and of Fluffy's well-being.'

I took the pen out of my mouth for a moment and said, 'Well, I think about that, too. That's what this whole damn custody business is about!'

There was a short pause. Then Clarissa said quietly, 'Is it, Annie?'

The plastic barrel splintered between my teeth. 'What do you mean?' I demanded.

'Out of here, Becky! No buts, I said out! I'm trying to have a private conversation with my friend. Yes, I know Annie's your friend, too, but she was mine first. And close the door behind you, please. Hey, I didn't say slam it! Look,' she went on, as I fished sharp fragments of plastic out of my mouth, 'don't hate me for saying this, but do you think – just perhaps – you and Mark might be using Fluffy as a means of getting at each other?'

'Well, he's certainly using him to get at me!' I protested. 'Though God knows why. What have I ever done to Mark, except be nice to him?'

'And?'

'And what?'

'What about you?'

'What about me?' I saw I'd bitten right through the Biro's plastic ink tube. 'Are you saying that I'm using Fluffy to get at Mark?' I asked, as I climbed off the bed, stepped into the bathroom and examined my reflection in the mirror. There was a big blue mark on my lips. I tried to rub it off with a towel, but only succeeded in spreading it.

'I'm not saying that you *are*, darling. I'm just posing the question.'

'Do you really think I'd do something as dreadful as that?' I shouted, as I threw myself back on to the bed. Clarissa didn't answer. 'You obviously do,' I went on huffily.

'I think you're very angry with him. And rightly so, of course. I just wonder if that might be clouding your judgement when it comes to Fluffy's best interest. I mean, his best interest at the moment.'

'I can't believe you're saying all this, Clarissa, when you're my closest friend.'

I heard her take a deep breath. 'Darling, I'm saying it *because* I'm your closest friend. Because I love you.' Suddenly I felt like weeping. 'And, frankly, I'm worried about you,' she went on. 'This battle over Fluffy – look what it's doing to you!'

'*It's* not doing anything to me. Mark bloody Curtis is!'

'Whatever. One way or another, trying to get custody of Fluffy is taking you over. It's beginning to obsess you.'

'It's hardly surprising, is it?' I said. 'Don't you understand, Clarissa? Mark's already taken practically everything away from me – my life, my future, my home. Not to mention my faith in my own judgement. I mean, I married the man, didn't I? Well, he's bloody well not going to take Fluffy from me, too! I'm not going to disappear from his life like my bloody –' My tirade came to an abrupt halt as I heard the words coming out of my mouth.

'Annie?' Clarissa asked, after a minute. 'What were you going to say?' She knew, because when I didn't answer she said softly, 'You're not your mother, darling. You're not walking out on Fluffy. And he's not a child.' I burst into tears. 'Oh, I'm sorry!' Clarissa said, in her most soothing voice. 'Darling, I didn't mean to upset you! But, look, if you can't take Fluffy into work again, and he can't stay at home alone, how on earth are you going to look after him during the weeks he's with you?'

'I don't know!' I sobbed. 'I'll have to manage somehow. It's impossibly hard, juggling work and looking after a dog. How on earth do single mothers manage with their children?'

'Mostly by working in low-paid part-time jobs, and basing their hours round their kids,' she said, becoming the know-it-all social worker. 'Alternatively, they pay a child-minder.'

We fell silent. Then we both exclaimed in unison, 'Oh, for God's sake!'

'I just need a new dog-walker, don't I?' I sniffed.

'But do yourself a favour, Annie. This time hire a woman. One who won't cause you any grief.'

I promised I would.

Twenty-three

'These letters, here, are references from all the owners of the dogs I'm, like, walking at the moment, right? I can give you their mobile numbers if you want to call them up and check on me. They won't mind, because they've all, like, become *really* close friends of mine. And these are references from the owners of the dogs I *used* to take out, if you want to read them. You probably can't be bothered, but you really should because they're incredibly amazing.'

The diminutive, dark-haired Darcie Wells, dog-walker to the cream of Fulham's canines, threw her references on to my sofa, then reached down and unzipped the rucksack that was lying beside her tiny, trainer-clad feet. I'd found her number by Googling 'Fulham, dog, walker' and 'reliable'. Then I'd called her between meetings, explained I had a slight problem, and that evening she'd rushed round to my flat.

'Hold on, Annie.' She rummaged among the scrunched-up plastic bags now spilling out of her rucksack. 'I really want to show you something. Where's my Sony? God, there's so much crap in here! I don't mean literally. Although I do pick it up, of course, that's what the bags are for – it's part of the service. Ah, here it is. Look! Aaah! That's Brandy on the screensaver. She's mine. I left her at home tonight because she got the runs really badly while we were in the park today. I didn't think you'd want me to bring her up in case Fluffy caught it.'

'Well, under the circumstances . . .'

'She's a Newfoundland–standard poodle cross,' Darcie interrupted me. With a petite pink hand, which boasted shell-like, well-scrubbed fingernails and a plethora of silver dolphin rings, she pushed her shoulder-length curls behind her tiny ears. A beaming smile lit her heart-shaped face as she gazed at the screen of her phone. 'I call her my Noodle, as in Labradoodle? She's *sooo* the best dog in the world. She comes out with me twice a day, because she *adores* being with the other dogs!'

'So, how much do you –'

'Somewhere in the memory there're some of the photos I took yesterday in Richmond Park. Ah, found them! See the boxer sniffing Brandy's bum? That's Max. He lives in Chelsea Harbour. His owner's a lawyer. A lesbian lawyer, actually. Says Max is the only man in her life. He's not gay, though – he can't keep his paws off Brandy. Follows her everywhere and always has to sit beside her in the van. He's, like, 'Helloo, keep away from her, you other guys, she's my bitch!' to the other dogs. It's *sooo* sweet! The springer spaniel there is Fanny. She belongs to an actress who's having an affair with some Conservative MP. It's all very hush-hush, actually, because he thinks he might lose his job as shadow minister of – Oops, I almost gave it away! You have to be very discreet in my job, y'know? My clients often confide in me – did I tell you most of them have become really good friends?'

'Yes, you –'

'I just know Fluffy's going to fit in *really* well. Especially with my afternoon dogs – if you want me to take him out then? You'll really like that, won't you, sweetie? Oh, my *God*!' she screeched, as Fluffy stuck his nose into the crotch of her skinny jeans. 'You can smell the bacon, can't you? You clever boy! I always keep treats in my jeans pockets, Annie, because I know my dogs'll come racing back when I call them. In fact, I just can't keep them away from me! I practically get raped every day! They're all like, "Hey, Darcie, gimme, gimme, gimmee!" Can I give him some bacon now, Annie?'

'Actually he's only just eaten and –'

'Just one little piece? So we'll be friends? I know there's some left in here somewhere.' She lifted her pert bottom off the sofa and stuck her hand into one of her back pockets, from which she extracted a greasy plastic bag. 'Here we are. Sit! Sit! Good boy!' Tail wagging, Fluffy darted forward, and snapped up the tiny morsel of dried-up meat she held out to him. 'Hey,' she laughed, 'you nearly got my finger there! You and I are going to be good mates, aren't we, Fluffy?' she continued, scratching his ears. 'You're going to be, like, "Wow, I'm having the best time ever on my walkies, Mum!" when you see Annie in the evenings, aren't you? You'll be best friends with all my doggies. See? He likes me already. I have a real connection with dogs, you know. In fact, some of the other dog-walkers call me the Dog Whisperer. Just like Cesar? You know the Dog Whisperer? I could do what he does, easily.'

She slipped from the sofa on to the laminate floor, the better to connect with Fluffy on an eye-to-eye level. She let him straddle her short slim legs, plant his front paws on the voluptuous breasts that threatened to burst out from under her shrunken green dog-hair-flecked T-shirt, and lick her face.

After a moment she turned towards me, one cheek glistening. 'So, what's with your situation then, Annie?'

'My situation?'

Darcie pointed to the open suitcase lying in the corner. 'It looks like you've just moved in.'

'Oh. Yes.'

'Nice builder, by the way. I *sooo* fancy those biceps.'

'You mean Vlad.'

'Is that his name? Is he single? Don't you think he's, like, "ooh, come and get me, baby"?'

'To tell the truth I'm not interested in men at the moment,' I confessed.

'Tell me about them!' Suddenly Darcie's brow clouded. 'They're fucking awful, the lot of them! I've tried everything to find a decent bloke. Speed-dating. Blind dating. Internet dating. I even put an ad in *Time Out*. You can't imagine what a load of wankers I've met. I met one guy on match.com last year. He seemed to be reasonable at first, but in the end it didn't work out because he didn't get on with Brandy. He was, like, "Hey, can't you kick that bloody dog off the bed while we're shagging?" I don't know what it was with him. One minute he was all over me, the next he was, like, "See ya, babe!" I mean, *hellooo*?'

'Actually, I'm getting divorced at the moment.'

'I knew it!' Darcie slapped her thigh. 'I sensed there was something up with you the moment I walked in. You see, I'm really good at reading auras. And do you know what? I could see this charcoal-grey cloud hovering over your head. That's depression. And a bit of viridian floating round your shoulders, which means you're weighed down by stress. Fluffy, now, he's like pure red, which indicates high energy and a healthy sex drive. As for me, I used to be dark brown – which is unenlightened – but now I'm a rainbow, which is a star person, with a strong blue-green bias because I'm good at spiritual healing. So, how is it? The divorce, I mean.'

'Pretty ghastly. My husband's trying to get custody of Fluffy.'

'He's *what*?' An expression of unmitigated horror spread across Darcie's face. She grabbed Fluffy and rained kisses on the top of his head. 'You poor baby! What's that fuck-face trying to do to you? I bet you anything he's a dark yellow or a dirty green – envious and spiteful!'

I was warming to Darcie. 'The awful part is, even though he's my dog, Mark's claiming he'd be better off living with him.'

'Well, you wouldn't be, would you?' Darcie almost wept into his coat. 'You need your mummy!'

'Yes, well, that's what I think, too. But Mark's saying I'm incapable of looking after him. Which means I have to prove to a judge that I am, to stop Mark getting him.'

'Well, it's crap, what he's claiming, isn't it? I mean, you've just hired me to help, haven't you? I tell you what, Annie, I could be a character witness. Or an expert witness. You know, a dog expert. And I could make a video of

257

Fluffy on my phone camera, showing how happy he is with you. It'd be, like, a sort of documentary. "A Day in the Life of Fluffy"! Show him getting up in the morning, having breakfast with you, having a bath, going out for walkies with Brandy. She'd love to be in films – she ought to be because she's, like, *sooo* beautiful. Everyone stops me in the street when they see her. They're, like, "Hey, where did you get that bitch?" And I'm really good with a camera. I was doing media studies at uni until I gave it up. So, what do you think?'

'It sounds wonderful!'

'Hey, have you got anything to drink, Annie?'

'No, I –'

'I don't want you to think I get wasted all the time or anything but there are just moments when I could, like, murder a glass of Chardonnay. There's a really sick bar just round the corner from here. We can take Fluffy with us because they're nice in there and they let dogs in – I know because I've been there absolutely millions of times with Brandy. The bar staff are like, "Hey, Brandy, have a bowl of peanuts!" whenever they see her. They just love her. It's a singles bar, actually, but the men won't bother us, because they're too fucking useless to make a move. Anyway, we could discuss how I can help you. So how about it?'

'Well, thanks, but I was planning to take Fluffy to the park now.'

'That's brilliant! We can go there on the way! I could even start doing some filming on my phone! You and Fluffy, walking together, catching a ball, that kind of thing. And at the same time Fluffy can get, like, used to being out with me, can't he? Which will be really good because, if you want me to, I can start walking him tomorrow. And maybe I can lift that viridian from your shoulders and bring you some sunlight yellow – that's happiness. I mean, if you want to, you can talk about the divorce and everything. I really think it might do you good to get it off your chest because you shouldn't, like, bottle things up, should you, because it's so bad for your karma?'

It was impossible to say no to Darcie. Besides, the idea of swapping my viridian for sunlight yellow was irresistible – and what else was I going to do all evening, except sit on the sofa with Fluffy feeling sorry for myself and watching the price of Antony Worrall Thompson saucepan sets plummet on Price-drop TV?

Frankly, I'd have done anything to get out of my attic for a couple of hours. Besides, as Darcie said, it was better for my karma to get things off my chest.

Which I did.

In fact, by the time Fluffy and I rolled home a bottle and a half later, there was nothing left on my chest at all except a thin Velvet T-shirt with a scooped neck.

Legless for the first time in years, I'd told Darcie everything about Mark, from the reasons for our marriage break-up to how good he'd been in bed.

I'd even told her exactly how I'd rescued Fluffy from the tramp.

The whole story.

The real story.

The one I'd sworn never to tell a soul.

Oh, what the hell did it matter if she knew the truth?

I reassured myself as, bumping my head on the sloping eaves again, I fell drunkenly into bed.

Darcie Wells wouldn't breathe a word to anyone, would she?

Of course not. She was my new best friend.

Twenty-four

Thanks to Darcie, my life as a single dog-owner quickly settled into a bearable routine. And so did Fluffy. Just about. On the weeks when he was staying with me, she collected him every noon from Monday through Saturday, and took him out for an energetic walk with Brandy and four or five other dogs. I didn't know where they went or what she did with them, but by the time she brought Fluffy back, he was sufficiently tired to sleep until I arrived home at seven when I'd take him out again. According to Vlad, who was still adding the finishing touches to the ground-floor flat, my dog no longer barked when he was alone in the attic. Nor did he always chew up my shoes. Instead he left them where I'd thrown them. Some of the time.

By some lucky fluke, it also turned out that Darcie had a relative in Islington, whom she often visited on a Sunday, which was the day when Mark and I swapped Fluffy. So, on the weeks when he'd been staying with me, she'd sometimes drive him over to the Workhouse on her way to her aunt. Then, the following Sunday, if she was seeing her aunt again, she'd collect Fluffy from Mark on the return journey, and drop him at my place. Because of this, I no longer had to see Mark very often, or suffer the pain of watching Fluffy run into his arms after being deprived of his company for seven days, without giving me a backward glance. That alone was worth the sixty quid a week I had to pay Darcie.

Annoying as she could be at times – her non-stop monologues often gave me a headache, and her new-age philosophy, which, as well as a belief in colour auras, encompassed UFOs, Buddhist chanting and 9/11 conspiracy theories – she was company for me when Fluffy was in Islington. My instinct was to stay in most evenings when I got home from work but, refusing to take no for an answer, Darcie often turned up on my doorstep and dragged me to the local singles bar where she'd spend half the time complaining about the men in her life, or lack thereof, and the other half trying to attract one. Though she claimed to be allergic to e-numbers, red meat, potatoes, dairy products, all wheat and pasta unless it was made with spelt, she had no trouble with alcohol and could easily get through a bottle of house red, or even two, on her own. On occasions, she left the wine bar legless, and spewed in the gutter when I walked her home – a process she said was as good for the digestive system as a coffee enema.

Necessity makes strange bedfellows or, in our case, drinking companions, so I put up with the things I didn't like about Darcie. After all, she was not only good with Fluffy, she was there for me. When I'd interviewed her, she'd promised to help me make a home movie, showing how happy Fluffy was with me, and she proved as good as her word. As far as I was concerned, she was a treasure – just like Mark had been when I'd first met him.

By the second week of August, the Haines and Hampton summer sale, which had started in July, was drawing to a close. The dregs of last season's fashions – odd skirts in large sizes, printed mini-dresses in neon yellow, and cutting-edge outfits, such as the lime-green linen catsuit with cropped legs, orange belt and mink-trimmed sleeves, which had brought its young British designer and our store a great deal of publicity yet had failed to find a buyer – had been reduced to seventy-five per cent of their normal prices and were languishing at the back of the designer concessions. Though it was approaching eighty-five degrees outside, Manny the doorman had abandoned his summer uniform in favour of shirtsleeves and the air-conditioning inside was on at full blast, the departments were being stocked with heavy overcoats, cashmere sweaters and long-sleeved woollen dresses – the winter fashions, which were now trickling in.

Since many of our wealthiest clients went away at the beginning of July and didn't return until September, Personal Shopping was at its quietest. Odd tourists drifted in for spur-of-the-moment consultations, many of them American, but they almost always left without buying anything, horrified by the value of the pound against the dollar, which made our clothes unaffordable. This after-noon, unusually, a new British client had booked in for two o'clock – a Mrs Redman from Brighton, who, when Charlotte had suggested on the phone that she see Eva, had insisted she wanted a consultation with me.

Since I was going over our sales figures on the computer during lunch, I'd asked Charlotte to take Mrs Redman through to our largest changing room when she arrived. Accordingly, at two o'clock prompt, there was a knock on my door, and Charlotte poked her head round it. 'Mrs Redman's here, Annie. She's waiting for you inside.'

'Thanks, Charlotte. *What's she like?*' I mouthed.

Charlotte shook her head. 'Home-counties fashion nightmare!' she whispered.

Smiling to myself, I went into the spacious changing room, where a petite, homely middle-aged woman was standing in front of the floor-to-ceiling plate-glass mirror. I did a double-take. In kitten-heeled navy blue court shoes, tan tights, a knee-length beige suit, with a white shoulder-bag hanging over one arm, she was the spitting image of my mother-in-law.

With a tentative smile, she took a step towards me. She was my mother-in-law. 'Hello, Annie, love,' she said.

'Jackie! What are you doing here?'

'I – I wanted to see you.'

'Did Mark ask you to come?'

She looked horrified. 'Oh, no! He doesn't know I'm here. And please don't tell him I came. He'd be furious.'

'Sure.' I went across to her and pecked her on both cheeks. 'Look, Jackie, it's lovely you're here, but I'm rather busy right now. I've got a new client coming in a minute. Actually, I thought you were her.'

She looked embarrassed. 'I am.'

'I don't understand. Her name's Mrs Redman. What's going on? Did you want a secret makeover or something?'

'Oh, no!' Jackie laughed and glanced down at her suit, which, I remembered, was the one she'd worn to our wedding, and the smartest outfit she possessed. 'I'm afraid I'm more make-do than makeover. Besides, those lovely clothes I saw on the way up here would get ruined in the pub kitchen, which is the only place I ever go. And as for the price tags, Annie, some of those dresses cost more than Dennis and I take at the pub in a fortnight! No, love, I just wanted to talk to you. I didn't know whether you'd see me if I phoned and asked you to, so I'm ashamed to say I booked in here – under a false name!'

The idea of my mother-in-law, the most straightforward person I'd ever met, resorting to such subterfuge made me smile. 'You didn't have to do that. Of course I would have seen you.'

'Oh, love!' The next moment she was hugging me tight, and weeping on my shoulder. 'I've wanted to ring you so often,' she sobbed, 'but Dennis kept telling me not to stick my nose in where it wasn't wanted. "Leave the kids alone and they'll sort it out themselves," he said.'

'Well, we don't seem to be doing a very good job of it, do we?' I admitted. Now there were tears in my eyes, too. I blinked them back and smiled at her. 'Oh, Jackie, it's so nice to see you.' And it was. Because my in-laws lived so far from London and worked in their pub seven days a week, Mark and I had only ever spent the occasional weekend or Sunday with them. But whenever we saw them, I was always overcome by how kind and warm-hearted Jackie was. She had a good word for everyone, a cup of tea at the ready and, more often than not, a big slice of delicious home-made cake to go with it. In fact, as I'd often told Mark, if I'd had to invent an ideal mother-in-law – or even an ideal mother – Jackie would have been she. 'I've missed you,' I said, as I hugged her again.

'I've missed you, too, Annie.'

'Come and sit down.' I led her to the big white sofa. 'Do you want something to drink? How about a glass of Bollinger? Don't look so shocked, we offer it to all our personal-shopping clients.'

'You know I never touch alcohol.'

'How about a cup of tea, then, and maybe some sandwiches?'

'Now, that would be lovely. I'd made some sandwiches for the journey, actually, but I left them behind. The ones on the train looked awful – and they were such a price I wouldn't buy one.'

'Did you come all the way from Norwich just to see me?'

'I'd go to the ends of the earth if it helped you and Mark to sort things out.'

I popped out to Reception, where Charlotte was busy brushing her long blonde hair and gazing at herself in a hand mirror, which she did at every opportunity. The moment she saw me, she lowered it behind her desk. 'May I help you, Annie?'

'Actually I think you mean, "*Can* I help you?" And, yes, Charlotte, you *can* and you *may*. Do you think you could rustle up some tea and sandwiches for – for Mrs Redman?'

'Of course, Annie. No problem.'

'Thank you. Tea for two, please. And, Charlotte?'

'Yes?'

'You look your usual glamorous self. There's no need to check in the mirror fifty times a day.'

She blushed scarlet. 'Thank you, Annie.'

Back in the changing room, I found Jackie dabbing her eyes with a tissue. I sat down close beside her. 'Actually, I wondered why I hadn't heard from you,' I confided.

'As I said, Dennis told me to keep out of it. But I've been ever so upset about this business. Both of us have. You know how fond we are of you.'

'Me you, too.'

'But Mark's our son, Annie, and we have to support him, no matter what he's done. Not that I wasn't very angry with him indeed when he told us. You know, about this affair he had. I can't understand why he did such a dreadful thing – and when he's married to someone like you! But to get divorced over it? I know I shouldn't say this but. . .' She looked at me very earnestly. 'Couldn't you try to forgive him, Annie?'

I took her hand. I was tempted to tell her it hadn't been the first time her beloved son had strayed off the marital straight and narrow, but I knew it would only upset her more. So I said, 'It's gone too far for that.'

'You mean this terrible business over Fluffy?'

'That, and other things.'

I let go of her hand as Charlotte pranced in on her five-inch heels, carrying a tray. 'Here's your tea, Mrs Redman. And your mini-sandwiches. I cut off the crusts for you myself,' she added, as proudly as if she'd thrown together a gourmet meal.

'Thank you, dear, but that really wasn't necessary.'

'My domestic-science teacher always used to say it looks nicer. And I think she was right. Don't you?' She put the tray carefully on the white coffee-table and beamed at my mother-in-law. 'May I pour you some tea?'

Jackie smiled up at her. 'No, thank you. I like it nice and strong, so I'll leave it to brew, if that's all right by you, dear.' Once Charlotte had left, she said, 'What a nice girl. Such good manners, and such a refined speaking voice. So, this is where you work, Annie. I must say, it's terribly posh.'

'Well, now that you're here, why don't you let me show you some of our clothes?'

'Oh, I couldn't afford to buy anything!'

'So what? Just for fun, I mean. You can't come to Haines and Hampton and not try anything on!'

For the next half-hour, Jackie and I walked round the store together, selecting garments from the new autumn collection, some of which she liked and others she didn't but I thought would suit her. Then, in the privacy of the personal-shopping suite, I made her try them on, no matter how outlandish they were. Neither of us could believe how sophisticated she looked in a red satin Hervé Léger evening dress, or in the fur-trimmed Chanel winter coat I'd picked out for her, particularly when I made her put on some deep plum lipstick with it. 'I'm almost tempted to buy it,' she said, as she marvelled at her reflection. 'I feel like a film star.' Then she looked at the price tag. '*How much?* Now I feel like a pauper.'

The time flew by. This was the first time I'd ever been alone with my mother-in-law – and, poignantly, it would probably be the last. I was discovering what fun she was.

When it came to trying on clothes, Jackie was as endearingly unselfconscious as a child with a dressing-up box. Before we knew it, it was three thirty – time for me to see my next client, and for her to catch her train.

'Well, I didn't expect to have such a marvellous time when I left home this morning,' she said, beaming at me. 'It's been wonderful, Annie. I feel quite refreshed.'

'It's been so nice seeing you, Jackie. I've had a great time too.'

'I'm only sorry I didn't come and visit you at work years ago – and that it's taken such terrible goings-on to get me here.' Her smile faded and, as she put her arms round me to hug me, she heaved a great sigh. 'You know, Annie, you're part of our family now, and I don't want to lose you. Neither does Dennis, or Mark's sisters.'

Choked as I was, I managed to say, 'Thank you.'

'Nor, I suspect, does Mark.'

'Well, if that's true, he has a funny way of showing it.'

She gave me a squeeze and then let go. 'Relationships as strong as yours once was don't come along often, darling. I know that marriage can be difficult. Sometimes you have to swallow your pride. But, in the end, it's worth persevering. It hasn't all been plain sailing with me and Dennis.' She searched my face. 'Do think about it.'

'I will. But I don't hold out much hope.'

'You never know, Annie, you and Mark may feel angry with one another now – you probably don't trust him, and you may both think you've burned all your bridges. But I'm sure if you both tried hard enough you'd mend them and get over this – this – Well, I won't call it a

269

glitch, it's much more serious than that. And, I probably shouldn't say this, but whatever bitterness there is between you and Mark at the moment, I'm absolutely sure that, deep down, he still loves you very much.'

I shook my head. I wished it were true, but it wasn't possible. Like a beautiful vintage dress, ripped apart at the seams, our marriage might once have been salvaged, but it had now deteriorated beyond the point of no return. There was no going back for us. Divorce was the only option.

Twenty-five

A week later, on Friday afternoon, I was back in Mr Williams's office. It was so hot and airless that he'd thrown open the tall sash windows and, after profuse apologies, had peeled off his dark grey suit jacket and hung it over the back of his chair. 'May I?' he said now, touching his dark blue tie.

'Feel free,' I said. 'Take everything off, for all I care.'

'Ha! I don't think I'll go that far.' After loosening the knot, he picked up the folded handkerchief lying on his desk and swiped away the bead of sweat that had settled in the overgrown thicket of one eyebrow. 'Look, I know we've gone over your statement, and the possible questions your husband's lawyers will ask you next week. But there's something I need to say to you before you leave here today, Mrs Curtis.'

'Yes? What?'

He took a deep breath. 'There's still time to call this off.'

I gazed in amazement at the figure sitting behind the piles of papers on his mahogany desk. I'd always thought he was slightly eccentric, but had he gone completely mad? 'Do you mean call off my divorce, Mr Williams?'

He shook his head, and a snowfall landed on his shoulders. 'No, though of course that's also a possibility. I was referring to the full hearing next week.'

'But it's – what? – only six days away now. I'm all prepared – and I thought you were, too.'

'That goes without saying, Mrs Curtis.' As it bloody well should, I thought, because I'd just paid his latest astronomical bill. 'However, we may have reached the edge of the Grand Canyon but we are not obliged to throw ourselves into it. Frankly, it's in your interest – in the interest of every divorcing couple, for that matter – to avoid going to court. Many a case is settled at the last minute. Indeed, deals between warring couples are often thrashed out on the court steps. If you want me to, I can lift up the telephone right now, speak to your husband's solicitor and suggest we try some last-minute mediation instead.'

I went to stand by the open sash window and gazed out across Lincoln's Inn Fields, where groups of office workers and tourists were sitting on the grass, many of them in what looked like their underwear, basking in the sun and eating their lunch. Enjoying normal life. Being carefree. Oh, how I longed to feel like that again. But I couldn't imagine that I ever would. I couldn't think past the full hearing on Thursday.

'Alternatively,' Williams went on, when I didn't answer, 'we could convene a meeting with Mr Curtis and Mrs Greenwood on Monday and try to reach a compromise. A little give here, a little take there. Fluffy weighed against your Banksy. Full residency rights over the animal in exchange for a slightly larger share of the flat, for instance.'

I turned back to him. 'Give me one good reason why I should strike any deal with Mark that wouldn't get me what I want, which is Fluffy. Mark's the one who's in the wrong.'

His eyes strayed from my face to the faint shadow of my bra, which showed through the thin silk of my Derek Lam blouse. 'As I've told you before,' he said to it, 'yours is not a clear-cut situation. You do have a good case, Mrs Curtis –'

'Of course I do,' I interrupted him.

He raised a hand to silence me. 'We do have a strong bundle of evidence to present to the judge next week, detailing your husband's work-shy attitude, his repeated infidelities, his unwillingness to make any substantial contribution to the marital finances, and so on and so forth. We also have this intriguing film.' He picked up the DVD of the film that Darcie had made on her mobile phone. '"A Day in the Life of Fluffy",' Williams read off the label. 'I watched it last night. I particularly liked the scene of you picnicking in that rowing-boat in Hyde Park.'

'Oh, yes, we filmed it a couple of Sundays ago.'

'I never knew dogs needed to wear life-jackets.'

'Darcie thought it'd look better if he was wearing some sort of safety device. She didn't want the judge thinking I didn't care about health-and-safety issues.'

'Ah, yes, Miss Darcie Wells. She seems to be a woman of many talents. I must say that her expert witness statement, though a little on the verbose side, might prove invaluable in swaying the judge in your direction. Though I'm not sure about the part on Fluffy's – what was it? His *colour aura*.' He leafed through the pile of documents in front of him and took out Darcie's statement. 'It was on page four, if I remember. Oh, yes.' He adjusted his glasses and cleared his throat. '"When I first saw Fluffy and Mrs Curtis together,"' he read out, in a deliberately flat voice, '"I could see that he was happy from the clear golden yellow light surrounding his wagging tail, indicating joyfulness and contentment. However, when I dropped him off at Mr Curtis's flat the other day on Mrs Curtis's behalf, the golden yellow definitely changed to a nasty sulphur during the journey there, indicating that Fluffy was in mental turmoil at being parted from her."' Williams looked up at me. 'I'm not sure how that will go down with the judge who happens to be sitting next Thursday.'

'Why? What's he like?'

'She's female, for a start, Mrs Curtis, though from her demeanour that's sometimes hard to tell. Mrs Justice Khan is a very striking woman in her fifties. Good figure, beautiful face. However, she lacks what one thinks of as the feminine attributes – kindness, empathy, warmth, that kind of thing. I'm afraid that the phrase "old battleaxe" doesn't begin to describe her. Behind her back they call her Genghis Khan.'

'That sounds like a good start.'

'I'm with you on that. Frankly, I'm not sure how she'll take to this case. The trouble is, as I've explained to you time and again, there's no legal precedent in this country for a custody battle over a pet. Dogs, cats, tame crocodiles – they're just pieces of furniture, as far as the law is concerned. Property.'

'Well, in that case there'll be no contest, will there? I mean, I bought Fluffy with my own money from that tramp before I ever laid eyes on Mark. So, he's my dog. Full stop. I win.'

'This is, of course, our best-case scenario. However, by your own admission you purchased Fluffy only a few days before you met your husband. And during the marriage Mr Curtis spent more time with the dog than you did. We already know through the disclosure process that his lawyers are basing *their* case on the fact that, because of his professional qualifications as a dog-walker –'

'Qualifications? You mean he knows how to hold a leash?'

'– because of his profession, and his long-standing role as Fluffy's primary carer, Mr Curtis is much better suited to looking after Fluffy than you are. He also has much more time to do so.'

Sometimes I wondered whose side Williams was on. 'But lately we've been sharing Fluffy, haven't we? And, as Darcie's DVD and statement prove, I can look after him perfectly well by myself, given the right help. Fluffy's happy living with me. Just as happy and cared-for as he is when he's with Mark.' But even as I said the words, I didn't quite believe them.

Williams paused, then picked up the felt-tip pen lying on his blotter, and twisted it in his fingers. He'd obviously decided against having his Mont Blanc on show when I was around. 'You can't have it both ways, Mrs Curtis. Either you ask the judge to consider Fluffy's well-being and his – well, his wishes, almost as if he were a child of the marriage, or you ask her to consider him merely as a piece of marital property – as he is in British law.

Either way, there are no guarantees that Mrs Justice Khan is going to rule in your favour. Frankly, the outcome will depend on the mood she's in. She may make a ruling you don't like at all, which leaves you in a worse position than if you'd settled beforehand. I can only say to you, *in dubiis non est agendum*.'

'Sorry?'

'Where the outcome is dubious, one should not act. Besides, as I've warned you repeatedly over the past few months, the full hearing is not only going to deplete your assets, it can be – it most certainly will be – a most unpleasant experience for both parties concerned. "*Contumeliam si dices, audies*", as Plautus put it.'

His habit of quoting Latin phrases at me seemed designed to make me feel ignorant. And the last thing I needed right then was to feel worse about myself than I already did. '*Please* speak English, Mr Williams.'

'"If you insult, you will be insulted." In other words, whatever dirt we throw at your husband, his counsel is bound to throw back at you in equal measure.'

'I've done nothing wrong. Unlike Mark. Why should I be afraid?'

'Why, indeed? Well, if you're absolutely sure you want to go ahead, all that remains is for me to remind you to keep your temper in court. You'll be under oath, remember, but don't let your husband's barrister rattle you, no matter what he or she asks. Keep your answers short and sweet. As for how you should present yourself . . .' his eyes dropped to my semi-transparent shirt again '. . . neat, ladylike and . . .'

I was about to remind Williams to whom he was talking:

if there was one thing I didn't need from him, it was sartorial advice. But, just then, his telephone rang.

'What is it, Sarah?' he said. 'I'm with a client. Oh? I see. Well, then, you'd better put her through.'

He covered the phone's mouthpiece with his hand and raised his eyebrows at me. 'Funnily enough, it's Miss Wells,' he said. 'She says it's urgent. You may as well sit down while I find out what this is about.'

I sat. I listened. It was not good news.

Twenty-six

'But, Darcie,' I sobbed into my BlackBerry, later that night, 'why have you decided to withdraw your statement supporting me?'

Though I'd never known her lost for words, Darcie took an extraordinarily long time to answer this question. 'It's not suddenly, Annie,' her voice came back at me through my earpiece, 'I've been thinking about it for absolutely ages. Like, even before I met you, I was getting vibes that something was going to come up I really shouldn't, like, get mixed up in. I'm sure I told you before I'm really psychic that way.'

Somehow, this excuse didn't ring true. 'You didn't seem to feel like this up till now,' I said. 'After all, I didn't ask you to help me with the court case, did I? It was you who offered, when we first met. In fact, being an expert witness and filming the DVD were your ideas.'

She sighed. 'Yes, but the thing is, Annie, I like to be helpful, I really do. You know I'm a kind and generous person and it's so, like, rewarding, isn't it, when people are grateful to you and stuff? But the moment I'd been to see that solicitor guy and discussed it with him, and made my statement, I realized I'd *sooo* made a mistake.'

A knot of anger formed inside me. Couldn't she have thought of this earlier? 'How could it be a mistake to support my fight for custody of Fluffy?'

'Because, well, it's just not the kind of thing I do, getting mixed up in other people's divorces, is it? I felt really kind of sick when I got home from your solicitor's. You know, unclean. I wasn't myself. Brandy noticed it the moment I came in. She's so sensitive, bless her, she picks things up straight away. She was, like, *ugh!* when she saw me. She actually ran away from me into the kitchen. So I followed her in there and I was, like, "Hey, what's going on with you, Brandy-babes?" And she just ran into the bedroom and hid under the bed with all my dirty knickers and socks, and she'd never done that before. I couldn't understand it. But then I looked in the mirror and realized what had happened to me, and I knew why she'd run away.'

The woman exasperated me. 'Why?' I sighed. 'What *had* happened to you?'

Darcie paused, then said dramatically, 'My rainbow aura had gone! Well, not exactly gone, but it had changed! I wasn't a star person any more. All my bright auric colours had, like, bled away. The violet. The purple. And the indigo. There wasn't a trace of golden solar magic left. Instead, there were these ugly dark grey and greenish-yellow rays coming out of the top of my head. And a halo of black. Black, Annie! You know what that means, don't you?'

'No.' By now I was having difficulty keeping my temper. 'What?'

'A black aura is pure evil.'

Darcie lapsed into silence. I, too, was speechless. I cursed myself for having employed such a flake to walk my dog. She'd changed colour, so I no longer had a witness to vouch for my ability to look after him. Great. 'Mr

Williams said you'd asked if you could withdraw the DVD, too,' I went on.

'Well, it's like part of the same thing, isn't it, Annie? It's all evidence. But the stupid wanker said I couldn't because apparently, even though I'd, like, filmed it on my camera, the DVD belongs to you.'

She lapsed into another uncharacteristic silence, during which I attempted to see things from her side. I failed. 'Well, I wish you'd told me all this before now,' I said, annoyed.

'Well, I could've, but I didn't want to, like, upset you.'

By now I wanted to, like, throttle her. Instead I said, in as understanding a voice as I could muster, 'Can't you see that it won't reflect well on me in court if my dog-walker has suddenly withdrawn her support? Please, Darcie, won't you change your mind? I really need your witness statement.'

'I would if I could, Annie, but I must get my rainbow aura back, and I really shouldn't be interfering in something that's, like, nothing to do with me.'

I thought the conversation was over, but then Darcie said, 'I mean, for all I know, in the long run Fluffy might be better off living with Mark, mightn't he?'

I felt myself go cold. 'What are you saying?'

'Because Mark's at home all the time,' she continued, 'or walking with other dogs on Hampstead Heath, and you're, like, out at work, aren't you? I mean, Annie, is that really fair to poor Fluffy?' I bit my lip, and struggled to come to terms with the uncomfortable truth of what she'd said. 'But, hey, what do I know?' Darcie added, as an afterthought. 'I'm just an outsider, really.'

And I'd thought she was a real friend. 'Well, I can't pretend I'm not upset that you've pulled out right at the last minute,' I said.

'I'm sorry. But I can't do anything that's against my principles.' I was going to ask her what these principles were when she went on brightly, as if the previous conversation hadn't taken place, 'I'm going over to see my aunt again this Sunday. Do you want me to pick up Fluffy from Mark's on my way back and drop him off at yours?'

'No, I don't. Thank you.'

'It'd save you having to, like, see Mark before the hearing on Thursday. It'd be no trouble, and Brandy'd just *love* Fluffy to drive back in the van with us. I think she's fallen for him. She's really missed him this week. She's *so* not interested in Max any more – the boxer I told you about? Poor Max! He's, like, "Hey, Brandy, don't you love me any more?" whenever he sees her. So, are you sure you don't want me to pick him up for you?'

'Yes.'

'Well,' she said, 'I only hope it doesn't upset you, seeing Mark just before the hearing.'

How could Darcie feign such interest when she'd just betrayed me? Or so I felt. 'Look, you're still coming to take Fluffy out for his midday walk this week, aren't you? Monday to Wednesday. He'll be coming to court with me on Thursday, so I won't need you then. I'll call you Thursday night and let you know what happened.'

'Annie, of course I'll turn up. Would I ever let you down?'

As soon as I'd hung up, I reached for the open bottle of Pinot Grigio in the fridge and took a tumbler out on to the balcony. The night sky glowed orange from the London street-lights, and below me, three bendy-buses thundered past, one after the other, like fat red snakes slithering down the road. A group of ladettes standing outside the pub on the corner were larking around with bottles of vodka, and somewhere down the street a couple were having a terrible row, so loud I could hear every insult they yelled at each other: *I swear I did! You never! You fucking bastard! Whore!* I turned round and looked through the French windows into the tiny living room. The place was unkempt and uncared-for. There were magazines all over the floor, one of the seat cushions had slipped off the sofa and the dirty crockery I hadn't bothered to wash up for days was piled in the sink.

As the fishy smell of yesterday's microwaved Wild Alaskan Salmon and Watercress Risotto wafted out at me, I was overwhelmed by doubt and despair. Once, my life had been full of good times and I'd known where I was going. Now every day was like wading upstream through a fast-moving river of sludge. I tried to comfort myself by thinking that, by this time next week, it'd be over: the full court hearing would have taken place, the divorce settlement would be finalized and my old home would be on the market. Most important of all, Mark would be in my past. Then I could move on and begin to rebuild my life.

But what would the outcome of the hearing be? Would there be enough money left after paying the court fees, the lawyers' fees, the estate agent's fees, and giving Mark his share of the profits for me to buy myself a decent flat?

More importantly, would Fluffy be mine?

For the first time since I'd decided to go to court, I'd lost confidence that I'd win the battle for him.

And even if I did win it, what then? What Darcie had said had struck home with me. Would Fluffy be happy if he was living with me full-time? Or, as she had suggested, would it be unfair on him?

Could I really cope with a dog single-handedly?

Bereft as I'd felt when she'd dropped Fluffy at Mark's for me the previous Sunday, there'd also been an element of relief in knowing that I wasn't going to have him on my conscience all week. I didn't like to admit it, even to myself, but nowadays spending time with him had become quite a strain. It wasn't just the stress of having to get up at the crack of dawn to take him out for a long, early-morning walk, or the panic of rushing home in the evenings to feed and take him out again, there was something else, something hard to put a finger on.

When Mark and I had lived together at the Workhouse, Fluffy had been content just to hang out with us and do his own thing. He'd nose around under the table in search of titbits, or spend hours destroying his toys. He'd trot into the bedroom by himself and burrow under the bed in search of trouble – didn't I know it? – or happily doze by the wow-factor gas-log fire.

But now that it was just him and me, closeted together every other week in the tiny attic, I felt unbelievably guilty every time I walked out of the door and left him alone. Even when I was there, Fluffy seemed to spend most of his time lying on the patch of floor between the sofa and the kitchen with his head between his paws, looking at me reproachfully. Whenever I was around I did what I could to stimulate him. I threw balls against the sloping walls for him, or got down on my hands and knees and played tag with him, or I stuffed dog biscuits into old socks or envelopes so that he could rip them apart in search of the hidden treasure. I talked to him, patted him, cuddled him and, even if he'd been out with Darcie, I took him for an hour-long stroll in the evenings when the weather allowed – as much to escape the claustrophobic flat as to give him some exercise.

But whatever I did, none of it felt natural, and Fluffy wasn't his old, cheerful self with me any more. He certainly never obeyed me. I sometimes wondered if he resented being shuffled like a pawn between two homes, and having to spend time with me in Fulham. Was living apart half the time inevitably making us grow apart? Or was I unwittingly making my dog unhappy?

Back inside the flat, I sat on the sofa and knocked back the dregs in my glass. I remembered what Clarissa had once said about Mark and me using Fluffy as a means of getting at each other. At the time I'd denied it vehemently, even to myself, but, when I thought about it now, wasn't there a kernel of truth in what she'd said? More than a kernel, in fact?

Just whose interests *had* I been putting first lately?

Fluffy's or mine?

Twenty-seven

'Hello?'

'It's me.'

It was midday on Sunday, and I was standing outside the Workhouse's tall iron gates, where I was due to collect Fluffy from Mark. I was wearing a pair of old, drainpipe Levi's teamed with a cropped, dip-dyed, Topshop T-shirt and the high-heeled, peep-toe Jonathan Kelseys that Mark, in our glory days, had once called my 'fuck-me' shoes. I'd spent ages deciding what to wear. I'd needed an outfit that would give me confidence for what I knew I had to do and, at the same time, that would give me a lift when I'd done it. By the time I'd finished getting dressed I'd discarded almost everything I possessed, and the flat had looked like the floor of Primark on a Saturday afternoon.

Mark buzzed me in and I took the lift upstairs. As it rose, my stomach sank. I remembered all the times Mark and I had snogged in there in the golden olden days. Once, on our way home from seeing a film at the Screen on the Green, we'd got so carried away in the lift that we'd practically undressed each other between floors. We were on our bed, half naked, before we'd realized we had to put our clothes back on and take our poor, desperate dog out for his late-night walk.

The moment I came out of the lift, Fluffy bounded

down the corridor and hurled himself at me. Mark had had him for the last seven days, and he appeared half crazed with joy to see me. Tongue hanging out, mouth open to reveal the jagged alpine peaks of his teeth, he stood on his hind legs and scrabbled at me as if he wanted to jump into my arms.

As I bent down to cuddle him, I looked over his head at Mark, who, in black baggy shorts and a loose sleeveless T-shirt, had come out into the corridor in his bare feet and was slouched casually – fetchingly – against the doorframe. With his rippling arm muscles, his long, dishevelled hair and his brooding expression, he was like a model in a Calvin Klein aftershave ad, and I cursed myself for finding him so attractive still.

'Hiya.' He looked me slowly up and down as I straightened and walked towards him. As I drew level, he said, 'Nice outfit.'

I felt myself blush. Damn! The last thing I wanted was for him to think I'd made an effort for him so, as I walked past him into the flat, with Fluffy leaping beside me, I said, off the top of my head, 'Well, I'm taking Fluffy out for lunch from here.'

He closed the door behind me. 'Oh? Who with?'

I turned towards him and smiled. 'No one you know.'

'I see. It's like that, is it?'

'Like what, Mark?'

'Like you're not going to tell me who you're having lunch with.'

I raised an eyebrow. 'I wouldn't have thought you'd be interested. Do you really want to know?'

He shrugged. 'I don't give a damn.'

'Well, then, Rhett.'

He gave a reluctant half-smile at the reference to *Gone With the Wind*, then shoved his hands into his shorts pockets and stared at the floor. There was a long silence. 'So, how are you?' he said eventually.

'I'm . . . okay. Just about. Considering that we're soon to go to court. And you?'

'The same.'

I wished I'd let Darcie pick up Fluffy after all. I thought back to what my mother-in-law had said when she'd come to see me – that, somewhere deep down, Mark still loved me and that, given the right circumstances, we might be able to bury the hatchet and get back together. Poor Jackie had been deluding herself. Since December Mark and I had become strangers – worse, hostile enemies. Even Fluffy seemed to sense it: he was now sitting midway between the two of us, slap in the middle of the bad atmosphere, turning his head back and forth as if he couldn't understand why we were so far apart.

'How's he been?' I asked.

'Great. We've had long walks on the Heath twice a day with the other dogs. I've got a couple of new ones to walk, actually. A German shepherd. And a boxer. Both from Kentish Town.'

'Fascinating.'

Mark glared at me. 'There's no need to be sarcastic, Annie. I'm just trying to earn a living.'

I remembered what Jackie had said about having to swallow one's pride. 'I'm sorry,' I said. 'I didn't mean to be horrid. It's just that – well, to be honest, Mark, this is difficult for me. Coming back to the flat. Seeing you.'

He nodded. 'Do you want a coffee before you rush off and have lunch with whoever he is?'

'I'd just like some water. Actually, there's something I wanted to talk to you about.'

'Oh?'

'Do you mind if I sit down?'

'You don't have to ask,' Mark said, over his shoulder, as he went to the sink and poured the water. 'This place is still yours.'

It didn't feel like it. Once I would have thrown myself down on the sofa, kicked off my shoes and tucked my feet under me. Now, an intruder in my own home, I perched primly on the edge. Meanwhile, acting as if I was a formal guest, Mark got ice from the dispenser in the American fridge – as big as my entire kitchen in Fulham – then asked politely if I wanted some lemon.

As least Fluffy was behaving normally. He put his paws on my knees and grinned at me. I scratched his ears. Mark handed me the clunking glass, then sat at the other end of the sofa with his feet planted on the floor. There was another excruciatingly awkward silence. Then we said in unison, 'Look . . .'

We stopped.

'You go first,' Mark said.

'No, you.'

'No, you.'

'Okay.' I took a deep breath. 'I was just going to say it doesn't have to be like this.'

'Like what?' His eyes met mine. 'You mean, like getting divorced?'

'Actually,' I went on slowly, 'I was talking about fighting over Fluffy.'

'Oh.' He looked away.

'I – I've been thinking things over, Mark.' I paused.

'And?' he prompted me belligerently.

'I've changed my mind.'

'How d'you mean?'

I took a deep breath and said the words I'd been turning over in my head all night: 'I want you to have him.'

Mark's head jerked round. His face had turned pale under his tan. I could see he didn't know whether or not to believe me. 'Is this some kind of trick?' he said. 'Because if it is, Annie . . .' I shook my head because I didn't trust myself to speak. 'You want me to have Fluffy?' I nodded. His mouth fell open. He was gob-smacked. 'I – I don't understand.'

'You were right,' I admitted. 'Fluffy'll be better off with you.' Tongue lolling, the subject of our conversation grinned up at me trustingly. He hadn't a clue what I was saying. I swallowed the lump that was now blocking my throat. 'I – I'm not around enough to take care of him properly.'

There was a long pause. Then Mark said my name. A moment later, he was sitting next to me, squeezing my hand. 'Annie, I don't know what to say,' he murmured. 'Thank you. I know how hard this must be for you. I promise I'll let you see him whenever you want to. Whenever, Annie.'

I nodded. By now tears were tumbling uncontrollably

down my cheeks. From being someone who never cried, I'd done quite a bit of it lately. 'Have you got a tissue?' I sniffed. Mark let go of my hand, ran to the kitchen units and tore off several yards of kitchen roll. 'I'm not going to cry *that* much,' I said, through my tears, as he brought it to me.

He flashed me a watery smile. 'Yeah, but I might.'

Before we knew it, we were sitting side by side, blubbering and, at the same time, half laughing at how ridiculous we were being. A minute before, we'd hated one another. Now it was as if a hole had appeared in the wall of hostility we had built between us. Relief coursed through me, but at the same time a terrible, cutting grief. I knew I was doing the right thing for Fluffy, but that didn't stop it being painful.

After I'd mopped my face and blown my nose, and Mark had done the same, I said, 'Mark, what did you want to say to me before, when you let me go first?'

'Just that this whole divorce business, Annie – it's been doing my head in.'

'I know what you mean.'

'Do you? I hate it. I hate being enemies with you. I wish the whole thing had never started. I know it was my fault. I behaved like a fucking idiot – literally, I guess – but I just can't believe it's all gone this far, and so fast. And the worst thing is, I . . .' He sighed. 'I miss you, Annie.'

I'd sometimes heard people say, 'It quite took my breath away,' but until that moment I'd never understood what they meant. Now I did. I felt winded, as if I'd just run a marathon and my lungs were about to burst.

'I miss all the little things about being with you,' Mark

went on. 'I miss waking up before you in the morning and making you a cappuccino. I miss the way you drop your towel on the bathroom floor, and the mess you leave behind when you go off to work. I miss texting you when you're there, and I miss knowing you'll be coming home at night. Most of all, I miss hanging out with you. You, me and Fluffy, the three of us together.' He glanced up at me again. 'I think the real reason I've not wanted to let go of him is because, well . . . because I haven't wanted to let go of you.'

I could hardly believe what I was hearing. 'Oh, Mark!' I breathed.

'The truth is, Annie . . .' He faltered. 'I'm not the same without you.'

'Really?'

'I don't feel whole. And, as for this divorce, I never meant it to be so fucking awful.'

'Neither did I,' I whispered.

'I never even wanted it to happen.'

'Didn't you?' I breathed.

He shook his head again. Our eyes met, and this time neither of us looked away. A moment later our arms were round each other. I felt I was coming home.

'Oh, darling!' Mark murmured, as he kissed my neck, my cheeks and then, finally, my lips. 'I've missed you so much, so very much.'

'Have you?' I said,

He broke off kissing me, and nodded. 'I love you so much, Annie. Let's go to bed.'

So we did.

Twenty-eight

'Oh!' Mark sighed, as he pulled me into the crook of his arm. 'That was really, really nice!'

I poked him in the ribs. '*Nice?*'

'Sorry. Fantastic. Incredible. Earth-shattering. So, how was it for you?'

'Am I bovvered?'

After a moment's silence, he said, 'You're a monster!' and began to tickle me. My screeches for help woke Fluffy, who'd fallen asleep on the floor beside us. Growling like a guard dog – no one was going to hurt his mistress! – he leaped on to the bed, ready to tear apart my attacker. But when he saw it was only Mark, he joined in the general hysteria, grabbed hold of the top sheet and dragged it off us, shaking it as if it was a live rat.

A few minutes later I left the two of them playing tug-of-war with a rolled-up newspaper, and slipped into the en-suite for a pee. As I washed my hands afterwards, and dried them on the rather grubby towel draped over the rail – Mark had obviously let standards slip now that only he was living here – I grinned at myself in the mirror above the basin. Darling Jackie had been right, I thought. Our relationship was salvageable. In fact, it was still very much alive. All it had needed was for me to take a step towards Mark, and for both of us to swallow our stupid pride.

Now I felt euphoric with relief. How brilliant it felt to be back in my gorgeous home! I'd go and collect my things from Fulham later – there was no time like the present and, besides, I wanted never to be parted from Mark again. Despite everything that had happened, and everything we'd put each other through, we still loved each other. And, as everyone knew, love conquered all. Thank God we'd come to our senses in the nick of time.

Was I a mess, though! All that kissing had turned my chin bright red, smudged my mascara and exfoliated my cheeks more thoroughly than micro-dermabrasion. As for my hair, I looked like Amy Winehouse in a wind tunnel. I certainly didn't want Mark to see me looking so wrecked, not when we'd just decided to get back together, so I splashed cold water on my skin, wiped off my smudged mascara with a tissue, then looked for my hairbrush but, of course, it wasn't in its usual place beside the basin. It was in Fulham. Even though his hair was always a tangled mess, Mark must have a brush or a comb somewhere, I thought, and flung open the bathroom cabinet in search of one.

A few minutes later, wearing the towelling bathrobe I'd once bought him as a Valentine's Day present, I left the bathroom and sat on the edge of the bed. Pushing Fluffy away, Mark drew me towards him, but I stayed so rigid in his arms that, after a moment, he let go. 'What's up, darling?' he said.

I sat up and looked at him with an expressionless face. 'Since when have you been using Protect and Perfect?'

Mark frowned. 'Protect and what, angel?'

I held up the opaque plastic tube of the Boots wrinkle-buster. 'It was in the bathroom cupboard.'

There followed a pause which, though short, was a fraction too long for my liking. Mark swallowed and said, 'It must be yours.'

'No, it isn't. I took mine with me when I moved out.'

'You couldn't have.'

'Of course I did. I use it every day. Besides, mine was bigger, and in a glass bottle. And, anyway, what about this?' I opened my other hand to reveal a small, smeary phial with a red pump-dispenser top. 'L'Oréal "Infallible. With Co-resistium Technology",' I read off the label. '"Resists Signs of Fatigue".'

Mark blanched. Then he said, 'Oh, *that*. Well, I'd been feeling completely washed out so last week I asked the chemist in Upper Street to recommend some sort of vitamin-tonic kind of thing.'

'And this is it?' He nodded. 'Does it work?'

'Yeah! I feel fine now.'

'That's good.' As good as his lying. Then I said, 'It's foundation, Mark.'

'What?'

'You know – makeup. "Continuous Perfecting Foundation",' I read out again. 'In a shade called Vanilla.'

We stared at each other. Mark bit his lip, then took a deep breath. 'Okay, I have seen someone a couple of times. But I swear to you it's over now that you and I are back together. It was just a casual thing.'

By now I knew it, of course, but hearing him say it

made me feel even sicker than I already did. 'It must be more than *casual*, if she's leaving her stuff in the bathroom.'

'Honestly, Annie. I didn't know she had.'

A pit the size of my Downtown seemed to open inside my stomach. 'You've slept with her. Here. In our bed.'

This wasn't a question but, rather, a statement of the bald facts. Mark sat up against the pillows, and crossed his arms over his chest defensively. 'It hasn't been *our* bed for a long time, Annie. You moved out. You were divorcing me, remember?'

I felt numb. He was right. We'd been getting divorced. Even though I was still paying the mortgage on this place, my husband was entitled to sleep with whomsoever he liked in what used to be our bedroom without feeling in the slightest bit guilty, and I no longer had any right to feel jealous or wronged. That didn't stop me doing so, though.

'Who is she?' I asked. He turned his head away. 'Who, Mark?'

He sighed. 'It doesn't matter. It's not a relationship, Annie.'

'No?'

'No! She's just someone I've shagged a couple of times, that's all.'

'I suppose that's what we've just been doing – *shagging*?' I said angrily. 'If you already have someone else, why did you sleep with me?'

'Because you and I still love each other,' he snapped back. 'Because *we*'re what's important!' He sighed again.

When he looked me in the eye he seemed torn between anger and guilt. 'I didn't have to force you, Annie. You wanted to as much as I did.'

He was right, damn him. And that made me feel even angrier – with him and with myself. 'I'd never have slept with you if I'd known you were going out with someone else. You knew that, didn't you?' He didn't answer. 'Is that why you didn't tell me about her?'

He sighed impatiently. 'I didn't tell you because the subject never came up. And because I'm not *going out* with her. She's not important!'

'Well, there's a familiar phrase.' I stood up and searched frantically among the discarded clothes lying on the floor for my Agent Provocateur knickers, which the bastard had torn off me when we'd gone to bed. Still wearing the bathrobe, I struggled back into them, then pulled on my jeans.

'What are you doing?' he said.

'What do you think? Going home.' Never mind that I *was* home, in the flat I was still paying for. I unearthed my bra from under his shorts and stomped into the bathroom to put it on. Meanwhile the bastard got out of bed, followed me in there, stark naked, and put his arms round me from behind as I was fastening it.

'Annie?' he wheedled. 'I thought we'd decided to make a go of things.'

'Let go of me, please!'

He attempted to kiss my neck. 'Look, can't we be grown-up about this?'

'I am being grown-up! Let go!' When he didn't, my elbow jerked back into him.

That seemed to do the trick, because he retreated, rubbing his ribs. 'Ouch! That really hurt!'

'Good.' I stormed back into the bedroom, where Fluffy was busy destroying a tissue he'd found on the floor. Stepping over the mess, I pulled on my T-shirt. Just then, Mark's Nokia rang in the living room. Diddle-ee-dee, diddle-ee-dee, diddle-ee-dee *dee*! He hesitated, but didn't move. 'Aren't you going to answer it?' I said, as I jammed the pins of my earrings through my pierced lobes. 'For all you know it could be your *girlfriend*!'

'I'm telling you, she's *not* my *girlfriend*!'

'Your *lover*, then. Whatever.'

'Annie, please! You've nothing to be jealous of!'

'HOW DARE YOU?' I yelled. 'I AM NOT, REPEAT, NOT, JEALOUS!'

His Nokia stopped ringing. Then, as I went back into the living room in search of my Jonathan Kelseys, it started up again. Diddle-ee-dee, diddle-ee-dee, diddle-ee-dee-*dee*. Whoever was calling was certainly persistent, I thought, as the shiny silver mobile danced a vibrating salsa across the glass coffee-table. 'Answer it!' I yelled.

'No, I won't!'

'Then I will!'

'Don't you dare!'

Mark tried to reach it before I did, but I got to the coffee-table first and snatched it. I ran for the spare loo and somehow managed to lock the door on him. A mobile number was flashing up on the screen. Though it seemed familiar I couldn't place it. By now Mark was yelling at me, and battering at the door to get in. I pressed the green button, and before I could say hello, a woman's voice said, 'Hiya, Sexy-pants! Has she, like, collected Fluffy yet?'

For a moment I was speechless.

'Hello?' said the caller. 'Mark, babes? Hello? Can you hear me?'

'Oh, yes, loud and clear,' I said.

There was a shocked silence at the other end.

'That's right, Darcie, it's Annie,' I continued. 'And please don't hang up. I'm glad you called because I've got something to tell you.'

'Wh – what?' she stuttered.

'You're fired.'

I pressed the off button. Suddenly everything was crystal clear. Mark must have realized it, because when I came out of the cloakroom he was sitting stark naked on the sofa with his head in his hands.

'How could you, Mark?' I said quietly.

He shook his head. 'I don't know. I'm truly sorry. It just kind of happened. I guess I was lonely. And missing you.'

'Please!'

He looked up. His face – his two-faced face – was a picture of misery. 'But it's the truth, Annie! She came round to drop Fluffy off a fortnight ago. I was feeling really low that night, and she kept me talking for ages, and then she just kind of threw herself at me. It's impossible to say no to Darcie. You know what she's like!'

'Obviously not as intimately as you do.'

'I'm sorry,' he murmured. 'Shit! It must seem awful.'

'*Seem* isn't the right word. I just can't believe you could be so devious!'

'What are you talking about, Annie?'

'You did it deliberately, didn't you?'

'Did what?'

'You slept with her so she'd withdraw from being my expert witness.'

'What? I didn't even know you had an expert witness!'

I almost laughed. 'Do you really expect me to believe that?'

'I promise you, Annie!' He shook his head again, then muttered, 'I don't know why you just sacked her.'

'*Helloo?* What planet are you living on?'

'She looks after Fluffy really well, doesn't she? And she hasn't done anything wrong.'

'Sleeping with your employer's husband is a pretty sackable offence. At least, it is in my book.'

'Oh, for God's sake!' Mark shouted. 'In a few days' time I'm going to be your ex-husband!'

'Yes – and, frankly, I can't wait!' I yelled back. 'However, we're still married at the moment, aren't we?'

'Look, I'm sorry. I admit it was a bad mistake. A terrible mistake.'

'You're not joking.' I grabbed my bag, swept into the hall, with Fluffy trotting after me, and clipped on his leash. 'Come on, Fluffy, we're getting out of here!'

Mark padded after me. 'Please don't run off like this, Annie! Please! We need to talk.'

I turned to face him. 'What about?'

'About the future. About us!'

I looked at him incredulously. 'Mark, there is no *us* any more,' I said. 'We have no future. I'll see you in court.'

Pulling Fluffy behind me, I slammed out of the flat and ran down the stairs, blinded by tears of humiliation.

Twenty-nine

With only days to go until the full hearing, a busy work schedule, and no dog-walker, I spent a good part of Monday and Tuesday in minicabs, ping-ponging between the Fulham attic and the store. It was the worst of all possible worlds. My work suffered. Fluffy suffered. I suffered. Even Vlad suffered. A leak sprang in one of the second-floor flats on Tuesday, flooding the one below, so he was back at the house, taking apart some kitchen units in search of the source. The splintering of MDF, combined with the sound of a Polish punk group played loudly though his iPhone, failed to drown the sound of barking when Fluffy was left alone for too long.

'That dog, he is giving me a bloody headache,' Vlad said, when I finally got home from work at seven o'clock on Tuesday evening to find him kneeling on one of the landings, ripping up the laminate strips he'd only recently laid, and exhibiting a glorious flash of builders' bum.

'I'm so sorry!' I said, as I ran up the stairs towards him. 'I tried to get back earlier, but I just couldn't get away.'

He stopped what he was doing and pulled out his earphones. 'That old cow who lives in number three, she come up complaining. The barking is getting on her nerves, she is going to call the council, noise pollution, pets aren't allowed in the lease. Yak, yak, yak. I tell to her, "Hey, I'm the landlord, lady, and I make rules around here. Besides, this dog belongs to my sister's boss, so fuck off, you old bag."' Vlad laughed good-naturedly. 'Maybe I didn't put it like that, Annie, but still, I tell her where to get off, innit.'

'I'm so sorry!'

'Hey, there's no need to lick my fucking boots, eh? The poor sod's lonely all by himself.' As he spoke, a heartrending howl came from upstairs, followed by scrabbling as Fluffy attempted to dig his way under the bottom of the door.

'Look, Vlad, I swear I'll pay for any damage he's caused. And I promise this won't go on for ever,' I said, as I clambered past him and headed upstairs. 'It's just that my bloody dog-walker . . . Well, let's just say she's let me down this week and I can't take Fluffy to work with me.'

'Yes, I hear from Eva what happened when you smuggle him in before. Some goings-on, eh?'

As I approached my front door, Fluffy heard or smelled me coming, and the howling changed back into frantic barking. The moment the door was open, he pushed past me and ran downstairs. By the time I'd found his leash, he was on the landing with Vlad, and they were larking around like two big puppies.

'You big bloody nuisance, innit, Fluffy?' Vlad was saying. 'I tell you what, Annie, I'm gonna be working here all day tomorrow. My friend can help me. There's no reason he should be locked up to drive everyone barking up the fucking wall. I look after him for you.'

'Oh, Vlad! Would you? You're an angel!'

The following morning, I rushed off to work, leaving the door of my flat ajar and Fluffy sitting beside Vlad in the semi-dismantled kitchen on the second floor, sharing his Polish-sausage sandwiches. 'You will take care of him?'

'No problem. He and I, we'll have good time together.'

'Thank you, Vlad, thank you!'

'You left Fluffy with my brother?' Eva said, when I told her. She seemed rather surprised.

'Why do you say it like that?' I asked uneasily. 'Do you think I shouldn't have?'

She flashed me a brisk smile. 'Not at all, Annie. Fluffy will be fine. I'm sure that nowadays Vlad is much more reliable than he used to be.'

What was Eva talking about? I had no time to ask. My morning was wall-to-wall consultations – my government-minister client, a television news presenter, and the recently discarded wife of a Russian oligarch. 'Ah, revenge shopping!' George Haines had said delightedly, when I told him she was coming in. 'That should be good for a six-figure sale!' Then, at half past two that afternoon, my favourite client, Marion Barclay, was popping in to change into the Armani suit and Burberry shirt I'd been keeping for her over the summer. 'I'll be coming from home and going straight on to my job interview,' she'd told me, over the phone the morning before. 'I know I shouldn't have left it till the last minute to pick everything up, but we've only just got back from Italy. Are you sure everything's ready for me?'

'Absolutely, Mrs Barclay. The alterations have been done, the suit's been steam pressed and it's hanging in a plastic bag on the back of my office door, waiting for you. So you can relax. I'll be here to help you get ready.'

'Bless you, Annie.'

Immediately after Mrs Barclay's appointment, I was booked to go up to George's office for an important meeting. Alexis Collins, the editor of *Zine*, the most influential and upmarket on-line style magazine in the USA, was in London for two days and George was taking her out to lunch at Nobu, then bringing her back to the store. 'I don't know why he's bothering,' I'd confided to Eva. 'She's rumoured never to eat anything at all. In fact, they say she doesn't have a stomach, or intestines. And no heart either.' Famously thin, famously beautiful, and infamously hard to please, Alexis – 'the wig on a stick', as one journalist had described her – was thinking of running a feature on Haines and Hampton in her spring issue. If she did, the publicity would be gold dust. My job was to help George impress her with our knowledge of up-to-the-minute fashion trends.

So, all in all, I didn't have a moment to think about Fluffy. That was, until my BlackBerry rang at one thirty, as I was totting up the discarded trophy wife's shopping list – a staggering £104,688.99, which she was charging to her ex's American Express. Mark's name flashed up on the screen. What did he want, today of all days?

I pressed the accept button, and snapped officiously, 'I'm extremely busy. If you have anything to say to me, it'll have to wait until we're in court tomorrow.'

'Well, that's too bad because I need to speak to you now,' Mark retorted, equally officiously.

'What about?'

'Where's Fluffy?'

'He's in my flat, of course.'

'I think you'll find he's not, Annie – that is, if you ever bother to go back there and check up on him.'

'How dare you be so rude? I look after him wonderfully!'

'Yeah, right!'

'Look, I'm at work. Do you know what work is? I left him at home only a few hours ago.'

'Well, he's not there now.'

'Of course he is!' I paused. 'Anyway, how would you know?'

'Because I've just had a phone call from the duty officer at Kensington police station. They've got Fluffy there.'

'Don't be ridiculous! They can't have!'

'Well, they have. Apparently he was picked up an hour ago in the Natural History Museum, trying to sink his teeth into a dinosaur bone.'

I laughed, somewhat bitterly. 'Okay, I've heard enough. This joke's in extremely poor taste.'

'I just can't believe you didn't call me when you lost him!'

'I didn't call you because I haven't lost him. He's at home!'

'Really? Before he got to the museum he apparently stole a slice of pizza from a sandwich bar in Old Brompton Road. He was also spotted in the basement of the Conran Shop, where he knocked over an expensive glass vase with his tail.'

'I don't understand,' I said. 'They must have the wrong dog. How come they phoned you?'

'Because my mobile number's on his collar, remember? And on his microchip details.'

'Look, it's impossible! I took him out for a long walk before work this morning and then I left him in my flat. Or, rather, in the house, with Vlad.'

'Who's Vlad?' Mark said suspiciously.

Suddenly I felt sick. Maybe Vlad had left the front door open and Fluffy had escaped. But the Natural History Museum was miles away from where I lived. How could he have got that far? And wouldn't Vlad have called me if Fluffy had gone missing?

'Annie, who's Vlad?' Mark repeated.

What had Eva said earlier, about Vlad being 'more reliable than he used to be'? 'He's the owner of the house,' I admitted. 'The developer. He's Eva's brother. He was working there today, and he volunteered to look after Fluffy for me. Fluffy must have got out. Oh, God – I'm so sorry.'

'How could you have been so fucking irresponsible as to leave him with a stranger?' Mark roared down the telephone.

'Vlad isn't a stranger! I honestly thought Fluffy was safe with him!'

'Well, you were wrong, weren't you? Frankly, it's a miracle he wasn't run over and killed!' He gave an exasperated sigh. 'Okay, you'll have to go and collect him from the police station straight away. It's in Earls Court Road.'

'What?' I glanced at my Dolce & Gabbana. It was ten past one. 'I can't, Mark! I've got an important client with me, and another coming in at two thirty. Then I've got

306

this magazine editor to deal with. I don't have a moment all afternoon.'

'Well, that's tough,' he said, 'because I'm in Islington, and I'm going to see my solicitor in the City. About *our* divorce. And apparently Fluffy just tried to shag a female deputy inspector or something. So, if he's not collected in the next half-hour, they're sending him to Battersea Dogs' Home. That won't look very good in court tomorrow, will it, Annie?'

Thirty

By the time I got back from collecting Fluffy from the police station it was gone two o'clock. Manny was on the staff door that afternoon and, like Cerberus guarding the gates of hell, he was standing outside it with his feet planted in a sea of crushed dog-ends, smoking a cigarette. His eyes widened when he saw me get out of the cab with my now over-excited mutt. I gritted my teeth, ready for the inevitable battle of wills.

'What 'appened to the 'andbag this time, Annie?' he inquired, discarding his cigarette after a final puff and grinding it underfoot with the others.

'Didn't you know? Big bags are out,' I quipped, as I walked determinedly up to the door. 'And Fluffy wouldn't fit in a tiny clutch.'

'Very funny, very droll.' He put himself between me and the entrance. 'You know yer can't bring 'im in 'ere again. Mr 'Aines says 'e'll give yer the sack if yer do.'

I'd said this to no one, but news travelled fast among the store's employees. 'Where on earth did you hear that rubbish?' I asked him.

'Through the grapevine,' he said, deadpan.

I narrowed my eyes at him. 'It was Eva, wasn't it? Or was it George's secretary?'

'You know better than to ask me that. My lips is sealed, love.'

'Oh, I don't care anyway! Look, please don't make a fuss,' I wheedled, as he continued to bar my way. 'Just let me through, darling. Go on!'

He shook his head slowly. 'Not with that wild animal. It's more than your job's worth, if I 'eard right. And mine, if I let 'im in.'

'But no one will know this time,' I persisted stubbornly. 'I truly promise he won't get into any trouble. Don't look so doubtful. Look, if George does find out, I swear I'll take total responsibility.' I glanced at my watch. It was getting perilously close to the time I was due to see George and I had to get Fluffy settled in my office first. I simply had to get past Manny. 'Come on!' I pleaded, somewhat desperately. 'Darling Manny! I wouldn't have brought him with me if it hadn't been a complete emergency.'

He narrowed his eyes at me. 'What's it wiv you and emergencies? You 'ad one a few years ago, if I remember rightly.'

'Did I?'

'Yes. You nicked my customer's taxi from under my nose outside the front door. Said your old man 'ad fallen over or somethink. What kind of emergency is this?' I could tell he was softening, despite the suspicious scowl.

'If you must know, Fluffy ran away from home this morning.'

'My 'eart bleeds, love. Cruel to 'im, were you?'

'It's a long story and I'd love to tell you every sordid detail but I've got a client arriving any minute. I swear I'll tell you on my way out. *Please* don't give me a hard time. I've just picked Fluffy up from the police and they weren't very pleased with me, either.'

'If Mr 'Aines finds out I seen him . . .'

'But you haven't, have you?' I smiled in what I hoped was my most irresistible manner, and said, 'Close your eyes. Go on! Please!'

Manny sighed in a long-suffering manner. Then he screwed his eyes shut and I pulled Fluffy past him, stopping only to peck his cheek. 'See? You've seen nothing at all,' I said, as I opened the iron gates of the old-fashioned goods lift and shoved Fluffy inside it. 'If Mr Haines ever finds out – which he won't – you can tell him so with a clear conscience.'

'Yeah, right!' Manny said, winking at me. 'You owe me one, Annie.'

'Anything. Anything you like,' I called, as I slammed the lift gates.

I got out on the second floor, and took the back corridor through to Personal Shopping. When she saw us emerge through the stockroom door, Charlotte, who was on Reception, jumped up and gave a thrilled shriek: 'It's the handbag gremlin again!' Tottering round the desk in her thigh-skimming denim boiler-shorts suit, teamed with some multicoloured Office platform peep-toe lace-ups with six-inch heels, she fell on to her bare knees and threw her arms round Fluffy's neck. 'Oh, he's so cute!' She grinned up at me. 'But won't you get into trouble again, Annie? I mean, didn't Mr Haines threaten to sack you if you brought him in again? Oops! I wasn't supposed to know that, was I?'

'Why not?' I said. 'Everyone else in the store seems to. Look, Charlotte, I need you to help me.'

'Of course, Annie! You know I'd do anything for you.'

'Thank you. I'm going to take Fluffy into my office right away, and settle him down in there,' I said, 'so keep watch, will you? Guard this reception desk with your life. Let no one past. It's vitally important that no one finds Fluffy, and that he doesn't get out this time, okay?'

'Okay! Wicked, Annie! Gosh, it's so thrilling. I feel like I'm in a James Bond movie. The one with Daniel Craig. But, Annie?' she said, trailing after me to my office door.

'Yes?'

'What are you going to do with him when Mr Haines comes down with Alexis Collins?'

'They're not coming here, Charlotte. I'm going up to George's office to see her at three o'clock.'

'Oh.' She seemed confused. 'Are you absolutely sure about that, Annie?'

'Yes, Charlotte, I am.'

'Phew. What a relief! Only when Tamara phoned just now, she said he was bringing Alexis Collins down here in five minutes.'

Tamara was George's secretary. 'Aren't they having lunch at Nobu?'

'Well, they were supposed to, but Tamara said Alexis cancelled lunch at the last minute and brought their meeting forward. Apparently she went to see a craniosacral therapist at the Mandarin Oriental Spa yesterday, and she told Alexis she's allergic to seafood. Alexis is, I mean. Not the craniosacral therapist.'

'Oh, my God! When did you say they were coming down here?'

'Well, Tamara did say in five minutes. But that was at least – what? – ten minutes ago.'

'Shit!' I was panic-stricken.

Charlotte bit her lip. 'Oh, Annie! Are you going to get into horrible trouble? May I help you in any way?'

'You may. You can. If you've got a gun you can shoot me. It'll save George having to do it later. Look, where's Eva?'

'She's still at lunch. She said she'd be back in half an hour. But, oh, Lord, I can't quite remember what time she left.'

By now Fluffy was getting impatient. Instead of tiring him out, his expedition to the Natural History Museum and his spell in a police cell seemed to have energized him. His eyes had a wild glint, and he was pulling friskily at the leather Versace belt I'd taken to the police station to serve as a temporary leash. I made him sit on my office floor, and told him not to bark under any circumstances. After ransacking my desk drawers I unearthed three biscuits and a bag of rather old Maltesers. He leaped up, but I wouldn't give them to him yet. I'd save them for keeping him quiet if and when George and Alexis Collins arrived.

I was about to get on the phone to Tamara and suggest we reschedule the meeting in George's office, when I heard his voice booming from Reception, 'And this is the way in to our personal-shopping department. This lovely young lady is, er . . .'

'I'm Charlotte, ma'am. The receptionist. How do you do, madam? Are you having a nice day?'

I put the box of Maltesers on the floor. Fluffy couldn't

believe his luck. As he fell on them, I went out into the corridor just in time to see Charlotte curtsy to a skeletally thin woman, of indeterminate age, who was wearing a long auburn wig and a huge pair of white-framed sunglasses. So, this was the famous Alexis Collins, the New York Upper East Side style icon, who only ever dressed in head-to-toe Chanel. True to her reputation, today she was wearing lime green Chanel shoes, opaque black textured Chanel tights, and the new-season black-and-white slashed-tweed Chanel suit, underneath which she wore an orange silk blouse. Her lime green tote handbag was also from the new season's Chanel collection, and her rings, necklace and earrings were emblazoned with the company's trademark double-C logo. I was surprised she hadn't had it tattooed on her forehead – a narrow, expressionless, Botoxed rectangle stretched between over-plucked eyebrows and the bottom of her fringe, and about the only part of her face visible, other than her lips.

'What charming English manners!' she drawled. 'And what a beautiful English-rose complexion you have.'

'Thank you so much,' Charlotte drawled back, coming into her own. 'My mother taught me always to wash my face in rainwater, so I still do. She says it softens the skin.'

'But isn't rainwater *toxic*?'

Charlotte frowned. 'I don't think so. At least, not the rainwater on our estate in Shropshire where Mummy collects it. She always has the chauffeur bring a bottle up to London when we're here.'

'That's so quaint and British, isn't it, George dahling?'

'Quite. Ah, Annie!' With relief, George had spotted me lingering by my office door, through which I was listening to the steady crunching of Maltesers between shark-like teeth. 'Come and meet Alexis.'

Pasting on a serene smile, but feeling anything but, I went to Reception and let George do the intros. 'Actually, I was just going to come up and see you in your office, Mr Haines,' I said. 'I've picked out a wonderful selection of our styles to show Miss Collins. I could bring them with me. I'm sure you'd both be more comfortable there.'

'Not at all!' Alexis surveyed our reception area with its luxurious contemporary white sofas and deep pile carpet. 'I don't mind roughing it.'

'Alexis wanted to come down to the shop floor, didn't you?' George said, giving her back an avuncular pat.

Her Rouge Noired lips smiled below the sunglasses. 'See, Annie, I like to experience life at the coal face. One can't have one's finger on the pulse of the fashion *zeitgeist* if one inhabits an ivory tower, can one, now?'

'No, I guess one can't,' I answered. I wanted to point out that our all-white personal-shopping suite could hardly be described as a coal face, but limited myself to saying, 'However, I have selected our most cutting-edge designs to show you. And it would be no trouble at all for me to bring them upstairs.'

'As I said, we're quite all right here. Sit down, Alexis.'

'Wouldn't you be more comfortable in one of our changing-room suites?' I said quickly. 'It'd be more private.'

'This is fine,' Alexis said. 'We don't need privacy. After

all, we aren't gonna fuck, are we, George? We're just gonna look at clothes!'

Shocked to the core, George tried to laugh, but didn't manage it. 'Um, may I offer you some Champagne, Alexis?'

The wig-on-a-Chanel-twig sat down and crossed her legs. 'Darling, I never touch alcohol. Only water.'

'Perrier? I think we have Buxton, too, don't we, Annie? Fizzy or flat?'

Alexis shuddered. 'No, no! Like this charming young lady's mother, I always travel with my own supply.' She smiled up at Charlotte. 'Do you think you could find your way to bringing me an empty glass? Sterile, if possible.'

'Sterile? Of course, ma'am.'

While Charlotte went to fetch a clean glass, Alexis delved into her tote and brought out a small dark blue bottle. 'See this, George? It's iceberg water from Greenland. It's over one hundred thousand years old.'

'I say!'

'It predates man and pollution, and it's the purest substance on earth. Purity in a bottle. Drop for drop, it costs more than Château Margaux.'

'In that case, I'd rather have the Bordeaux.'

'Believe me, this *eau* is worth every cent – and it costs a hell of a lot of them. A litre of this a day, and you'll live for ever. You really should try it. I tell you, it's changed my life. I bring it over from the States with me. This is the last bottle I have left. God knows what I'll do when I've drunk it. Die of thirst, I guess.'

George nodded. 'Fascinating! Um, perhaps you could show us what you've selected, Annie? Oh – what's that noise?' A terrible rumpus was now coming from my office.

'Just the cleaners,' I said hurriedly. God, what was Fluffy destroying? 'They're doing the carpet in my office. I'll go and tell them to stop, shall I?'

'No, no. I was just curious.'

'It won't take me a second, honestly.'

'Don't bother, Annie.' George slapped his thigh. 'Just bring on those glorious cutting-edge designs!'

As Charlotte came back with a glass for Alexis's melted iceberg water, I rushed into the stockroom for the rail of garments Eva and I had selected the previous day. They included floor-length Marios Schwab jersey sheaths, colourful Duro Olowu frocks, and some padded Giles Deacon sleeveless jackets that looked as if they belonged in a sci-fi film – just the sort of clothes we'd thought would look good on the e-pages of *Zine*. By the time I'd come back with the rail, a woman was standing in the reception area. She'd already introduced herself to George as one of my clients, and Alexis Collins was staring at her in horror.

It was Marion Barclay. Nervous about getting to her important interview on time, she'd arrived ten minutes early for her appointment, wearing a pair of unflattering old jeans, a shabby brown fleece jacket and trainers. A Tesco carrier-bag containing her good shoes was tucked under her arm. Just then Eva returned from her lunch-break so I left her to deal with George and Alexis Collins while I helped Mrs Barclay get ready.

'Look at me! I'm a right old mess!' Marion Barclay said, as we walked towards my office to collect her clothes. 'I was in such a hurry to leave the house I just threw on the first things I could lay my hands on.' She pulled at her fleece. 'This thing's my husband's. Not exactly chic!'

'Well, we'll soon have you spruced up for your interview,' I told her. 'I'll just get your things.'

Without thinking, I opened my office door and reached for the clothes hanging behind them. The moment I did, Fluffy bounded out.

On a sugar rush he galloped into the reception area and, leaving Marion Barclay where she was, I ran after him. 'What the devil?' George yelled, as Fluffy jumped on to the sofa, trampled across his legs and threw himself at Alexis Collins, knocking her glass of hundred-thousand-year-old water all over her. Straddling her legs, he stuck his nose in the crotch of her skirt and lapped up the liquid iceberg.

'My water!' Alexis screamed, as I lunged for Fluffy's collar.

But he was too quick for me. He leaped off the sofa and disappeared into the store. Without waiting to explain to George – what could I say, anyway? – I followed him towards the escalators and, pushing past the surprised customers, pursued him down to the first floor.

'Excuse me! Stop, Fluffy! Sorry, madam! Come back here immediately!'

Knowing I was after him, and with no intention of being caught, Fluffy swerved through the Burberry concession, knocking over one of the display mannequins, which was dressed in the new season's fashions – a short brown cashmere coat and slinky bronze leggings – and sending four others on the same stand toppling like dominos. I tried to right them, but they kept falling over, so I left them to the assistants, who'd come running over to see what had happened. 'Must go! There's a wild animal on the loose!' I told them, as I glimpsed Fluffy's tail disappear through an archway and into the lift hall.

I arrived there in time to see a set of lift doors close. From the loud voices and squeals that were coming from inside it, I knew he was in there. I watched the digital indicator: the lift went past the ground floor and down to the basement. Instead of waiting for the next lift to arrive, I dashed for the staff stairs and clattered down them.

I emerged in the men's department on the lower ground floor. I didn't have to look for Fluffy, because I could tell where he was by the commotion coming from the store's Italian café. I pushed through its frosted-glass doors into the airy space of minimalist white linen tablecloths and bleached-lime chairs. The frozen faces of the diners and the maître d' were turned to the kitchen, situated in a box in the centre of the room. The usual spectacular view through its plate-glass windows of white-coated chefs slaving over the industrial steel ranges was today eclipsed by an even more spectacular view of my dog, who was standing on one of the counters wagging his tail, his teeth stuck into a leg of Parma ham.

I took a deep breath, and pushed through the double doors into the kitchen, where I was almost deafened by the string of expletives issuing from the mouth of Carlo, the head chef, who was standing next to Fluffy, brandishing a carving knife. I elbowed my way through the gaggle of shouting, white-coated catering staff clustered round him, I grabbed Fluffy by the collar, prised the Parma ham out of his mouth, then lifted him into my arms. Everyone fell silent. Carlo gaped at me as I smiled and said, 'Well done for finding him!' As I carried him towards the door, everyone's eyes followed me. Head lowered, I made my way through the silent restaurant, Fluffy squirming in my arms and ostentatiously licking his lips.

Still carrying him – he wasn't going to escape again, if I could help it – I took the customer lift up to the second floor, and walked slowly back to Personal Shopping with my heart in my black suede ankle boots. I knew I'd have to face George some time, and it might as well be now. I certainly had some explaining to do.

But George wasn't interested in my excuses. He was too busy trying to appease Alexis Collins for her ruined suit, not to mention Marion Barclay who, white-faced and near to tears, was standing by the reception desk, still wearing her husband's fleece and her jeans. As I approached, they fell ominously silent, even Eva, whose hand was on Marion Barclay's shoulder. Mrs Barclay glared at me as if she'd like to kill me, and George's expression turned from merely stormy to positively tornado-like. The only one who seemed remotely sympathetic was Charlotte. From her post behind the desk, she gave me a watery smile, then bit her lower lip.

'What's the matter?' I asked lamely. As if it wasn't obvious. But there was worse to come. Eva jerked her head towards my office and, as I trudged towards it, still carrying Fluffy, I remembered the loud noises that had been coming from inside it earlier on. It was the cleaners,

I'd told George and Alexis. But what had Fluffy been doing?

I opened the door. Mrs Barclay's Armani suit was lying scrunched up on the floor, half in and half out of its protective plastic cover. The skirt was ripped, and the jacket was covered with semi-digested Maltesers. Of the Burberry shirt, only one arm, five buttons, and a collar remained.

The interview outfit was in ruins.

Likewise, my career.

Thirty-one

The following morning was the hearing. Mark and I happened to arrive at the Royal Courts of Justice in Fleet Street at exactly the same time. He was accompanied by Greenwood and her squat, dark-haired female brief, and I was with Williams and Simon, the young, tall, upper-class barrister to whom Williams had introduced me an hour earlier and who was going to represent my case in court.

Full of bounce after his adventures in the Natural History Museum and the store, Fluffy arrived with me. He leaped up at Mark the moment he saw him, and Mark bent to pat the top of his head. Glaring at my soon-to-be-ex as if he were some kind of animal molester, I pulled Fluffy away from him, hoisted the handles of my Downtown on to my shoulder and, like a prize boxer on the way into a big match, swept down the corridor in my black Teenflo trouser suit, surrounded by my legal team.

Clarissa, Dad and Norma were waiting for me outside the courtroom, huddled together a few feet from Mark's parents. Dennis avoided looking at me as I passed him, but Jackie and I exchanged a sad smile, and the briefest greeting.

'Hello, Jackie.'

'Hello, Annie.'

In a bottle-green skirt and peach blouse, my mother-in-law seemed like a different woman from the one who'd had such fun trying on designer clothes with me – could it only have been a few weeks ago? It seemed an age. The fun-filled Jackie had gone. This was the real one – uncomplicated, loyal, down-to-earth, anxious-looking – and I loved her all the more for it. I wanted to tell her that I'd done what she'd suggested and tried to make things better with Mark, but that my efforts had ended in disaster. However, there was no opportunity. The intimacy we'd fleetingly enjoyed when she'd visited me at work would never happen again. My mother-in-law and I were in opposite camps.

Clarissa looked equally anxious. There were shadows under her eyes, and, in a faded dress and dark linen jacket, she was more washed out than ever under the bright fluorescent lights. 'Of course I'll be there, darling,' she'd assured me when I'd asked her if she'd come and support me on the day of the hearing; I simply couldn't have faced it without her. Now she threw her arms round me and hugged me tightly.

'I feel so sick!' I whispered. 'I'm so scared. I want to run away.'

'Nonsense!' she whispered back. 'You can do it! Remember what Miss Davis used to say?'

Miss Davis had taught us ancient history at school. With her large, bulbous eyes and her tiny, upturned nose, she'd looked exactly like a Chihuahua as she'd trotted up and down in front of the class of bored girls, firing the names of Greek and Roman heroes, and intermittently rapping her ruler on the desk of any girl who wasn't concentrating. Clarissa and I had been the worst offenders.

'Miss Davis? Do you mean, "If you two don't stop passing notes to each other, I'll send you to see the head"?' I asked now.

'No! I mean "With your shield or on it".' Those, reputedly, had been the words Spartan women had said as they'd waved off their sons to battle, *'Return with your shield or on it'* had meant the boys should enter battle in the understanding that they should either win or die an honourable death and be carried home. 'I suppose I should say, *"With your dog or on it,"* today,' Clarissa muttered, before she let go of me.

Next, Dad put his arm round my shoulders and gave me a squeeze. 'How's my beautiful girl bearing up?'

'Never better.' I forced a smile. Though we'd had our differences over Mark in the past, I was glad he was there for the final battle. In one of his bespoke grey Savile Row suits, with a red silk handkerchief poking out of his jacket pocket, he looked magnificent and solid; his very presence reassured me. So did Norma's: she'd jettisoned her uniform of skin-tight jeans, high-heeled boots and voluptuous sweaters in favour of a demure, knee-length navy skirt suit, teamed with kitten-heeled pumps. Still, the long black silk waterfall of her straightened hair, her big dangly silver earrings and her shimmering dark purple eye makeup ensured that she was as sexy as ever – as was the back of her skirt, which clung to her voluptuous behind.

'It's so nice of you to come,' I said, as we hugged.

'I wouldn't have stayed away for the world,' she said,

323

as her strong arms encircled me. 'I'll always be here for you, babe.' I felt like crying.

Mrs Justice Khan, a petite Asian beauty in her early fifties, was already sitting at the bench when we entered the courtroom. Williams had been right when he'd told me she was striking: with her finely chiselled features, her pinched little mouth and her cold dark eyes, which could narrow in a second to arrow slits, she struck terror into everyone who saw her. And that included not just the humans but Fluffy, who took one look at her as I led him in, growled nervously and then, ears flattened, slunk under the desk at which Williams, my barrister and I were sitting.

First, the judge granted permission for it to be an open hearing, as Mark and I had requested; otherwise our families would have been excluded from the courtroom. Then my barrister stood up, and stated the grounds on which I'd petitioned Mark for divorce – the irretrievable breakdown of our marriage due to Mark's adultery – then outlined the settlement I had proposed. While he spoke, Mrs Justice Khan flicked through the bundle of evidence in front of her, nodding every now and then, and occasionally shaking her head. Several times she took up a pencil and scribbled notes in the margins of the pages. But when the barrister came to the part concerning Fluffy, she put down her pencil and looked up.

'Even the respondent has agreed that the petitioner has been – and I quote from his lawyer's words at the Financial Dispute Resolution – "more than generous" in the financial offer she has made to him,' the barrister said. 'Mr Curtis is an able-bodied man, but her offer will provide him with a substantial sum of money, which, if wisely invested, will allow him to continue living in the style to which he has become accustomed due to the petitioner's hard work. One must recall that Mr Curtis entered the marriage five years ago with no capital of his own, and that in the intervening period any contribution he made to the marital finances has been negligible. All that Mrs Curtis asks in return for a generous settlement, which amounts to half her assets, is that she be allowed to keep just one of her personal possessions – Fluffy, the dog she had purchased with one hundred pounds of her own money before she even met the respondent, let alone married him.'

Here Mrs Justice Khan got to her feet, took off her black-rimmed spectacles and peered down her elegant nose at Fluffy, who was now lying on the floor at my feet, with his head between his paws and his eyes closed. 'Am I to understand that the petitioner and respondent are in dispute solely over who gets *that*?' she said.

'Yes, my lady.'

She leaned further over the bench, the better to observe Fluffy, and the sides of her long white horsehair wig flapped forward at either side of her face, like a spaniel's ears. As if he knew he was being talked about, Fluffy pricked up his own ears, opened his eyes and rolled them in her direction. After giving her a long stare, punctuated by another low growl, he closed them again and went back to sleep. 'What breed of dog is it?'

After conferring with Williams, my barrister said, 'He's what they call a crossbreed, my lady.'

'Oh. A mongrel.' Her nostrils flared. She sat down in

the judge's seat, her back ramrod straight against its leather padding. 'I'm surprised that either party wants it,' she remarked tersely. 'If it was mine, I'd probably pay for it to be put down.' I was about to leap to my feet in protest and, I suspect, Mark was going to do the same. But Williams put a hand on my sleeve. 'Well, I suppose we'd better get on with it,' Mrs Justice Khan continued. 'If Mr and Mrs Curtis have nothing better to do with their money than to waste it in wasting my time, we'll indulge them, shall we?' Her lips parted in a chilling smile, which made the hair on the back of my neck stand on end.

When my barrister had concluded, Mark's brief got to her feet. For a while she droned on about how Mark's role as a house-husband had enabled me to pursue my career unfettered by any domestic obstacles that might have otherwise held me back from promotion. Then she began an impassioned plea on Fluffy's behalf.

'For thousands of years in this country a pet animal has been considered merely part of the marital estate. It is this fact that the petitioner's case rests on. However, in these more enlightened times I think it is accepted that our relationship with animals, and dogs in particular, is held to be far more complex than our relationship with, say, a chair, a car or even a house. Thus it is surely reasonable for the court to take a broader view, and to direct that the animal's welfare be taken into account when deciding its future. In the United States it is now so commonplace to consider the interests of a family pet that more than a hundred and ninety accredited law schools offer courses in animal-related law. I would like to draw attention to several high-profile divorce cases in the States concerning the same issues we're dealing with here today, most notably, the actor Drew Barrymore, who fought her ex-husband over the custody of their dog, Flossie, and the case of Dita von Teese versus Marilyn Manson, who went to court over the custody of their Dachshunds and cats.'

'Enough, *please*!' Genghis Khan's imperious voice cut her short as effectively as a machete blow. 'Counsel, as far as I am aware we are not in the United States of America, and Mr and Mrs Curtis are not Dita Striptease and Marilyn Monroe – isn't she dead, by the way? Can you please limit yourself to British law and the case in question? Otherwise we'll be here for ever. In other words, cut to the chase.'

The barrister cleared her throat. 'Yes, my lady. To cut to the chase, then. Mrs Curtis's claim for the dog rests solely on the fact that she says he was hers before she met the respondent. In this hearing I aim to show that Mr Curtis has as much right, if not more, to claim owner-ship of Fluffy. Mr Curtis has been almost solely responsible for looking after the dog for the last five years. In his capacity as a dog-walker, he has walked Fluffy at least twice a day every day. It is Mr Curtis who has been at home for Fluffy . . .'

'Helping him with his homework,' Williams muttered under his breath.

'. . . and Mr Curtis who has taken Fluffy to the vet when the dog has been sick, and Mr Curtis who has trained him, fed him and in all other ways acted as the dog's main carer. If the court were to direct that Mr Curtis should be awarded sole residency of Fluffy, this stability in Fluffy's lifestyle would continue, and the dog's welfare would be assured. If, on the other hand, Fluffy were to be given into Mrs Curtis's custody, he would face an uncertain future. He would be left alone six days a week, locked up in unsuitable accommodation for hours on end, a virtual prisoner, with no access to the great outdoors – a dog's natural habitat. In effect, he would be the canine equivalent of a latch-key child.'

Genghis Kahn sighed. 'Let us not demean one of the most important roles of the family division – deciding who should have residency of the children of divorcing couples – by making such tasteless comparisons. It would do us all good to remember that a dog is a dog.'

Williams pursed his lips in a tight smile. It was clear that things were going our way. However, Mark's female counsel had an unpleasant surprise up her white shirtsleeve.

'In short, my lady,' she continued, 'Mr Curtis feels so strongly about Fluffy's welfare that he has instructed me to say that he is willing to forgo the entire financial settlement due to him in order to secure sole residency of the dog.'

I should have felt pleased, but I was outraged. The offer was tantamount to financial blackmail. My father, however, jumped to his feet and called across the courtroom, 'Take the money, Annie!'

'Order,' rapped Mrs Justice Khan. 'Silence, or I will close this hearing to the public.'

'I'm not the bloody public, I'm her father!' Dad grumbled, as Norma yanked him back into his chair.

'Mrs Curtis,' Mrs Justice Khan said, turning to me,

'perhaps we can cut this hearing short. Mr Curtis has made you an offer you surely can't refuse. If you accept it and let him have ... What's the animal's name again?' she said, in an aside to the clerk of the court.

'Fluffy, my lady.'

'Thank you. If you let your husband have Fluffy, you stand to make a huge financial gain by it. More than enough to buy yourself dozens of new dogs.'

'But I don't want dozens of new dogs!' I protested. 'I just want Fluffy. I love *him*, not dogs in general! You wouldn't say to a mother, "You can always get yourself another child", would you? Don't you see how important Fluffy is to me?'

She glared at me as if I was a slug. 'Obviously. Otherwise, I presume, you wouldn't be here, and we'd be spared this exhibition. But, as a mother and grandmother myself, and not a dog-owner, I don't claim to understand your attachment to a mere animal. Well, this is all very stirring stuff, but where is the law in it? As far as I can see, there are two questions. One: to whom does Fluffy actually belong? To the one who purchased him, or the one who nurtured him? Two, should we treat the dog as a chattel, as the law prescribes, or take his wishes and well-being into consideration when determining his future, as one would with a child? If Mr and Mrs Curtis truly have their dog's welfare at heart, perhaps we should do the latter and, as we do with children who are considered old enough to express their own wishes, let him have his own say in the matter – that is, if he is of an age to make a sensible decision. How old *is* the dog, by the way?'

'Five, your honour,' Mark and I said in unison. 'But every human year is the equivalent of seven in a dog's life, which makes him thirty,' Mark continued.

'Thirty-*five*!' my father interjected, with disgust. 'Hopeless!' he added in a loud aside to Norma. 'He doesn't even know his five times table!'

'I, too, have done a little research into the way similar cases are being handled in the United States,' Mrs Justice Khan said, with another of her hydrochloric-acid smiles. 'Mr Curtis's lawyers are not the only ones here who know how to use the search engine Google – and I have come across the so-called "call test", which I mean to use now. Just as a little diversion. Since everyone's determined to waste time, I may as well waste some myself.'

I swallowed hard as dread overwhelmed me. I knew what was about to happen. Mark did, too. Our eyes met for an instant across the courtroom, and I knew we were thinking exactly the same thing: of that time when we'd looked after Clarissa and James's children for the weekend. When we'd got home on the Sunday night we'd gone to bed and watched a DVD of *The Awful Truth*, in which Lucy and Gerry Warrener, a.k.a. Irene Dunne and Cary Grant, had gone to court over the custody of their fox terrier, Mr Smith. The judge in the film had also used the so-called "call test". At the time, we'd sworn that nothing like that could ever happen in our relationship. Now here we were in an identical situation.

'Mr and Mrs Curtis,' Mrs Justice Khan ordered, 'would you mind standing up and walking to opposite sides of the court?' As we did so, Fluffy opened his eyes, raised his head and watched us curiously. 'You, Mr Curtis, a little more towards the window, and Mrs Curtis, more to the other side. Thank you. Right! Now, Mr Williams, will you please lead that animal into the centre of the room? That's it. We want to make this as fair as possible.'

As he stood beside Williams in the centre of the room, Fluffy realized that all eyes were upon him. His face lit up, and his tail was wagging like a metronome set to *allegro*.

'Now, Mr and Mrs Curtis, when I count to three I'd like both of you to call your dog at the same time, so everyone can see who he'd rather be with. At the same time, I'd like you, Counsel, to unclip his leash. Are you ready?'

No, I wasn't. So much would depend on the outcome. As I stood at the side of the court, I wished that, like Irene Dunne, I had my dog's favourite toy hidden in a fur muff to tempt him to me. I cursed myself for not having thought of this, or used Darcie's trick of keeping bacon scraps in my pockets. I also wondered if she'd told Mark about it – or if he'd found that bacon in her jeans pocket for himself. But now wasn't the time to dwell on what the two of them had got up to. I had to concentrate all my energy on persuading Fluffy to come to me, rather than going to Mark.

'One, two, *three*!' said Mrs Justice Khan.

While Williams struggled with the clip of the leash, Mark and I started to call Fluffy as loudly as we could. 'Fluffy! Fluffyball!'

'Here, boy, *here*!'

'Fluffy, darling, come to *me*! *Darling*!'

As we shouted at him across the room, Fluffy looked

first at me, and then at Mark, then back to me again, and then to Mark. Then he got to his feet and wandered over to Clarissa. Norma giggled, which set Clarissa off, Mark's parents, and then everyone else in the courtroom – everyone, that is, with the exception of Mark, me and Mrs Justice Khan.

'Well, he's made his wishes plain enough!' she said, pursing her lips. 'I can't say I blame him. Do you want the dog, madam?' she asked Clarissa. 'He's yours for the asking.'

An hour or so passed, during which the bundles of evidence we'd presented to the court were sifted through in detail and the barristers' hourly fees clocked up and up. It was sickening, listening to our relationship being pulled apart in front of strangers; at times I wanted to die. Both Mark and I were called to the witness box to answer questions about each other's behaviour. How many times had Mark been unfaithful to me? How much had I relied on him to take care of our domestic situation? Did I know how to use the oven? How many hours a week did I actually spend at home?

Then Mark's brief presented a photograph album, showing shots Mark had taken of Fluffy playing with the other dogs he walked on Hampstead Heath. She also played a recording of Fluffy barking frantically, which was said to have been made clandestinely while I was at work, but which my barrister Simon pointed out could have been recorded anywhere.

My side countered by screening Darcie's 'A Day in the Life of Fluffy' on PowerPoint. 'Very touching,' Mrs Justice Khan remarked sarcastically, as the final image of me cuddling Fluffy on a bench in Regent's Park faded to black. 'Though I doubt it'll win an Oscar.' She leafed through her notes, then looked up again. 'Wasn't some expert witness meant to be testifying on behalf of the petitioner?'

'Yes, my lady,' Simon said. 'In fact, it was the same woman who put that film together. Mrs Curtis's dog-walker, Miss Darcie Wells. But I'm afraid Miss Wells withdrew as a witness at the last minute.'

'Withdrew? For what reason?'

He took a deep breath and a step forward, like an actor about to deliver a killer line. 'She had a change of heart, my lady, after Mr Curtis seduced her, apparently with the express purpose of persuading her to withdraw her state-ment in support of his wife.'

Jackie and Dennis gasped. So did Dad and Norma. But Mark jumped to his feet and said, 'That's a complete lie!'

Genghis Khan glared at him over the top of her spec-tacles. 'Mr Curtis, interfering with a witness – no *double-entendre* intended – is a very serious offence. Please explain yourself. And remember that you are still on oath. Are you saying that you did *not* have sex with Miss Wells?'

Mark had enough of a conscience to look embar-assed. 'Well, we did have sex,' he explained, turning scarlet, 'but it wasn't for that reason. I didn't even know Darcie was one of Annie's witnesses, for God's sake. How was I supposed to? She never mentioned it to me!'

'I suppose you were too busy discussing more important

matters at the time – Ugandan affairs, no doubt,' Mrs Justice Khan said tersely. 'Well, Counsel, have we finished with all this yet?'

'Not quite,' said Mark's brief, rising to her feet again. 'I would like to recall Mrs Curtis as a witness.'

What was going on? Williams and I frowned at each other and, after a word with him, Simon said, 'Objection, my lady. To make Mrs Curtis take the stand again seems unnecessarily tedious.'

'This whole affair is unnecessarily tedious,' Genghis Kahn put in. 'Or should I say unnecessary *and* tedious?' She turned to Mark's barrister. 'Counsel?'

She cleared her throat. 'Since the ownership of Fluffy is of crucial importance, my lady, I'd like to question the petitioner again on one more point.'

'Very well. Objection overruled. But can you be as brief as possible?'

What was going on? I looked at Williams, who raised his eyebrows and gave a small shrug. Feeling slightly uneasy, I went back to the witness box. The judge reminded me that I was still on oath, and the brief began questioning me. 'Mrs Curtis, can you please tell the court in your own words how you acquired your dog?'

I looked at Williams, who looked at Simon. 'Objection, my lady,' he said immediately. 'The petitioner has already been examined on this point.'

'Overruled. Answer the question, please.'

I hesitated. There was a horrible sinking feeling in my stomach. But I had no choice but to go on. 'As I said earlier, I bought him from a tramp in Camden Town.

Fluffy was a small puppy at the time, and the man was obviously mistreating him. Fluffy was dehydrated, and almost starving.'

The brief pushed her long black hair behind her ears and adjusted her thick spectacles. 'And could you tell the court again exactly how much you paid the tramp for him?'

I felt extremely uneasy. All eyes were upon me. I cleared my throat and said, 'A hundred pounds.'

'Let me just get this clear.' She flashed me a simpering smile. 'The tramp said, "You can have this puppy for a hundred pounds," so you opened your handbag and handed over the money to him?'

I hesitated, then said, 'Yes.'

'I see.' Now she cleared her throat. 'Did you have a hundred pounds in cash in your handbag at the time, Mrs Curtis?'

'Yes,' I stammered. And then I felt myself go red. 'Well – no,' I added. 'Not all of it.' I stopped.

There was a long pause, during which I glanced round the court. Was I imagining it, or was everyone staring at me in a peculiar way? Dad, Norma, Jackie, Dennis, Mark – even Clarissa. Then Mark's barrister said, 'Can you clarify that, please?'

I tore my eyes away from the other people, and looked down at my hands. 'I had . . . well, thirty or forty pounds on me. So I handed it all to the tramp – as a sort of deposit. Then I – I went round the corner to the bank and I got out the rest.'

'On a Sunday?'

'Yes. From a cashpoint machine.'

'I see. And can you tell us what happened afterwards, Mrs Curtis?'

'Well, I . . . I . . .' Everyone was still watching me. I hesitated again. And as I did so, Simon got to his feet and cried, 'Objection!' again.

'Overruled,' snapped Mrs Justice Khan. 'Frankly, I fail to see where this line of questioning is going, but wherever it is, I'd like us to get there as soon as possible. Please answer the question, Mrs Curtis.'

'Shall I repeat it for you, Mrs Curtis? What did you do after you'd got the money out of the cashpoint machine?'

Suddenly I could scarcely breathe. She knew! I told myself it was impossible. How could Mark's lawyers have found out about him? How could they know what had happened, when I'd told no one about it? Not Clarissa, not Dad, and not even Mark.

No one knew the real story of how I'd got Fluffy.

No one, that was, except Darcie bloody Wells.

My mind flashed back to the first night she and I had got drunk together in the local singles bar. Though I was not normally a big drinker, we'd got through a whole bottle of wine, then ordered another and drunk at least half of it. The following morning I'd woken up with a splitting headache, made worse by the memory that I'd told her much more than I'd ever revealed to anyone else. At the time, I'd dismissed it from my mind. What did it matter? It had all happened so long ago.

Besides, Darcie was on my side.

Then, a few weeks later, she'd had an affair with Mark. And I'd sacked her.

Suddenly I pictured her naked in Mark's arms after they'd made love, and she was gabbling away to him in her usual fashion. Mark must have lapped it up – he'd always liked a bit of pillow-talk. I could almost hear her spill the poisonous beans in her sweet little-girl voice: 'Annie was, like, *right* . . . and she was, like, *so* . . . and the tramp was, like, *hey* . . . And Fluffy was, whatever.' Had she repeated every little detail I'd told her in the wine bar? Even the bit I'd said about Mark being good in bed? Had Mark then told Greenwood about the tramp? Or had Darcie gone to Greenwood off her own bat in search of vengeance?

'Mrs Curtis? Can you please tell us what happened then?'

I stared at Mark's brief. Loudly, like the beat of a warning drum, the blood started pounding in my ears. Even if she knew, how could she prove anything? I could say that Darcie was lying! Who could disprove it? No one had been there that day, except me and the tramp.

Clarissa was right: today was a case of 'With your shield or on it.' I raised my chin defiantly and said, 'I went straight back to Jamestown Road, where I'd left the tramp, and gave him the rest of the money.'

'Thank you, Mrs Curtis. No further questions.'

'The witness can stand down.'

As I returned to my seat, flooded with the relief of having got that over with, Mark's brief smiled at me, like a snake that had just caught a fly on its tongue. Then she turned to the judge. 'My lady, I would like to call one final witness.'

Mrs Khan yawned. 'Must you, Counsel?'

'He's a crucial witness. Mr Joseph Holtby.'

'Who's Joseph Holtby?' Williams whispered, as I sat down next to him.

'I haven't a clue,' I whispered back. 'I've never heard of him.' Needing reassurance, I reached down and stroked Fluffy, who was now stretched out under my chair.

Simon stood up. 'I object, your honour,' he said. 'There was nothing in the disclosure about calling Joseph Holtby as a witness. My client doesn't know anyone of that name. Anything he has to say would therefore be irrelevant to her claim for full custody of her pet.'

'On the contrary, my lady,' Mark's brief said. 'Mr Holtby's testimony is extremely relevant. In fact, it will show that not only is the petitioner unfit to look after Fluffy, she is not even his rightful owner. On top of that, she has given false testimony to this court, and she has lied to her husband since the day she met him.'

'Nonsense!' Clarissa shouted, jumping out of her seat. 'That's impossible!'

At the same time my father sprang up, red in the face. 'How dare you call my Annie a liar?' he yelled.

Even Mark looked alarmed as he tugged at Greenwood's arm and said, 'Hey, c'mon! That's a bit much!'

'Order, order! Will everyone please sit down? Order!'

Simon looked at Williams, who turned to me. 'What she's talking about?' he muttered.

'I haven't a clue!' I hissed back. But I had.

'Very well, then, Counsel,' said Mrs Justice Khan, in a long-suffering voice. 'Call your witness, if you want to.

But I hope you have a very good reason for making such serious allegations against the petitioner.'

'I do, my lady,' the brief said. 'I call Mr Joseph Holtby.'

Thirty-two

We all turned as the double doors at the back of the courtroom swung open. In came a man who might have been any age from thirty-five to fifty-five, walking with a jerky limp. His long, grey-streaked hair looked as if it had been chopped off at shoulder-level with a pair of garden shears, and his chin was covered with clumps of stubble and drops of dried blood, as if he had recently shaved himself with a blunt razor. An ill-fitting grey jacket hung awkwardly from his bony shoulders. From the way he kept fingering the lapels, he was uncomfortable in it, almost as if, like his all-too-shiny shoes, he'd put it on for the first time that day. Perhaps he had – as he walked towards us, I noticed a shop label swinging below the hem. Whoever Joseph Holtby was, he'd been scrubbed up for his court appearance but, as one could tell from the state of his long, ragged, dirt-engrained fingernails, not thoroughly enough.

'Do you recognize him?' Williams whispered urgently, as Holtby approached the judge.

'I don't think so,' I said. But as I scrutinized the man's face my unease grew. There was a large cold-sore scab on his lip, alongside the scars of many others. Beneath his eyebrows blinked a pair of bright blue eyes, overlaid with a yellow, rheumy cast.

Could it be him? It wasn't possible. And yet, as Joseph

Holtby climbed into the witness box and took an oath to tell the truth, the whole truth and nothing but the truth, he pushed back the lock of hair that was flopping over his forehead, and the Harry Potter scar was there for all to see.

Williams tapped my wrist. 'Well? Do you recognize him?'

Someone else certainly did, even after all these years. His nose twitched, his ears flattened against his skull and he growled menacingly. Joseph Holtby, who was by now sitting in the witness box, pointed a nicotine-stained finger towards him. 'Seamus!' he cried. 'My little darling!'

Teeth bared in a snarl, Fluffy jumped to his feet and lunged at him, but I grabbed hold of his leash just in time to stop him getting away.

Mark's brief stood up. 'Mr Holtby, could I ask you to tell the court a little about yourself?'

'Why do they want to know about me?' he said suspiciously. 'I thought I was here as a witness. I haven't done anything wrong.'

'Quite the contrary. I'm trying to explain who you are. Would you mind telling us where you live?'

'To be sure, I'm what they call "of no fixed abode". I stick around Camden Town, mostly.'

'And how long have you been sticking around there, as you put it?'

'Six or seven year, mebbe, now.'

'And do you recognize this dog?'

He nodded. 'I'd know him anywhere by his colouring and that tuft o' hair on his forehead. Though I haven't seen him since he was a wee pup. He's my little Seamus.'

'Can you please explain what you mean when you say that he's yours?'

'I had him when he was a puppy.'

'When you say you had him, do you mean that you bought him?'

'Yes. Off a friend.'

'And how much did you pay for him?'

'Oh, I forget the exact amount. But I t'ink it was a pack of Silk Cut.'

'And how long did you have him for?'

'Sure it was only a matter of weeks. I loved that puppy as if he was my own flesh and blood. And he helped me in my profession.'

'Could you please tell us what your profession is?'

He scratched his head thoughtfully. 'I guess I'm in what you'd call wealth redistribution.'

'Can you explain that a little more fully, please?'

'I'm a little like Robin Hood. I ask money off them who can afford it, and use it to live on.'

'In other words, you beg?'

He drew himself up. 'It's an honest job. And I can't work, see? I'm on disability benefit,' he explained to the judge.

'Mr Holtby, can you tell the court what happened to Seamus?'

His eyes flashed with anger. 'He was stolen from me.'

There was a general intake of breath. Though my eyes were now downcast, I sensed Williams glance at me. 'Stolen?' the barrister repeated.

'Aye, stolen. By a young lady.'

'And where did this theft take place?'

'In Camden Town. Behind the bingo hall.'

'Can you explain when that was, and what happened that day?'

'It were a few years ago, on a Sunday – I'd just been thrown out of the church where I'd been sleeping because the service was about to start. So, I went for a walk, and settled down in a doorway. To be honest wid you, I might have had a drop too much to drink.'

'And what happened next?'

'I fell asleep. And when I came to, this young woman was standing in front of me, with Seamus clasped in her arms, ready to make off with him. I'd caught her in the act. She pretended she wanted to buy him from me. At first I said no, but then I changed my mind. You see, I thought she might be able to offer him a better life than I could.'

'And how much did she offer to pay you for Seamus?'

'A hundred pound.'

'A hundred pounds?' the barrister went on. 'That's a great deal of money, Mr Holtby.'

'It would have been – enough to start a new life wid, if she'd only paid it me. She handed over a small deposit, see, and then she ran off, saying it was all she had on her, and she'd be back soon wid the rest.'

'And did she return with the rest of the money?'

'To be sure, I waited a long while, and she didn't come back. And while I was waiting, I changed my mind about selling the dear little t'ing. I couldn't bear to part wid him,

343

see? I thought, Joseph, you need this little puppy, he's the only one in the whole wide world who loves you. So I waited for her, t'inking I'd give her back her money when she returned. I waited and I waited. I t'ink I must have fallen asleep again. Then . . .'

'Yes?'

'Then, some time later . . .'

Some time later . . . My mind went back to that scorching hot Sunday afternoon. I was dressed in my white jeans and black T-shirt, standing right at the back of the long, long queue to use the cash machine on the corner of Parkway. Directly in front of me was a tall, skeletally thin Goth wearing skintight black trousers and a sleeveless vest. There was a tattoo on his arm, in the shape of a crucifix held up by a monstrous hand. It occurred to me as I was staring at that quasi-religious image that the tramp would have disappeared from Jamestown Road by the time I got back there, taking with him the puppy and the money I'd already paid.

The moment I'd got my money out, I ran back towards Jamestown Road, weaving my way along the crowded pavement and twisting my ankle more than once.

At last I turned the corner. As I'd suspected, the tramp had gone, taking with him the puppy, my thirty pounds, and his soiled blue sleeping-bag. All that was left of him was the strong stench of urine and a trickle of some sinister, sticky liquid snaking across the ground. Seething with anger, I ran up to the corner with Arlington Road, thinking he might have staggered towards the old hostel for the homeless, but he was nowhere in sight. I hung about outside the hostel for a while, convinced that he must have gone in, but when I plucked up the courage to ask at the door, the man in charge said he knew who I was describing but hadn't seen him since that morning.

I honestly didn't care about the money. I just wanted to save the puppy. I remembered the way the drunk had ill-treated it, and the way it had looked up at me – as if it was begging me to rescue it.

I spent the next two hours tracing and retracing the surrounding streets, asking everyone I met if they'd seen anything of the man with the puppy, but no one had.

It had been around five fifteen when I'd left Clarissa's house, slightly tipsy from downing two glasses of Pimm's. Suddenly it was getting dark, Camden Market was closed, and I'd been searching for the tramp for hours. My arches were killing me, and the straps of my sandals were cutting into my insteps. There were blisters under my toes, and, even though I'd bought a large bottle of freshly squeezed orange juice from a stall near the canal, and gulped at it constantly, my head was aching and my throat was parched. Utterly defeated, I decided to give up the search, and headed for the Tube station.

Which was when I noticed the alleyway beside the bingo hall – a narrow, dark canyon between high brick walls. About ten metres or so from the street, it turned sharply to the left, so I couldn't see where it led. It was the kind of alleyway that, under normal circumstances, I wouldn't have dreamed of walking down, certainly not alone and at night.

I hesitated, wondering what sort of dodgy situation might be lurking down there. Then, thinking of the puppy,

I turned down the alleyway, walking as quickly and confidently as I could. Round the corner it ended in a barred doorway, painted with the words 'Emergency Exit'. I was about to turn back when I noticed something lurking behind a large, industrial-sized waste-bin beside the door. Holding my breath against the stench, I walked round it. The tramp wasn't there, but his stained blue sleeping-bag was. I stood there, looking at it. And then I heard a muffled whimper from underneath.

There was no way I was going to touch the disgusting thing with my hands, so I lifted it off gently with one foot. Underneath was a sodden cardboard box with 'New Zealand Apples' printed on the side – and inside it, in a bed of his own filth, was a trembling Fluffy.

Without another thought I scooped him up, tucked him under my arm and scurried back down the alleyway. As I came out into the road, I bumped straight into the tramp. He smelled even more strongly of whisky than he had before, and he was carrying a plastic bag of bottles in one hand.

'Oy!' he said. 'What're you doin'?'

Without stopping to explain, I ran in the direction of the station.

It wasn't until I was on the train home that I realized I should have thrown the rest of the money at him. But no way was I going to risk returning to find him again.

Thirty-three

'And is the woman who stole your dog in this courtroom today?' Mark's barrister asked, when Holtby had finished speaking.

Holtby pointed at me. 'She's the one,' he said. 'I never forget a face.'

'Thank you, Mr Holtby,' she said. 'No more questions.'

A flush of shame crept up my throat. I couldn't speak. Williams picked up his Biro, scribbled something on a piece of paper and pushed it towards me. 'Say nothing under any circumstances,' it read. Then he whispered something to my barrister, who stood up and addressed the judge.

'My lady, I have some questions for Mr Holtby.'

Mrs Justice Khan glanced at her watch and sighed. 'Very well. But make it quick, please. It's almost lunchtime, and I'm sure Mr and Mrs Curtis have no wish to drag this expensive case on into the afternoon. I certainly haven't.'

Simon stuck his thumbs in his armpits and turned towards Holtby. 'Mr Holtby, are you an alcoholic?' he asked bluntly.

The tramp lifted his chin proudly. 'Yes, I am.'

'And had you been drinking on the afternoon of the so-called puppy theft?'

'I always take a drop in the afternoons.'

'Any idea how many drops it was that particular afternoon?'

'I don't recall.'

'Are we talking one unit of alcohol? More than one? Two? Three units, perhaps? Four? Six? Eight?'

Holtby frowned. 'I don't know what you mean by units but it couldn't have been more than a litre of Strongbow and half a bottle o' whisky.'

'Not more than a litre of Strongbow *and* a half-bottle of whisky?' The barrister smiled. 'Thank you. So, would it be fair to say that you were somewhat inebriated at the time?'

Holtby looked affronted. 'Not so that it would cloud my memory.'

'Mr Holtby, do you have any proof that you ever owned any puppy, let alone this one? A purchase invoice, perhaps? A photograph, showing you and your pet enjoying happy times together? Or are we simply to take your word for it? The word of a homeless alcoholic,' he announced, turning to the judge, 'against that of a hard-working woman who, through her industry and generosity, kept her impecunious husband in luxury for years.'

'Objection, my lady!' Mark's brief stood up. 'This line of questioning is –'

'Overruled. Answer the question, please, Mr Holtby.'

'No, to be sure I don't have that kind of proof.'

'And if we were to give you the benefit of the doubt and say that you did once own a puppy – even this one – do you have any proof that it was stolen? For example, did you report the theft to the police and get a crime number from them?'

Holtby grimaced 'Go to *the police*? I certainly did not!'

Mark's brief jumped to her feet again. 'Objection, your honour. We've already established that Mr Holtby was homeless at the time, and in a state of slight inebriation. It is highly unlikely that the police would have shown the slightest interest or sympathy had he reported the theft.'

'Sustained. Get to the point, please, Counsel.'

'I am trying to establish the facts, my lady. They are, first, that Mr Holtby is a self-confessed alcoholic, who has admitted that he'd been drinking on the afternoon of the so-called puppy-theft. Second, even if he is telling the truth, and someone did steal his puppy, there is no proof that my client took it, or even that Fluffy is the same dog. Given how much a puppy changes as it grows —'

'Yes, yes, I take your point. Perhaps we should just ask Mrs Curtis if she has any comment to make about Mr Holtby's claim.'

'I object, my lady. My client is . . .'

'. . . willing to explain,' I said, standing up.

'My lady, I object,' said Simon.

'Objection overruled. If your client wishes to clear this matter up, I'm not going to prevent her speaking. This case is starting to get interesting, and not before time.'

Williams turned towards me, and whispered, 'I strongly advise you not to say anything at all, Mrs Curtis.'

'But I've got nothing to be ashamed of.'

'Mrs Curtis, please, listen to me. I know what I'm talking about.'

By now I'd had enough of taking his advice. It was getting me nowhere. Feeling headstrong and slightly reckless, I stood up and walked back towards the witness box. The judge nodded at me as I sat down. 'Thank you, Mrs Curtis. But before you speak, I'd like to remind you that you are still on oath.'

'Yes, I know.' I took a deep breath, and the truth flooded out of me. 'Well, yes, Fluffy is Mr Holtby's puppy,' I admitted. 'I bought Fluffy from him because otherwise he would have died. I agreed to pay Mr Holtby a hundred pounds, but I only had thirty on me, so I gave him what I had, then went off to get some more from the bank, just like he said. But when I came back to Jamestown Road, Holtby had run off with Fluffy *and* my money. *He'd* stolen from *me*. I searched for him for hours – not because I wanted my money back but because I wanted to save Fluffy. In the end I found him – he'd been abandoned all alone in a cardboard box behind a dustbin in an alleyway. He had no water or food, and he was lying in his own filth. Crying. You can't imagine how cruel it was. So I took him away. I didn't *steal* him, because I'd already paid Mr Holtby thirty pounds for him.'

'The price was a hundred,' Holtby shouted.

'Which, I think, is the price that, earlier this morning, you swore on oath you'd paid,' Mrs Justice Khan said. 'So, you were lying, Mrs Curtis?'

I looked around me, unsure of my territory. 'Well, not really.'

'I asked you a simple question. Please answer yes or no.'

'Well, in that case the answer's yes.' I saw Williams put

his head into his hands. 'But it wasn't really a lie. I mean, I would have given Mr Holtby the rest of the money if he'd kept to his side of the bargain. I'd just been to get it for him, for heaven's sake!'

Mrs Justice Khan looked at me disapprovingly. 'Did it not occur to you that Mr Holtby might have changed his mind about parting with the animal?'

'No! I just thought he'd stolen my money. Which he had!'

'So you took the dog out of revenge?'

'No!' I insisted. 'I took him because otherwise he would have died within a matter of hours. And I'd already paid thirty pounds for him – more, actually, because I'd given Mr Holtby money earlier on that day to buy himself some food.'

'That was charity!' Holtby cried out. 'Alms for the poor!'

I looked round the room in dismay. 'Surely the actual price I paid isn't that important?'

'What you think is or isn't important is irrelevant,' Mrs Justice Khan said. 'What is important is, that, having affirmed that you would tell the truth, you have lied in a court of law. By doing so, you have committed perjury.'

'*What?*' I couldn't believe this was happening. I turned to my father. Surely he'd stand up and tell the judge she was mistaken. But Dad was biting his lip and staring at his knees.

'Perjury is considered one of the most serious crimes in the criminal calendar,' Mrs Justice Khan continued, with more enthusiasm than she'd shown all morning. 'It is punishable by up to seven years' imprisonment and

351

heavy fines. I have no choice but to order you to be charged with this offence, Mrs Curtis. As for this divorce hearing, and your dispute over who should get residency of your dog, Mr and Mrs Curtis, I rule that, from this moment on, he should live with his rightful owner – Mr Joseph Holtby.'

As Holtby raised his clenched fist and shouted, 'Long live British justice!' Mark and I both jumped to our feet and shouted 'No!' in unison.

'You can't do that!' Mark shouted.

She gave him a withering look. 'Mr Curtis, do I have to remind you that I am in charge of this court, and that I can do what I like, as long as it's within the law? And if you make another remark like that, in that tone of voice, I'll have *you* for contempt.'

'But Annie doesn't deserve to be charged with perjury!' he went on. 'And Mr Holtby hasn't a clue how to look after Fluffy. He doesn't know him. He's not even got anywhere to take him.'

'Well, Mr Curtis, it was your counsel who introduced Mr Holtby as a witness. You should have thought about this before. Frankly, you have only yourself to blame if you don't like the outcome of this hearing. Would you like me to order that the dog should be put down instead?'

'No!' we both shouted again.

And I added, 'Your honour, I mean, my lady, I beg you not to give Fluffy to that man! Let Mark have him, please!'

Mrs Justice Khan froze me with an icy stare. 'Am I to understand, Mrs Curtis, that having just wasted tens of thousands of pounds of your own money on this ridiculous hearing, not to mention hours of my precious time, *and* committed perjury into the bargain, you're now telling me how to do my job?'

'No, of course not, but –'

'Right! I've now had enough of this circus. As I said, in the case of Curtis versus Curtis, the dog goes to Mr Holtby. As for the couple's assets – if there are any assets left after costs are paid and the fine for perjury that Mrs Curtis will no doubt get – they should be divided equally between the petitioner and the respondent. Now, Mr Holtby, I suggest you take that animal as far away from here as possible. Mrs Curtis, you must report to your local police station tomorrow morning to face charges. If you don't turn up, I'll have a warrant issued for your arrest. Understand? This court is now adjourned. I want my lunch.' She swept out of the court, leaving us all reeling.

The moment she'd left, all the women present – Clarissa, Norma, even Jackie Curtis – burst into tears. Meanwhile my father sprang to his feet and ran towards Mark with his fists raised. Jackie screamed, and Norma pulled Dad back, saying, 'Don't, Bob! Don't! You'll only make things worse!' Meanwhile Clarissa ran to me and threw her arms around me. As I looked over her shoulder, my eyes met Mark's, and we stared at each other across the ruins of our marriage, aghast at what we'd done.

Williams broke off from his conference with Simon. 'Not the outcome we'd hoped for, I'm afraid,' he muttered, as he stood up and shuffled his papers into a neat pile.

'You're not joking,' Clarissa said furiously, releasing me.

'How could you have let this happen? It's a complete disaster for Annie.'

'Yes, well, the perjury business is most unfortunate,' he went on. 'I did advise her not to say anything. You'll be needing a lawyer again, I expect, Mrs Curtis. You have my email address and telephone number. Perhaps we should have a word about it outside. I'm sure we can come to some arrangement over fees.'

At that moment, Holtby came to me, grabbed the leash and started to pull Fluffy away from me. Fluffy dug his heels in. 'Come on, you stupid mutt,' Holtby grumbled, yanking him roughly towards the doors. Fluffy strained away from him, and snarled dangerously, showing his teeth. I knew he was on the point of attacking. Mark did, too. He ran over to them, and when he approached, Fluffy jumped up at him.

'Look, you don't *really* want this dog, do you?' Mark said to Holtby.

The tramp looked at him blankly. 'Now, what makes you think that?'

By now Fluffy was snarling again. 'I'll buy him off you,' Mark said.

'Buy him? So, another one wants to buy my dog! Well, this time he's not for sale.'

'Oh, come on! *Stop that, Fluffy! Sit!*'

'This here's a valuable animal, I'll have you know.' Holtby yanked roughly at the leash again. 'He must be – with all the trouble you've taken to try and keep him. And now he's mine again. Ouch! Get off, you vicious brute!' For Fluffy had fastened his teeth round one of Holtby's trouser legs.

'Stop, Fluffy!' Mark shouted. Just then, Holtby leaned down and struck Fluffy on the head with his fist. Fluffy flew sideways with a whimper, and a second later Mark grabbed Holtby by the lapels. 'Don't you ever hurt this dog again, understand?' As he let go of him Holtby toppled backwards. 'Okay, let's stop playing games and cut to the chase,' Mark went on masterfully, grabbing Fluffy's leash as he lunged at the tramp a second time, snarling and barking. 'This dog's never going to be any use to you – look at him! So, how much do you want for him?'

Looking shaken, Holtby dusted down his suit jacket. Then he grabbed the leash back from Mark. 'To be sure, he's my meal ticket.'

'How much?' Mark repeated.

'Twenty.'

Now Mark looked taken aback. 'Twenty quid?' he said quietly.

'I'll give you forty!' my father called.

'Sixty!' shouted Dennis.

Holtby threw back his head and laughed, showing brown teeth. 'You all think I'm stupid, don't you? Just because I like a drink now and then and have nowhere to live. Twenty, forty, sixty quid? Pah! I want twenty grand for him!'

We all gasped, even my father, who sank down on one of the benches, leaned forward and put his head in his hands, muttering, 'That's all we need – a fucking comedian!'

Meanwhile, Mark glanced at me. The colour had drained from his face. Then he turned back to Holtby. 'That's ridiculous,' he said.

Holtby shrugged. 'Not so. It's simple economics, the law of supply and demand. I haven't always been on the street, see,' he added, as he saw the astonishment on Mark's face – on all our faces. 'I used to be a schoolteacher – oh, yes, before my wife left me and took everything, including my kids. So.' He tightened his hold on the leash. 'For once in my life I have a monopoly on a product, and I can name my price. If you want it, you can pay up. Take it or leave it. It's your choice.'

Mark glanced at me again. By now I was sobbing. Poor Fluffy! It was all so hopeless. 'You're holding me to ransom,' Mark said to Holtby. 'Look, I'll give you five hundred for him. Okay, a thousand.'

'What?' cried Dennis.

'No way!'

'Five thousand, then? Ten?' Everyone gasped again.

'Come to your senses, lad!' Dennis said, running forward and grabbing Mark by the elbow. 'Are you mad?'

Holtby walked off, dragging Fluffy after him.

Shaking off his father, Mark followed him. 'Fifteen thousand,' he said. Holtby kept on walking. 'Okay! I'll give you what you want,' Mark said as Holtby clasped the handle. 'Twenty thousand pounds.'

Holtby froze. Then he turned. A huge grin spread across his face. Just as he was about to shake Mark's hand I heard myself call, 'Thirty thousand!'

'Annie!' Clarissa gasped, 'What are you saying?'

'Shut up, Annie!' my father yelled.

'Forty!' cried Mark.

'Forty-five!' I shouted.

Clarissa shook my arm. 'For God's sake, stop it!'

Mark looked at me again. 'Fifty thousand!'

I hesitated. 'Don't, Annie, don't!' Clarissa hissed at me. 'You haven't got that kind of money!'

The courtroom was completely silent for a moment. Then Holtby said, 'You did say fifty thousand? For this piece of living shite?' Mark nodded slowly. By now he was ashen. Holtby smiled and held out his hand. Mark gulped, then shook it. 'Now, that's more like it,' Holtby said. 'You're what I call a real gentleman.'

Thirty-four

Maybe I was in shock, because the next thing I knew we were standing outside the court – me, Norma, Dad, Clarissa, Williams and Simon, Dad and Clarissa supporting me by the arms. All I could think was that Mark and I had just been involved in a bidding war for our own dog, and Mark had agreed to pay fifty thousand pounds for him, which was probably all of the money he'd get out of the divorce once we'd paid off the lawyers and the court expenses.

'What a waste of dosh!' my father was saying. 'As for that bastard Curtis, I'll fucking kill him.'

'Stop it, Bob!' said Norma.

'No, I won't! He's ruined my Annie's life! Mark my words, I'll get him for it if it's the last thing I do. As for you, young lady,' he went on, turning to me, 'telling lies in court, stealing that dog, marrying that idiot in the first place – this whole thing has been a monumental cock-up from beginning to end.'

Williams tried to butt in: 'Now, now, Mr Osborne –'

But my father interrupted him. 'I don't want to hear another word from you! Understand? Call yourself a solicitor? Why, you couldn't solicit if you was a tart on a street corner!'

Just then, Mark, his parents and his lawyer came out of the building. Jackie was still weeping, Mark looked paler than ever and was holding Fluffy's leash. As they drew closer, Fluffy strained towards me, wagging his tail madly. When my father saw Mark coming, he lunged at him again.

'You stupid bastard!' This time his right fist caught Mark a blow on the cheek. Mark staggered backwards, knocking Greenwood's briefcase to the ground. As her papers fluttered into the air I threw myself at Dad. Clarissa attempted to pull me away, and Fluffy jumped up at us, barking, and suddenly Dennis's fists were flying at my father. Next, Fluffy sank his fangs into Dad's bespoke jacket – the bottom part of the sleeve came away in his teeth – and Dad went for Mark again. I became aware of flashes going off: a couple of passers-by had stopped to watch the brawl, and one was taking photographs of us on her mobile phone.

Suddenly Norma was in the middle of the mayhem, pushing Mark and Dad apart. 'Stop it!' she yelled. 'That's enough!' Arms akimbo, she drew herself up to her full height and glared at us. 'What are you thinking of, brawling like a street gang? Hasn't this morning been terrible enough without you making such a scene? And what the hell do you think *you*'re doing? Happy slapping?' she said, turning on the owner of the still flashing mobile phone. 'And you a grown woman! You should be ashamed! Go home and put your own house in order!' Mortified, the woman pocketed her phone and walked off. Norma drew a deep breath, and turned on my father. 'Bob Osborne, hasn't Annie already been through enough today without you making things worse?'

'Keep out of this, Norma,' he said roughly. 'This is family business.'

Norma froze. Then she pushed back her fringe, crossed her arms over her breasts and glared at Dad defiantly. 'And what am I, pray, if not family? I may only be a few years older than Annie but, God knows, I've loved her as if she was my own child from the first day I met her. But you – you've always kept me at arm's length from her. Oh, yes! Just like you've kept me at a distance from yourself.'

'Shut up, Norma, this isn't the time or place to . . .' Dad began.

He didn't stand a chance against this new, fiery woman who now uncrossed her arms and flicked her decorative acrylic talons dismissively against his lapel. 'Don't you give me orders!' she said. 'I'm my own woman! Who are you to tell me what I should or shouldn't talk about? You think I'm just your mistress? Well, I'm my own mistress first! I'm a mother and a businesswoman. And I've had more than enough of you treating me like some kind of – I don't know – some kind of bitch on the side.'

Jackie gasped, as did Dad. 'I never –'

There was no stopping Norma now. 'Oh, it suits you very well, having me as your temporary plaything,' she went on. 'Here when you want me, gone when you don't. But I've had enough of being sidelined, right? I've bitten my tongue for far too long. Let me tell you something, Bob, you were against Annie's marriage from the very start. And maybe, if you'd been a bit more supportive of your son-in-law, instead of criticizing him all the time, this fiasco would never have happened.'

Dad's mouth fell open. 'So it's my fault now? My fault that, because of that unfaithful, idle bastard, my daughter's lost her home and is going to have a criminal record?'

'Our son's not a bastard!' Jackie interjected.

'And I suppose it's also my fault,' Dad continued, 'that the pair of them have thrown thousands of quid down the drain on this stupid divorce?'

While he and Norma wrangled on, I sank down on the stone steps.

Meanwhile Martha Greenwood tapped Williams's shoulder. 'I'll be in touch about the settlement. Perhaps you can arrange the payment to Holtby out of the money your client owes mine.' Williams nodded vaguely, but his eyes stayed glued to Norma. He was entranced, as if he'd never seen anything like her. Greenwood turned to Mark. 'I think it's time we took your dog and left.'

'Not before I've spoken to Annie,' Mark said. He walked over to where I was sitting, with the over-excited Fluffy pulling ahead of him. As he attempted to give me an exfoliating facial with his tongue, Mark hovered over me. 'I'm sorry,' he said at last.

I looked up at him. 'Why? You've won. Isn't that what you wanted?'

'I just wanted Fluffy to be well cared-for, that's all. You know you can't look after him when you're at work all day.'

'Well, as it happens that wouldn't have been a problem any more,' I said.

'What do you mean?'

'If you must know, George Haines sacked me yesterday.'

'*What?*'

'Which is a good thing really,' I added bitterly, 'because I don't think I had enough holiday leave owing to cover the prison sentence I'm about to get.'

Mark had the decency to look horrified. 'Shit! This has turned into nightmare.'

Yes, it was a nightmare. All the love I'd once felt for him had turned to pure hatred. And it was poisoning me.

'I'm so sorry, Annie.'

'What about? Being fifty grand down, or ruining my life?'

'Believe me, I wasn't trying to get you into trouble. My solicitor wanted to know everything, so when Darcie told me what you'd told her, I kind of passed it on without thinking it through. If only I hadn't been so fucking stupid! If only I'd realized what might happen, I'd never in a million years have mentioned it.'

I stood up. 'Too little too late. I really don't want to hear any more of your grovelling apologies.'

'I honestly never intended . . .' he went on lamely. His voice trailed away. 'I wish we could turn the clock back.'

'Not as much as I do, believe me.' I pushed Fluffy off me and stood up. 'And do you know when to? To the day I first telephoned Wag the Dog Walks. I'd never, ever have called you.'

Mark bit his lip. Then he said, 'I want you to have him.'

'What?'

'I want you to have Fluffy.'

For a few seconds I was speechless. Then I laughed at the irony of it. 'After all this? You've got to be joking.'

He held out the leash to me. 'Go on – take him.'

I glared at him. 'Regretting you spent all my hard-earned money on him, are you? Well, sorry, but, unlike you, I don't have fifty thousand pounds to spare.'

As Mark's face creased in a grimace, I suddenly remembered how long it was since he'd looked at me lovingly. 'I'll pay Holtby,' he said. 'I mean, out of my share of the settlement. I never wanted any money from you in the first place. It was you who insisted I take it.'

'I didn't notice you protesting,' I countered.

'I tried, but I didn't have a chance. You just assumed that was what we'd do.' His eyes flashed at me. 'In control of the purse strings to the very last. Anyway, take him, before I change my mind.' Mark reached for one of my clenched fists, prised open the fingers, and thrust the end of Fluffy's leash into my hand.

At that moment, a series of yaps came from the other side of Fleet Street. Fluffy's ears pricked, and all three of us turned our heads. Between the cars and buses that were driving past we saw a woman on the opposite pavement walking a beautiful Cavalier King Charles Spaniel. As it trotted along, its raised tail swung back and forth, as tantalizingly as a stripper's feather fan. The moment Fluffy saw it, he was barking and pulling to get to it. I thrust his leash back into Mark's hand. 'Thanks, but no thanks. I don't want *anything* from you.'

He looked amazed. 'Not even Fluffy?'

'No. And do you know why, Mark? Because every time I'll look at him, I'll think of our marriage.'

By now the Cavalier's wagging tail was receding into the distance, and Fluffy was yanking violently to get to it before it disappeared.

Mark tried to press the leash back into my hand. 'Take him, for God's sake.'

'I don't want him!'

'I said, take him!'

'No!'

'Take him, Annie!'

And as we thrust the leash back and forth between us, Fluffy pulled free and hurtled down the steps in pursuit of the sexy bitch on the other side of the road. Mark and I ran after him, yelling for him to stop, but he took absolutely no notice of us; we were powerless where his sex drive was concerned.

Ears flopping, black-and-white fringe flying, tail wagging in expectation of a fabulous shag, Fluffy leaped off the kerb and straight into the path of an oncoming car.

Thirty-five

It was Christmas Day and, for the first time in years, I wasn't celebrating in the Workhouse. The flat was being sold to some City slicker who'd lost his job in the sub-prime mortgage crisis, found himself in negative equity and been forced to downsize from his penthouse pad in Clerkenwell to what was in effect the back-streets of Islington. 'The poor sod's down to his last million!' my father had commented, when he'd made his offer. 'My heart bleeds for him! It's what happened in the olden days, isn't it, love? When you was unemployed, it was straight into the workhouse with you.'

The estate agent who was handling the sale had said that Mark and I were lucky to find a buyer so quickly, even though he'd offered much less than the asking price. Rather than accept such a low sum, Dad had offered to buy Mark's share, and rent the flat until such time as I was able to afford it again. But there were reasons why I couldn't accept his generosity. For a start, I needed the capital to pay the huge court and legal fees I'd been landed with, not to mention my fine for perjury – due to a hole in the court timetables, my trial had taken place on the heels of my divorce. I also had to give Mark his share of our joint assets.

Besides, I never wanted to see my old flat again. The place where I'd once been so happy now held nothing but painful memories for me.

Consequently my furniture, along with most of my personal possessions, was now in storage in a warehouse beneath a flyover somewhere on the North Circular Road, and, since I'd come out of prison at the beginning of the month, I'd been effectively homcless.

Not that I was suffering. Since I'd been released I'd been staying with Dad in Hampstead Garden Suburb. In the past, I'd taken for granted the scale and luxury of our detached mock-Georgian house with its wood-panelled entrance hall, its sweeping staircase and spacious reception rooms: the living room with its bright chande-liers and buttoned chesterfields; the cosy TV room, with its comfortable, squashy sofas and shelves of books; and the formal dining room, dominated by a highly polished, Regency-style, oval table and ten dining chairs – chairs that were rarely sat on, because in the past Dad and I had had our meals in the sunny kitchen, or in the TV room, our sock-clad feet resting companionably side by side on the coffee-table, and our plates balanced on our laps.

But after serving a ten-week prison sentence, I had a very different perspective on my old home. In jail, I'd been confined most of the time to a minuscule overheated cell where I could touch all four walls while I was lying on the narrow bed, and my view of the outside world had consisted of a sliver of an exercise yard, seen through the reinforced glass of a narrow, barred window. Even Vlad's attic was huge in comparison, and my father's house now seemed like the Palace of Versailles. I had the run of what seemed like acres of space, and unlimited freedom to do whatever I wanted, whenever I wanted.

There was no one to tell me when to get up or when to go to bed. If I felt like it, I could stay in my room all day, reading books or watching television. I could luxuriate for hours in a hot bath brimming with bubbles. I could open a door all by myself, rather than waiting for a prison officer to come and let me out. I could run up and down the stairs just for the hell of it, go into the kitchen and raid the well-stocked fridge when I was hungry and even when I wasn't. Most wonderful of all, perhaps, was that I could step outside into the well-kept garden at any time of day or night, and drink in the cold, crisp, fresh air.

'You can stay here as long as you like, love,' Dad had said, after he'd collected me from prison a fortnight before, and brought me back. 'It's still your home, and it always will be.'

Dad had been totally supportive ever since the full hearing, and my subsequent short trial for perjury. But, however luxurious, his house wasn't my home any more. I didn't belong there. I didn't belong anywhere. The divorce, and being in prison, had changed me.

I'd pleaded guilty to the perjury charge, and the lawyers my father had engaged to represent me had warned me that I might be sent down. But even when I was escorted out of the dock, and taken to the court cells to await transportation, the knowledge that I was going to prison seemed unreal. As in so many American movies, any minute now some kindly policeman or lawyer – Atticus Finch, perhaps, in *To Kill a Mockingbird* – would open the cell door, tell me that it had all been a big mistake and I was free to go home. Because I, formerly Annie Curtis, now once again Annie Osborne, just wasn't the sort of person who went to prison, was I? I wasn't a criminal, I was a hard-working, law-abiding model citizen. I hadn't beaten up any old ladies, or crashed a car into a bus queue while out joyriding, or robbed a bank at gunpoint. I'd simply been rather stupid when it came to my divorce.

'How long did you get?' The bag-lady sitting beside me lifted her stained skirt and scratched a blotchy thigh.

I swallowed hard. 'Six months.'

She laughed, revealing more gaps in her mouth than teeth. 'That's not a sentence, that's a doddle!' she said. 'Your ARD'll be in three months' time, so with any luck you'll be out for Christmas.'

I hadn't a clue that an ARD was my Automatic Release Date, and when she spoke her breath smelled so foul that I didn't want to ask. I'd entered a brand-new world with its own rules and its own vocabulary of words and acronyms, and it would take me until the end of my sentence to get to grips with it.

I waited numbly. We both waited. I felt queasy, and asked to go to the lavatory, but nobody let me out for half an hour. When, finally, a police officer did, she not only escorted me to the lavatory but came in with me. As I sat on the loo, doubled up with stomach cramps, I didn't know who to feel sorrier for, myself or her.

Back in the cell again, with three other women prisoners, I waited. Eventually the doors opened again and we were all ushered out. But instead of being sent home with an apology, I was handcuffed and then marched upstairs to one of those large white prisoner-transport vans you often see being pursued by snapping paparazzi on the TV news. I'd always wondered what they were like inside, and what the people behind those blacked-out windows were thinking. Now it was me, locked into a tiny steel cubicle that stank of urine, sitting on a hard plastic seat with my view of the outside world blurred by tears. And all the time I was thinking, *This can't be happening*.

We arrived at what looked like a medieval gatehouse in front of an ugly modern building pierced with tiny barred windows. A sign outside said 'Highridge Prison', and I realized that it was indeed happening, and to me, and that nothing was going to stop it. I was taken into a room and robbed of all I held most precious: my BlackBerry with its screensaver photo of Fluffy, my Dolce & Gabbana watch, my Downtown, my spirit and my dignity; all but the two last were sealed up in plastic bags, which, I was informed, would be returned to me at the end of my sentence.

I was used to other people's near-nudity in the changing rooms at work, but now, in a curtained cubicle, I was the one being ordered to remove all my clothing. After a day of hanging around nervously, I was grubby and sweaty, and felt horribly exposed, even in the cotton gown they handed me. 'Pretty,' said the hard-faced female prison officer, as with latex-gloved fingers, she picked up the delicate white lace bra I'd been wearing and examined it. Then she added, with satisfaction, 'You can't keep it.'

'But it's my bra!' I protested, covering my bare breasts with my hands.

Slowly she looked me up and down. 'It's underwired,' she said.

'So?'

'That makes it a potential hazard, to both yourself and the other inmates.'

'No, that makes it the best kind of bra to give my size of breasts the correct support,' I answered, on the verge of losing it. 'What do you think I'm going to do? Take the bones out and stab someone with them? Or make a noose and hang myself?'

Her nostrils flared. She'd got my number all right, and she didn't like it one little bit. 'Violence and self-harm are two of the biggest problems we face in here, Osborne,' she snapped. 'So, if you feel tempted to top yourself, I'll recommend you for twenty-four-hour suicide watch. Okay?' I bit my tongue, and she returned her close attention to the bra. 'There's only one way you can keep this, and that's if you let us cut the wires out.'

'Have you seen the label?' I gasped. 'It's a Rigby and Peller! Do you have any idea how much it cost?'

I was told to shower in an open cubicle with hair blocking the drains. I lathered myself thoroughly with gel that smelled of lavatory cleaner. By the time I'd dried myself on the towel I was given, I felt as grubby as ever. Braless, but back in the white shirt and black trouser suit I'd worn to court that morning, I was taken to an induction room, told my prison number, which I immediately forgot, and sent in to see a nurse, who asked if I was on any medication and if I'd ever had suicidal thoughts. Not until now, I wanted to say.

Clanking gates; locked doors; an old woman shuffling past in a pair of slippers, swearing under her breath; an explosion of angry voices echoing down a fluorescent-lit corridor; a snatch of Jay-Z coming through an open doorway – 'Show Me What You Got'. Groups of unsmiling women pushing past roughly, or staring at me as if they could smell my fear; an indescribably sickening sour-sweet smell halfway between that of old menstrual tampons, vomit, and the mess of tinned tomatoes, gristle, instant mash and baked beans that my primary school had dished up for our revolting dinners. I tried to take it in my stride, but I couldn't help gagging with revulsion. I wanted to run back down the corridor and beat my fists on the prison gates, screaming, 'I swear I'll be good in future! Just let me out of here now!' The two hours I'd spent in Highridge had felt like a torturous eternity. How could I bear it for my entire sentence?

I would stay in my cell the whole time, I decided, as I was shown into an overheated box so narrow that, if I stretched out my arms, I could flatten my palms on the opposite walls. A small table, a plastic chair and, tucked behind a half-screen just beyond the narrow bed, the *pièce de résistance*: my own en-suite facilities, a cracked basin and a stinking lavatory with a broken lid.

I sat on the edge of the bed, took off my jacket and hung it over the back of the chair. Since there was nothing else to do, I stared numbly at the pale green walls. I thought of my ruined marriage, and I thought of my ruined life, and I thought, most painfully of all, of what Mark and I had done to Fluffy, so stupidly, in the name of love. I was overwhelmed with loss and guilt.

A few minutes later, a young woman in her twenties appeared at the door, told me her name was Tanya, and said she'd been asked to show me round before we were banged up for the night. She led me down the corridor, and by the time I got back, five minutes later, my jacket had gone.

It was the last straw. Outraged, I was about to report the theft to one of the prison officers when Tanya grabbed my arm. 'Don't,' she warned. 'Your life won't be worth living, love. Believe me, there's only one way to survive in here, and that's to button your lip, watch your back, and keep your head down.'

Thirty-six

My father was the first to visit me, a fortnight after I'd gone inside. The moment I saw him in the visiting room, I allowed myself to do something I hadn't done since I'd arrived at Highridge: I cried. Dad held me tight and let me sob on to the lapels of his precious bespoke camel coat. I felt his chest heave, as he let out a deep sigh. 'Oh, Annie, Annie! A fine pickle you've got yourself into.'

I drew away, blew my nose and we sat down on opposite sides of a small Formica table. Dad put his hand comfortingly over mine. He looked wonderful. I'd never noticed it before but prosperity literally shone from him. His cheeks and balding head gleamed as if they'd been scrubbed by a team of barbers. His suntanned fingers were adorned with the usual selection of gold rings, and his evenly shaped fingernails had been buffed to a mirror finish.

'It's so good to see you,' I said. 'You look as dapper as ever.'

My father's eyes flicked over me. 'Wish I could say the same for you, love. You're a right old mess.'

'Thanks, Dad. That's just what I needed to hear.'

He rocked back in his plastic chair. 'Where's my beautiful Annie? You've let yourself go, love. In just two weeks! Your hair's rubbish. Don't they let you wash it? And what's the matter with your face? It's all pasty.'

I put my hand up to my cheek. 'Well, prison rations aren't the ideal detox diet. Besides, I'm not wearing any makeup.'

'And why not?'

'My makeup bag was stolen. Shortly after my jacket.' Dad shook his head, but he didn't look surprised. He knew from experience what life inside was like. 'So, this is probably the first time you've seen me without mascara since I was thirteen,' I went on. 'Anyway, there doesn't seem much point in slapping on warpaint when I've already lost the battle.'

He gave me a measured look. 'It's not like you to give up, Annie.'

I sighed. 'Yes, well I guess there's a first time for everything.'

Dad's face clouded. 'I'll kill that bastard husband of yours for what he's done to you, if I ever cross paths with him again!'

'My ex-husband, you mean. And I wouldn't bother. He's not worth it. You'd only end up in here, too.'

'What? Banged up with all these women?' My father raised an eyebrow, and his lips twisted into a smile. 'I can think of worse fates.'

I laughed, despite myself. 'Oh, I've missed you, darling Dads.'

'I've missed you, too, kiddo. Can't you break out of this dump for a few hours and come to the Wolseley for supper?' He patted the lapel of his coat and said, in a stage-whisper, 'I've got a crow-bar hidden in here.'

'Dad!' I glanced at the grim female officer standing by

the door, well within earshot. But my father just turned and winked at her.

'She knows I'm joking. Don't you, gorgeous?' To my astonishment, she struggled not to smile. 'I've already been rubbed down half a dozen times since I got here this afternoon. And very enjoyable it was, too. I was only disappointed it wasn't a strip-search. I'm coming back next week – and it's not to see my daughter!' She laughed. I had to hand it to my father, at the age of sixty-five and with very little hair, he could still charm any woman he chose to. 'So, you're all right, are you, love?' he said, turning back to me.

I shrugged. 'I'm surviving. Look, I haven't had a chance to say so before, Dad, but I'm so terribly sorry about all of this. I've really let you down.'

'Well, it's certainly been a major fuck-up – if you'll excuse my French,' he added over his shoulder to the officer. 'Because of that bastard, you've lost everything you worked so hard for – the job you loved, your flat . . .'

There was a lump in my throat. 'And darling Fluffy.'

He leaned back in the plastic chair. 'Don't talk to me about that mutt! You and Mark were as stupid as each other over it. I mean, look where it's got you!' He squeezed my hand. 'But you're a soft-hearted kid and you've certainly been punished enough for it. Far too much. You don't deserve this. Any of it.' Tears were rolling down my cheeks again. 'And to think that fucker's still walking around outside. Here.' He delved into his inside pocket, drew out a freshly laundered, initialled handkerchief and handed it to me. 'Well, Annie, it's a good thing your nan's not around to see what's happened to you.'

'Would she be terribly ashamed of me?'

'Are you kidding? She'd crack open a bottle of Guinness and drink a toast. Doing time's a family tradition, isn't it?'

We smiled at each other. 'How are *you* doing?' I asked.

'Me? Other than missing you, love, and worrying if you're okay, I'm fine. Never been better.'

'Really?' I looked at him doubtfully.

'But . . . there's something I need to tell you. About Norma and me . . .'

My heart sank with a familiar feeling. 'Oh, no, Dad, don't tell me you've broken up with her.'

'Well, actually, love . . .' he said shiftily.

Suddenly I felt terribly angry with him. 'Why now? Why at all? Norma's so nice.'

'Oh. D'you like her, then?'

'Of course I like her! Actually, I more than like her. I think she's fantastic. I only wish you could see it.'

'Hold on there, Annie. I never said I didn't. Norma's a great girl, I admit –'

'She's a woman!' I protested.

He blinked at me uncomprehendingly. 'That's what I said. She's a great girl.'

Why was I bothering? The last thing my father would ever be was politically correct. 'Dad, you've been going out with her for five and a half years, longer than I was married to Mark.'

Dad gave a disapproving sniff. 'And that's supposed to be an advertisement for long-term relationships, is it?' He reached over the table and squeezed my hand. 'The thing is, Annie, you got to remember that I'm a quarter of a century older than Norma. Lately I've been feeling I can't keep up with her. Frankly, I'm too old to go out clubbing till dawn on a Saturday night. I've been getting itchy feet – more like aching feet, if the truth be told. I suddenly realized I wanted someone to grow old with. Someone I could stay in with, put my slippers on with, curl up and watch telly with.'

'So why go off with someone else?' I persisted.

He shook his head. 'Will you give me a chance to finish? I've not gone off nowhere.'

'Then I don't understand.'

He flushed. 'I, er . . . I popped the question the other day,' he mumbled.

'You did *what*?' I gasped.

He raised a hand to stop me saying any more. 'Now, I know it's well out of character, love, but after what happened with her and that bastard solicitor of yours outside the court, well, I didn't have much choice.'

'Mr Williams? What's he got to do with it?'

Dad grimaced. 'When we went rushing after Fluffy, he only stopped Norma and asked her out, didn't he? Told her he was really impressed by the way she'd stood up to me. Apparently he likes his women sparky and dominating.' He shuddered inside his camel coat. 'Well, when Norma told me about it a few days later, and said she was thinking about having lunch with him, it gave me a bit of a shock. I suddenly thought, She's not such a bad old cow . . . What if I lose her? So, I did what any self-respecting man would do in the same situation. I tried to put it out of my mind. But I couldn't. So, a couple of days ago, I asked her to marry me.'

'Dad! And did she say yes?' I breathed.

Incredulous that I needed to ask, my father grimaced at me. 'What do you *think*? Bloody hell! Who could resist me?'

'Oh, Dad!' I was so thrilled I wanted to burst out laughing. Yet I found myself choked by emotion and sobbing into his handkerchief. I'd often worried about how he'd manage as he grew older – surely a time would come when his ever-younger girlfriends would tire of him, and my fear had always been that he'd end up lonely and alone. Now I knew that Norma would be there for him. Kind, independent and with a mind of her own, she had a loving nature, endless good sense and the strength of character any woman would need to deal with my strong-willed father. On top of that, she loved him and, I knew, was as fond of me as I was of her. And yet, pleased as I was, part of me felt bereft, as if I was losing my father when I needed him most. I think Dad sensed it, too, because he said gruffly, 'Don't think of it as losing your dad, Annie. Between you, me and the prison walls, you'll always come first. Think of it as gaining two teenage hoodlums as step-brothers, and a step-mum you can go out clubbing with.'

When I'd reassured him I was thrilled, and scrawled a note congratulating Norma, my father left. I tried to be brave, but inside I was in agony. It was so painful to say goodbye to him, knowing he was going home to Hampstead Garden Suburb and I couldn't go with him – like having a limb torn away. I'd tried not to think of Fluffy too much during the past two weeks, but suddenly I was overcome with longing to have him bounding along

378

at my side, his muzzle open in a demented grin and his cartoon hair flopping over his glinting eyes. What a comfort that would be.

What a ridiculous fantasy.

I was on my way back to my cell when one of the screws shouted down the corridor, 'Osborne, the new governor wants to see you right away.'

'I want to go back to my cell,' I called out to her. 'I don't feel well.'

'It wasn't a request, Osborne, it was an order. The governor wants to see you so get a fucking move on!'

What had I done? I wondered, as I followed her slouched, bulging, uniformed back through a series of locked gates, up and down concrete stairs, past communal bathrooms where, through the half-open doorways, you could hear the splash of showers and smell shampoo. The rulebook, which I'd been given on my first day, stated that there were twenty-five possible offences against prison discipline I could commit so it wasn't hard to infringe one. Had I intentionally obstructed an officer in the execution of her duty? Had I unwittingly administered a controlled drug to myself? Had I used threatening, abusive or insulting words or behaviour? Or had some other prisoner – someone with a grudge against me – planted drugs in my cell or grassed me up for something I hadn't done? Plenty of women might have done that. I'd tried to do as Tanya told me, keep my head down and watch my back – two things that were physically impossible to do at the same time – but I rarely talked to anyone, and I had the distinct feeling that everyone loathed me.

The new governor had taken over at Highridge shortly

before I'd arrived, and one of the things I'd learned in the past fortnight was that being called in to see her was certainly not an everyday event. I must be in serious trouble, but in my present state I didn't care. Whatever I was accused of, I'd admit to it. Whatever punishment was meted out – a spell in solitary, peeling spuds with my fingernails or scrubbing lavatories with a toothbrush – I'd take it without complaint.

After negotiating the maze of long, faceless corridors and locked gates in the modern wing of the prison, we emerged in the ground-floor hallway of the original Victorian building. A set of mahogany double doors set with reinforced-glass panels took us into a stone-floored corridor, where the officer ordered me to sit on a bench opposite a door with the words 'Governor's Office' painted on it. After five minutes it swung open and a bespectacled woman in a mini-skirt came out clutching some files. Before she disappeared into the next office, she said, 'She'll see you now.'

While the officer waited for me in the corridor, I went in on my own. The room was panelled in dark wood and illuminated by modern uplighters, which reflected off a lofty plaster ceiling. A line of tall grey filing cabinets dominated one wall, topped with piles of papers, and on an adjoining wall, built into the panelling, there was a small fireplace with a dingy cast-iron grate. The institutional effect was softened by several silver-framed photos, a vase of chrysanthemums on the mantelpiece and a small sofa covered with faded chintz.

What particularly struck me about the office, though, were its windows. For the last fourteen days my horizons had been limited to long, artificially lit corridors and the view through my filthy cell window of an internal prison courtyard. Now, through two long sashes barred on the outside, I could see the branches of plane trees, cars driving past, and people waiting at a bus stop, going about their everyday lives. The outside world – which I used to be part of – was now so tantalizingly close to me, yet so impossible to reach. Though in reality it was a very ordinary main road, to me it was beautiful.

So entranced was I by the view, and by the sunlight flooding in through the windows' gleaming panes, that I didn't notice the woman sitting in front of them behind a big old-fashioned pedestal desk. I jumped when she spoke to me.

'Hello, Annie. Please take a seat while I finish this.'

Her tone was businesslike, yet somehow soothing. There was something familiar about it, too, but I didn't think anything of it. I scraped back one of two wooden chairs on the other side of her desk, sat down and looked at her. At first all I could see was a silhouette against the light of a slightly stocky woman with neatly coiffed brown hair, busy writing something in a ledger, but as my eyes focused, and she took off her spectacles, I realized who she was, and gasped.

Thirty-seven

'Mrs Barclay!'

Marion Barclay. The same Mrs Barclay who'd decided to change career and had needed the perfect outfit for her job interview. How could I ever forget the navy blue, fine-wool suit I'd found for her, with its flared knee-length skirt, or the cream silk Burberry shirt I'd teamed with it? I hadn't seen her since the fateful day when she'd rushed into the store to collect the outfit on the way to her interview, only to find that Fluffy had destroyed it.

Mrs Barclay was the new governor of Highridge Prison. Great, I thought bitterly.

She put down her pen and sighed. 'Well, Annie, I never thought I'd see you here.'

I swallowed. 'I never thought I'd be here, Mrs Barclay.'

'But here you are. Here we both are. On opposite sides of the desk.'

'Yes.'

She smiled rather coldly. 'For my part, I got the job I wanted, despite having to turn up for it in an old fleece and a pair of my husband's jeans.'

'You mean, this was it?' I said. 'You were applying to be the governor of Highridge?' She nodded. 'Look, I know I said it before, but I'm truly sorry about what happened to your suit.'

She waved a hand dismissively. 'They were just clothes, Annie. There are more important things in life, as I realized after the initial shock had worn off.' She paused. 'I read about your divorce. And your trial, of course. It was in the newspapers. I must say, I'm surprised. Perjury is a very serious offence.'

A lump rose up in my throat. 'Yes, I know that now.'

'As is theft. Even from a tramp.'

'Yes.'

She looked right through me with her piercing eyes, and I dropped my head in shame. I felt worse than I had when I was eleven years old and my maths teacher had chastised me for cheating in an exam. 'And then, to my surprise, I saw your name on the list of our new inmates,' she continued. 'How did your parents take it?'

'Well ... My father was upset, of course ...'

'And your mother?'

The lump in my throat got bigger. 'Oh ... My mother ...' I started. 'I don't have a ...' Suddenly I could say no more. The next thing I knew, I was slumped on the squashy sofa, sobbing my heart out for the second time that afternoon while Marion Barclay perched on the edge of the cushion next to me, holding my hot hand in her cool one and proffering a box of tissues. I don't know how long it took, but I told her everything: about Mum running away when I was eight, about saving Fluffy and meeting Mark, and Fern's thong, and the pink lead, and Mrs Weimaraner, and Fluffy getting run over after the court case.

'It's amazing,' she said, when I'd cried myself out. 'You and I have come into contact several times. And over the years I must have told you many intimate things about myself. To me, you always seemed a cheerful young woman. I had no idea all these problems were festering beneath the surface. I'm sorry, Annie. You've been punished enough without me adding to your woes by rubbing your nose in it.' She smiled. 'Look, I probably shouldn't say this, but you're in good company in the perjury stakes. Many well-known people have committed the same crime, paid the price for it, as you're doing, then gone on to rebuild their lives and even salvage their reputations. Think of Jonathan Aitken and Jeffrey Archer. And Martha Stewart, of course, the first lady of American home makeovers, who, if I remember, got into serious trouble by making false statements to federal agents. You'll have your career back when you get out, Annie, just like she did.'

I shook my head. 'George Haines sacked me.'

'I hope that wasn't because of me.'

'It was my fault. He was livid I'd brought Fluffy into the store. You see, I'd done it before and I'd promised him I wouldn't again.'

Marion Barclay sighed. 'It's a bloody stupid move on Haines's part, commercially speaking. No one else in Personal Shopping has half your flair. They'll lose a lot of customers. And I'll be one of them. Haines and Hampton isn't the only store in London that has a personal-shopping department. I'm sure you'll find a new employer.'

'With a criminal record? I don't think so.' By now I'd worked my way through the entire box of tissues. I blew my nose noisily on the last one. 'Anyway,' I said, 'I don't care any more. I'm through with high fashion. Makeovers and personal shopping and designer clothes – that world's so superficial.'

'Let me tell you something, Annie.' She took my hand and squeezed it. 'There was nothing superficial about what you did for me. You made me feel confident again after I'd had my mastectomy. In charge of my life. And, as it happens, more desirable – though I don't think I should be talking about that, certainly not here. Look,' she went on, letting go of my hand, 'I'm sure you'll find something to do when you're released. Which, I believe, will be just before Christmas.'

'Well, I don't care about personal shopping any more,' I said. 'Frankly, I don't care about anything. I've lost everything that was important to me, Mrs Barclay. My marriage. My home. My self-respect. And Fluffy.'

'You can't afford not to care, Annie,' she said, rather sternly. 'We only get one chance at life – one crack of the whip – and you're far too young, and too gifted in your own way, to give up. One day you'll probably get married again –'

'Never!' I interrupted.

'– and maybe have children, something I've always regretted not doing. Given your history with your mother, you might find it a healing experience. As for losing Fluffy . . .' she stood up and walked back to her desk '. . . you say you loved him, but . . .' She sat down, and indicated for me to take my place opposite her. 'You may not like me saying this, Annie, but, well, he was just a dog. Losing him may seem bad now. It may seem terrible. But if it's the worst thing in the world you ever have to deal with

. . . you'll get over it. People lose their *children* and find a reason to carry on living. Are you telling me that you're going to let losing a *dog* destroy you? Get a grip, young lady! Stop wallowing in self-pity and thinking about yourself all the time. Think about what you could do for others, others who are much worse off than you.'

'Why are you lecturing me like this?' I asked, as I resumed my seat opposite her.

'Because you're worth lecturing, Annie. And because I have a suggestion to make.' She clasped her hands, put them on the desk and leaned forward in her chair. 'Look, I can't be seen to give you special privileges while you're here. You'll have to earn them like everyone else. Doing you favours would be more than my job's worth. And since you went to so much trouble to help me get it in the first place – Fluffy aside – it would be rather too ironic if I lost it because of you, wouldn't it? However, Annie, there is something you could do for me.'

'Oh?'

'It's a kind of experiment I want to try. This prison is full of women who feel worthless. They've no self-esteem or self-respect, and no ambition. And most have had little education. As you probably know by now, many of them also have mental-health problems. Some are depressed, even suicidal. On the whole they come from abusive homes, or extremely deprived backgrounds – backgrounds that make yours seem like Paradise, even though your mother ran off and left you. The only thing a lot of these women have is their children, and many have lost those too – lost them into the care system because they're drug addicts, or they have nowhere to live, or they just can't cope with them for some reason. The odd thing is that many of these women are also very bright. They've no idea what they could attain if they put their minds to it. I'd like you to help them get their self-confidence back, and a bit of self-respect.'

'Me? How can I help them?'

Marion Barclay smiled. 'Isn't it obvious, Annie? By doing for them what you did for me. By making them feel better about themselves. By helping them to make the most of what they have – which is precious little, in many cases.'

'You mean you want me to do makeovers? In here?' Mrs Barclay nodded. I almost laughed. 'But it's impossible! At the store I had a team of helpers and four floors of expensive designer clothes to choose from. And hairdressers and makeup artists and every cosmetic in the world. Money was no object.'

'Yes, yes, I know all that. And, of course, that's going to be a big challenge for you. But … couldn't you do *something*? Look, I can supply you with a room – some sort of office. And I'm sure we can get the cosmetics firms, or some department store or other – maybe even Haines and Hampton – to donate some makeup. We could make enquiries. As for clothes, well, there's a big store room I've discovered in the basement that's full of lost property – things past prisoners have left behind. They're not what you'd call designer outfits, but … Well, you'd have to improvise. I'm sure you're resourceful. Do the best you can with what you have. Maybe you could set up some kind of swap shop among the inmates.' She smiled warmly. 'Will you do this for me, Annie? I have a feeling that, by doing something for the others, you may get something out of it for yourself.'

For the rest of my stay in Highridge, I threw myself into setting up Marion Barclay's makeover scheme. She got her friends to donate their old clothes and, after putting up a poster in the dining room, I found a hair-stylist and a couple of dressmakers among the inmates to help me transform my new 'clients'. In addition, Mrs Barclay allowed me to telephone Eva, who, since my dismissal, had been appointed acting head of Personal Shopping at Haines and Hampton – a job I knew she deserved. But that didn't stop me feeling sick at heart as I imagined her sitting in my tiny office, with her coat hanging on the back of the door and her neat feet pressed close together under what I still felt was my desk. And was I imagining it, or was there an officious, slightly gloating tone in her voice when she said, 'I'll do what I can, Annie. I'll certainly have a word with Mr Haines. But I can't promise anything'?

Two weeks later, I was summoned back to the governor's office to find three large cardboard boxes and four Haines and Hampton carrier-bags on the floor. Charlotte was standing in the middle of them. Dressed in a sober black trouser suit, carrying a quilted leather Marc Jacobs Cecilia, and with her blonde hair pulled back in a tight ponytail, she looked nervous and subdued. She frowned when I walked in – I think it took her a moment to recognize me, but when she did her face lit up, and she tottered over to me on a pair of killer red Manolos, flapping her hands. 'Annie! Annie!' She stopped short a foot away from me, turned towards the governor and frowned. 'Might I touch her, Mrs Barclay?' she asked. 'I mean, can I? Is it allowed?'

'Well, I don't care if it isn't. Let them throw me into solitary for a week!' I said, and threw my arms round her. As we hugged, my nostrils filled with the wonderful smells that emanated from her: Chanel Naturally Luminous Foundation, if I wasn't mistaken, and Aveda Pure Abundance Volumizing Shampoo and, yes, a Breath of Joy, the exclusive Jean Patou perfume that Charlotte's mother always gave her for her birthday. In the past all these scents had been so much a part of my daily life that I'd scarcely noticed them, but now they conjured up a world that seemed a million miles away – exotic, expensive, luxurious. I longed for it so much I could scarcely bear it.

Charlotte drew back, and although her painted lips were smiling, her eyes weren't. Up till now, she'd only ever seen me at work, smartly dressed and groomed, and I became conscious of how dreadful I must look in my crumpled T-shirt and sweatpants, my hair unwashed, my bare skin greasy and emanating the fusty smell of prison from every open pore. I'd spent the morning cleaning the dusty office Mrs Barclay had found for me to do my makeovers in so I probably smelled of sweat too. I felt ashamed of myself, and somehow at a disadvantage.

'It's wonderful to see you, Charlotte,' I said, backing off slightly, 'and I can see you've brought lots of goodies with you.'

'Well, Eva asked Mr Haines, and he said we could have some of the ex-sale stock that was in the warehouse,' she explained. 'So I went down there and sorted through them and although, of course, there's nothing from this season, I did find some quite nice pieces from last winter, like a couple of Miu Miu jackets and some Nicole Farhi trousers. There's even a last season Julien Macdonald dress that was a return – the zip's broken, but I'm sure it could be mended. This box has got belts and bags in it, and that one's all tops. And these,' she went on, pointing at the carrier-bags, 'have got makeup and cleansers in them. I told the girls in Cosmetics why I needed them, and they coughed up lots of free samples and testers. This little bag is for you. They all send their love, Annie.'

I'd tried not to think about Haines and Hampton too much since I'd been sacked, but while I listened to Charlotte over-enunciate her vowels, the place came back to me in a vivid flash. I pictured myself in the ground-floor cosmetics department, with its steel-and-glass counters, its acres of mirrors and white paint, its vastly expensive lotions and potions in their beautiful pots and packets, and its staff of friendly beauticians dressed in pristine white, like nurses in an intensive-care unit. In the past, just walking in there had lifted my spirits and made me feel safe. How much I'd loved being a part of it all. Now I'd blown it. I was *persona non grata*. I'd never belong there again.

I think Marion Barclay must have realized I was upset, because she suddenly said, 'Why don't you take those boxes down to the office now, Annie? Perhaps Charlotte would like to go with you – that is, if you have time, Charlotte? I'm sure I could rustle up a special visitor's pass for the occasion. And maybe even a goods trolley to put the boxes on.'

Twenty minutes later, Charlotte and I were trundling a blue metal laundry trolley loaded with boxes and bags down the corridors, closely followed by a prison officer and the curious stares of my fellow inmates. Compared to all of us, Charlotte looked like a being from another planet. Which in a way she was: Planet Upper Class.

After a month in Highridge, I took for granted the endless metal gates and locked doors we had to go through, but I could see her flinching as each one slammed shut behind us. She kept glancing over her shoulder nervously, as if she expected to be jumped by a lunatic wielding an axe, and at times I saw her struggle valiantly not to gag at the smell. By the time we arrived at the room that had been designated as the makeover office, she was looking quite unwell. I asked if she wanted to leave, but she insisted on staying for a while so that we could open the boxes she'd brought. Thankfully, after my cleaning marathon of that morning, the room smelled of bleach, rather than stewed cabbage and cauliflower.

The first thing I did, once we'd unloaded the trolley, was to sort through the carrier-bags from the cosmetics department, find an *eau de toilette* tester – it was Oscar, by Oscar de la Renta – and spray the air with it.

'Ah! That's better!' I said, breathing in deeply. 'Mmmm! I feel almost human again.'

Charlotte dusted the trolley with a tissue, then sat on it glumly. 'Annie, might you mind if I speak my mind frankly to you?'

It wasn't the time or place to correct her grammar, so I simply said, 'Fire away, Charlotte.'

'You seem awfully cheerful but ... this place!' Her powdered face crumpled. 'It's just *horrible*! All those locked doors and things! And it smells disgusting, too. It looks so dirty that I don't want to touch anything in case I catch germs. And, well, some of the people we passed in the corridors ... Well, to put it mildly, most of them are so, well ...' she lowered her voice to a whisper '... so overweight and, well, badly dressed! This is a style-free zone, Annie! How can you bear it, being locked up in here for weeks and weeks? I couldn't stand it for a day!'

My jaw dropped. I'd tried to put a brave face on things since I'd arrived in the prison. I'd even told myself I was nothing but a spoiled middle-class brat, and that this place wasn't nearly as bad as I thought it was. After all, from what I could tell, none of the other inmates seemed to mind it half as much as I did. Now here was Charlotte, putting the feelings I'd attempted to suppress into the sentences I'd dared not formulate even in my mind.

It was the first time I'd found anything remotely funny since the full hearing. I started to laugh. Charlotte was perplexed. 'What is it, Annie? Have I said something wrong?'

'No,' I managed to say, 'you've put your finger on it exactly. It's just that I haven't dared admit it before, even to myself. Come and give me a hug! I love you!'

Thirty-eight

The clothes, accessories and makeup Charlotte had brought from Haines and Hampton, combined with the clothes Mrs Barclay had collected, were more than enough to get my makeover studio going. About a dozen women – all reluctant guinea-pigs – were made over during the first five days of operation, and agreed to take part in a small fashion show, which we held in the gymnasium at the weekend. The event was such a hit, and the women so thrilled by what the hairdressers and I had done for them, that by the end of the second week everyone wanted to be friends with me. News of my makeovers soon spread beyond the prison walls to an independent television company in Soho, who were banging on the prison gates, wanting to do a six-part series, to be entitled *Jailbird Makeover*. Mrs Barclay turned them down, of course. She wanted to do something for the women's confidence, not turn them into media fodder and give them a five-minute fame fix.

By then, it was the beginning of December, and my Automatic Release Date – or ARD, as I now called it – had come up, and it was time for me to leave Highridge. Marion Barclay had asked me to come back in a voluntary capacity to carry on the scheme. I'd promised I would, after Christmas. But first, I needed to get my head together. There were a couple of very important issues I had to sort out.

Number one: where was I going to live?

Number two: how was I going to keep body and soul together, now that I was an ex-con? An ex-con, moreover, who was about to join the vilified ranks of Britain's single mothers.

Oh, I'd made a big mistake on my first night in Vlad's flat when I'd flushed my contraceptive pills down the loo.

During the first few weeks of my sentence I'd presumed fear was making me feel queasy every morning; either that, or my stomach was unaccustomed to prison food. Then, when I'd developed a craving for the kind of chocolates I'd not eaten since my childhood – Wispas, Munchies, Crunchie Bars – I'd told myself I was comfort-eating, which I was surely entitled to do under the circumstances. As I continued alternately to stuff my face with every bit of chocolate I could buy or cadge off my fellow inmates, then thow it up, I piled on the pounds. Did I care? No. Did I suspect anything? Not when my period was late, because they'd always been rather erratic. And not even when my breasts spilled over the top of the cotton Agent Provocateur B-cup bra that Norma had sent me to take the place of that boned Rigby & Peller.

So, by the time the penny dropped – or, rather, was pointed out to me in mid-November by a fellow inmate, who asked who'd knocked me up – I was probably about three months gone, although, from the size of me, it looked nearer five.

Had I gone to the prison doctor straight away, I suppose I could have done something about it, but a strange lethargy overtook me. The only people I told were Clarissa and Norma, when they turned up together to visit me a fortnight before my release.

'Congratulations, babe!' My step-mother-to-be beamed at me as if I'd given her the best news in the world. A second later her face fell, and she exclaimed, 'My God, I'm going to be a grandmother!'

Clarissa glanced at her, then back at me. 'Brilliant timing, Annie,' she said.

'It is rather, isn't it?'

'I mean, after all those years of Mark wanting a family, and you saying you weren't ready, you wait until four days before your final divorce hearing to have unprotected sex with him!'

'Ah! Too much information!' Norma covered her ears, but too late.

'Why don't you rub it in?' I said to Clarissa.

My best friend stifled a giggle. 'Sorry. But you have to admit it is pretty spectacular.' Then she took my hand across the table, and continued seriously, 'So, what do you plan to do about it, darling?'

'What should she plan to do about it?' Scandalized, Norma grabbed my other hand. 'You're not suggesting she has an abortion, I hope?'

'I'm not suggesting anything, Norma,' Clarissa said, clasping my other hand more firmly. 'I'm just asking Annie what she wants to do.'

'Well, I'm *telling* her!' Norma said, squeezing my fingers so hard that I thought the bones would pulverize. 'She should have this baby!'

'Don't argue, please,' I begged. 'Truthfully, I don't know

what I want to do. I'll think about it when I get out of here.'

'Well, if you're – what? – thirteen or fourteen weeks gone, you'll have to make up your mind pretty quick.' Norma sniffed.

Clarissa let go of my hand and sat back in her chair. 'If you want my opinion, darling . . .'

'No, I don't, thank you.'

'As I said, if you want my opinion –'

'She doesn't!' Norma put in. 'You heard what she said!'

Clarissa ignored us both and carried on '– which I know is of absolutely crucial importance to you, well, I agree with Norma.'

Norma looked shocked. 'You do?'

'Yes. Of course.' Clarissa turned back to me. 'Darling, you're forty-one now.'

'Oh, give me a break! Not that tick-tock rubbish, please.'

'Well, it's true, isn't it?'

'And believe me, Annie,' Norma said, 'motherhood is a blessing. It may not always be easy, but it's a blessing. I tell you, girl, there's nothing better in the world than family.'

I thought of what Marion Barclay had told me about her own regrets at not having had children. Then I thought of my mother, and smiled ruefully. 'We don't seem to do motherhood very well in my family. Or marriage, for that matter.'

'Up till now, please!' put in the future Mrs Bob Osborne. 'I intend to change all that.'

'Besides, being a crap mother's not in the genes,' said Clarissa. 'I mean, look at me. I may not be perfect, but I'm certainly a better mother to my children than Mummy is to me. Annie, I just think that if you don't have this baby, you'll regret it. You'll come out of your marriage with absolutely nothing.'

'Wrong,' I said morosely. 'You're forgetting my criminal record.'

After a quick pause, Clarissa said, 'Okay, except that!' and all three of us giggled.

But having a baby was no joke. And having your ex-husband's baby, when you'd just got divorced, was not something to undertake lightly. True, Norma had promised to give me all the help she could; she'd even promised to come with me to some fancy restaurant and, over steak, chips and a bottle of something red and expensive, help me break the news to Dad. As for Mark, the baby's father, he had exhibited a slightly more civilized side of himself since the full hearing. He'd even written to me in prison, apologizing for what he described as 'the terrible shit my lawyer landed you in by bringing in Holtby'. He'd added that he'd 'honestly had no idea what trouble it would cause. If I had, believe me, I'd never have allowed it – even if it had meant you got Fluffy. I'm absolutely gutted about it all.'

Included in the letter had been a cheque for all the money he'd been awarded in our divorce settlement, less the fifty thousand he'd promised to pay Holtby before Fluffy had been run over. 'I'll pay that back to you as soon as I can,' his letter had concluded. 'Shit, Annie, what a fucking fiasco!'

397

There was no arguing with that.

None of this amounted to an incentive to have Mark's baby, though.

I'd not written back to him.

Thirty-nine

I spent Christmas morning at Dad's, curled up on the sofa in the TV room, wearing a pair of my old cotton pyjamas, which I'd found in my chest of drawers, and one of Dad's silk bathrobes. *It's a Wonderful Life* was on again, but as mine wasn't any more, I didn't watch it. Instead I saw an old *Vicar of Dibley* Christmas special, followed by the 1999 made-for-TV film of *A Christmas Carol*, starring Richard E. Grant as Bob Cratchit and Patrick Stewart as Scrooge. 'In just one night, he has seen his past, his present and his future,' was the film's tagline, read by the announcer beforehand, 'and they've all come back to haunt him.' This seemed to sum up my predicament perfectly.

Afterwards, I wandered in my socks through the marble-floored hallway into the kitchen, where I picked at the Marks & Sparks Traditionally Cured Scottish Gravad Lax Salmon with Creamy Mustard and Dill Sauce that Norma had left for me, shoved some Golden Roast Parsnips Coated with Wild Flower Honey and Wholegrain Mustard Dressing into the oven and, while I waited for them to cook, picked all the white chocolates out of a big Belgian selection. The house seemed uncannily quiet, even with the television at full blast. I began to wonder if I should have said yes when Dad had invited me to join him, Norma and my soon-to-be step-brothers on holiday in Marbella. The thought of staying in a luxury hotel, and the Spanish sunshine, had been unbelievably tempting. But something had stopped me saying yes. I hadn't told Dad about the baby yet, so parading around in a swimming costume in front of him – even my black Speedo Chi Tank with built-in bust and tummy control – was probably best avoided. And after being forced into such close proximity with so many strangers in prison, I was looking forward to being alone.

Anxious about how I was coping, Clarissa had repeatedly begged me to come over to Primrose Hill, where she was cooking Christmas lunch for fifteen, but much as I loved her, James and the children, I couldn't bring myself to tag on to another family's Christmas celebrations. I wouldn't have been any fun, not in the mood I was in. Neither did I particularly want to see the Hon. Mrs Garland. Thirty years after she'd first hinted at my 'bad breeding', I'd lived up to her expectations.

'I don't blame you wanting to avoid her,' Clarissa had said, when she'd called on Christmas Eve. 'James thinks she's poisonous, and even I wish she wasn't coming. So do the girls. They'd much rather you were with us instead. Please, change your mind, darling.'

'No, I won't,' I'd told her. 'I'll be fine. I really want to be alone.'

But, as Clarissa was well aware, I wasn't doing a complete Marlene Dietrich on Christmas Day. Thanks to her, if thanks were appropriate, I wasn't quite on my own.

Three days before, and just after Dad had left for the airport, she'd drawn up in the driveway in her battered

Volvo, hooting madly. Looking and feeling like the mini-whale I was becoming, I'd trudged out to greet her in my dressing-gown and slippers, with a coat thrown over the top. 'Hi! What are you doing here?' I'd asked. 'And – what's that in your car?'

'That's your Christmas present, darling,' she'd said rather nervously. 'A few days early, I'm afraid. I'm sorry it's not wrapped.'

I'd looked at the little head peering anxiously out of the Volvo's back window. It had the worried, foxy face of a small wire-haired brown and white Jack Russell, with flattened ears and sad black eyes. Then, feeling incredibly angry, I'd turned on Clarissa. 'You can take it away right now,' I said. 'I don't want it.'

'It isn't an it, it's a she, and she's called Molly,' Clarissa had replied, after a brief hesitation. 'And before you send her and me packing, Annie, I think you ought to meet her, and hear what I've got to say, and not be so ungrateful.'

'Don't you understand? I don't want another dog!' I'd almost shouted.

Clarissa had regarded me in silence. Then she'd raised her chin defiantly and opened the back door of the car. 'Come on, Molly,' she'd said. 'This is where you get out.' The Jack Russell walked slowly to the edge of the car seat, gave Clarissa a somewhat cautious glance, then scrabbled down from the high precipice on to the gravel. Tail down, she stood there trembling, while my best friend lectured me.

'Molly's five years old,' she said. 'She belongs – or I should say belonged – to one of my clients, a wonderful ninety-two-year-old lady called Miss Chips. Until last week, they lived together in a rather grotty basement flat off the Seven Sisters Road. Miss Chips has survived for years on an appallingly low basic pension – the sort that wouldn't keep you or me for a single day, let alone a week – but she'd rather have starved herself than let Molly go hungry, and I'm sure she did half the time. Two years ago, she broke her hip and was on a Zimmer frame for months. But, even so, she managed to take Molly out for a walk every day – that's how devoted to her she was. Anyway, since then she's been getting more and more infirm. I tried several times to persuade her to move into sheltered accommodation, but she always refused because none of the places would accept dogs.

'Then, last week, Miss Chips had a stroke, fell over and broke her other hip. Although she's still got all her marbles, she's now bedridden and stuck in some miserable, mixed-sex geriatric ward. I went to see her yesterday, and she couldn't stop crying. And do you know why, Annie? Not because she knows she's probably going to die in the next few weeks, and is almost completely paralysed down one side, and can only just make herself understood, but because she's worried sick about what's going to happen to Molly, who was being looked after temporarily by one of her neighbours.' Clarissa stopped, choked by her story.

'Look, I admit it's very sad,' I said, 'but it's not my problem. Surely somewhere like Battersea Dogs' Home would find Molly a new family?'

'Well, as it happens, that's what I suggested. But Miss Chips wouldn't have it. She became even more distressed.

She was convinced that Molly would be sent to people who'd mistreat her or turn her into cat meat or something. Anyway, I suddenly thought of you and told Miss Chips I knew the perfect new owner for her – my very best friend, who doted on dogs and had recently lost her own.'

'Did you tell Miss Chips how?' I interrupted.

'I'm not sure she would have understood if I'd told her the whole sorry saga. Well, Annie, you should have seen her face. It lit up with such joy. At least, the half of her face that still moves did. She looked beautiful, almost beatific. She said she could now die a happy woman. And then . . . then she did.' Clarissa retrieved a scrunched-up tissue from her sleeve and blew her nose.

'Hold on, you said before that she was alive and in hospital.'

She sniffed, and stuffed the remains of the tissue back up her sleeve. 'Okay, I admit I added the last part for dramatic effect. But the rest of it's true.'

I sighed. 'Look, I know you mean well but it's just not on. You see, I'm not upset about not having a dog, Clarissa. It's Fluffy I wanted.' I looked at the small creature who was trembling between us and bent down to stroke her head. 'Can't you keep her?'

'Actually, I would,' Clarissa said, 'but James and I are out at work all day. Besides, Miranda's allergic.'

'Since when?' I asked suspiciously.

My friend waved her hand. 'Oh, months ago,' she said vaguely. 'Well, if you really don't want Molly, I'll have to take her away. After Christmas.'

'But . . .'

She pushed a stray lock of uncombed hair behind an ear. 'Look, Annie, the girls are on school hols, I've got to pick up my monstrous twenty-two-pound turkey from the butcher within the next twenty minutes, and I don't have time to find Molly another home now. You'll have to keep her until I do. Okay?'

'Oh, you're infuriating!'

'Thank you. I'm glad that's settled.'

Smiling rather smugly to herself, she handed me Molly's leash, then opened the boot of the Volvo and dumped an old basket with a plastic bag of dog food on the drive. 'But remember, Clarissa,' I said, through the open car window as she started the engine, 'this dog is mine just for Christmas, not for life.'

Head to one side, as if she didn't understand what was happening, Molly watched the Volvo drive off. When I tugged gently on her leash she looked up at me, thoroughly confused. 'Don't worry, you're only stuck with me for a few days,' I told her. 'Then Clarissa will find you a proper new home with someone who loves you.' She must have got used to being passed from hand to hand in the last few days because, though she didn't have a clue who I was or what she was doing there, she obediently trotted after me into the house.

Since then, she'd followed me everywhere, a small, silent, cautious shadow that never barked, never got excited and showed no trace of personality. Extremely obedient, she sat when instructed, came when called, ate her food as soon as I put it down for her, and did her business in the garden the moment I let her out. At night, she curled up in a tight little ball in her basket, which I'd put in the upstairs corridor, just outside my bedroom door. Whenever I got up to go to the loo in the night – a common occurrence in my present state – she opened an eye, lifted her head and watched me pad past her into the bathroom. Perhaps she sensed that her stay with me was merely temporary because she made no move to get close to me, and I, in turn, made no overtures towards her, even though I knew she must be missing Miss Chips. I simply couldn't bring myself to. Though she seemed a nice enough dog, Molly wasn't Fluffy. I felt as detached from her as I did from the foetus growing in my womb.

By the time I'd eaten my Christmas lunch of Honey Roast Parsnips, however, I felt guilty that I wasn't paying the poor, pathetic dog enough attention. I remembered what Clarissa had said about Miss Chips taking her for walks even when she'd been on a Zimmer frame, and although I didn't feel like getting dressed, I struggled into my jeans, stole one of my father's many cashmere sweaters, and zipped my anorak over my spreading hips.

'We're just going round the block,' I told Molly firmly, as I double-locked Dad's front door behind us. But the moment we left the drive, her ears pricked up in the bitterly cold wind, her stumpy tail wagged, and she pulled ahead of me.

I was about to turn the corner of the block and head home when I decided to walk on a little further. The fresh air had woken me up, too, and after days of sloth-fulness I felt like some exercise. Before long I found myself on the long, wide sweep of Hampstead Lane. With sudden determination to face some of my demons,

I crossed and entered the grounds of Kenwood House. I would go no further than the wide gravel terrace behind the white stucco mansion, I told myself, a terrace where Mark, Fluffy and I had walked many a time. When I got there, and found I hadn't fallen to pieces, I looked down the long, grassy slope to the ornamental lake and told myself I'd go no further than there, where we'd often picnicked on Sundays.

Before I knew it, I'd walked Molly past the pretty white *trompe l'oeil* bridge, and into the dense woods behind where at last I let her off the leash. Nose to the ground, she scampered ahead down the muddy paths, between the low fences, glancing over her shoulder every minute or so to make sure I was still there. When we got to the iron gate that led out on to Hampstead Heath, I called her back. To venture on to the Heath itself, on this of all days, was a step too far.

Molly, however, had other ideas. She refused stubbornly to come back to me. Before I knew it I was following her across the sloping meadows, past the railed-in mound with the clump of trees on top, which Mark had always referred to as the Magic Circle, and up Parliament Hill – the last place on earth I wanted to be on Christmas Day.

When she reached the top, Molly stopped. Panting heavily – though not as heavily as I – she walked deliberately up to one of the benches, jumped on to it and sat down, ears pricked, almost as if she was waiting for something. She seemed to know exactly what she was doing, so much so that I could only think Miss Chips had brought her here in the past. Making my way through the dozen-odd families who, like me, had decided to brave the elements for a post-prandial Christmas Day walk, I joined my foster-dog on the damp bench. Side by side, we stared out across the London skyline below us – the Post Office Tower, the Houses of Parliament, the London Eye, Centrepoint, the dome of Wren's St Paul's.

As if she wanted reassurance, Molly shuffled towards me and attempted to snuggle up to me, but I couldn't bring myself to touch her. By now I was feeling at rock bottom. It had been sheer masochism on my part, allowing her to lead me up here. I thought about Mark, and all our previous Christmas Day walks with Fluffy, how Mark had proposed to me on this very spot, six years ago to the day – almost to the minute. How much we'd loved each other in those days! And how I still missed him – well, not missed him exactly but, rather, missed the relationship we'd had in the early days. It had seemed so wonderful at the time. How had it gone so disastrously wrong? Who'd been responsible? Mark? Me? Both of us?

Whoever. What did it matter now? Our marriage was over, and the happiness and ease we'd once felt in each other's company was a thing of the past. I shivered into my anorak. The sky above me was like I imagined my future – bleak, gloomy, unremittingly grey. I was glad when Molly gave up trying to get close to me and jumped down on to the grass. I didn't want her near me, because I didn't feel anything for her. I couldn't feel anything any more – nothing, that was, except grief.

Then, all of a sudden, I did feel something. I sat up straight, tore off my gloves, slid my hands under my anorak, and spread out my fingers across my skin. For a while nothing happened. But just when I'd convinced myself I'd imagined it, the sensation happened again – a fluttering movement inside my belly, not unlike indigestion or wind.

However, something told me it wasn't indigestion.

No, it was the foetus.

Or, as I suddenly thought of it, the baby.

My baby.

It struck me like a thunderbolt that a real human being was growing inside me. Not just growing, but moving.

I jumped up excitedly, and looked around, wanting to share this incredible newsflash with someone. I was having a baby! And, as God and Scarlett O'Hara were my witnesses, I was going to be a better mother to it than my mother had been to me! The future might be difficult, but it certainly wasn't going to be bleak or lonely, because I was having a baby, and there were going to be two of us from now on.

No – there'd be three of us. I'd forgotten Molly. Poor little Molly, who'd lost Miss Chips, the owner who'd loved her. Dear, good little Molly, who needed a new home as urgently as I needed to create one for my future child.

Suddenly I couldn't wait to pick Molly up, muddy as she was, give her a big hug and share the good news with her that she wasn't going to be shunted off to live with yet another stranger after Christmas. From now on she'd be staying with me. For ever.

But where was Molly?

I couldn't see her. I stood up and called her name, but she didn't come. I walked back up the Tarmac pathway to the summit of the hill and scoured the undulating field, but she was nowhere to be seen. Feeling increasingly panicky, I rushed around, asking everyone in sight if they'd seen a Jack Russell terrier with a stumpy tail and a brown patch over one eye. One woman said she'd seen one outside the café on the Dartmouth Park side of the Heath but it had been on a leash and with some children. Another said she'd seen one down by the lido – she pointed to a far-off building at the southern tip of the hill – and it had been heading for the road. I was about to run down there in search of Molly when someone else told me they'd just seen a little Jack Russell heading into a wooded area – 'Over there,' he said, pointing to a small copse about a hundred yards down the hill.

I half ran towards the trees, desperately calling her name. Just as I got there, she emerged from the tangled undergrowth and, looking very pleased with herself, trotted towards me, tail wagging. 'Oh, thank God!' I sighed. 'Molly! You silly girl! I thought I'd lost you.'

Then another dog hopped out of the bushes in Molly's wake – a thin, wiry, odd-looking, lurcher-like creature, with a long face topped with a flopping, demented fringe. His ears pointed in opposite directions, and his mouth hung open in what looked like a grin. As he came out of the bushes, ungainly on three legs, he seemed extremely pleased with himself. In fact, he had the familiar, vacant look in his eyes that I'd often seen after he'd had sex.

Fluffy.

Forty

I hadn't seen him since the day of the full hearing, when he'd run down the steps of the court in pursuit of the Cavalier bitch and disappeared under the wheels of a Honda Civic. His yelps as he lay bleeding in the road had been heartrending. Mark had picked him up, and carried him out of the traffic, while Dad had tried to reassure the devastated driver that it hadn't been his fault. While I'd sat on the pavement holding Fluffy's trembling body across my lap, Mark had taken off his jacket and wrapped him in it.

Five of us had crammed into a taxi for the journey to an animal hospital in Camden Town – me, Dad, Norma, Dennis and Mark, who sat there white-faced while Fluffy writhed on his lap. No one had spoken – I don't think anyone trusted themselves to say anything. While we'd waited for the vet to examine Fluffy, Mark and I had sat on opposite sides of the waiting room, he with his father, me with Dad and Norma, but we hadn't even looked at one another. We'd both presumed Fluffy was going to die. And when he did, it would be our fault.

Eventually a nurse in green overalls had come out and told us that Fluffy had been badly injured, and that they might have to amputate his right hind leg. But first he had to recover from shock, which was a dangerous condition in itself. It was touch and go as to whether he'd pull through, but as soon as his condition stabilized – if it stabilized – they'd need to anaesthetize him and operate. If we wanted to, we could go through and see him, but he was very poorly, and heavily sedated.

Mark had got to his feet and walked to where I was sitting with my father. Dad had glared up at him. If looks could have killed, Mark would have dropped dead that instant. 'Are you coming?' he'd asked me. I'd shaken my head and, after giving me a long, backward glance, Mark had gone in by himself to see Fluffy. By the time he'd come out into the waiting room, Dad, Norma and I had left.

At that moment I'd thought I'd never see Fluffy again. But here he was, following Molly towards me. Amazingly, he seemed perfectly happy on only three legs. He sniffed my feet curiously, looked up at me with a frown – and went wild, hopping up and down on his remaining back leg, pawing my chest with his front ones and barking like a maniac. I'd thought he might have forgotten me, but no, he was overjoyed.

I was crouching and hugging him before I realized that if Fluffy was there Mark must be, too. He was probably with bloody Darcie, or the Weimaraner's owner, or whoever his latest fling was. I grew furious at the mere thought of it. How could he bring another woman to Parliament Hill on Christmas Day – a day that had always been so special to us and the day he'd proposed to me here?

I looked around but couldn't see him, so I crashed into the copse that Molly and Fluffy had just come out of and headed for a large holly bush. Still barking and leaping

411

for joy, Fluffy romped at my heels, with Molly trundling loyally behind him. I tried to push Fluffy away, but he wouldn't go.

Then, looking a bit like Colin Firth's Mr Darcy in *Pride and Prejudice*, Mark strode over the crest of Parliament Hill. He seemed to be alone. I dived into the holly and peered at him through its thick, prickly foliage. In his jeans and black anorak, his hair long and windswept, he was craggier and more attractive than ever. My stomach lurched again, but this time it wasn't the baby. Why did I still find him so attractive? Damn him!

Mark looked around for Fluffy, and when he couldn't see him he put his fingers into his mouth and gave a piercing whistle. Then he called Fluffy's name. Fluffy left my side and cantered lopsidedly up the hill towards him. I breathed a sigh of relief. However, just before he reached Mark he began to bark and run in circles. I watched Mark try to calm him, but Fluffy wouldn't have it. He ran up to Mark, fastened his teeth to the hem of his anorak and tried to pull him in my direction. When Mark shook him off, he lolloped back to the copse. Crashing through the tangled undergrowth, he made his way towards my hiding-place.

It was too late to make a run for it so I dived into the holly bush, throwing myself on the ground and dragging Molly with me by her collar. I heard Mark whistle and call to Fluffy again, but Fluffy kept circling us, then turning back and barking at him.

'Shoo! Go away!' I hissed, as Fluffy stuck his nose under the branches. But he wouldn't leave. As I tried to push him off, Molly broke free and ran out from under the bush. My heart thumped against my ribs, and I squeezed my eyes shut. I heard footsteps coming towards me through the undergrowth.

'Who's this, Fluffs?' I heard Mark say. 'Your new friend, eh?' I opened my eyes in time to see Molly trot up to him. He crouched and stroked her ears. A moment later she scrambled back towards the bush, where Fluffy was now nosing dangerously close to my feet. Mark's footsteps came ever closer. 'What have you guys found in there?' he said. 'A squirrel or something?'

A moment later, with an 'Ouch!' as the holly leaves pricked him, Mark pulled apart the branches and peered into the gloom. First he glimpsed my boots, and started back as if he'd discovered a dead body. 'Christ!' he muttered. Then he saw my face and turned white. '*Annie?*'

'Go away!'

'But . . .' He frowned. 'Are you okay?'

'Yes, thank you,' I said crisply.

'Then . . .' He shook his head. 'What are you doing in there?'

I racked my soggy brains. I had to come out with something. 'I – I'm just . . . looking for mushrooms.'

'Really?'

'Yes. Oyster mushrooms. Shiitakes. That kind of thing.'

'Shiitakes, eh?' His mouth twitched into the beginnings of a smile. 'On Hampstead Heath?'

'Yes,' I persisted, as if that was the most natural thing in the world.

'But . . . don't shiitakes only grow in the Far East?'

413

I sighed impatiently. 'Oh, for heaven's sake, Mark! What do you think I'm doing under here?'

'I haven't got a clue.'

God, he could be remarkably dense at times. 'I'm hiding, of course,' I snapped.

'Who from?'

'Who do you think? You!'

His smile broadened. 'Not very effectively, if you don't mind me saying so.'

'Not as it turns out,' I admitted.

'Well, now that I've found you, you might as well come out. Unless you're enjoying lying in the cold mud?'

'As a matter of fact, I'm perfectly happy where I am.'

'Is it some new kind of cutting-edge beauty treatment? Mud therapy or something?'

His attempt at humour was too infuriating. I sighed impatiently. 'Look, just go away, will you?'

His smile died. 'Sure.' But he didn't move. Neither did I want him to go, I realized, with a sick feeling. Angry as I was with him, I couldn't help being glad to see him in a perverse way. It seemed that he didn't want to go away either, because after a short pause he tried to strike up a normal conversation. 'So, um, how are you?'

'How do you think? Wonderful,' I said sarcastically. 'And you?'

'Oh, you know . . .' Those big shoulders heaved inside his anorak, and I suddenly remembered how wonderful his bare skin had felt against mine. I swept away the thought as briskly as I could. 'I didn't think I'd see you up here,' he went on. 'Not today of all days.'

So, he'd remembered. I looked daggers at him. 'Nor I you.'

'I didn't know you'd even been released. I tried to find out, but no one would tell me. Clarissa won't even answer my phone calls.'

'Really? I can't imagine why.'

Sighing, he crouched so that we were nearly at the same level. 'I hope you got my letter?' I nodded. 'You never replied.'

I stopped avoiding his eyes and looked directly at him. 'There didn't seem to be anything to say.'

'I suppose not.'

'Thanks for the cheque,' I added grudgingly.

'It was your money. I thought you might need it when you got out.'

I nodded. There was another excruciating pause. And to think that conversation had once flowed as easily between us as kisses! Oh, this was painful. 'Are you still dog-walking?' I said eventually.

Mark looked embarrassed, and I had a horrible feeling he was going to tell me he was shacked up with some new, high-earning career woman. Instead he surprised me: 'I've succumbed to the inevitable and got a job.'

Curiosity got the better of my intention not to engage with him. 'A proper one?' I asked. He nodded. 'That sounds a bit drastic.'

'I know. But it was time. More than time. Forty-one's too old to become a rock star. I mean, it was a pipe-dream, wasn't it? A fantasy I'd clung to – for a couple of decades too long.' He scratched his head absently. 'I'm still playing and writing music, though. In fact, I'm working on a new song at the moment. I think it could be quite good, actually, but ... Well, I guess music's more of a spare-time occupation than a career. Anyway, I've started working for a catering company, doing dinner parties and stuff in people's homes. It kind of works out with Fluffy because I'm at home most of the day, preparing everything, and I just go out at nights to serve it.'

'Well, you always were a wonderful cook.'

'At least I did something right, then.' He smiled sadly. 'Look, are you sure you don't want to come out of there?'

I shook my head, even though the damp was seeping through my jeans and the cold was permeating my whole body. I'd begun to shiver, and my teeth were chattering. Molly must have been wondering if something was wrong with me. Sniffing loudly, she squeezed past Mark, joined me under the bush and tried to lick my face. 'Okay, Molly,' I said. 'I'll be out soon.'

'She's yours?' Mark seemed astonished. Just then, Fluffy stuck his nose under the bush and, in a playful fashion, nipped Molly's tail.

'He's doing all right as a tripod,' I said.

'Yeah. It's amazing how he's adapted. Pissing's the only problem. Since he's only got one back leg, he can't lift it without toppling over.'

'Poor boy.' My eyes met Mark's again. 'But at least he's still alive. He could have been killed. Because of us.'

'I know. God, we were stupid.'

There was another pause, this one pregnant with thoughts of every thing that had happened. 'I've just got Molly,' I said, to break it, as I pushed her gently away from my face. 'Clarissa gave her to me for Christmas.'

'She and Fluffy seem to have taken quite a shine to each other.'

'I have a feeling it's more than a shine. I saw them come out of the bushes just now, and Fluffy was wearing his just-shagged look.'

Mark grinned, and patted Fluffy's head. 'That's my boy! Three legs or four, that dog just can't control himself.'

'It must run in the family, then.' The remark had slipped out before I could stop myself. Mark's grin died. 'Sorry,' I said. 'I didn't mean to say that.'

He shook his head. 'I'm the one who should apologize, Annie. It was me who fucked things up. Literally.'

'Well, I guess I did my fair share, too. Though I'm not sure my father sees it that way. If he ever claps eyes on you again, I think he'll kill you.'

'I wouldn't blame him.' He sighed. 'After you got sent down, I thought my parents would kill me, too. At times I felt like killing myself.'

I think we both realized at this point that our chance meeting had gone on long enough. Mark got to his feet and held out his hand to me. I let him haul me out of the bushes. His hand in mine felt warm and wonderfully familiar. Despite everything that had happened, yes, despite everything, he was the person to whom I felt closest in the world, and I was hit by a deep pang of regret.

'You're heavy!' he said as, a second after they should have done, our fingers slipped apart. He looked me up and down rather curiously.

I crossed my arms over my stomach. 'Yes, okay, I've put on weight. It was the prison food. Thanks for noticing.'

During the long pause that followed, the cold wind whistled in the bare wintry branches above us and the dogs foraged happily in the undergrowth. The sadness in the air was almost tangible. Maybe it was a form of masochism, but there was something I had to ask Mark. I knew I shouldn't, but I couldn't stop myself. 'So, are you still seeing her, then?'

'Who?' he asked. I raised my eyebrows. 'Oh, Mrs Weimaraner? Look, I told you at the beginning it wasn't a big thing. I mean,' he said hurriedly, when he saw my expression harden, 'not for her or me. We were both kind of unhappy in our own way, and it just sort of happened. So, no, I'm definitely not seeing her.' I nodded. 'And anyway,' he added, 'I've made up my mind not to have any more casual affairs. Not while I'm married.'

'*What?*' I felt as if a bucket of iced water had just been thrown over me. 'You're *married*? *Already*?'

Mark stuck his hands in his anorak pockets. 'I'm afraid so,' he said.

There was no reason on earth why I should care. Nevertheless, a feeling of utter desolation swept over me. 'Oh. Who to?' I said, trying to sound as indifferent as I could. 'Darcie, I suppose?'

He seemed horrified. 'Give me a break! That was a big mistake. Or should I say another of my many?'

'Not to mention a lapse in taste.'

'Yeah. Sorry. She was pretty ghastly.'

'Like, yeah, you're *sooo* right!' I mimicked her. Mark

sniggered. Then there was yet another pause. 'So, who are you married to, then?' I asked at last.

He stared at me for a moment. Then he said slowly, 'To my wife, of course.'

How could he be so insensitive? This was no time for jokes. 'I know *that*,' I snapped. 'But who is she?'

He bit his lip, paused, then pointed at me.

Suddenly I was overcome with fury. 'What sick game are you playing, Mark Curtis? We're divorced! Or have you forgotten that memorable day in court?'

'Please, let's not mention it. But the thing is,' he went on earnestly, 'that was only the final hearing, do you see?'

'No,' I said rudely. 'I don't.'

'Well, you and I still hadn't been granted our decree absolute. Apparently you have to apply to the courts for it *after* the final hearing.'

'*What?*' I was incredulous. 'Williams never told me that! At least, I don't remember if he did.'

'You probably had other things on your mind at the time. Like facing a charge of perjury.'

'Well, didn't *you* apply for the decree absolute?'

Mark shook his head. 'The petitioner has to do that.'

'Couldn't that Martha woman have done anything about it?'

'She said she could write to your solicitor and remind him. But I told her not to bother.'

'Why?' I demanded.

He shrugged. 'I dunno. I just couldn't bring myself to do it. It seemed so horribly . . . well, so horribly final, I guess.' His eyes met mine again, and this time they had a vulnerable look in them. 'Apparently,' he went on, after clearing his throat, 'if a decree absolute hasn't been granted, a couple are still officially married.'

'Really? How do you know that?'

'I Googled it. Plus I checked with Greenwood. So, I'm sorry to tell you that the dreaded knot between us still hasn't been fully untied.'

'You mean, all that money we spent, and losing the flat, and me going to prison, and Fluffy's accident – it was for nothing?'

Mark nodded. 'I'm afraid so.'

It was so incredible that I almost laughed. 'I can't believe it!'

Suddenly he seemed very anxious. 'Oh, you can apply for the decree absolute now. We both can. We could even sort of do it together.' He paused. 'That is, if you want to, Annie?'

'Well, don't you?'

'Sure. I mean, yes. If that's what you want?'

Why was he asking such a stupid question? Wasn't the answer obvious? Of course that's what I wanted. Didn't I? Hadn't that been what the whole disastrous divorce saga had been about? So, if that was the case, why didn't I say *yes* immediately he asked me? Why was I so pleased to see Mark, even though I was still angry with him? Surely I couldn't still love him, when I hated him so much.

He gazed at his boots. 'Are you very upset? That we're still hitched, I mean?'

I hesitated. 'Are you?'

'I asked you first.'

'Oh, for heaven's sake, Mark, we could go on like this all day.'

'I guess we could.' He kicked at a stone that was embedded in the mud and, instead of giving me a straight answer, he said, 'Actually, there was another reason why I didn't want the decree to be granted.'

He lapsed into silence, which I prodded him out of by asking, 'Which was?'

'Well, because . . .' He kicked the stone again. 'Because I missed you terribly, Annie,' he confessed to the mud. 'I still do. I miss being with you. Not how things were at the end, of course, but how they were before.' His words uncannily echoed my own feelings. 'And the fact that I know we're still officially married has made me feel, I dunno, closer to you in some way. Stupid, really, isn't it?'

I was so taken aback that I didn't know what to say. 'No, not stupid at all,' I murmured.

'I thought you'd be really angry. I mean, that we're not divorced.'

'Well, I should be, I suppose. Not with you, but with myself. And Williams, of course. But the funny thing is I'm not.'

'Really?'

I shook my head, and found myself smiling sadly at him. 'Oh, Mark! We've both been so stupid, haven't we? Neither of us knew the first thing about getting divorced. We just rushed into it. Just like we rushed into getting married.'

'Do you wish we hadn't?'

'Hadn't what? Rushed into getting married or rushed into getting divorced?'

He spread his hands. 'Both, I guess.'

'Yes and no,' I said.

'Meaning what, precisely? Yes, you're not sorry we

rushed into getting married, and no, you're not sorry we got divorced. Not that we're divorced yet. Or do you mean it the other way round?'

I started to giggle. 'I can't work it out.'

'Neither can I now!' He, too, snorted with laughter.

'So,' I said, after we'd straightened our faces, as we knew we should. 'You and I are still married. The baby's going to born *in wedlock*, after all.'

I'd blurted it out by mistake. But Mark had to know some time.

He looked suitably shocked. 'The *baby*?' he said. 'What baby?'

I took a deep breath and unzipped my anorak. 'This isn't all prison stodge,' I said, putting my hands on my belly.

He stared at it. 'You're pregnant?' he breathed. He came over to me and, after asking if he could, laid his hands reverently on the tiny bump. 'But . . . I don't understand. How did this happen?' he said.

'Oh, in the normal way. It's not an immaculate conception or anything.'

'I mean, when, Annie?' he said urgently. 'When did it happen?'

'Not while I was doing time in an all-female prison, that's for sure.'

'So . . . Before that, then?' I nodded. Mark was being remarkably quick at catching on. But then he took his hand off the bump, drew back and said nervously, 'Give it to me straight, Annie, please. Who's the father?'

I looked him straight in the eyes. 'Well, as it turns out, he's my husband.'

He gulped. 'Me? You mean, that one time when . . . ?'

'Yes. That one time when.'

'But . . .'

'Darcie might have been using Boots Protect and Perfect at the time, but I wasn't.'

Mark drew a long breath, and a huge smile spread slowly across his face. 'You and I are having a baby?' he whispered.

'Well,' I said matter-of-factly, 'to be perfectly accurate, I'm the one having it. Losing my figure and throwing up every morning. But you're welcome to take over those jobs, if you want. Otherwise your work's done. That is, until it's time to change nappies. I mean, if you want to help look after it when it comes out . . .'

'You bet your ass I do!'

'My newly fat ass, you mean.'

'Yes. Your beautiful newly fat ass!' Impulsively he clasped me to him and gave my newly fat arse a gentle squeeze under my anorak. Then he drew back and his smile faded. 'But . . . Look . . . Do you want me to help? Could we, Annie?'

'Could we what?' I held my breath.

'Well, do you think we could get back together, after all that's happened? We've been so horrible to each other. Said and done such appalling things.'

'I hadn't noticed.'

'Seriously. Could you ever get over it?'

'Seriously, I don't know, Mark,' I said. 'How about you?'

His expressive face crumpled. 'I already am over it. I behaved like a prize prick. I was so upset you wanted to divorce me that I couldn't think straight. But you . . . Could you ever trust me again, Annie? Could you ever forgive me for being unfaithful? Not to mention everything else.'

I thought about it. Could I put Fern's thong and the Weimaraner's pink collar and leash behind me? Even if I wanted to, could I get over Mark's fight to take Fluffy from me, and put aside the anger and bitterness that had swamped us during the past year? I knew now that it wasn't all his fault, that both of us bore some responsibility for what had happened. But still . . . Could I ever forget my trial for perjury and those ghastly weeks in prison? 'I don't know,' I said again.

Mark took my hands in his. 'I swear that things would be different if . . . if, well, you felt you wanted to give me another chance. *I*'d be different. I already *am* different. A bit more responsible, I mean.'

'I suppose I could also try to be different myself,' I said. 'Not quite so bossy and controlling. A little less perfect, maybe.' I smiled. 'Plus not such a workaholic. Not that I have any work.'

'It's a good thing I have, then,' Mark said. 'You'd have to be a kept woman for a while.'

'I don't think I'd like that.'

'Oh, it's not such a bad life. I used to be one myself.' He grinned at me and I found myself grinning back. 'It wouldn't be just us any more, though, would it, Annie?' he said more seriously. 'It'd be us and the baby.'

'And Fluffy and Molly,' I added. 'Let's not forget them.'

'I don't think there's much chance of that. Look, shall we go home now?' he asked. 'I'm bloody freezing standing here. And your lips are turning blue. Even the dogs are shivering.'

I turned towards them. Poor little Molly was standing in a puddle of mud, and was indeed trembling with cold. But Fluffy was nosing happily through the undergrowth on his three legs, still bathed in his warm, after-sex glow. 'Okay,' I said cautiously. Then I said, 'No, we can't.'

'Can't what?'

'We can't do it, Mark. We can't go home.'

He looked crestfallen. 'Why not?'

'Because we don't have a home to go to.'

'Shit!' Mark said. And then, terrible as it was, we were laughing. 'I completely forgot,' he went on. 'Sold to pay the legal fees.'

'And my fine. And Joseph bloody Holtby.'

'What a fuck-up!'

'So,' I asked, 'where are you living?'

'A grotty one-bed flat in Tufnell Park. Cheap, not cheerful, but at least they don't mind dogs. How about you?'

'I'm staying at my father's. Don't look so frightened. He won't kill you – not today, that is. He's in Spain, on holiday with Norma and the boys.'

'Phew. Shall I walk you back there, then?'

I zipped up my anorak over my bump, and we picked our way out of the copse, then took the path that led north back to Kenwood House. Fluffy lolloped in circles around us, with Molly scampering at his heels.

Overcome by all that we'd said, Mark and I walked side by side, in silence, without touching. But as we entered the woods I reached for his hand and, despite everything that had happened between us, our fingers locked as if it was the most natural thing in the world.

Acknowledgements

I would like to thank Grant Howell, LLB, of the law firm Charles Russell, for so generously taking the time to advise me throughout the writing of this book, and for doing so with such good humour; and Rebecca Haynes of Harvey Nichols in London, for her invaluable advice about the world of personal shopping. I would also like to thank solicitor Trevor Cooper of doglaw.co.uk, a website specializing in canine law; and Deborah Rothfield.